Praise for Sophie Kinsella's Novels

REMEMBER ME?

"Kinsella delights again! . . . Winning . . . Kinsella keeps things fresh and frothy with workplace politicking, romantic intrigue and a vibrant . . . cast. . . . Readers will be rooting for Lexi all along."   —*Publishers Weekly*

"Buoyed by Kinsella's breezy prose, this winning offering boasts a likable heroine and an involving story."
                                                                        —*Booklist*

"A delicious page-turner, filled with hearty chuckles and heartache . . . [Kinsella] finds a way to make losing one's memory seem refreshingly funny."   —*USA Today*

"Comfort food for the brain . . . A perfect pick for a spring-break read."   —*Fort Worth Star-Telegram*

"Kinsella is a witty writer and the novel is consistently funny."   —*Rocky Mountain News*

"A lively new novel . . . a breezy blend of romantic comedy and cautionary fairy tale . . . Kinsella is hilarious."
                                                                        —*New York Post*

THE UNDOMESTIC GODDESS

"Kinsella is at the top of the chick-lit game. . . . [She] skewers high-powered city life while delivering a romantic comedy anyone who subsists on takeout will appreciate. . . . Light yet filling."   —*New York Post*

"*The Undomestic Goddess* is a fast, fun read that delves a little deeper."   —*Cleveland Plain Dealer*

ALSO BY SOPHIE KINSELLA

Confessions of a Shopaholic
Shopaholic Takes Manhattan
Shopaholic Ties the Knot
Can You Keep a Secret?
Shopaholic & Sister
The Undomestic Goddess
Shopaholic & Baby

Sophie Kinsella

Remember
Me?

A DELL BOOK

REMEMBER ME?
A Dell Book

PUBLISHING HISTORY
Dial Press hardcover edition published March 2008
Dell international mass market edition / November 2008

Published by Bantam Dell
A Division of Random House, Inc.
New York, New York

This is a work of fiction. Names, characters, places,
and incidents either are the product of the author's imagination
or are used fictitiously. Any resemblance to actual persons,
living or dead, events, or locales is entirely coincidental.

Book design by Laurie Jewell

Library of Congress Catalog Card Number: 2007039423

Dell is a registered trademark of Random House, Inc., and the
colophon is a trademark of Random House, Inc.

ISBN 978-0-440-29691-1

Printed in the United States of America

www.bantamdell.com

OPM   10 9 8 7 6 5 4

To Atticus

Prologue

Of all the crap, crap, crappy nights I've ever had in the whole of my crap life.

On a scale of one to ten we're talking . . . a minus six. And it's not like I even have very high standards.

Rain spatters down my collar as I shift from one blistered foot to the other. I'm holding my denim jacket over my head as a makeshift umbrella, but it's not exactly waterproof. I just want to find a taxi, get home, kick off these stupid boots, and run a nice hot bath. But we've been waiting here for ten minutes and there's no sign of a cab.

My toes are *agony*. I'm never buying shoes from Cut-Price Fashion again. I bought these boots last week in the sale (flat black patent; I only ever wear flats). They were half a size too small, but the girl said they would stretch and that they made my legs look really long. And I believed her. Honestly, I'm the world's biggest sucker.

We're all standing together on the corner of some street in southwest London that I've never been to

before, with music pounding faintly from the club below our feet. Carolyn's sister is a promoter and got us
discounted entry, so that's why we schlepped all the
way here. Only now we have to get home, and I'm the
only one even *looking* for a cab.

Fi has commandeered the only nearby doorway and
has her tongue down the throat of the guy she chatted
up earlier at the bar. He's cute, despite the weird little
mustache. Also, he's shorter than Fi—but then, a lot of
guys are, given she's nearly six feet tall. She has long
dark hair and a wide mouth, and an oversized laugh to
match. When Fi is really tickled by something, she
brings the whole office to a standstill.

A few feet away, Carolyn and Debs are sheltering
underneath a newspaper arm in arm, caterwauling
"It's Raining Men" as if they're still on the karaoke
stage.

"Lexi!" Debs yells, extending an arm for me to join
in. "It's raining men!" Her long blond hair is all ratty
in the rain, but she's still bright-faced. Debs's two favorite hobbies are karaoke and jewelry making—in
fact, I'm wearing a pair of earrings she made me for my
birthday: teeny silver *L*s with dangling seed pearls.

"It isn't bloody raining men!" I call back morosely.
"It's just raining!"

I normally love karaoke too. But I'm not in a singing
mood tonight. I feel all sore inside, like I want to curl
up away from everyone else. If only Loser Dave had
turned up like he promised. After all those *luv u Lexi*
texts; after vowing faithfully to be here at ten. I sat
waiting all that time, watching the door, even when the

other girls told me to give up on him. Now I feel like a sappy moron.

Loser Dave works in car telesales and has been my boyfriend since we got together at Carolyn's friend's barbecue last summer. I don't call him Loser Dave to insult him—it's just his nickname. No one remembers how he got it and he won't tell; in fact, he's always trying to make people call him something else. He started referring to himself as Butch a while ago, because he reckons he looks like Bruce Willis in *Pulp Fiction*. He has a buzz cut, I suppose—but the resemblance ends there.

Anyway, it didn't catch on. To his workmates he just *is* Loser Dave, the way I'm Snaggletooth. I've been called that since I was eleven. And sometimes Snagglehair. To be fair, my hair is pretty frizzy. And my teeth are kind of crooked. But I always say they give my face character.

(Actually, that's a lie. It's Fi who says they give my face character. Personally, I'm planning to fix them, as soon as I've got the cash and can psych myself up to having braces in my mouth—i.e., probably never.)

A taxi comes into sight and I immediately stick out my hand—but some people ahead flag it down first. Great. I shove my hands in my pockets and miserably scan the rainy road for another yellow light.

It's not just Loser Dave standing me up that's bothering me: it's the bonuses. Today was the end of the financial year at work. Everyone was given paper slips saying how much they'd got and started jumping about with excitement, because it turns out the company's

2003–2004 sales were better than anyone expected. It was like Christmas came ten months early. Everyone was gabbing all afternoon about how they were going to spend the money. Carolyn started planning a holiday to New York with her boyfriend, Matt. Debs booked highlights at Nicky Clarke—she's always wanted to go there. Fi called Harvey Nichols and reserved herself a new cool bag called a Paddington or something.

And then there was me. With nada. Not because I haven't worked hard, not because I didn't meet my targets, but because to get a bonus you have to have worked for the company for a year, and I missed qualifying by a week. One *week*. It's so unfair. It's so penny-pinching. I'm telling you, if they asked me what I thought about it—

Anyway. Like Simon Johnson would ever ask the opinion of an associate junior sales manager (flooring). That's the other thing: I have the worst job title ever. It's embarrassing. It hardly even fits on my business card. The longer the title, I've decided, the crappier the job. They think they'll blind you with words and you won't notice you've been stuck in the corner of the office with the lousy accounts no one else wants to work on.

A car splashes through a puddle near the pavement and I jump back, but not before a shower of water hits me in the face. From the doorway I can hear Fi hotting things up, murmuring into the ear of the cute guy. I catch a few familiar words and, despite my mood, have to clamp my lips together so I don't laugh. Months ago, we had a girls' night in, and ended up confessing all our dirty-talk secrets. Fi said she uses the same line each time and it works a treat: "I think my underwear's melting off."

I mean. Would any guy fall for that?

Well, I guess, by Fi's record, they do.

Debs confessed that the only word she can use without cracking up during sex is *hot*. So all she ever says is "I'm hot." "You're so hot." "This is really hot." Mind you, when you're as stunning as Debs, I wouldn't think you'd need much of a repertoire.

Carolyn has been with Matt for a million years and declared she never talks in bed at all except to say "ow" or "higher," or once, as he was about to come, "Oh crap, I left my hair straighteners on." I don't know if she really meant it; she's got a pretty quirky sense of humor, just like Matt. They're both super-bright—almost geeky—but cool with it. When we're all out together the two of them throw so many insults at each other, it's hard to know if they're ever serious. I'm not sure even *they* know.

Then it was my turn, and I told the truth, which is that I compliment the guy. Like, with Loser Dave, I always say "You have beautiful shoulders" and "You have such beautiful eyes."

I didn't admit that I say these things because I'm always secretly hoping to hear back from a guy that I'm beautiful too.

Nor did I admit that it's never yet happened.

Anyway. Whatever.

"Hey, Lexi." I look up to see that Fi has unsuckered

herself from the cute guy. She ducks under my denim jacket and gets out a lipstick.

"Hi," I say, blinking rainwater off my lashes. "Where's lover boy gone?"

"To tell the girl he came with that he's leaving."

"Fi!"

"What?" Fi looks unrepentant. "They're not an item. Or much of one." She carefully redoes her mouth in pillar-box red. "I'm getting a whole new load of makeup," she says, frowning at the blunt end of the lipstick. "Christian Dior, the whole lot. I can afford it now!"

"You should!" I nod, trying to sound enthusiastic. A moment later Fi looks up with realization.

"Oh, bollocks. Sorry, Lexi." She puts an arm around my shoulder and squeezes. "You should have got a bonus. It's not fair."

"It's fine." I try to smile. "Next year."

"You okay?" Fi narrows her eyes at me. "You want to go for a drink or anything?"

"No, I need to get to bed. I've got an early start in the morning."

Fi's face clears suddenly and she bites her lip. "*Jesus.* I forgot all about that, too. What with the bonuses and everything . . . Lexi, I'm sorry. This is a really shit time for you."

"It's fine!" I say at once. "It's . . . I'm trying not to make it a huge deal."

No one likes a whinger. So somehow I make myself smile brightly, just to show I'm fine with being the snaggly-toothed, stood-up, no-bonus girl whose dad just died.

Fi is silent for a moment, her green eyes glittering in the passing headlights.

"Things'll turn around for you," she says.

"You think?"

"Uh-huh." She nods, with more energy. "You just have to believe it. Come on." She squeezes me. "What are you, woman or walrus?" Fi's been using that expression since we were both fifteen, and it makes me smile every time. "And you know what?" she adds. "I think your dad would have *wanted* you to turn up to his funeral hungover."

She met my dad a couple of times. She's probably right.

"Hey, Lexi." Fi's voice is suddenly softer, and I brace myself. I'm in a pretty edgy mood as it is, and if she says something nice about my dad, I might cry. I mean, I didn't know him that well or anything, but you only get one dad.... "Do you have a spare condom?" Her voice pierces my thoughts.

Right. So I probably didn't need to worry about the sympathy overload.

"Just in case," she adds with a wicked grin. "I mean, we'll probably just chat about world politics or whatever."

"Yeah. I'm so sure." I root around inside my green birthday-present Accessorize bag for the matching coin purse and produce a Durex, which I discreetly hand to her.

"Thanks, babe." She kisses me on the cheek.

"Listen, d'you want to come to mine tomorrow night? After it's all over? I'll make spaghetti carbonara."

"Yeah." I smile gratefully. "That would be great. I'll call you." I'm already looking forward to it. A plate of delicious pasta, a glass of wine, and telling her all about the funeral. Fi can make the grimmest things seem funny... I know we'll end up in stitches.

"Hey, there's a taxi! Taxiii!" I hurry to the edge of the pavement as the cab pulls up and beckon to Debs and Carolyn, who are screeching out "Dancing Queen." Carolyn's glasses are spattered with rain-drops, and she's about five notes ahead of Debs. "Hi there!" I lean through the window to the taxi driver, my hair dripping down my face. "Could you possibly take us first to Balham, and then—"

"Sorry, love, no karaoke." The taxi driver cuts me off with a baleful glance at Debs and Carolyn.

I stare at him, confused. "What d'you mean, no karaoke?"

"I'm not 'aving them girls in 'ere, doin' me 'ead in with their bloody singing."

He has to be joking. You can't ban people for *singing*.

"But—"

"My cab, my rules. No drunks, no drugs, no karaoke." Before I can reply, he puts the taxi into gear and roars away down the road.

"You can't have a 'no karaoke' rule!" I shout after the cab in outrage. "It's... discrimination! It's against the law! It's..."

I trail off helplessly and look around the pavement.

Fi has disappeared back into Mr. Cutie's arms. Debs and Carolyn are doing the worst "Dancing Queen" routine I've ever seen; in fact, I don't blame that taxi driver. The traffic is whooshing by, drenching us with spray; rain is drumming through my denim jacket into my hair; thoughts are circling around my head like socks in a dryer.

We'll never find a taxi. We'll be stuck out here in the rain all night. Those banana cocktails were noxious—I should have stopped after four. I have my dad's funeral tomorrow. I've never been to a funeral before. What if I start sobbing and everyone stares at me? Loser Dave's probably in bed with some other girl right this second, telling her she's beautiful while she moans "Butch! Butch!" My feet are blistered *and* they're freezing—

"Taxi!" I instinctively scream the word, almost before I've registered the distant yellow light. It's coming up the road, signaling left. "Don't turn!" I wave frantically. "Over here! Here!"

I have to get this cab. I *have* to. Clutching my denim jacket over my head, I run along the pavement, skidding slightly, yelling till I'm hoarse. "Taxi! Taxi!" As I reach the corner the pavement is crowded with people, and I skirt around them and up the steps to some grand municipal building. There's a balustraded platform with steps going right and left. I'll hail the taxi from up here, then run down and jump in. "TAXI! TAAA-XIII!"

Yes! It's pulling up. Thank God! At last—I can get home, run a bath, forget all about today.

"Here!" I call out. "Just coming, wait a sec—"

To my consternation I notice a guy in a suit on the pavement below heading toward the taxi. "It's ours!" I roar, and start pelting down the opposite steps. "It's ours! I hailed that cab! Don't you even dare— Argh! *Aaaaargh!*"

Even as my foot skids on the wet step I'm not sure what's happening. Then, as I start falling, my thoughts rush with disbelief: I've slipped on my stupid, cheap, shiny-soled boots. I'm tumbling right over, down the steps, like a three-year-old. I scrabble desperately at the stone balustrade, scraping my skin, wrenching my hand, dropping my Accessorize bag, grabbing for anything, but I can't stop myself—

Oh shit.

The ground's coming straight toward me—there's nothing I can do—this is really, *really* going to hurt . . .

Chapter One

How long have I been awake? Is it morning yet?

I feel so rough. What happened last night? God, my head hurts. Okay, I'm never drinking again, *ever*.

I feel so woozy I can't even think, let alone...

• • •

Oww. How long have I been awake?

My head is splitting and kind of foggy. And my mouth is parched. This is the most monster hangover I've ever had. I'm never drinking again, *ever*.

Is that a voice?

No, I have to sleep...

• • •

How long have I been awake? Five minutes? Half an hour, maybe? It's kind of hard to tell.

What day is it, anyway?

For a moment I just lie still. My head is pounding with a rhythmic pain, like some sort of massive concrete-breaker. I'm dry-throated and aching all over. My skin feels like sandpaper.

Where was I last night? What's wrong with my brain? It's like a fog has descended over everything.

I'm never drinking again. I must have alcohol poisoning or something. I'm trying to remember last night as hard as I can—but all that's coming into my head is stupid stuff. Old memories and images from the past, flashing by in random order, like some kind of iPod shuffle in my brain.

Sunflowers waving against a blue sky...

Amy as a newborn baby, looking like a little pink sausage in a blanket...

A plate of salty french fries on a wooden pub table; hot sunshine on my neck; my dad sitting opposite in a Panama hat, blowing out cigar smoke and telling me, "Eat up, sweetheart"...

The sack race at school. Oh God, *not* this memory again. I try to block it out, but too late, it's rushing in.... I'm seven years old, it's sports day, and I'm winning by miles, but it feels so uncomfortable to be out front that I stop and wait for all my friends. They catch up—then somehow in the melee I trip and wind up coming in last. I can still feel the humiliation, hear the laughter, feel the dust in my throat, the taste of bananas...

Hang on. Somehow I force my brain to hold steady for a moment.

Bananas.

Through the fog another memory is glimmering. I'm desperately trying to retrieve it, to reach for it...

Yes. Got it. Banana cocktails.

We were drinking cocktails at some club. That's all I can remember. Bloody banana cocktails. What on earth did they put *in* them?

I can't even open my eyes. They feel heavy and stuck down, like that time I used false eyelashes with dodgy glue from the market, then tottered into the bathroom the next morning to find one eye glued shut with what looked like a dead spider on top of it. Really attractive, Lexi.

Cautiously, I move a hand up to my chest and hear a rustle of sheets. They don't sound like the ones at home. And there's a weird lemony smell in the air, and I'm wearing some soft cottony T-shirt thing I don't recognize. Where am I? What on earth—

Hey. I didn't score, did I?

Oh wow. Was I unfaithful to Loser Dave? Am I wearing some hot guy's oversize T-shirt that I borrowed to sleep in after we had passionate sex all night and that's why I feel so bruised and sore—

No, I've never been unfaithful in my life. I must have stayed overnight with one of the girls or something. Maybe I'll get up, have a shower . . .

With a huge effort I wrench my eyes open and incline my head a few inches.

Shit. What the hell—

I'm lying in a dim room, on a metal bed. There's a panel of buttons to my right, a bunch of flowers on the nightstand. With an inward gulp I see an IV drip in my left hand, attached to a bag of fluid.

This is unreal. I'm in hospital.

What's going on? What *happened*?

I mentally prod my brain, but it's a big, stupid, empty balloon. I need a strong cup of coffee. I try peering around the room for clues—but my eyes don't want to peer. They don't want information, they want eyedrops and three aspirin. Feebly I flop back onto the pillows, close my eyes, and wait a few moments. Come on. I have to be able to remember what happened. I can't have been *that* drunk . . . can I?

I'm holding on to my one fragment of memory like it's an island in the ocean. Banana cocktails . . . banana cocktails . . . think hard . . . *think* . . .

Destiny's Child. Yes! A few more memories are coming back to me now. Slowly, slowly, in patches. Nachos with cheese. Those crummy bar stools with the vinyl all split.

I was out with the girls from work. At that dodgy club with the pink neon ceiling in . . . somewhere. I can remember nursing my cocktail, totally miserable.

Why was I so down? What had happened—

Bonuses. Of course. A familiar cold disappointment clenches my stomach. And Loser Dave never showed up. Double whammy. But none of that explains why I'm in hospital. I screw up my face tight, trying to focus as hard as I can. I remember dancing like a maniac to Kylie and singing "We Are Family" to the karaoke machine, all four of us, arm in arm. I can vaguely remember tottering out to get a cab.

But beyond that . . . nothing. Total blanko.

This is weird. I'll text Fi and ask her what happened. I reach toward the nightstand—then realize there's no phone there. Nor on the chair, or the chest of drawers.

Where's my phone? Where's all my stuff gone?

Oh God. Was I *mugged*? That has to be it. Some teenager in a hoodie clonked me over the head and I fell down in the street, and they must have called an ambulance and—

An even more horrendous thought grips me. *What underwear was I wearing?*

I can't help giving a small moan. This could be seriously bad. This could be the scaggy gray knickers and bra I only put on when the hamper is full. Or that faded lemon thong with the fraying edge and cartoon of Snoopy.

It wouldn't have been anything posh. I mean, you wouldn't for Loser Dave—it'd be a waste. Wincing, I swivel my head from side to side—but I can't see any clothes or anything. The doctors must have incinerated them in the special Hospital Incinerator for Scaggy Underwear.

And I still have no idea what I'm doing here. My throat's feeling really scratchy and I could die for a nice cool glass of orange juice. Now that I think of it, where are all the doctors and nurses? What if I were dying?

"Hello?" I call out feebly. My voice sounds like someone dragging a grater over a wooden floor. I wait for a response, but there's silence. I'm sure no one can hear me through that thick door.

Then it occurs to me to press a button on the little panel. I select the one that looks like a person, and a few moments later the door opens. It worked! A gray-haired nurse in a dark blue uniform enters and smiles at me.

"Hello, Lexi!" she says. "Feeling all right?"

"Um, okay, thanks. Thirsty. And my head hurts."

"I'll fetch you a painkiller." She brings me a plastic cup full of water and helps me up. "Drink this."

"Thanks," I say after gulping the water. "So...I'm guessing I'm in hospital? Or, like, a really high-tech spa?"

The nurse smiles. "Sorry. Hospital. You don't remember how you got here?"

"No." I shake my head. "I'm a bit hazy, to be honest."

"That's because you had quite a bump on the head. Do you remember anything about your accident?"

Accident...accident...And suddenly, in a rush, it all comes back. *Of course.* Running for the taxi, the paving stones wet with rain, slipping on my stupid cheap boots...

Jeez Louise. I must have really bashed my head.

"Yeah. I think so." I nod. "Kind of. So...what's the time?"

"It's eight o'clock at night."

Eight o'clock? Wow. I've been out of it for a whole *day*?

"I'm Maureen." She takes the cup from me. "You were only transferred to this room a few hours ago. You know, we've already had several conversations."

"Really?" I say, surprised. "What did I say?"

"You were a little slurred, but you kept asking if something was 'baggy.'" She frowns, looking perplexed. "Or 'scaggy'?"

Great. Not only do I wear scaggy underwear, I talk about it to strangers.

"Scaggy?" I try to appear baffled. "I've no idea what I meant."

"Well, you seem fully coherent now." Maureen plumps up my pillow. "Is there anything else I can get you?"

"I'd love some orange juice, if there is any. And I can't see my phone anywhere, or my bag."

"All your valuables will have been put somewhere safe. I'll just check." She heads out and I look around the silent room, still dazed. I feel like I've put together only a tiny corner of the jigsaw puzzle. I still don't know which hospital I'm in...how I got here...Has anyone told my family? And there's something else nagging at me like an undertow...

I had been anxious to get home. Yes. That's right. I kept saying I needed to get home, because I had an early start the next day. Because—

Oh no. Oh *fuck*.

My dad's funeral. It was the next day, eleven o'clock. Which means...

Did I *miss* it? Instinctively I try to get out of bed— but even sitting up makes my head lurch. At last, reluctantly, I lie back down. If I've missed it, I've missed it. Nothing I can do about it now.

It's not like I really knew my dad well. He was never around that much; in fact, he felt more like an uncle. The kind of jokey, roguish uncle who brings you sweets at Christmas and smells of drink and cigarettes.

Nor was it a massive shock him dying. He was having some big heart bypass operation, and everyone knew there was a 50-50 risk. But still, I should have been there today, along with Mum and Amy. I mean, Amy's only twelve—and a timid little twelve at that. I suddenly have a vision of her sitting in the crematorium next to Mum, all grave under her Shetland pony fringe, clutching her raggedy old Blue Lion. She's not ready to see her dad's coffin, not without her big sister to hold her hand.

As I lie there, imagining her trying to look brave and grown up, I suddenly feel a tear rolling down my face. It's the day of my dad's funeral, and here I am in hospital with a headache and probably a broken leg or something.

And my boyfriend stood me up last night. And no one's come to visit me, I suddenly realize. Where's all my anxious friends and family, sitting around the bed and holding my hand?

Well, I suppose Mum's been at the funeral with Amy. And Loser Dave can sod off. But Fi and the others—where are they? When I *think* how we all went to visit Debs when she had her ingrown toenail removed. We all practically camped on the floor, and brought her Starbucks and magazines, and treated her to a pedicure when it was healed. Just for a toenail.

Whereas I've been unconscious, with an IV drip and everything. But obviously no one cares.

Great. Just bloody . . . brilliant.

Another fat tear trickles down my face, just as the door opens and Maureen comes in again. She's holding a tray, and a plastic bag with *Lexi Smart* written on it in thick marker.

"Oh dear!" she says as she sees me wiping my eyes.

"Is the pain very bad?" She hands me a tablet and a little cup of water. "This should help."

"Thanks very much." I gulp down the pill. "But it's not that. It's my life." I spread my arms hopelessly. "It's total rubbish, from start to finish."

"Of course it's not," Maureen says reassuringly. "Things might look bad—"

"Believe me, they *are* bad."

"I'm sure—"

"My so-called career is going nowhere, and my boyfriend stood me up last night, and I haven't got any money. And my sink keeps leaking rancid brown water into the flat below," I add, remembering with a shudder. "I'll probably get sued by my neighbors. And my dad just died."

There's silence. Maureen looks flummoxed.

"Well, that does all sound rather . . . tricky," she says at last. "But I expect things will soon turn around for the better."

"That's what my friend Fi said!" I suddenly have a memory of Fi's eyes shining in the rain. "And look, I end up in hospital!" I make a despairing gesture at myself. "How is this turning around for the better?"

"I'm . . . not sure, dear." Maureen's eyes are darting helplessly from side to side.

"Every time I think everything's crap . . . it just gets even crapper!" I blow my nose and heave a massive sigh. "Wouldn't it be great if just once, *just one time,* life fell magically into place?"

"Well, we can all hope, can't we?" Maureen gives me a sympathetic smile and holds out her hand for the cup.

I pass it back—and as I do so, I suddenly notice my nails. Bloody hell. What on earth—

My nails have always been bitten-down stumps that I try to hide. But these look amazing. All neat and varnished pale pink...and long. I blink at them in astonishment, trying to work out what's happened. Did we go for a late-night manicure last night or something and I've forgotten? Did I get acrylics? They must have some brilliant new technique, because I can't see the join or anything.

"Your handbag's in here, by the way," Maureen adds, putting the plastic bag on my bed. "I'll just go and get you that juice."

"Thanks." I look at the plastic bag in surprise. "And thanks for the bag. I thought it had been nicked."

That's something good, anyway, to have got my bag back. With any luck my phone will still be charged up and I can send a few texts.... As Maureen opens the door to leave, I reach into the shopping bag—and pull out a smart Louis Vuitton tote with calfskin handles, all glossy and expensive-looking.

Oh, *great*. I sigh in disappointment. This isn't my bag. They've got me mixed up with someone else. Like I, Lexi Smart, would possess a Louis Vuitton bag.

"Excuse me, this bag isn't mine," I call out, but the door has already closed.

I gaze at the Louis Vuitton wistfully for a while, wondering who it belongs to. Some rich girl down the corridor, must be. At last I drop it onto the floor, flop back on my pillows, and close my eyes.

Chapter Two

I wake up to find chinks of morning light edging underneath the drawn curtains. A glass of orange juice is on the nightstand and Maureen is bustling about in the corner of the room. The IV drip has magically disappeared, and I feel a lot more normal.

"Hi, Maureen," I say, my voice scratchy. "What time is it?" She turns around, her eyebrows raised.

"You remember me?"

"Of course," I say in surprise. "We met last night. We talked."

"Excellent! That shows you've come out of post-traumatic amnesia. Don't look alarmed!" she adds, smiling. "It's a normal stage of confusion after a head injury."

Instinctively I put my hand up to my head and feel a dressing. Wow. I must really have whacked it on those steps.

"You're doing well." She pats my shoulder. "I'll get you some fresh orange juice."

There's a knock at the door. It opens and a tall, slim

woman in her fifties comes in. She has blue eyes, high cheekbones, and wavy, graying blond hair in straggly layers. She's wearing a red quilted waistcoat over a long printed dress and an amber necklace, and she's holding a paper bag.

It's Mum. I mean, I'm ninety-nine percent certain it is. I don't know why I'm even hesitating.

"The *heating* in this place!" she exclaims in her familiar thin, little-girl voice.

Okay, it's definitely Mum.

"I feel quite faint!" She fans herself. "And I had such a stressful journey. . . ." She glances toward the bed almost as an afterthought, and says to Maureen, "How is she?"

Maureen smiles. "Lexi's much better today. Far less confused than she was yesterday."

"Thank goodness for that!" Mum lowers her voice a fraction. "It was like talking to a lunatic yesterday, or some . . . *retarded* person."

"Lexi isn't a lunatic," says Maureen evenly, "and she can understand everything you say."

The truth is, I'm barely listening. I can't help staring at Mum. What's *wrong* with her? She looks different. Thinner. And kind of . . . older. As she comes nearer and the light from the window falls on her face, she looks even worse.

Is she ill?

No. I'd know about it if she was ill. But honestly, she seems to have aged overnight. I'll buy her some Crème de la Mer for Christmas, I resolve.

"Here you are, darling," she says in overly loud,

clear tones. "It's me. Your mo-ther." She hands me the paper bag, which contains a bottle of shampoo, and drops a kiss on my cheek. As I inhale her familiar smell of dogs and tea-rose perfume, it's ridiculous, but I feel tears rising. I hadn't realized quite how marooned I felt.

"Hi, Mum." I reach to hug her—but my arms hit thin air. She's already turned away and is consulting her tiny gold watch.

"I can't stay more than a minute, I'm afraid," she says with a kind of tension, as though if she lingers too long the world will explode. "I'm due to see a specialist about Roly."

"Roly?"

"From Smoky's latest litter, darling." Mum shoots me a glance of reproach. "You remember little Roly."

I don't know how Mum expects me to keep track of all her dogs' names. There's at least twenty of them and they're all whippets, and every time I go home there seems to be another one. We were always an animal-free family—until the summer when I was seventeen. While on holiday in Wales, Mum bought a whippet puppy on a whim. And overnight it triggered this total mania.

I do like dogs. Kind of. Except when six of them jump up at you every time you open the front door. And whenever you try to sit down on a sofa or a chair, there's a dog on it. And all the biggest presents under the Christmas tree are for the dogs.

Mum has taken a bottle of Rescue Remedy out of her bag. She squeezes three drops onto her tongue, then breathes out sharply. "The traffic coming here was terrible," she says. "People in London are so aggressive. I had a *very* unpleasant altercation with a man in a van."

"What happened?" I say, already knowing that Mum will shake her head.

"Let's not talk about it, darling." She winces, as though being asked to recall her days of terror in the concentration camp. "Let's just forget about it."

Mum finds a lot of things too painful to talk about. Like how my new sandals could have got mangled last Christmas. Or the council's continual complaints about dog mess in our street. Or, to be honest, mess in general. In life.

"I've got a card for you," she says, rooting in her bag. "Where is it, now? From Andrew and Sylvia."

I stare at her, bemused. "Who?"

"Andrew and Sylvia, next door!" she says, as though it's obvious. "My neighbors!"

Her next-door neighbors aren't called Andrew and Sylvia. They're Philip and Maggie.

"Mum—"

"Anyway, they send their love," she says, interrupting me. "And Andrew wants to ask your advice on skiing."

Skiing? I don't know how to ski.

"Mum..." I put a hand to my head, forgetting about my injury, and wince. "What are you *talking* about?"

"Here we are!" Maureen comes back into the room, bearing a glass of orange juice. "Dr. Harman's just coming along to check you over."

"I must go, darling." Mum gets to her feet. "I left the car on some extortionate parking meter. And the congestion charge! Eight pounds I had to pay!"

That's not right either. The congestion charge isn't eight pounds. I'm *sure* it's only five quid, not that I ever use a car—

My stomach plunges. Oh my God—Mum's getting dementia. That has to be it. She's already going senile, at the age of fifty-four. I'll have to speak to one of the doctors about her.

"I'll be back later with Amy and Eric," she says, heading to the door.

Eric? She really calls her dogs some odd names.

"Okay, Mum." I smile brightly, to humor her. "Can't wait."

As I sip my juice I feel a bit shaken up. Everyone thinks their mum is a bit crazy. But that was seriously crazy. What if she has to go into a home? What will I do with all the dogs?

My thoughts are interrupted by a knock at the door, and a youngish doctor with dark hair enters, followed by three other people in medical uniforms.

"Hello there, Lexi," he says in a pleasant, brisk manner. "I'm Dr. Harman, one of the resident neurologists here. These are Nicole, a specialist nurse, and Diana and Garth, our two trainee doctors. So, how are you feeling?"

"Fine! Except my left hand feels a bit weird," I admit. "Like I've been sleeping on it and it isn't working properly."

As I lift up my hand to show him, I can't help

admiring my amazing manicure again. I *must* ask Fi
where we went last night.

"Right." The doctor nods. "We'll take a look at
that; you may need some therapy. But first I'm going to
ask you a few questions. Bear with me if some of them
seem blindingly obvious." He flashes a professional
smile and I get the feeling he's said all this a thousand
times before. "Can you tell me your name?"

"My name's Lexi Smart," I reply promptly. Dr.
Harman nods and adds a tick mark in his folder.

"And when were you born?"

"Nineteen seventy-nine."

"Very good." He makes another note. "Now, Lexi,
when you crashed your car, you bumped your head
against the windshield. There was a small amount of
swelling to your brain, but it looks as though you've
been very lucky. I still need to do some checks,
though." He holds up his pen. "If you'd like to look
at the top of this pen, I'm going to move it from side
to side."

Doctors don't let you get a word in, do they?

"Excuse me!" I wave at him. "You've mixed me up
with someone else. I didn't crash any car."

Dr. Harman frowns and flips back two pages in his
folder. "It says the patient was involved in a traffic accident." He looks around the room for confirmation.

Why is he asking them? *I'm* the one it happened to.

"Well, they must have written it down wrong," I say
firmly. "I was out clubbing with my friends and we
were running for a taxi and I fell. That's what happened. I remember it really well."

Dr. Harman and Maureen exchange puzzled looks.

"It was definitely a traffic accident," murmurs Maureen. "Two vehicles, side-on. I was down in Emergency and I saw her come in. *And* the other driver. I think he had a minor arm fracture."

"I couldn't have been in a car crash." I try to keep my patience. "For a start, I don't have a car. I don't even know how to drive!"

I'm intending to learn to drive one day. It's just that I've never needed to since living in London, and lessons are so expensive, and it's not like I can afford a car.

"You haven't got a..." Dr. Harman flips over a page and squints at the writing. "A Mercedes convertible?"

"A *Mercedes*?" I snort with laughter. "Are you serious?"

"But it says here—"

"Look." I cut him off as politely as I can. "I'll tell you how much twenty-five-year-old sales associates at Deller Carpets earn, okay? And you tell me if I can afford a Mercedes convertible."

Dr. Harman opens his mouth to answer—but is interrupted by one of the trainees, Diana, who taps his shoulder. She scribbles something on my notes and Dr. Harman's mouth snaps open again in shock. His eyes meet the trainee's; she raises her eyebrows, glances at me, then points at the paper again. They look like a pair of mime-school rejects.

Now Dr. Harman is coming closer and gazing intently at me with a grave expression. My stomach starts flip-flopping. I've seen *ER*, I know what that ex-pression means.

Lexi, we did a scan and we saw something we weren't expecting to find. It could be nothing.

Except it's never nothing, is it? Otherwise why would you be on the show?

"Is something really wrong with me?" I say almost aggressively, trying to suppress the sudden wobble of terror in my voice. "Just tell me, okay?"

My mind is already ripping through the possibilities. Cancer. Hole in the heart. Lose a leg. Maybe I've al-ready *lost* a leg—they just didn't want to tell me. Surreptitiously I feel through the blankets.

"Lexi, I want to ask you another question." Dr. Harman's voice is gentler. "Can you tell me what year it is?"

"What *year* it is?" I stare at him, thrown.

"Don't be alarmed," he says reassuringly. "Just tell me what year you think it is. It's one of our standard checks."

I look from face to face. I can tell they're playing some kind of trick on me, but I can't work out what.

"It's 2004," I say at last.

There's a weird stillness in the room, as if no one wants to breathe.

"Okay." Dr. Harman sits down on the bed. "Lexi, today is May 6, 2007."

His face is serious. All the others appear serious too. For an instant a frightening chink seems to open up in my brain—but then, with a rush of relief, I get it. This is a windup!

"Ha-ha." I roll my eyes. "Very funny. Did Fi put you up to this? Or Carolyn?"

"I don't know anyone called Fi or Carolyn," Dr. Harman replies without breaking his gaze. "And I'm not joking."

"He's serious, Lexi," one of the trainees chimes in. "We're in 2007."

"But...that's the *future*," I say stupidly. "Are you saying they've invented time machines?" I force a little laugh, but no one else joins in.

"Lexi, this is bound to be a shock," Maureen says kindly, putting a hand on my shoulder. "But it's true. It's May 2007."

I feel as if the two sides of my brain aren't connecting or something. I can hear what they're saying, but it's just ludicrous. Yesterday it was 2004. How can we have jumped three years?

"Look, it can't be 2007," I say at last, trying not to give away how rattled I am. "It's 2004. I'm not *stupid*—"

"Don't get upset," Dr. Harman says, sending warning glances to the others. "Let's take this slowly. Why don't you tell us what you last remember?"

"Okay, well..." I rub my face. "The last thing I remember is going out with some friends from work last night. Friday night. We went clubbing...and then we were trying to get a taxi in the rain and I slipped on the steps and fell. And I woke up in hospital. That was February 20, 2004." My voice is trembling. "I know the date exactly, because it was my dad's funeral the next day! I missed it, because I'm stuck here!"

"Lexi, all of that happened more than three years ago," Maureen says softly. "You're remembering the wrong accident."

She seems so sure. They all seem so sure. Panic is rising inside me as I look at their faces. It's 2004, I know it is. It *feels* like 2004.

"What else do you remember?" asks Dr. Harman. "Working back from that night."

"I don't know," I say defensively. "Being at work... moving into my flat...everything!"

"Is your memory foggy at all?"

"A...a bit," I admit reluctantly as the door opens. The trainee named Diana left the room a moment ago and now she's back, holding a copy of the *Daily Mail*. She approaches the bed and glances at Harman. "Should I?"

"Yes." He nods. "That's a good idea."

"Look, Lexi." She points to the dateline at the top. "This is today's paper."

I feel a massive jolt of shock as I read the date: *May 6, 2007*. But I mean...that's just words printed on paper—it doesn't prove anything. I look farther down the page, at a photograph of Tony Blair.

"God, he's aged!" I exclaim before I can stop myself. *Just like Mum* flashes through my mind, and a sudden coldness trickles down my spine.

But...that doesn't prove anything either. Maybe the light was just unflattering.

Hands trembling, I turn the page. There's total silence in the room; everyone is watching me, agog. My gaze travels uncertainly over a few headlines—*Interest rates to rise . . . Queen on States visit*—then is drawn by a bookshop ad.

Half price on all fantasy, including
Harry Potter and the Half-Blood Prince.

Okay. Now my skin is really prickling. I've read all the Harry Potter books, all five of them. I don't remember any half-blood prince.

"What's this?" Trying to sound casual, I point at the ad. "What's *Harry Potter and the Half-Blood Prince?*"

"That's the latest book," Garth, the other trainee, says. "It came out ages ago."

I can't help gasping. "There's a sixth Harry Potter?"

"There's a seventh out soon!" Diana steps forward eagerly. "And *guess* what happens at the end of book six—"

"Shh!" exclaims Nicole, the other nurse. "Don't tell her!"

They continue bickering, but I don't hear them anymore. I stare at the newspaper print until it jumps about in front of my eyes. That's why nothing made sense. It's not Mum who's confused—it's me.

"So I've been lying here in a coma"—I swallow hard—"for three years?"

I can't believe it. I've been Coma Girl. Everyone's been waiting for me to wake up for three whole years. The world's been going on without me. My family and friends have probably made me tapes, kept vigils, sung songs, and everything. . . .

But Dr. Harman is shaking his head. "No, that's not it. Lexi, you were only admitted five days ago."

What?

Enough. I can't cope with this anymore. I came into hospital five days ago in 2004—but now magically it's 2007? Where are we, bloody Narnia?

"I don't understand!" I say helplessly, thrusting the paper aside. "Am I hallucinating? Have I gone *crazy*?"

"No!" Dr. Harman says emphatically. "Lexi, I think you're suffering from what we call retrograde amnesia. It's a condition which normally arises following head injuries, but it seems that yours might be quite lengthy."

He carries on speaking, but his words aren't fixing properly in my brain. As I look around at the staff, I suddenly feel suspicion. They look fake. These aren't real medical professionals, are they? Is this a real hospital?

"Have you stolen my kidney?" My voice erupts in a panicky growl. "What have you done to me? You can't keep me here. I'm calling the police...." I try to struggle out of bed.

"Lexi." Nicole holds me by the shoulders. "No one's trying to hurt you. Dr. Harman's speaking the truth. You've lost your memory and you're confused."

"It's natural for you to panic, to believe that there's some kind of conspiracy. But we're telling you the truth." Dr. Harman looks me firmly in the eyes. "You've forgotten a chunk of your life, Lexi. You've *forgotten*. That's all."

I want to cry. I can't tell if they're lying, if this is all some massive trick, whether I should trust them or make a run for it. . . . My head's whirling with confusion—

Then suddenly I freeze. My hospital-gown sleeve got hitched up as I was struggling and I've just spotted a small, distinctive V-shaped scar near my elbow. A scar I've never seen before. A scar I don't recognize.

It's not new, either. It must be months old.

"Lexi, are you all right?" asks Dr. Harman.

I can't reply. My eyes are riveted on the unfamiliar scar.

Heart thumping, I slowly move my gaze down to my hands. These nails aren't acrylics, are they? Acrylics aren't that good. These are my real, genuine nails. And there's no way they could have grown this long in five days.

I feel like I've swum out of the shallows and found myself in mile-deep gray water.

"You're saying"—I clear my hoarse throat—"I've lost three years of my memory."

"Well, it's difficult to be precise, but that's what it looks like at the moment." Dr. Harman nods.

"Can I see the newspaper again, please?" My hands are trembling as I take it from Diana. I turn over the pages and every single one has the same dateline. *May 6, 2007. May 6, 2007.*

It really is the year 2007. Which means I must be . . .

Oh my God. I'm twenty-eight.

I'm *old*.

Chapter Three

They've made me a nice strong cup of tea. Because that cures amnesia, doesn't it, a cup of tea?

No, stop it. Don't be so sarky. I'm grateful for the tea. At least it's something to hold on to. At least it's something *real*.

As Dr. Harman talks about neurological exams and CT scans, I'm somehow managing to keep it together. I'm nodding calmly, as if to say, "Yeah, no problem. I'm cool with all of this." But inside I'm not remotely cool. I'm freaking. The truth keeps hitting me in the guts, over and over, till I feel giddy.

When at last he gets paged and has to leave, I feel a huge sense of relief. I can't be talked at anymore. I'm not following any of what he says, anyway. I take a gulp of tea and flop back on my pillows. (Okay, I take it all back about the tea. It's the best thing I've tasted for a long time.)

Maureen has gone off duty and Nicole has stayed in the room and is scribbling on my chart. "How are you feeling?"

"Really, really . . . *really* weird." I try to smile.

"I don't blame you." She smiles back sympathetically. "Just take it easy. Don't push yourself. You've got a lot to take in. Your brain is trying to reboot itself."

She consults her watch and writes down the time.

"When people get amnesia," I venture, "do the missing memories come back?"

"Usually." She gives a reassuring nod.

I shut my eyes tight and try throwing my mind back as hard as I can. Waiting for it to net something, snag on *something*.

But there's nothing. Just black, frictionless nothing.

"So, tell me about 2007." I open my eyes. "Who's prime minister now? And president of America?"

"That would be Tony Blair," replies Nicole. "And President Bush."

"Oh. Same." I cast around. "So . . . have they solved global warming? Or cured AIDS?"

Nicole shrugs. "Not yet."

You'd think a bit more would have happened in three years. You'd think the world would have moved on. I'm a bit unimpressed by 2007, to be honest.

"Would you like a magazine?" Nicole asks. "I'm just going to sort you out some breakfast." She disappears out the door, then returns and hands me a copy of *Hello!* I run my eyes down the headlines—and feel a jolt of shock.

" 'Jennifer Aniston and Her New Man.' " I read the words aloud uncertainly. "What new man? Why would she need a new man?"

Nicole follows my gaze, unconcerned.
"... he split up from Brad Pitt?"

"... r and Brad *split*?" I stare up at her, aghast.
"... n't be serious! They can't have done!"

"He went off with Angelina Jolie. They've got a daughter."

"*No!*" I wail. "But Jen and Brad were so perfect together! They looked so good, and they had that lovely wedding picture and everything...."

"They're divorced now." Nicole shrugs, like it's no big deal.

I can't get over this. Jennifer and Brad are divorced. The world is a different place.

"Everyone's pretty much got used to it." Nicole pats my shoulder soothingly. "I'll get you some breakfast. Would you like full English, continental, or fruit basket? Or all three?"

"Um...continental, please. Thanks very much." I open the magazine, then put it down again. "Hang on. Fruit basket? Did the NHS suddenly get a load of money or something?"

"This isn't NHS." She smiles. "You're in the private wing."

Private? I can't afford to go private.

"I'll just refresh your tea..." She picks up the smart china pot and starts to pour.

"Stop!" I exclaim in panic. I can't have any more tea. It probably costs fifty quid a cup.

"Something wrong?" Nicole says in surprise.

"I can't afford all this," I say in an embarrassed rush. "I'm sorry, I don't know why I'm in this posh room. I should have been taken to an NHS hospital. I'm happy to move..."

"It's all covered by your private health insurance," she says. "Don't worry."

"Oh," I say, taken aback. "Oh, right."

I took out private health insurance? Well, of course I did. I'm twenty-eight now. I'm sensible.

I'm twenty-eight years old.

It hits me right in the stomach, as though for the first time. I'm a different person. I'm not me anymore.

I mean, obviously I'm still *me*. But I'm twenty-eight-year-old me. Whoever the hell that is. I peer at my twenty-eight-year-old hand as though for clues. Someone who can afford private health insurance, obviously, and gets a really good manicure, and...

Wait a minute. Slowly I turn my head and focus again on the glossy Louis Vuitton.

No. It's not possible. This zillion-pound, designer, movie-star-type bag couldn't really be—

"Nicole?" I swallow, trying to sound nonchalant. "D'you think...Is that bag...*mine*?"

"Should be." Nicole nods. "I'll just check for you..." She opens the bag, pulls out a matching Louis Vuitton wallet, and snaps it open. "Yes, it's yours." She turns the wallet around to display a platinum American Express card with *Lexi Smart* printed across it.

My brain is short-circuiting as I stare at the embossed letters. That's my platinum credit card. This is my bag.

"But these bags cost, like...a thousand quid." My voice is strangled.

"I know they do." Nicole suddenly laughs. "Go on, relax. It's yours!"

Gingerly I stroke the handle, hardly daring to touch it. I can't believe this belongs to me. I mean . . . where did I *get* it? Am I earning loads of money or something?

"So, I was really in a car crash?" I look up, suddenly wanting to know everything about myself, all at once. "I was really driving? In a *Mercedes*?"

"Apparently." She takes in my expression of disbelief. "Didn't you have a Mercedes in 2004, then?"

"Are you joking? I can't even drive!"

When did I learn to drive? When did I suddenly start to afford designer handbags and Mercedes cars, for God's sake?

"Look in your bag," suggests Nicole. "Maybe the things inside will jog your memory."

"Okay. Good idea." There are flutters in my stomach as I pull open the bag. A smell of leather, mixed with some unfamiliar perfume, rises from the inside. I reach in—and the first thing I pull out is a tiny gold-plated Estée Lauder compact. At once I flip it open to have a look.

"You've had some cuts to the face, Lexi," Nicole says quickly. "Don't be alarmed—they'll heal."

As I meet my own eyes in the tiny mirror, I feel sudden relief. It's still me, even if there's a huge graze on my eyelid. I move the mirror about, trying to get a good view, flinching as I see the bandage on my head. I tilt it farther down: there are my lips, looking weirdly full and pink, as if I was snogging all last night, and—

Oh my God.

Those aren't my teeth. They're all white. They're all gleamy. I'm looking at a stranger's mouth.

"Are you okay?" Nicole interrupts my daze. "Lexi?"

"I'd like a proper mirror, please," I manage at last. "I need to see myself. Have you got one you could bring me?"

"There's one in the bathroom." She comes forward. "In fact, it's a good idea for you to get moving. I'll help you."

I heave myself out of the high metal bed. My legs are wobbly, but I manage to totter into the adjoining bathroom.

"Now," she says, before she closes the door. "You have had some cuts and bruising, so your appearance may be a little bit of a shock. Are you ready?"

"Yes. I'll be fine. Just show me." I take a deep breath and steel myself. She swings the door shut to reveal a full-length mirror on the back of it.

Is that . . . *me*?

I can't speak. My legs have turned to jelly. I grip a towel rail, trying to keep control of myself.

"I know your injuries look bad." Nicole has a strong arm around me. "But believe me, they're just surface wounds."

I'm not even looking at the cuts. Or the bandage or the staple on my forehead. It's what's underneath.

"That's not . . ." I gesture at my reflection. "That's not what I look like."

I close my eyes and visualize my old self, just to make sure I'm not going crazy. Mouse-colored frizzy hair, blue eyes, slightly fatter than I'd like to be. Nice-ish face but nothing special. Black eyeliner and bright pink Tesco lipstick. The standard Lexi Smart look.

Then I open my eyes again. A different girl is staring back at me. Some of my hair has been messed up by the crash, but the rest is a bright, unfamiliar shade of chestnut, all straight and sleek with not one bit of frizz. My toenails are perfectly pink and polished. My legs are tanned golden brown, and thinner than before. And more muscled.

"What's changed?" Nicole is looking at my reflection curiously.

"Everything!" I manage. "I look all . . . sheeny."

"Sheeny?" She laughs.

"My hair, my legs, my *teeth* . . ." I can't take my eyes off those immaculate pearly whites. They must have cost a bloody fortune.

"They're nice!" She nods politely.

"No. No. No." I'm shaking my head vigorously. "You don't understand. I have the worst teeth in the world. My nickname is 'Snaggletooth.' "

"Shouldn't think it is anymore." Nicole raises an amused eyebrow.

"And I've lost loads of weight. . . . And my face is different; I'm not sure exactly how . . ." I scan my features, trying to work it out. My eyebrows are thin and groomed . . . my lips seem fuller somehow. . . . I peer more closely, suddenly suspicious. Have I had something *done*? Have I turned into someone *who has work done*?

I tear myself away from the mirror and pull the door open, my head spinning.

"Take it easy," Nicole warns, hurrying after me.

"You've had a shock to the system. Maybe you should take things one step at a time...."

Ignoring her, I grab the Louis Vuitton bag and start yanking things out of it, examining each item closely as though it might impart a message. God, just *look* at this stuff. A Tiffany key fob, a pair of Prada sunglasses, a lip gloss: Lancôme, not Tesco.

And here's a small, pale-green Smythson diary. I hesitate for a moment, psyching myself up—then open it. With a jolt I see my own familiar handwriting. *Lexi Smart, 2007* is scribbled inside the front cover. I must have written those words. I must have doodled that feathery bird in the corner. But I have absolutely no recollection of doing so.

Feeling as if I'm spying on myself, I start leafing through the tiny pages. There are appointments on every page: *Lunch 12:30. Drinks P. Meeting Gill—artwork.* But they're all written in initials and abbreviations. I can't glean much from this. I flick onward to the end and a bunch of business cards falls out of the diary. I pick one up, glance down at the name—and freeze.

It's a card from the company I work at, Deller Carpets—although it's been given a trendy new logo. And the name is printed in clear charcoal gray.

LEXI SMART

DIRECTOR, FLOORING

I feel as though the ground has fallen away from me.

"Lexi?" Nicole is regarding me in concern. "You've gone very pale."

"Look at this." I hold the card out, trying to keep a grip on myself. "It says 'director' on my business card. That's, like, boss of the whole department. How could I possibly be the boss?" My voice rises more shrilly than I intended. "I've only been at the company a year. I didn't even get a bonus!"

Hands trembling, I slot the card back between the diary pages and reach into the bag again. I have to find my phone. I have to call my friends, my family, *someone* who knows what's going on. . . .

Got it.

It's a sleek new model that I don't recognize, but it's still pretty simple to work out. I haven't got any voice messages, although there's a new unread text. I select it and peer at the tiny screen.

Running late, I'll call when I can.
E.

Who's "E"? I rack my brains but can't think of a single person I know whose name begins with *E*. Someone new at work? I go to my stored texts—and the first one is from "E": *I don't think so. E.*

Is "E" my new best friend or something?

I'll trawl through my messages later. Right now I have to talk to someone who knows me, who can tell me exactly what's been going on in my life these last three years . . . I speed-dial Fi's number and wait, drumming my nails, for a reply.

"Hi, you've reached Fiona Roper. Please leave a message."

"Hey, Fi," I say as soon as the beep sounds. "It's me, Lexi! Listen, I know this'll sound weird, but I've had an accident. I'm in hospital and I just...I need to talk to you. It's quite important. Can you give me a call? Bye!" As I close the phone, Nicole puts a hand on it reprovingly.

"You're not supposed to use these in here," she says. "You can use a landline, though. I'll set you up with a receiver."

"Okay." I nod. "Thanks." I'm about to start scrolling through all my old texts, when there's a knock on the door and another nurse comes in, holding a pair of bags.

"I've got your clothes here." She puts a shopping bag down on my bed. I reach in, pull out a pair of dark jeans, and stare at them. What are these? The waist is too high and they're *way* too narrow, almost like tights. How are you supposed to get a pair of boots on under those?

"Oh, 7 For All Mankind," says Nicole, raising her eyebrows. "Very nice."

Seven for what?

"I'd love a pair of those." She strokes a leg admiringly. "About two hundred quid a pop, aren't they?"

Two hundred pounds? For *jeans*?

"And here's your jewelry," adds the other nurse, holding out a transparent plastic bag. "It had to come off for the scans."

Still stunned by the jeans, I take the bag. I've never been a jewelry-type person, unless you count TopShop earrings and a Swatch. Feeling like a kid with a

Christmas stocking, I reach into the bag and pull out a tangle of gold. There's an expensive-looking bracelet made of hammered gold, and a matching necklace, plus a watch.

"Wow. This is nice." I run my fingers cautiously over the bracelet, then reach in again and retrieve two chandelier earrings. Caught up among the knotted strands of gold is a ring, and after a bit of careful unweaving I manage to untangle it.

There's a general intake of breath. Someone whispers, "Oh my God."

I'm holding a huge, shiny, diamond solitaire ring. The type you get in movies. The type you see on navy-blue velvet in jewelers' windows with no price tag. At last I tear my gaze away and see that both nurses are riveted too.

"Hey!" Nicole suddenly exclaims. "There's something else. Hold out your hand, Lexi. . . ." She tips up the bag and taps the corner. There's a moment's stillness—then out onto my palm falls a plain gold band.

There's a kind of rushing in my ears as I stare down at it.

"You must be married!" Nicole says brightly.

No. No way. Surely I'd *know* if I was married? Surely I'd sense it deep down, amnesia or no amnesia. I turn the ring over in my clumsy fingers, feeling hot and cold all over.

"She is." The second nurse nods. "You are. Don't you remember, love?"

I shake my head dumbly.

"You don't remember your wedding?" Nicole looks

agog. "You don't remember anything about your husband?"

"No." I look up suddenly with horror. "I didn't marry Loser Dave, did I?"

"I don't know!" Nicole gives a giggle and claps her hand over her mouth. "I'm sorry. You just looked so appalled. D'you know what his name is?" She looks at the other nurse, who shakes her head.

"Sorry. I've been on the other ward. But I know there's a husband."

"Look, the ring's engraved!" Nicole exclaims, taking it from me. " 'A.S. and E.G. June 3, 2005.' Coming up on their two-year anniversary." She hands it back. "Is that you?"

I'm breathing fast. It's true. It's carved here in solid gold.

"I'm A.S.," I say at last. "*A* for Alexia. But I have no idea who E.G. is."

The *E* from my phone, I suddenly realize. That must have been him texting me. My husband.

"I think I need some cold water. . . ." Feeling giddy, I totter into the bathroom, splash water on my face, then lean forward across the cold enamel basin and stare at my bashed-up, familiar-unfamiliar reflection. I feel like I'm about to have a meltdown. Is someone still playing a gigantic prank on me? Am I hallucinating?

I'm twenty-eight, I have perfect white teeth, a Louis Vuitton bag, a card saying "director," and a husband.

How the hell did all *that* happen?

Chapter Four

Edward. Ethan. Errol.

It's an hour later and I'm still in a state of shock. I keep looking in disbelief at my wedding ring resting on the bedside cabinet. I, Lexi Smart, have a husband. I don't feel *old* enough to have a husband.

Elliott. Eamonn. Egbert.

Please, God, not Egbert.

I've ransacked the Louis Vuitton bag. I've looked all the way through the diary. I've skimmed through all my stored mobile numbers. But I still haven't found out what *E* stands for. You'd think I'd remember my own husband's name. You'd think it would be engraved in my psyche.

When the door opens, I stiffen, almost expecting it to be him. But it's Mum again, looking pink and harassed.

"Those traffic wardens have *no* hearts. I was only twenty minutes at the vet, and—"

"Mum, I've got amnesia." I cut her off in a rush. "I've lost my memory. I've lost a whole chunk of my life. I'm really ... freaked out."

"Oh. Yes, the nurse mentioned it." Her gaze briefly meets mine, then flicks away again. Mum's not the greatest at eye contact; she never has been. I used to get quite frustrated by it when I was younger, but now I just see it as one of those Mum things. Like the way she won't learn the names of TV programs properly, even after you've told her five hundred times it's not *The Simpsons Family*.

Now she's sitting down and peeling off her waistcoat. "I know *exactly* how you feel," she begins. "My memory gets worse every day. In fact, the other day—"

"Mum..." I inhale deeply, trying to stay calm. "You don't know how I feel. This isn't like forgetting where you put something. I've lost three years of my life! I don't know anything about myself in 2007. I don't look the same, none of my things are the same, and I found these rings which apparently belong to me, and I just have to know something..." My voice is jumping about with apprehension. "Mum...am I really *married*?"

"Of course you're married!" Mum appears surprised that I need to ask. "Eric will be here any minute. I told you that earlier."

"Eric's my husband?" I stare at her. "I thought Eric was a dog."

"A *dog*?" Mum raises her eyebrows. "Goodness, darling! You *did* get a bump on the head!"

Eric. I'm rolling the name around my head experimentally. *My husband, Eric.*

It means nothing to me. It's not a name I feel either way about.

I love you, Eric.

With my body I thee worship, Eric.

I wait for some sort of reaction in my body. Surely I should respond? Surely all my love cells should be waking up? But I feel totally blank and nothing-y.

"He had a very important meeting this morning. But otherwise he's been here with you night and day."

"Right." I digest this. "So . . . so what's he like?"

"He's *very* nice," says Mum, as though she's talking about a sponge cake.

"Is he . . ." I stop.

I can't ask if he's good-looking. That would be really shallow. And what if she avoids the question and says he has a wonderful sense of humor?

What if he's obese?

Oh God. What if I got to know his beautiful inner soul as we exchanged messages over the Internet, only now I've forgotten all about that and I'll have to pretend his looks don't matter to me?

We lapse into silence and I find myself eyeing up Mum's dress—Laura Ashley, circa 1975. Frills come in and out of fashion, but somehow she doesn't notice. She still wears the same clothes she wore when she first met my dad, and the same long flicky hair, the same frosted lipstick. It's like she thinks she's still in her twenties.

Not that I would ever mention this to her. We've never been into cozy mother-daughter chats. I once tried to confide in her, when I split up with my first boyfriend. Big mistake. She didn't sympathize, or hug me, or even really listen. Instead she got all pink and defensive and sharp with me, as if I was deliberately trying to wound her by talking about relationships. I felt like I was negotiating a land-mine site, treading on sensitive bits of her life I didn't even realize existed.

So I gave up and called Fi instead.

"Did you manage to order those sofa covers for me, Lexi?" Mum interrupts my thoughts. "Off the Internet," she adds at my blank look. "You were going to do it last week."

Did she listen to *anything* I said?

"Mum, I don't know," I say, slowly and clearly. "I don't remember anything about the last three years."

"Sorry, darling." Mum hits her head. "I'm being stupid."

"I don't know what I was doing last week, or last year ... or even who my own husband is." I spread my arms. "To be honest, it's pretty scary."

"Of course. Absolutely." Mum is nodding, a distant look in her eyes, as though she's processing my words. "The thing is, darling, I don't remember the name of the Web site. So if you *did* happen to recall—"

"I'll let you know, okay?" I can't help snapping. "If my memory returns, the first thing I'll do is call you about your sofa covers. Jesus!"

"There's no need to raise your voice, Lexi!" she says, opening her eyes wide.

Okay. So in 2007 Mum still officially drives me up the wall. Surely I'm supposed to have grown out of being irritated by my mother? Automatically I start picking at my thumbnail. Then I stop. Twenty-eight-year-old Lexi doesn't shred her nails.

"So, what does he do?" I return to the subject of my so-called husband. I still can't really believe he's real.

"Who, Eric?"

"Yes! Of course Eric!"

"He sells property," Mum says, as though I ought to know. "He's rather good at it, actually."

I've married a real-estate agent called Eric.

How?

Why?

"Do we live in my flat?"

"Your flat?" Mum looks bemused. "Darling, you sold your flat a long time ago. You have a marital home now!"

"I *sold* it?" I feel a pang. "But I've only just bought it!"

I love my flat. It's in Balham and is tiny but cozy, with blue-painted window frames which I did myself, and a lovely squashy velvet sofa, and piles of colorful cushions everywhere, and fairy lights around the mirror. Fi and Carolyn helped me move in two months ago, and we spray-painted the bathroom silver, and then spray-painted our jeans silver too.

And now it's all gone. I live in a marital home. With my marital husband.

For the millionth time I look at the wedding ring and diamond solitaire. Then I automatically shoot a glance at Mum's hand. She still wears Dad's ring, despite the way he's behaved toward her over the years—

Dad. Dad's funeral.

It's like a hand has gripped hold of my stomach, tight.

"Mum..." I venture cautiously. "I'm really sorry I missed Dad's funeral. Did it... you know, go all right?"

"You didn't miss it, darling." She peers at me as though I'm crazy. "You were there."

"Oh." I stare at her, confused. "Right. Of course. I just don't remember anything about it."

Heaving a massive sigh, I lean back on my pillows. I don't remember my own wedding and I don't remember my dad's funeral. Two of the most important events in my life, and I feel like I've missed out on them. "So, how was it?"

"Oh, it all went off as well as these things ever do..." Mum's looking twitchy, the way she always is when the subject of Dad comes up.

"Were many people there?"

A pained expression comes to her face.

"Let's not *dwell* on it, darling. It was years ago." She gets up as though to remove herself from my questioning. "Now, have you had any lunch? I didn't have time to eat *anything*, just a snatch of a boiled egg and toast. I'll go and find something for us both. And make sure you eat properly, Lexi," she adds. "None of this no-carbs obsession. A potato won't kill you."

No carbs? Is that how I got this shape? I glance down at my unfamiliar toned legs. It has to be said, they look as if they don't know what a potato *is*.

"I've changed in appearance quite a lot, haven't I?" I can't help saying, a bit self-consciously. "My hair... my teeth..."

"I suppose you are different." She peers at me vaguely. "It's been so gradual, I haven't really noticed."

For God's sake. How can you not even notice when your daughter turns from a manky, overweight Snaggletooth into a thin, tanned, groomed person?

"I won't be long." Mum picks up her embroidered shoulder bag. "And Amy should be here any moment."

"Amy's here?" My spirits lift as I visualize my little sister in her pink fleecy vest and flower-embroidered jeans and those cute sneakers that light up when she dances.

"She was just buying some chocolate downstairs." Mum opens the door. "She loves those mint Kit Kats."

The door closes behind her and I stare at it. They've invented *mint* Kit Kats?

2007 really is a different world.

• • •

Amy's not my half sister or stepsister, like most people assume. She's my full, one-hundred-percent sister. But people get confused because: 1. There's thirteen years between us. 2. My mum and dad had split up before she was born.

Maybe "split up" is too strong. I'm not sure what went on exactly—all I know is, my dad was never around much when I was growing up. The official reason was that his business was based abroad. The *real* reason was that he was a feckless chancer. I was only eight when I heard him described like that by one of my aunts at a Christmas party. When they saw me they got flustered and changed the subject, so I figured *feckless* was some really terrible swear word. It's always stuck in my mind. *Feckless*.

The first time he left home, I was seven. Mum said he'd gone on a business trip to America, so when Melissa at school said she'd seen him in the co-op with a woman in red jeans, I told her she was a fat liar. He came back home a few weeks later, looking tired— from the jet lag, he said. When I pestered him for a souvenir, he produced a pack of Wrigley's gum. I called it my American gum and showed everyone at school— until Melissa pointed out the co-op price sticker. I never told Dad I knew the truth, or Mum. I'd kind of known all along that he wasn't in America.

A couple of years later he disappeared again, for a few months this time. Then he started up a property business in Spain, which went bust. Then he got involved in some dodgy pyramid scheme and tried to get all our friends involved. Somewhere along the line he became an alcoholic...then he moved in for a bit with some Spanish woman....But Mum kept taking him back. Then, at last, about three years ago, he moved to Portugal for good, apparently to get away from the tax man.

Mum had various other "gentlemen friends" over the years, but she and Dad never divorced—never really let go of each other at all. And, evidently, on one of his jovial, the-drinks-are-on-me-darlings Christmas visits, she and he must have...

Well. I don't exactly want to picture it. We got Amy, that's the point. And she's the most adorable little thing, always playing on her disco dance mat and wanting to plait my hair a million times over.

The room is quiet and dim since Mum left. I pour

myself a glass of water and sip it slowly. My thoughts are all cloudy, like a bomb site after the blast. I feel like a forensics expert, picking through the different strands, trying to work out the full picture.

There's a faint knocking at the door and I look up. "Hello? Come in!"

"Hi, Lexi?"

An unfamiliar girl of about fifteen has edged into the room. She's tall and skinny, with jeans falling off her midriff, a pierced navel, spiky blue-streaked hair, and about six coats of mascara. I have no idea who she is. As she sees me, she grimaces.

"Your face still looks fucked up."

"Oh," I say, taken aback. The girl's eyes narrow as she surveys me.

"Lexi...it's me. You do know it's me, don't you?"

"Right!" I make an apologetic face. "Look, I'm really sorry, but I've had this accident and I'm having some problems with my memory. I mean, I'm sure we have met—"

"Lexi?" She sounds incredulous; almost hurt. "It's me! It's *Amy*."

• • •

I'm speechless. I'm beyond speechless. This cannot be my baby sister.

But it is. Amy's turned into a tall, sassy teenager. Practically an adult. As she saunters around the room, picking things up and putting them down, I'm mesmerized by the height of her. The *confidence* of her.

"Is there any food here? I'm starving." She has the same sweet, husky voice she always did—but modulated. Cooler and more street-wise.

"Mum's getting me some lunch. You can share if you like."

"Great." She sits down in a chair and swings her long legs over the arm, displaying gray suede ankle boots with spiky heels. "So, you don't remember anything? That's so cool."

"It's not cool," I retort. "It's horrible. I remember up to just before Dad's funeral...and then it just goes fuzzy. I don't remember my first few days in hospital, either. It's like I woke up for the first time last night."

"Way out." Her eyes are wide. "So, you don't remember me visiting you before?"

"No. All I remember is you being twelve. With your ponytail and braces. And those cute hair clips you used to wear."

"Don't remind me." Amy mimes puking, then frowns in thought. "So...let me get this straight. The whole of the last three years is a total blank."

"Like a big black hole. And even before that it's a bit foggy. Apparently I'm *married*?" I laugh nervously. "I had no idea! Were you a bridesmaid at the wedding or anything?"

"Yeah," she says distractedly. "It was cool. Hey, Lexi, I don't want to bring this up when you're feeling so ill and everything, but..." She twists a strand of hair, looking awkward.

"What?" I look at her in surprise. "Tell me."

"Well, it's just that you owe me seventy quid." She

shrugs apologetically. "You borrowed it last week when your cash card wasn't working and you said you'd pay me back. I don't suppose you'll remember..."

"Oh," I say, taken aback. "Of course. Just help yourself." I gesture at the Louis Vuitton bag. "I don't know if there's any cash in there..."

"There will be," Amy says, swiftly unzipping it with a tiny smile. "Thanks!" She pockets the notes and swings her legs over the arm of the chair again, playing with her collection of silver bangles. Then she looks up, suddenly alert. "Wait a minute. Do you know about—" She stops herself.

"What?"

She surveys me with narrowed, disbelieving eyes. "No one's told you, have they?"

"Told me what?"

"*Jesus.* I suppose they're trying to break things to you gradually, but, I mean..." She shakes her head, nibbling her nails. "Personally, I think you should know sooner rather than later."

"Know what?" I feel a beat of alarm. "What, Amy? Tell me!"

For a moment Amy seems to debate with herself, then she gets up.

"Wait here." She disappears for a few moments. Then the door opens again and she reappears, clutching an Asian-looking baby about a year old. He's wearing overalls and holding a beaker of juice, and he gives me a sunny smile.

"This is Lennon," she says, her expression softening. "This is your son."

I stare at them both, frozen in terror. What's she talking about?

"I guess you don't remember?" Amy strokes his hair fondly. "You adopted him from Vietnam six months ago. It was quite a story, actually. You had to smuggle him out in your rucksack. You nearly got arrested!"

I adopted a baby?

I feel cold to my guts. I can't be a mum. I'm not ready. I don't know anything about babies.

"Say hello to your child!" She carts him over to the bed, clicking in her spiky heels. "He calls you Moo-mah, by the way."

Moo-mah?

"Hi, Lennon," I say at last, my voice stiff with self-consciousness. "It's . . . it's Moo-mah!" I try to adopt a motherly, cooing voice. "Come to Moo-mah!"

I look up to see Amy's lips trembling strangely. Suddenly she gives a snort of laughter and claps a hand over her mouth. "Sorry!"

"Amy, what's going on?" I stare at her, suspicion dawning. "Is this really my baby?"

"I saw him in the corridor before," she splutters. "I couldn't resist it. Your face!" She's in paroxysms of laughter. " 'Come to Moo-mah!' "

I can hear muffled cries and shouts coming from outside the door.

"That must be his parents!" I hiss in consternation. "You bloody little . . . Put him *back*!"

I collapse on my pillows in relief, my heart pounding. Thank fuck. I don't have a child.

And I cannot get over Amy. She used to be so sweet

and innocent. She used to watch *Barbie Sleeping Beauty* over and over with her thumb in her mouth. What's *happened* to her?

"I nearly had a heart attack," I say reproachfully as she comes back in, holding a can of diet Coke. "If I died, it would be your fault."

"Well, you need to get savvy," she retorts with an unrepentant grin. "People could feed you all kinds of bullshit."

She takes out a stick of chewing gum and starts unwrapping it. Then she leans forward.

"Hey, Lexi," she says in a low voice. "Have you really got amnesia or are you just making it up? I won't tell."

"*What?* Why would I make it up?"

"I thought there might be something you wanted to get out of. Like a dentist's appointment."

"No! This is genuine!"

"Okay. Whatever." She shrugs and offers me the gum.

"No, thanks." I wrap my arms around my knees, suddenly daunted. Amy's right. People could take total advantage of me. I have so much to learn and I don't even know where to start.

Well, I could start with the obvious.

"So." I try to sound casual. "What's my husband like? What does he ... look like?"

"Wow." Amy's eyes open wide. "Of course! You have no idea what he's like!"

"Mum said he was nice ..." I try to hide my apprehension.

"He is lovely." She nods seriously. "He has a real

sense of humor. And they're going to operate on his hump."

"Yeah. Nice try, Amy." I roll my eyes.

"Lexi! He'd be really hurt if he heard that!" Amy looks taken aback. "This is 2007. We don't discriminate because of looks. And Eric is such a sweet, loving guy. It's not *his* fault his back was damaged when he was a baby. And he's achieved so much. He's awe-inspiring."

Now I'm hot with shame. Maybe my husband does have a hump. I shouldn't be hump-ist. Whatever he looks like, I'm sure I chose him for a very good reason.

"Can he walk?" I ask nervously.

"He walked for the first time at your wedding," says Amy, her eyes distant with memory. "He got up out of his wheelchair to say his vows. Everyone was in tears ... the vicar could hardly speak...." Her mouth is twitching again.

"You little cow!" I exclaim. "He doesn't bloody well have a hump, does he?"

"I'm sorry." She starts giggling helplessly. "But this is *such* a good game."

"It's not a game!" I clutch at my hair, forgetting my injuries, and wince. "It's my life. I have no idea who my husband is, or how I met him, or anything...."

"Okay." She appears to relent. "What happened was, you got talking to this grizzled old tramp on the street. And his name was Eric—"

"Shut up! If you won't tell me, I'll ask Mum."

"All right!" She lifts her hands in surrender. "You seriously want to know?"

"Yes!"

"Okay, then. You met him on a TV show."

"Try again." I lift my eyes to heaven.

"It's true! I'm not bullshitting now. You were on that reality show *Ambition*. Where people want to get to the top in business. He was one of the judges and you were a contestant. You didn't get very far on the show, but you met Eric, and you hit it off."

There's silence. I'm waiting for her to crack up laughing and produce some punch line, but she just swigs from the can of diet Coke.

"I was on a reality show?" I say skeptically.

"Yeah. It was really cool. All my friends watched, and we all voted for you. You should have won!"

I eye her closely, but her face is totally serious. Is she telling the truth? Was I really on the *telly*?

"Why on earth did I go on a show like that?"

"To be the boss?" Amy shrugs. "To get ahead. That's when you had your teeth and hair done, to look good on TV."

"But I'm not ambitious. I mean, I'm not *that* ambitious..."

"Are you kidding?" Amy opens her eyes wide. "You're, like, the most ambitious person in the world! As soon as your boss resigned you went for his job. All the bigwigs at your company had seen you on telly and they were really impressed. So they gave it to you."

My mind flashes back to those business cards in my diary. *Lexi Smart, Director*.

"You're the youngest director they've ever had in the company. It was so cool when you got the job,"

Amy adds. "We all went out to celebrate, and you bought us all champagne..." She pulls her chewing gum out of her mouth in a long strand. "You don't remember *any* of this?"

"No! Nothing!"

The door opens and Mum appears, holding a tray bearing a covered plate, a pot of chocolate mousse, and a glass of water.

"Here we are," she says. "I've brought you some lasagne. And guess what? Eric's here!"

"*Here?*" The blood drains from my face. "D'you mean...here in the hospital?"

Mum nods. "He's on his way up right now to see you! I told him to give you a few moments to get ready."

A few *moments*? I need more than a few moments. This is all happening way too fast. I'm not even ready to be twenty-eight yet. Let alone meet some husband I allegedly have.

"Mum, I'm not sure I can do this," I say, panicked. "I mean...I don't feel up to meeting him yet. Maybe I should see him tomorrow. When I'm a bit more adjusted."

"Lexi, darling!" remonstrates Mum. "You can't turn your husband away. He's rushed here from his business especially to see you!"

"But I don't know him! I won't know what to say or what to do..."

"Darling, he's your *husband*." She pats my hand reassuringly. "There's nothing to worry about."

"He might trigger your memory," chimes in Amy, who has helped herself to the chocolate mousse pot and is ripping the top off. "You might see him and go 'Eric! My love! It all comes back to me!'"

"Shut up," I snap. "And that's *my* chocolate mousse."

"You don't eat carbs," she retorts. "Have you forgotten that too?" She waves the spoon tantalizingly in front of my face.

"Nice try, Amy," I say, rolling my eyes. "There's no way I would ever have given up chocolate."

"You *never* eat chocolate anymore. Does she, Mum? You didn't eat any of your own wedding cake because of the calories!"

She has to be bullshitting me. I wouldn't have given up chocolate, not in a million years. I'm about to tell her to piss off and hand over the mousse, when there's a knock at the door and a muffled male voice calls, "Hello?"

"Oh my God." I look wildly from face to face. "Oh my God. Is that him? Already?"

"Hold on a moment, Eric!" Mum calls through the door, then she whispers to me. "Tidy yourself up a bit, sweetheart! You look like you've been dragged through a hedge."

"Give her a break, Mum," says Amy. "She was dragged through the wreckage of a *car*, remember?"

"I'll just comb your hair quickly..." Mum comes over with a tiny handbag comb and starts jerking at my head.

"Ow!" I protest. "You'll make my amnesia worse!"

"There." She gives a final tug, and wipes at my face with the corner of a hanky. "Ready?"

"Shall I open the door?" says Amy.

"No! Just...wait a sec."

My stomach is churning in dread. I can't meet some total stranger who's apparently my husband. It's just...too freaky.

"Mum, please." I turn to her. "It's too soon. Tell him to come back later. Tomorrow. Or we could leave it a few weeks, even."

"Don't be silly, darling!" Mum laughs. How can she *laugh*? "He's your husband. And you've just been in a car accident and he's been worried sick, and we've kept him waiting long enough, poor chap!"

As Mum heads toward the door I'm gripping the sheets so hard, the blood is squashed out of my fingertips.

"What if I hate him? What if there's no chemistry between us?" My voice shoots out in terror. "I mean, does he expect me to go back and *live* with him?"

"Just play it by ear," Mum says vaguely. "Really, Lexi, there's nothing to worry about. He's *very* nice."

"As long as you don't mention his toupee," puts in Amy. "Or his Nazi past."

"Amy!" Mum clicks her tongue in reproof and opens the door. "Eric! I'm so sorry to keep you. Come in."

There's an unbearably long pause. Then into the room, carrying an enormous bouquet of flowers, walks the most drop-dead gorgeous man I've ever seen.

Chapter Five

I can't speak. All I can do is gaze up at him, a bubble of disbelief rising inside me. This man is seriously, achingly good-looking. Like, Armani model good-looking. He has medium-brown curly hair, cropped short. He has blue eyes, broad shoulders, and an expensive-looking suit. He has a square jaw, impeccably shaved.

How did I land this guy? How? How? *How?*

"Hi," he says, and his voice is all deep and rounded like an actor's.

"Hi!" I manage breathlessly.

Look at his huge chest. He must work out every day. And look at his polished shoes, and his designer watch...

My eyes drift back to his hair. I never thought I'd marry someone with curly hair. Funny, that. Not that I have anything *against* curly hair. I mean, on him it looks fabulous.

"My darling." He strides to the bed in a rustle of expensive flowers. "You look so much better than yesterday."

"I feel fine. Um . . . thanks very much." I take the bouquet from him. It's the most amazing, trendy designer-looking bouquet I've ever seen, all shades of white and taupe. Where on earth do you get *taupe* roses?

"So . . . you're Eric?" I add, just to be one hundred percent sure.

I can see the shock reverberate through his face, but he manages a smile. "Yes. That's right. I'm Eric. You still don't know me?"

"Not really. In fact . . . not at all."

"I told you," Mum chips in, shaking her head. "I'm *so* sorry, Eric. But I'm sure she'll remember soon, if she makes a real effort."

"What's that supposed to mean?" I shoot her an affronted look.

"Well, darling," she says, "these things are all a matter of willpower, I've read. Mind over matter."

"I'm trying to remember, okay?" I say indignantly. "You think I *want* to be like this?"

"We'll take it slowly," Eric says, ignoring Mum. He sits down on the bed. "Let's see if we can trigger some memories. May I?" He gestures toward my hand.

"Um . . . yes. Okay." I nod, and he takes my hand in his. It's a nice hand, warm and firm. But it's a stranger's hand.

"Lexi, it's me," he says in firm, resonant tones. "It's Eric. Your husband. We've been married for nearly two years."

I'm too mesmerized to reply. He's even better-looking up close. His skin is really smooth and tan, and his teeth are a perfect gleaming white . . .

Oh my God—I've had sex with this man shoots through my mind.

He's seen me naked. He's ripped my underwear off. We've done who-knows-what together and I don't even *know* him. At least . . . I assume he's ripped my underwear off and we've done who-knows-what. I can't exactly ask, with Mum in the room.

I wonder what he's like in bed. Surreptitiously I run my eyes over his body. Well, I married him. He must be pretty good, surely. . . .

"Is something on your mind?" Eric has noticed my wandering gaze. "Darling, if you have any questions, just ask away. . . ."

"Nothing!" I flush. "Nothing. Sorry. Carry on."

"We met nearly three years ago," Eric continues, "at a reception at Pyramid TV. They make *Ambition,* the reality show we were both involved in. We were attracted instantly. We were married in June and honeymooned in Paris. We had a suite at the George V. It was wonderful. We went to Montmartre, we visited the Louvre, we had café au lait every morning. . . ." He breaks off. "Do you recall any of this?"

"Not really," I say, feeling guilty. "Sorry."

Maybe Mum's right. I should try harder to remember. Come on. Paris. The *Mona Lisa*. Men with stripy shirts. *Think*. I cast my mind back, desperately trying to match his face with images of Paris, to trigger some memory. . . .

"Did we go up the Eiffel Tower?" I say at last.

"Yes!" His face lights up. "Are you starting to remember? We stood in the breeze and took photos of each other—"

"No." I cut him off. "I just guessed. You know, Paris...Eiffel Tower...it seemed quite likely."

"Ah." He nods with obvious disappointment, and we lapse into silence. To my slight relief, there's a knock at the door and I call out, "Come in!"

Nicole enters, holding a clipboard. "Just need to do a quick blood pressure check—" She breaks off as she sees Eric holding my hand. "Oh, I'm sorry. I didn't mean to interrupt."

"Don't worry!" I say. "This is Nicole, one of the nurses who's been looking after me." I gesture around the room. "This is my mum, and sister...and my husband, who's called"—I meet her eyes significantly—"Eric."

"*Eric!*" Nicole's eyes light up. "Very nice to meet you, Eric."

"It's a pleasure." Eric nods at her. "I'm eternally grateful to you for looking after my wife."

Wife. My stomach flips over at the word. I'm his wife. This is all so grown-up. I bet we have a mortgage, too. And a burglar alarm.

"My pleasure." Nicole gives him a professional smile. "Lexi's a great patient." She wraps the blood pressure cuff around my arm and turns to face me. "I'll just pump this up...."

"*He's gorgeous!*" she mouths, giving me a surreptitious thumbs-up, and I can't help beaming back.

It's true. My husband is officially gorgeous. I've never even had a *date* with anyone in his league before.

Let alone get married to them. Let alone go and eat croissants in the George V hotel.

"I'd very much like to make a donation to the hospital," Eric says to Nicole, his deep, actory voice filling the room. "If you have any special appeal or fund..."

"That would be wonderful!" exclaims Nicole. "We've got an appeal right now for a new scanner."

"Maybe I could run the marathon for it?" he suggests. "I run every year for a different cause."

I'm nearly bursting with pride. None of my other boyfriends has ever run the marathon. Loser Dave could barely make it from the sofa to the TV.

"Well!" says Nicole, raising her eyebrows as she lets the blood pressure cuff deflate. "It's a real pleasure to meet you, Eric. Lexi, your pressure looks fine..." She writes something on my notes. "Is that your lunch there?" she adds, noticing the untouched tray.

"Oh yes. I forgot all about it."

"You must eat. And I'm going to ask everyone not to stay *too* much longer." She turns to Mum and Amy. "I know you want to spend time with Lexi, but she's still fragile. She needs to take it easy."

"I'll do whatever it takes." Eric clasps my hand. "I just want my wife well again."

Mum and Amy start to gather their things—but he stays put.

"I'd like a few moments, just the two of us," he says. "If that's okay, Lexi?"

"Oh," I say with a dart of apprehension. "Er... fine!"

Mum and Amy both come over to hug me good-bye,

and Mum makes another quick attempt to straighten my hair. Then the door closes behind them and I'm left alone with Eric, in a still, strange silence.

"So," Eric says at last.

"So. This is...weird." I attempt a little laugh, which immediately peters out to nothing. Eric is gazing at me, his brow furrowed.

"Have the doctors said whether you'll ever retrieve your memories?"

"They think I will. But they don't know when."

Eric gets up and strides to the window, appearing lost in thought. "So it's a waiting game," he says at last. "Is there anything I can do to speed the process?"

"I don't know," I say helplessly. "Maybe you could tell me some more about us and our relationship?"

"Absolutely. Good idea." He turns, his frame silhouetted against the window. "What do you want to know about? Ask me anything at all."

"Well...where do we live?"

"We live in Kensington in a loft-style apartment." He proclaims the words as though they're capitalized. "That's my business. Loft-style living." As he says the phrase *loft-style living* he makes a sweeping, parallel-hands gesture, as though he's moving bricks along a conveyor belt.

Wow. We live in Kensington! I cast around for another question to ask, but it all seems so arbitrary, like I'm padding out time in an interview.

"What sort of things do we do together?" I say eventually.

"We eat fine food, we watch movies...We went to the ballet last week. Had dinner at The Ivy afterward."

"The Ivy?" I can't help gasping. I've been to dinner at The Ivy?

Why can't I remember any of this? I shut my eyes tightly, trying to mentally kick-start my brain into action. But...nothing.

At last I open my eyes again, feeling a bit dizzy, to see Eric has noticed the rings on the cabinet. "That's your wedding ring, isn't it?" He looks up, puzzled. "Why is it here?"

"They took it off for the scans," I explain.

"Shall I?" He picks up the ring and takes hold of my left hand.

I feel a sudden prickle of alarm.

"I...um...no..." Before I can stop myself I yank my hand away and Eric flinches. "I'm sorry," I say after an awkward pause. "I'm really sorry. I just... you're a stranger."

"Of course." Eric has turned away, still holding the ring. "Of course. Stupid of me."

Oh God, he looks really hurt. I shouldn't have said "stranger." I should have said "friend I haven't met yet."

"I'm really sorry, Eric." I bite my lip. "I do want to know you and...love you and everything. You must be a really wonderful person or I wouldn't have married you. And you look really good," I add encouragingly. "I wasn't expecting anyone nearly so handsome. I mean, my last boyfriend wasn't a *patch* on you."

I look up to see Eric staring at me.

"It's strange," he says at last. "You're not yourself. The doctors warned me, but I didn't realize it would be so...extreme." For a moment he looks almost overcome, then his shoulders straighten. "Anyway, we'll get you right again. I know we will." He carefully puts the ring back on the cabinet, sits down on the bed, and takes my hand. "And just so you know, Lexi...I love you."

"*Really?*" I beam delightedly before I can stop myself. "I mean...fab. Thanks very much!"

None of my boyfriends has ever said "I love you" like that—i.e., properly, in the middle of the day, like a grown-up, and not just pissed or while having sex. I have to reciprocate. What shall I say?

I love you too.

No.

I probably love you too.

No.

"Eric, I'm sure I love you too, deep down somewhere," I say at last, clasping his hand. "And I'll remember. Maybe not today. And maybe not tomorrow. But...we'll always have Paris." I pause, thinking this through. "At least, you'll have it. And you can tell me about it."

Eric looks slightly mystified.

"Eat your lunch and take a rest." He pats my shoulder. "I'll leave you in peace."

"Maybe I'll wake up tomorrow and remember everything," I say hopefully as he gets to his feet.

"Let's hope." He scans my face for a moment or

two. "But even if you don't, my darling, we'll sort this out. Deal?"

"Deal." I nod.

"See you later."

He lets himself out quietly. I sit still in the silence for a moment. My head's starting to throb again and I'm a bit dazed. It's all too much. Amy has blue hair and Brad Pitt has a love child with Angelina Jolie and I have a gorgeous husband who just said he loves me. I'm half-expecting to go to sleep and wake up back in 2004, hungover on Carolyn's floor, and find this was all a dream.

Chapter Six

But it was no dream. I wake up the next morning and it's still 2007. I still have shiny perfect teeth and bright chestnut hair. And I still have a big black hole in my memory. I'm just eating my third piece of toast and taking a sip of tea when the door opens and Nicole appears, wheeling a trolley laden with flowers. I gape at it, impressed by the array. There must be about twenty arrangements on there. Tied bouquets...orchids in pots...grand-looking roses...

"So...is one of these mine?" I can't help asking.

Nicole looks surprised. "All of them."

"*All* of them?" I splutter, almost spilling my tea.

"You're a popular girl! We've run out of vases!" She hands me a stack of little cards. "Here are your messages."

"Wow." I take the first card and read it.

Lexi—darling girl. Look after yourself, get well, see you very soon, all my love.

Rosalie.

Rosalie? I don't know anyone called Rosalie. Bemused, I put it aside for later and read the next one.

Best wishes and get well soon.
Tim and Suki.

I don't know Tim and Suki, either.

Lexi, get well soon! You'll soon be back to three
hundred reps! From all your friends at the gym.

Three hundred reps? Me?

Well, I guess that would account for the muscled legs. I reach for the next card—and at last, it's from people I actually know.

Get well soon, Lexi. All best wishes from Fi,
Debs, Carolyn, and everyone in Flooring.

As I read the familiar names, I feel a warm glow inside. It's stupid, but I almost thought my friends had forgotten all about me.

Nicole interrupts my thoughts. "So your husband's quite a stunner!"

"D'you think so?" I try to appear nonchalant. "Yeah, he is quite nice-looking, I suppose...."

"He's amazing! And you know, he came around the ward yesterday, thanking us all again for looking after you. Not many people do that."

"I've never been out with a guy like Eric in my life!"

I abandon all pretense at being nonchalant. "To be honest, I still can't believe he's my husband. I mean, *me*. And him."

There's a knock on the door and Nicole calls, "Come in!"

It opens and in come Mum and Amy, both looking hot and sweaty, lugging between them about six shopping bags stuffed with photograph albums and envelopes.

"Good morning!" Nicole smiles as she holds the door open. "Lexi's feeling a lot better today, you'll be glad to hear."

"Oh, *don't* tell me she's remembered everything!" Mum's face drops. "After we've carried all these pictures all this way. Do you know how heavy photograph albums are? And we couldn't find a space in the car park—"

Nicole cuts her off. "She's still experiencing severe memory loss."

"Thank goodness for that!" Mum suddenly notices Nicole's expression. "I mean...Lexi, darling, we've brought some pictures to show you. Maybe they'll trigger your memory."

I eye the bag of photos, suddenly excited. These pictures will tell my missing story. They'll show me my transformation from Snaggletooth to...whoever I am now. "Fire away!" I put down all the flower messages and sit up. "Show me my life!"

• • •

I'm learning a lot from this hospital stay. And one thing I've learned is, if you have a relative with amnesia and want to trigger her memory, *just show her any old picture—it doesn't matter which one*. It's ten minutes later, but I haven't seen a single photo yet, because Mum and Amy keep arguing about where to start.

"We don't want to *overwhelm* her," Mum keeps saying as they both root through a bag of pictures. "Now, here we are." She picks up a photo in a card-board frame.

"No *way*." Amy grabs it from her. "I've got a zit on my chin. I look gross."

"Amy, it's a tiny pimple. You can hardly see it."

"Yes, you can. And this one is even grosser!" She starts ripping both photographs into shreds.

Here I am, waiting to learn all about my long-lost life, and Amy's destroying the evidence?

"I won't look at your zits!" I call over. "Just show me a picture! Anything!"

"All right." Mum advances toward the bed, holding an unframed print. "I'll hold it up, Lexi. Just look at the image carefully and see if it jogs anything. Ready?" Mum turns the print around.

It's a picture of a dog dressed up as Santa Claus.

"Mum..." I try to control my frustration. "Why are you showing me a dog?"

"Darling, it's Tosca!" Mum appears wounded. "She would have looked very different in 2004. And here's Raphael with Amy last week, both looking lovely..."

"I look *hideous*." Amy snatches the picture and rips it up before I can even see it.

"Stop ripping up the pictures!" I almost yell. "Mum, did you bring photographs of anything else? Like people?"

"Hey, Lexi, do you remember this?" Amy comes forward, holding up a distinctive necklace with a rose made out of jade. I squint at it, trying desperately to dredge some memory up.

"No," I say at last. "It doesn't jog anything at all."

"Cool. Can I have it, then?"

"Amy!" says Mum. She riffles through the pictures in her hand with dissatisfaction. "Maybe we should just wait for Eric to come with the wedding DVD. If that doesn't trigger your memory, nothing will."

The wedding DVD.

My wedding.

Every time I think about this, my stomach curls up with a kind of excited, nervous anticipation. I have a wedding DVD. I had a wedding! The thought is alien. I can't even imagine myself as a bride. Did I wear a pouffy dress with a train and a veil and some hideous floral headdress? I can't even bring myself to ask.

"So . . . he seems nice," I say. "Eric, I mean. My husband."

"He's super." Mum nods absently, still leafing through pictures of dogs. "He does a lot for charity, you know. Or the company does, I should say. But it's his own company, so it's all the same."

"He has his own company?" I frown, confused. "I thought he was a real-estate agent."

"It's a company that *sells properties,* darling. Big loft developments all over London. They sold off a large part of it last year, but he still retains a controlling interest."

"He made ten million quid," says Amy, who's still crouched down by the bag of photos.

"He *what*?" I stare at her.

"He's stinking rich." She looks up. "Oh, come on. Don't say you hadn't guessed that?"

"Amy!" says Mum. "Don't be so vulgar!"

I can't quite speak. In fact, I'm feeling a bit faint. Ten million quid?

There's a knock at the door. "Lexi? May I come in?"

Oh my God. It's him. I hastily check my reflection and spray myself with some Chanel perfume that I found in the Louis Vuitton bag.

"Come in, Eric!" calls Mum.

The door swings open—and there he is, manhandling two shopping bags, another bunch of flowers, and a gift basket full of fruit. He's wearing a striped shirt and tan trousers, a yellow cashmere sweater, and loafers with tassels.

"Hi, darling." He puts all his stuff down on the floor, then comes over to the bed and kisses me gently on the cheek. "How are you doing?"

"Much better, thanks." I smile up at him.

"But she still doesn't know who you are," Amy puts in. "You're just some guy in a yellow sweater."

Eric doesn't look remotely fazed. Maybe he's used to Amy being bolshy.

"Well, we're going to tackle that today." He hefts one of the bags, sounding energized. "I've brought along photos, DVDs, souvenirs. . . . Let's reintroduce you to your life. Barbara, why don't you put on the wedding DVD?" He hands a shiny disc to Mum. "And to get you started, Lexi...our wedding album." He heaves an expensive-looking calfskin album onto the bed and I feel a twang of disbelief as I see the embossed words.

ALEXIA AND ERIC
JUNE 3, 2005

I open it and my stomach seems to drop a mile. I'm staring at a black-and-white photograph of me as a bride. I'm wearing a long white sheath dress; my hair's in a sleek knot; and I'm holding a minimalist bouquet of lilies. Nothing pouffy in sight.

Wordlessly I turn to the next page. There's Eric standing next to me, dressed in black tie. On the following page we're holding glasses of champagne and smiling at each other. We look so *glossy*. Like people in a magazine.

This is my wedding. My actual, real live wedding. If I needed proof...this is proof.

From the TV screen suddenly comes the mingled sound of people laughing and chattering. I look up and feel a fresh shock. Up there on the telly, Eric and I are posing in our wedding outfits. We're standing next to a huge white cake, holding a knife together, laughing at someone off screen. I can't take my eyes off myself.

"We chose not to record the ceremony," Eric is explaining. "This is the party afterward."

"Right." My voice is a tad husky.

I've never been sappy about weddings. But as I

watch us cutting the cake, smiling for the cameras, posing again for someone who missed the shot... my nose starts to prickle. This is my wedding day, the so-called happiest day of my life, and I don't remember a thing about it.

The camera swings around, catching the faces of people I don't recognize. I spot Mum, in a navy suit, and Amy, wearing a purple strappy dress. We're in some huge, modern-looking space with glass walls and trendy chairs and floral arrangements everywhere, and people are spilling out onto a wide terrace, champagne glasses in their hands.

"Where's this place?" I ask.

"Sweetheart..." Eric gives a disconcerted laugh. "This is our home."

"Our *home*? But it's massive! Look at it!"

"It's the penthouse." He nods. "It's a nice size."

A "nice size"? It's like a football field. My little Balham flat would probably fit on one of those rugs.

"And who's that?" I point at a pretty girl in a baby-pink strapless dress who's whispering in my ear.

"That's Rosalie. Your best friend."

My *best friend*? I've never seen this woman before in my life. She's skinny and tanned, with huge blue eyes, a massive bracelet on her wrist, and sunglasses pushed up on her blond, California-girl hair.

She sent me flowers, I suddenly remember. *Darling girl... love, Rosalie.*

"Does she work at Deller Carpets?"

"No!" Eric smiles as though I've cracked a joke. "This bit is fun." He gestures toward the screen. The camera is following us as we walk out onto the terrace, and I can just hear myself laughing and saying, "Eric, what are you up to?" Everyone is looking up for some reason. I have no idea why—

And then the camera focuses and I see it. Skywriting. *Lexi I will love you forever.* On the screen, everyone is gasping and pointing, and I see myself staring up, pointing, shading my eyes, then kissing Eric.

My husband organized surprise skywriting for me on my wedding day and *I can't bloody remember it?* I want to weep.

"Now, this is us on holiday in Mauritius last year . . ." Eric has fast-forwarded the DVD and I stare disbelievingly at the screen. Is that girl walking along the sand *me*? My hair's braided and I'm tanned and thin and wearing a red string bikini. I look like the kind of girl I'd normally gaze at with envy.

"And this is us at a charity ball . . ." Eric's fast-forwarded and there we are again. I'm wearing a slinky blue evening dress, dancing with Eric in a grand-looking ballroom.

"Eric is a *very* generous benefactor," Mum says, but I don't respond. I'm riveted by a handsome, dark-haired guy standing near the dance floor. Wait a moment. Don't I . . . know him from somewhere?

I do. I do. I definitely recognize him. At last!

"Lexi?" Eric has noticed my expression. "Is this jolting your memory?"

"Yes!" I can't help a joyful smile. "I remember that guy on the left." I point at the screen. "I'm not sure who he is exactly, but I *know* him. Really well! He's warm, and funny, and I think maybe he's a doctor . . or maybe I met him in a casino—"

"Lexi . . ." Eric gently cuts me off. "That's George Clooney, the actor. He was a fellow guest at the ball."

"Oh." I rub my nose, discomfited. "Oh right."

George Clooney. Of course it is. I'm a moron. I subside back onto my pillows, dispirited.

When I think of all the hideous, mortifying things I *can* remember. Having to eat semolina at school when I was seven, and nearly vomiting. Wearing a white swimsuit when I was fifteen and getting out of the pool, and it was transparent and all the boys laughed. I remember that humiliation like it was yesterday.

But I can't remember walking along a perfect sandy beach on Mauritius. I can't remember dancing with my husband at some grand ball. Hello, brain? Do you have *any* priorities?

"I was reading up on amnesia last night," Amy says from her cross-legged position on the floor. "You know which sense triggers memory the best? Smell. Maybe you should *smell* Eric."

"It's true," Mum puts in unexpectedly. "Like that chap Proust. One whiff of a fairy cake and everything came flooding back into his mind."

"Go on," Amy says encouragingly. "It's worth a try, isn't it?"

I glance over at Eric, embarrassed. "Would you mind if I . . . smelled you, Eric?"

"Not at all! It's worth a go." He sits on the bed and freeze-frames the DVD. "Should I lift my arms up, or . . ."

"Um ... I guess so ..."

Solemnly Eric lifts his arms. I lean forward gingerly and sniff his armpit. I can smell soap, and aftershave, and a mild, manly kind of smell. But nothing's rushing back into my brain.

Except visions of George Clooney in *Ocean's Eleven*.

I may not mention those.

"Anything?" Eric is frozen, rigid in his arms-up position.

"Nothing yet," I say after sniffing again. "I mean, nothing very strong ..."

"You should smell his crotch," says Amy.

"*Sweetheart*," Mum says faintly.

I can't help glancing down at Eric's crotch. The crotch I've married. It looks pretty generous, although you can never quite tell. I wonder—

No. Not the point right now.

"What you two should do is have sex," Amy says into the awkward silence, then snaps her gum. "You need the pungent smell of each other's bodily—"

"Amy!" Mum cuts her off. "Darling! That is quite enough!"

"I'm just saying! It's nature's own amnesia cure!"

"So." Eric drops his arms again. "Not exactly the greatest success."

"No."

Maybe Amy's right. Maybe we should have sex. I glance at Eric—and I'm convinced he's thinking the same thing.

"Never mind. It's still early days." Eric smiles as he

closes the wedding album, but I can tell he's disappointed too.

"What if I never remember?" I look around the room. "What if all those memories are lost for good and I can never get them back? *Ever?*"

As I look around at the concerned faces I suddenly feel powerless and vulnerable. It's like that time my computer crashed and I lost all my e-mail, only a million times worse. The techy guy kept telling me I should have backed up my files. But how do you back up your own brain?

• • •

In the afternoon I see a neuropsychologist, Neil. He's a friendly guy, in jeans. I sit at a table with him, taking tests—and I have to say, I'm pretty good! I remember most of twenty words in a list; I remember a short story; I draw a picture from memory.

"You're functioning extremely well, Lexi," Neil says after he fills in the last check box. "Your executive skills are there, your short-term memory is pretty good considering, you have no major cognitive problems . . . but you're suffering from a severe focal retrograde amnesia. It's very unusual, you know."

"But *why?*"

"Well, it has to do with the way you hit your head." He leans forward, animated, draws an outline of a head on his pad of paper, and starts to fill in a brain. "You've had what we call an acceleration-deceleration injury. When you hit the windshield, your brain was thrown around in your skull, and a small area of your brain was, shall we say, tweaked. It could be you've done damage to your warehouse of memories...or it could be that you've done damage to your ability to *retrieve* memories. In that case the warehouse is intact, if you like, but you're unable to open the door."

His eyes are shining, as though this is all really fabulous and I should be thrilled with myself.

"Can't you give me an electric shock?" I say in frustration. "Or hit me over the head or something?"

"I'm afraid not." He looks amused. "Contrary to popular belief, hitting an amnesiac over the head is not going to bring their memory back. So don't try that at home." He pushes his chair back. "Let me walk you to your room."

We arrive back at my room to find Mum and Amy still watching the home DVD while Eric talks on his cell phone. Immediately he finishes his conversation and claps his phone shut. "How did you get on?"

"What did you remember, darling?" Mum chimes in.

"Nothing," I admit.

"Once Lexi gets back to familiar surroundings, she'll probably find her memory returns quite naturally," says Neil reassuringly. "Although it may take time."

"Right." Eric nods earnestly. "So, what next?"

"Well." Neil flips through my notes. "You're in good shape physically, Lexi. I would say you'll probably be discharged tomorrow. I'll make an appointment for you in a month's time as an outpatient. Until then, the best place for you is home." He smiles. "I'm sure that's where you want to be too."

"Yes!" I say after a pause. "Home. Great."

Even as I'm saying the words I realize I don't know what I mean by *home*. Home was my Balham flat. And that's gone.

"What's your address?" He takes out a pen. "For my notes."

"I'm . . . not sure."

"I'll write it down," Eric says helpfully, and takes the pen.

This is crazy. I don't know where I live. I'm like some confused old lady.

"Well, good luck, Lexi." Neil looks at Eric and Mum. "You can help by giving Lexi as much information as possible about her life. Write things down. Take her back to places she's been. Any problems, just call me."

The door closes behind Neil and there's silence, apart from the chatter of the telly. Mum and Eric are exchanging looks. If I was a conspiracy theorist I'd say they were hatching a plan.

"What is it?"

"Sweetheart, your mother and I were talking earlier about how we would"—he hesitates—"tackle your release."

Tackle my release. He sounds like I'm a dangerous, psychotic prisoner.

"We're in a pretty strange situation here," he continues. "Obviously I would love it if you wanted to come home and resume your life again. But I appreciate that you may find it uncomfortable. After all . . . you don't know me."

"Well, no." I chew my lip. "I don't."

"I said to Eric, you're very welcome to come and stay with me for a bit," puts in Mum. "Obviously it will be a *little* disruptive, and you'll have to share with Jake and Florian, but they're good dogs."

"That room smells," says Amy.

"It does not *smell*, Amy." Mum seems affronted. "That builder chap said it was simply a question of dry something-or-other." She makes a vague gesture.

"Rot," says Amy, without moving her gaze off the television. "And it does smell."

Mum is blinking hard in annoyance. Meanwhile, Eric has come over, his face showing concern.

"Lexi, please don't think I'll be offended. I understand how tough this is for you. I'm a stranger to you, for Christ's sake." He spreads his arms. "Why on earth would you want to come home with me?"

I know it's my cue to answer—but I've suddenly been distracted by an image on the TV screen. It's of me and Eric on a speedboat. God knows where we are, but the sun is shining and the sea is blue. We're both wearing sunglasses and Eric is smiling at me as he drives the boat and we look totally glamorous, like something out of a James Bond movie.

I can't help staring at it, mesmerized. *I want this life* rushes through my brain. *It belongs to me. I earned it. I'm not going to let it slip through my fingers.*

Eric is still talking. "The last thing I want to do is get in the way of your recovery. Whatever you want to do, I will completely understand."

"Right. Yes." I take a sip of water, playing for time. "I'll just . . . think about it for a few moments."

Okay, let's just get my options absolutely clear here:

1. A rotting room in Kent which I have to share with two whippets.
2. A palatial loft in Kensington with Eric, my good-looking husband who can drive a speedboat.

"You know what, Eric?" I say carefully, measuring out my words. "I think I *should* come and live with you."

"Are you serious?" His face lights up, but I can tell he's taken aback.

"You're my husband," I say. "I should be with you."

"But you don't remember me," he says uncertainly. "You don't know me."

"I'll get to know you again!" I say with growing enthusiasm. "Surely the best chance I have of remembering my life is to live it. You can tell me about yourself, and me, and our marriage. . . . I can learn it all again! And that doctor *said* familiar circumstances would help. They'll trigger my retrieval system or whatever."

I'm more and more positive about this. So I don't know anything about my husband or my life. The point is, I've married a good-looking multimillionaire who loves me and has a huge penthouse and brought me taupe roses. I'm not going to throw it all away just because of the small detail that I can't remember him.

Everyone has to work at their marriage in some way

or another. I'll just have to work at the "remembering your husband" part.

"Eric, I really want to come home with you," I say as sincerely as I can. "I'm sure we have a great, loving marriage. We can work it out."

"It would be wonderful to have you back." Eric still looks troubled. "But please don't feel any sense of obligation—"

"I'm not doing this out of obligation! I'm doing it because . . . it just feels right."

"Well, I think it's a *very* good idea," Mum puts in.

"That's it, then," I say. "Settled."

"Obviously you won't want to . . ." Eric hesitates awkwardly. "I mean . . . I'll take the guest suite."

"I would appreciate that," I say, trying to match his formal tone. "Thank you, Eric."

"Well, if you're sure about this . . ." His whole face has brightened. "Let's do this properly, shall we?" He glances questioningly at my wedding ring, still lying on the cabinet, and I follow his gaze.

"Yes, let's!" I nod, suddenly excited.

He picks up both rings and self-consciously I hold out my left hand. I watch, transfixed, as Eric slips the rings onto my finger. First the wedding band, then the enormous diamond solitaire. There's a hush in the room as I gaze down at my beringed hand.

Fuck, that diamond's huge.

"Are you comfortable, Lexi?" Eric asks. "Does that feel right?"

"It feels . . . great! Really. Just right."

A huge smile licks across my face as I turn my hand this way and that. I feel like someone should throw confetti or sing the "Wedding March." Two nights ago I was being stood up in a crappy club by Loser Dave. And now ... I'm married!

Chapter Seven

It has to be karma.

I must have been amazingly noble in a previous existence. I must have rescued children from a burning building, or given up my life to help lepers, or invented the wheel or something. It's the only explanation I can think of for how I've landed the dream life.

Here I am, zooming along the Thames Embankment, with my handsome husband, *in his open-top Mercedes.*

I say *zooming.* Actually we're going at about twenty miles an hour. Eric is being all solicitous and saying he knows how hard it must be for me to get back in a car, and if I feel traumatized to tell him straightaway. But really, I'm fine. I don't remember anything about the crash. It's like a story I've been told that happened to someone else, the kind where you tilt your head politely and say "Oh no, how awful" but you've already stopped listening properly.

I keep glancing down at myself in wonder. I'm wearing a pair of cropped jeans, *two sizes* smaller than I used to wear. And a top by Miu Miu, which is one of those names I only used to know about from magazines. Eric brought me a bag of clothes to choose from, and they were all so posh and designer I hardly dared touch them, let alone put them on.

On the backseat are all the bouquets and presents from my hospital room, including a massive basket of tropical fruit from Deller Carpets. There was a letter attached from someone called Clare, which said she would send me the minutes of the latest board meeting to read at my leisure, and she hoped I was feeling better. And then she signed it "Clare Abrahams, assistant to Lexi Smart."

Assistant to Lexi Smart. I have my own personal assistant. I'm on the board of directors. Me!

My cuts and bruises are a lot better and the plastic staple has been taken out of my head. My hair is freshly washed and glossy and my teeth are as moviestar perfect as ever. I can't stop smiling at every shiny surface I pass. In fact, I can't stop smiling, full stop.

Maybe in a previous life I was Joan of Arc and I got tortured horrifically to death. Or I was that guy in *Titanic*. Yes. I drowned in a cruel, freezing sea and never got Kate Winslet, and this is my reward. I mean, people don't just get presented with a perfect life for no good reason. It just doesn't happen.

"All right, darling?" Eric briefly puts his hand on mine. His curly hair is all ruffled in the wind and his expensive sunglasses are glinting in the sunshine. He looks like the kind of guy the Mercedes PR people would *want* to be driving their cars.

"Yes!" I beam back. "I'm great!"

I'm Cinderella. No, I'm *better* than Cinderella, because she only got the prince, didn't she? I'm Cinderella with fab teeth and a shit-hot job.

Eric signals left. "Well, here we are..." He pulls off the road into a grand pillared entrance, past a porter in a glass box, into a parking space, and then turns off the engine. "Come and see your home."

• • •

You know how some hyped-up things are a total letdown when you actually get to them. Like, you save up for ages to go to an expensive restaurant and the waiters are snooty and the table is too small and the dessert tastes like Mr Whippy.

Well, my new home is approximately the opposite of that. It's way *better* than I imagined. As I walk around, I'm awestruck. It's massive. It's light. It has views over the river. There's a vast, L-shaped cream sofa and the coolest black granite cocktail bar. The shower is a whole marble-clad room, big enough for about five people.

"Do you remember any of this?" Eric is watching me intently. "Is it triggering anything?"

"No. But it's absolutely stunning!"

We must have some cool parties here. I can just *see* Fi, Carolyn, and Debs perched at the cocktail bar, tequila shooters going, music blaring over the sound system. I pause by the sofa and run my hand along the plushy fabric. It's so pristine and plumped up, I don't think I'll ever dare sit down on it. Maybe I'll just have to hover. It'll be great for my bum muscles.

"This is an amazing sofa!" I look up at Eric. "It must have cost a packet."

He nods. "Ten thousand pounds."

Shit. I draw my hand back. How can a sofa cost that much? What's it stuffed with, *caviar*? I edge away, thanking God I didn't sit down on it. Memo to self: do not ever drink red wine on / eat pizza on / ever go near the ten-grand posh cream sofa.

"I really love this . . . er . . . light fitting." I gesture to a free-standing undulating piece of metal.

Eric smiles. "That's a radiator."

"Oh right," I say, confused. "I thought *that* was a radiator." I point to an old-fashioned iron radiator that has been painted black and fitted halfway up the opposite wall.

"That's a piece of art." Eric corrects me. "It's by Hector James-John. *Disintegration Falls*."

I walk over to it, cock my head, and gaze up alongside Eric, with what I hope is an intelligent art-lover's expression.

Disintegration Falls. Black radiator. Nope, no idea.

"It's so . . . structural," I venture after a pause.

"We were lucky to get this," Eric says, nodding at the piece. "We tend to invest in a piece of nonrepresentational art about every eight months. The loft can take it. And it's about the portfolio as much as anything else." He shrugs as though this is self-explanatory.

"Of course!" I nod. "I would have thought the portfolio...aspect would be...absolutely..." I clear my throat and turn away.

Keep your mouth shut, Lexi. You know fuck-all about modern art or portfolios or basically what it's like being rich and you're giving it all away.

I turn away from the radiator-art-thing and focus on a giant screen, which almost fills the opposite wall. There's a second screen across the room, by the dining table, and I noticed one in the bedroom. Eric clearly likes the telly.

He notices me looking at it. "What would you like?" He picks up a remote control and flicks it at the screen. "Try this." The next minute I'm looking at a massive blazing, crackling fire.

"Wow!" I stare at it in surprise.

"Or this." The picture changes to brightly colored tropical fish weaving through fronds of seaweed. "It's the latest in home screen system technology," he says proudly. "It's art, it's entertainment, it's communication. You can e-mail on these things, you can listen to music, read books...I have a thousand works of literature stored on the system. You can even have a virtual pet."

"A pet?" I'm still gazing at the screen, dazzled.

"We each have one." Eric smiles. "This is mine, Titan." He flicks his control and an image appears on the screen of a massive stripy spider, prowling around a glass box.

"Oh my *God*!" I back away, feeling sick. I've never been great with spiders, and that one is about ten feet high. You can see the hairs on its horrible legs. You can see its *face*. "Could you possibly switch that off, please?"

"What's wrong?" Eric looks surprised. "I showed Titan to you on your first visit here. You said you thought he was adorable."

Great. It was our first date. I said I liked the spider to be polite, and now I'm stuck with it.

"You know what?" I say, trying to keep my gaze averted from Titan. "The crash could have given me a spider phobia." I try to sound knowledgeable, like I heard this from a doctor or something.

"Maybe." Eric has a slight frown, as though he's about to pick holes in this theory. As well he might.

"So I have a pet too?" I say quickly, to distract him. "What is it?"

"Here you go." He zaps at the screen. "Here's Arthur." A fluffy white kitten appears on the screen and I cry out in delight.

"He's so *cute*!" I watch him playing with a ball of string, batting it and tumbling over. "Does he grow up into a cat?"

"No." Eric smiles. "He stays as a kitten indefinitely. All your life, if you want. They have a life capacity of one hundred thousand years."

"Oh, right," I say after a pause. Actually, that's freakish. A one-hundred-thousand-year-old virtual kitten.

Eric's phone beeps and he flips it open, then zaps at the screen again to restore the fish. "Sweetheart, my driver's here. I'm going to have to go to the office briefly. But Rosalie is on her way to keep you company.

Until then, if anything bothers you, just call me at once—or you can e-mail me through the system." He hands me a rectangular white gadget with a screen. "Here's your remote control. It controls heating, ventilation, lighting, doors, blinds...Everything here is intelligent. But you shouldn't need to use it. All the settings are in place."

"We have a remote-control *house*?" I want to laugh.

"It's all part of loft-style living!" He makes the parallel hand gesture again, and I nod, trying not to give away how overwhelmed I am.

I watch as he shrugs on his jacket. "So...how exactly does Rosalie fit in?"

"She's the wife of my partner, Clive. You two have a great time together."

"Does she hang out with me and the other girls from the office?" I ask. "Like Fi and Carolyn? Do we all go out together?"

"Who?" Eric looks blank. Maybe he's one of those guys who doesn't keep up with his wife's social life.

"Never mind," I say quickly. "I'll work it all out."

"Gianna will be back later too. Our housekeeper. Any problems, she'll help you." He comes over, hesitates, then takes my hand. His skin is smooth and immaculate, even up close, and I can just smell a gorgeous sandalwood aftershave.

"Thanks, Eric." I put my hand over his and squeeze it. "I really appreciate it."

"Welcome back, darling," he says a little gruffly. Then he disengages his hand and heads toward the door, and a moment later it closes behind him.

I'm alone. Alone in my marital home. As I look around the huge space again, taking in the Lucite cube coffee table, the leather chaise, the art books...I realize I can't see that many signs of *me*. There are no brightly colored pottery jugs or fairy lights or piles of paperbacks.

Well, Eric and I probably wanted to start again, choosing things together. And we probably got loads of amazing wedding presents. Those blue-glass vases on the mantelpiece look like they cost a fortune.

I wander over to the huge windows and peer down at the street below. There's no noise or draft or anything. I watch a man carry a package into a taxi far below and a woman struggling with a dog on a lead. Then I pull out my phone and start texting Fi. I *have* to talk to her about all of this. I'll get her to come around later. We'll curl up on the sofa and she can fill me in on my life, starting with Eric. I can't help smiling with anticipation as I press the buttons.

Hi! Back home—give me a call! Can't wait to c u!!!
Lxxxx

I send the same text to Carolyn and Debs. Then I put my phone away and swivel around on the shiny wooden floor. I've been trying to keep up a nonchalant air in front of Eric, but now that I'm alone I can feel a beam of elation popping through. I never thought I'd live anywhere like this, *ever*.

A laugh suddenly bubbles to my lips. I mean, it's crazy. Me. In this place!

I swivel again on the floor, then start twirling, my arms out, laughing madly. I, Lexi Smart, live here in this state-of-the-art remote-controlled palace!

Sorry, Lexi Gardiner.

This thought makes me giggle even more. I didn't even know my own married name when I woke up. What if it had been Pratt-Bottom? What would I have said then? "Sorry, Eric, you seem a lovely guy, but there's absolutely no way on earth..."

Crash. The sound of breaking glass interrupts my thoughts. I stop twirling in horror. Somehow I accidentally caught my hand on a glass leopard that was leaping through the air on a display shelf. Now it's lying on the floor in two pieces.

I've broken a priceless ornament, and I've only been in the place about three minutes.

Shit.

I cautiously bend down and touch the bigger tail-end piece. There's a nasty jagged edge and some splinters of glass on the floor. There's no way this can be mended.

I'm hot with panic. What am I going to do? What if it was worth ten thousand quid, like the sofa? What if it's some family heirloom of Eric's? What was I *thinking*, twirling around?

Gingerly I pick up the first piece, and then the second. I'll have to sweep up the splinters of glass and then—

An electronic beep interrupts me and my head jerks up. The giant screen opposite has turned bright blue with a message in green capitals.

HI, LEXI—HOW ARE YOU DOING?

Fuck! He can see me. He's watching me. It's Big Brother!

In terror I leap to my feet and shove the two pieces of glass under a cushion on the sofa.

"Hi," I say to the blue screen, my heart pounding. "I didn't mean to do that, it was an accident..."

There's silence. The screen isn't moving or reacting in any way.

"Eric?" I try again.

There's no reply.

Okay... maybe he can't see me after all. He must be typing this from the car. Cautiously I venture over to the screen and notice a wall-mounted keyboard and tiny silver mouse, discreetly tucked away to the side. I click on Reply and slowly type FINE, THANKS!

I could leave it there. I could find a way to fix the leopard... or replace it somehow....

No. Come on. I can't start off my brand-new marriage by keeping secrets from my husband. I have to be brave and own up. HAVE BROKEN GLASS LEOPARD BY MISTAKE, I type. REALLY SORRY. HOPE IS NOT IRREPLACEABLE?

I press Send and pace about as I wait for the reply, telling myself over and over not to worry. I mean, I don't know for certain that it's a priceless ornament, do I? Maybe we won it in a raffle. Maybe it's mine, and Eric's always hated it. How am I supposed to know?

How am I supposed to know anything?

I sink down onto a chair, suddenly overwhelmed by how little I know about my own life. If I'd known I was going to get amnesia, I would have at least written my-self a note. Given myself a few tips. *Be careful of the glass leopard, it's worth a bloody fortune. P.S., you like spiders.*

There's a beep from the screen. I catch my breath and look up. OF COURSE IS NOT IRREPLACE-ABLE! DON'T WORRY.

I feel a huge whoosh of relief. It's all right.

THANKS! I type, smiling. WON'T BREAK ANY-THING ELSE, PROMISE!

I can't believe I overreacted like that. I can't believe I hid the pieces under a cushion. What am I, five years old? This is my own house. I'm a married woman. I have to start behaving like it. Still beaming to myself, I lift up the cushion to retrieve the pieces—and freeze.

Fuck.

The bloody glass has ripped the bloody cream sofa. I must have caught it as I shoved the pieces underneath. The plushy fabric's all ragged.

The ten-thousand-pound sofa.

I automatically glance up at the screen—then quickly look away, hollow with fear. I can't tell Eric I've ruined the sofa too. I *can't.*

Okay. What I'll do is . . . is . . . I won't tell him today. I'll wait for a better moment. Flustered, I rearrange the cushions so the rip isn't visible. There. Good as new. No one looks under cushions, do they?

I grab the bits of glass leopard and head into the kitchen, which is all glossy gray-lacquer cupboards and rubber floor. I locate a roll of kitchen paper, wrap up the leopard, manage to track down the trash behind a streamlined unit door, and chuck the bits in. Okay. That's it. I am not wrecking anything else.

A buzzer sounds through the apartment and I look up, my spirits lifting. This must be Rosalie, my new best friend. I can't wait to meet her.

• • •

Rosalie turns out to be even skinnier than she looked on the wedding DVD. She's dressed in black capri pants, a pink cashmere V neck, and huge Chanel sunglasses pushing her blond hair back. As I open the door she gives a small shriek and drops the Jo Malone gift bag she's holding.

"*Oh* my God, Lexi. Look at your poor face."

"It's fine!" I say reassuringly. "Honestly, you should have seen me six days ago. I had a plastic staple in my head."

"You poor thing. What a *night*mare." She retrieves her gift bag, then kisses me on each cheek. "I would have come around earlier, only you *know* how long I waited to get that slot at Cheriton Spa."

"Come in." I gesture to the kitchen. "Would you like a cup of coffee?"

"Sweetie..." She looks puzzled. "I don't drink coffee. Dr. André banned me. You know that."

"Oh right." I pause. "The thing is...I don't remember. I have amnesia."

Rosalie is gazing at me, politely blank. Doesn't she know? Didn't Eric tell her?

"I don't remember anything about the last three

years," I try again. "I hit my head and it's all been wiped from my memory."

"*Oh* my God." Rosalie's hand goes to her mouth. "Eric kept saying things about amnesia and you wouldn't know me. I thought he was joking!"

I want to giggle at her horrified expression. "No, he wasn't joking. To me you're ... a stranger."

"I'm a stranger?" She sounds hurt.

"Eric was a stranger too," I add hastily. "I woke up and I didn't know who he was. I still don't, really."

There's a short silence during which I can see Rosalie processing this information. Her eyes widen and her cheeks puff out and she chews her lip.

"*Oh* my God," she says at last. "*Night*mare."

"I don't know this place." I spread my arms around. "I don't know my own home. I don't know what my life is like. If you could help me out, or ... tell me a few things ..."

"Absolutely! Let's sit down ..." She leads the way into the kitchen area. She dumps the Jo Malone bag on the counter and sits down at the trendy steel breakfast table—and I follow suit, wondering if I chose this table, or Eric chose it, or we both chose it together.

I look up to see Rosalie staring at me. At once she smiles—but I can see she's freaked out.

"I know," I say. "It's a weird situation."

"So, is it *permanent*?"

"Apparently my memory could come back, but no one knows if it will. Or when it will, or how much."

"And apart from that, are you okay?"

"I'm fine, except one of my hands is a bit slow." I lift

up my left hand to show her. "I've got physio exercises to do." I flex my hand like the physiotherapist taught me, and Rosalie watches in fascinated horror.

"*Night*mare," she breathes.

"But the real problem is...I don't know anything about my life since 2004. It's just a big black hole. The doctors said I should try and talk to my friends and build up a picture, and maybe that'll trigger something."

"Of *course*." Rosalie nods. "Let me fill you in. What do you want to know?" She leans forward expectantly.

"Well..." I think for a moment. "How did we two meet?"

"It was about two and a half years ago." Rosalie nods firmly. "I was at a drinks party, and Eric said, 'This is Lexi.' And I said, 'Hi!' And that's how we met!" She beams.

"Right." I shrug apologetically. "I don't remember."

"We were at Trudy Swinson's? You know, who used to be an air hostess, but she met Adrian on a flight to New York, and everyone says she zeroed in on him as soon as she spotted his black Amex..." She trails off, as if the enormity of the situation is hitting her for the first time. "So you don't remember any *gossip*?"

"Well...no."

"*Oh* my God." She blows out sharply. "I have so much to fill you in on. Where shall I start? Okay, so there's me." She pulls a pen out of her bag and starts writing. "And my husband, Clive, and his evil bitch ex, Davina. *Wait* till you hear about her. And there's Jenna and Petey—"

"Do we ever hang out with my other friends?" I interrupt her. "Like Fi and Carolyn? Or Debs? Do you know them?"

"Carolyn. Carolyn." Rosalie taps the pen against her teeth, frowning thoughtfully. "Is she that lovely French girl at the gym?"

"No, Carolyn my friend from work. And Fi. I must have talked about them, surely. I've been friends with Fi forever . . . we go out every Friday night . . ."

Rosalie looks blank.

"Sweetie, to be honest, I've never heard you mention them. As far as I know, you never socialize with colleagues from work."

"What?" I stare at her. "But . . . it's our thing! We go clubbing and we dress up and we have cocktails . . ."

Rosalie laughs. "Lexi, I've never even *seen* you with a cocktail! You and Eric are both so serious about wine."

Wine? That can't be right. All I know about wine is that it comes from Oddbins.

"You look confused," Rosalie says anxiously. "I'm bombarding you with too much information. Forget the gossip." She pushes aside her sheet of paper, on which I can see she's written a list of names with "bitch" and "sweetheart" next to them. "What would you like to do?"

"Maybe we could just do whatever we normally do together?"

"Absolutely!" Rosalie ponders for a moment, then her brow clears. "We should go to the gym."

"The gym," I echo, trying to sound enthused. "Of course. So . . . I go to the gym a lot?"

"Sweetie, you're addicted! You run for an hour every other morning at six a.m."

Six a.m.? Running?

I never run. It's painful and it makes your boobs bounce around. I once did a mile-long fun run with Fi and Carolyn, and I nearly died. Although at least I was better than Fi, who gave up running after two minutes and walked the rest of the way, smoking a cigarette, and then got into a row with the organizers and was banned from any future Cancer Research fund-raisers.

"But don't worry, we'll do something lovely and restful today," Rosalie says reassuringly. "A massage, or a nice gentle stretch class. Just grab your exercise clothes and we'll go!"

"Okay!" I hesitate. "Actually, this is a bit embarrassing... but I don't know where my clothes are. All the cupboards in our bedroom are full of Eric's suits. I can't find any of mine."

Rosalie looks utterly pole-axed. "You don't know where your *clothes* are?" Tears suddenly spring to her huge blue eyes and she fans her face. "I'm sorry," she gulps. "But it's just come home to me how horrific and scary this must be for you. To have forgotten your entire wardrobe." She takes a deep breath, composing herself, then squeezes my hand. "Come with me, sweetie. I'll show you."

• • •

So the reason I couldn't find my clothes is they're not in a wardrobe, they're in a whole other room, behind a concealed door which looks like a mirror. And the reason they need a whole other room is because there's *so bloody many of them.*

As I stare at the racks I feel faint. I've never seen so many clothes, not outside a shop. Crisp white shirts, tailored black trousers, suits in shades of mushroom and taupe. Chiffony evening wear. Tights rolled up in their own special drawer. Folded silky knickers with La Perla labels. I can't see anything that doesn't look brand-new and immaculate. There are no baggy jeans, no sloppy sweaters, no comfy old pj's.

I leaf through a row of jackets, all pretty much identical apart from the buttons. I can't believe I've spent so much money on clothes and they're all versions of beige.

"What do you think?" Rosalie is watching me, her eyes sparkling.

"Amazing!"

"Ann has a great eye." She nods sagely. "Ann, your personal shopper."

"I have a personal shopper?"

"Just for the main pieces each season..." Rosalie pulls out a dark blue dress with spaghetti straps and the tiniest ruffle around the hem. "Look, this is the dress you wore when we first met. I remember thinking, 'Ah, *this* is the girl Eric's smitten with.' It was the talk of the party! And let me tell you, Lexi, there were a *lot* of disappointed girls out there when you two got married...." She reaches for a long black evening dress. "This is the dress you wore to my murder mystery evening." She holds it up against me. "With a little fur shrug and pearls...Don't you remember?"

"Not really."

"What about this Catherine Walker? You *must* remember that... or your Roland Mouret..." Rosalie is whipping out dress after dress, none of which looks remotely familiar. She reaches a pale garment carrier and stops with a gasp. "Your wedding dress!" Slowly, reverently, she unzips the garment carrier and pulls out the silky white sheath I recognize from the DVD. "Doesn't that bring it all back?"

I stare at the dress, trying as hard as I can to will my memory to return... but nothing.

"*Oh* my God." Rosalie suddenly claps a hand over her mouth. "You and Eric should have a renewal of vows! I'll plan it for you! We could have a Japanese theme, you could wear a kimono—"

"Maybe!" I cut her off. "It's early days. I'll... think about it."

"Hmm." Rosalie looks disappointed as she packs the wedding dress away. Then her face lights up. "Try the shoes. You *have* to remember your shoes."

She heads to the other side of the room and flings open a cupboard door. And I stare in disbelief. I've never seen so many shoes. All in neat rows, most of them high-heeled. What am I doing with high-heeled shoes?

"This is unbelievable." I turn to Rosalie. "I can't even *walk* in heels, God knows why I bought them."

"Yes, you can." Rosalie looks puzzled. "Of course you can."

"No." I shake my head. "I've never been able to do heels. I fall over, I twist my ankle, I look stupid..."

"Sweetie." Rosalie's eyes are wide. "You *live* in heels. You were wearing these last time we had lunch." She pulls out a pair of black pumps with four-inch stiletto heels. The kind I'd never even look at in a shop.

The soles are scuffed. The inside label has been rubbed away. Someone's been wearing these.

Me?

"Put them on!" says Rosalie.

Cautiously I slip off my loafers and step into the pointy heels. Almost at once I topple over and grab Rosalie.

"You see? I can't balance."

"Lexi, you can walk in these," Rosalie says firmly. "I've seen you do it."

"I can't." I make to take them off, but Rosalie grabs my arm.

"No! Don't give up, sweetie. It's *in* you, I know it is! You have to ... unlock it!"

I try another step, but my ankle bends like plasticine. "It's no good." I exhale in frustration. "I wasn't meant to do this."

"Yes, you were. Try again! Find the zone!" Rosalie sounds like she's coaching me for the Olympics. "You can do it, Lexi."

I totter to the other side of the room and cling to the curtain. "I'll never crack this," I say despairingly.

"Of course you will. Just don't think about it. Distract yourself. I know! We'll sing a song! 'Land of hope and glor-eeee ...' Come on, Lexi, *sing*!"

Reluctantly I join in. I really hope Eric doesn't have a CCTV camera trained on us at this moment.

"Now walk!" Rosalie gives me a little push. "Go!"

"'Land of hope and gloreeee...'" Trying to keep my mind focused on the song, I take a step forward. Then another. Then another.

Oh my God. I'm doing it. I'm walking in high heels!

"You see?" Rosalie crows in triumph. "I told you! You *are* a heels girl."

I get to the other side of the room, swivel around confidently, and walk back, an elated grin on my face. I feel like a model!

"I can do it! It's easy!"

"Yay!" Rosalie lifts her hand and gives me a high-five. She opens a drawer, scoops up some gym clothes, and pops them into an oversize tote. "Come on, let's go."

• • •

We drive to the gym in Rosalie's car. It's a sumptuous Range Rover with the license plate ROS 1. Designer shopping bags are strewn all over the backseat.

"So, what do you do?" I say as she winds her way between two lanes of traffic.

"I do a lot of volunteer work." She nods earnestly.

"Wow." I feel a bit shamefaced. Rosalie didn't strike me as the volunteer-work type, which just shows how prejudiced I am. "What kind?"

"Event planning, mainly."

"For a particular charity?"

"No, mostly for friends. You know, if they need a helping hand with the flowers or party favors or whatever..." Rosalie's smiling winsomely up at a truck driver. "*Please* let me in, Mr. Lorry-driver...Thank you!" She pulls over into the next lane and blows him a kiss.

"I do the odd bits for the company, too," she adds. "Eric's such a sweetie, he always gets me involved in launches, that kind of thing. Oh shit, road works!" She swerves, to a cacophony of angry hooting, and turns the radio up higher.

"So you like Eric?" I try to sound casual, although I'm dying to hear what she thinks of him.

"Oh, he's the perfect husband. Absolutely perfect." She draws up at a crosswalk. "Mine's a *monster*."

"Really?" I stare at her.

"Mind you, I'm a monster too." She turns to face me, her blue eyes deadly serious. "We're so volatile. It's a total love-hate relationship. Here we are!" She zooms off again and drives into a tiny car park, pulls up next to a Porsche, and turns off the engine.

"Now, don't worry," she says as she ushers me toward the glass double doors. "I know this will be really hard for you, so I'll do all the talking....Hi there!" She pushes her way into a smart reception area furnished with tan leather seating and a pebbled fountain.

"Hi, ladies." The receptionist's face falls as she sees me. "Lexi! You poor thing! We heard about the accident. Are you all right?"

"I'm fine, thanks." I venture a smile. "Thanks very much for the flowers."

"Poor Lexi has amnesia," says Rosalie impressively. "She doesn't remember this place. She doesn't remember *anything.*" She casts around as though for a way to illustrate. "Like, she doesn't remember this door . . . or . . . or this plant . . ." She gestures to a large frondy fern.

"Goodness!"

"I know." Rosalie is nodding solemnly. "It's a *night*mare for her." She turns to me. "Is this bringing back any memories, Lexi?"

"Er . . . not really."

Everyone in the reception area is staring at me, agog. I feel like a member of the Amnesia Freak Circus.

"Come on!" Rosalie firmly takes hold of my arm. "We'll get changed. You might remember once you're in your exercise clothes."

The changing rooms are the most palatial ones I've ever seen, all smooth wood and mosaic showers and gentle music playing over the speakers. I disappear into a cubicle and pull on a pair of leggings. Then I pull on the leotard bit.

It's got a thong, I realize to my horror. My bum will look *massive*. I can't wear this.

But I don't have anything else. Reluctantly I pull it on, then edge out of the cubicle, hands over my eyes. This could be really, really gross. I count to five, then force myself to take a peek.

Actually . . . I don't look too bad. I remove my hands completely and stare at myself. I look all long and lean and . . . different. Experimentally I flex my arm—and a biceps muscle I've never seen before pops up. I stare at it in astonishment.

"So!" Rosalie bustles up to me, dressed in leggings and a crop top. "This way . . ." She ushers me into a large, airy exercise studio, where rows of well-groomed women are already in position on yoga mats.

"Sorry we're late," she says momentously, looking around the room. "But Lexi has got amnesia. She doesn't remember *anything*. About *any* of you."

I get the feeling Rosalie is enjoying this.

"Hi." I do a shy wave around the room.

"I heard about your accident, Lexi." The exercise teacher is coming over wearing a sympathetic smile. She's a slim woman with cropped blond hair and a headset. "Please take it easy today. Sit out whenever you like. We're starting with some mat work..."

"Okay. Thanks."

"We're trying to trigger her memory," Rosalie chimes in. "So everyone just *act normal*."

As all the others raise their arms, I nervously take a mat and sit down. Gym has never exactly been my strong point. I guess I'll just follow as best I can. I stretch my legs out in front of me and reach for my toes, although there's no way I'll ever be able to—

Bloody hell. I can touch my toes. In fact, I can put my head right down on my knees. What's *happened* to me?

In disbelief I follow the next maneuver—and I can do that one too! I'm bendy! My body is moving into each position as if it can remember everything perfectly, even if I can't.

"And now, for those that are up to it," the teacher is saying, "the advanced dancer position..."

Cautiously I start tugging on my ankle—and it

obeys me! I'm pulling my leg right above my head! I feel like yelling "Look at me, everyone!"

"Don't overdo it, Lexi." The teacher looks alarmed. "Maybe take it easy now. I'd leave out splits this week."

No way. I can do *splits*?

• • •

Afterward in the changing room I'm exhilarated. I sit in front of the mirror, drying my hair, watching as it turns from damp mouse back to shiny glowing chestnut. "I can't get over it," I keep saying to Rosalie. "I was always so crap at exercise!"

"Sweetie, you're a natural!" Rosalie is slathering body lotion all over herself. "You're the best in the class."

I switch off the hair dryer, pull my hands through my dry hair, and survey my reflection. For the millionth time, my gaze is drawn to my gleaming white teeth— and my full pink lips. My mouth never looked like that in 2004—I *know* it didn't.

"Rosalie." I lower my voice. "Can I ask you a . . . a personal question?"

"Of course!" Rosalie whispers back.

"Did I ever have anything done? To my face? Like Botox? Or"—I lower my voice still further, hardly able to believe I'm saying this—"*surgery?*"

"Sweetie!" Rosalie looks appalled. "Shh!" She puts her finger to her lips.

"But . . ."

"Shh! Of course we haven't had anything done! All totally, one-hundred-percent natural." She winks.

What does that wink mean?

"Rosalie, you *have* to tell me what I've had done..." I trail off suddenly, distracted by my reflection in the mirror. Without noticing what I've been doing, I've been taking hairpins from the jar in front of me and putting my hair up on autopilot. In about thirty seconds, I've constructed the most perfect chignon.

How the fuck did I do that?

As I survey my own hands I can feel slight hysteria rising inside me. What else can I do? Defuse a bomb? Assassinate someone with one blow of my hand?

"What is it?" Rosalie catches my gaze.

"I just put my hair up." I gesture at the mirror. "Look. It's incredible. I've never done that before in my life."

"Yes, you have." She looks puzzled. "You wear it like that for work every day."

"But I don't *remember*. It's like...it's like Superwoman's taken over my body or something. I can walk in heels, I can put my hair up, I can do splits.... I'm like this überwoman! It's not *me*."

"Sweetie, it *is* you." Rosalie squeezes my arm. "You better get used to it!"

• • •

We have lunch in the juice bar and chat with a couple of girls who seem to know me, and then Rosalie drives me home. As we travel up in the lift I'm suddenly exhausted.

"So!" Rosalie says as we enter the apartment. "Do you want to have another look at your clothes? Maybe swimwear!"

"Actually, I feel pretty wiped out," I say apologetically. "Do you mind if I go and have a rest?"

"Of course not!" She pats my arm. "I'll wait out here for you, make sure you're okay..."

"Don't be silly." I smile. "I'll be fine until Eric comes home, really. And...thanks, Rosalie. You've been so kind."

"Darling girl." She gives me a hug and picks up her bag. "I'll give you a call. Look after yourself!" She's halfway out the door when something occurs to me.

"Rosalie!" I call. "What should I make Eric for dinner tonight?"

She turns and gazes at me uncomprehendingly. I suppose it is quite a strange question, out of the blue.

"I just thought you might know what sort of thing he likes." I laugh awkwardly.

"Sweetie..." Rosalie blinks several times. "Sweetie, *you* don't make the dinner. Gianna makes the dinner. Your housekeeper? She'll be out shopping right now, then she'll come back, make dinner, turn down your bed..."

"Oh, right. Of course!" I nod hastily, trying to look like I knew that all along.

But bloody hell. This really is a different life. I've never even had a *cleaner* before, let alone a five-star-hotel-type housekeeper.

"Well, I guess I'll go to bed, then," I say. "Bye."

Rosalie blows me a kiss and closes the door behind her, and I head into the bedroom, which is all cream and luxurious dark wood, with a massive suede-upholstered bed. Eric has insisted that I take the main bedroom, which is very kind and noble of him. Mind you, the spare room is pretty sumptuous too; in fact, I think he gets his own Jacuzzi, so he can't complain.

I kick off my heels, climb under the duvet, and feel myself instantly relax. This is the most comfortable bed I have ever been in, *ever*. I wriggle around a bit, luxuriating in the smooth sheets and perfect squashy pillows. Mmm, that's good. I'll just close my eyes and have a tiny kip...

I wake to a dim light and the sound of chinking crockery.

"Darling?" comes a voice from outside the door. "Are you awake?"

"Oh." I struggle to a sitting position and rub my eyes. "Er...hi."

The door opens and in comes Eric, holding a tray and a shopping bag.

"You've been asleep for hours. I've brought you some supper." He heads toward the bed, puts down the tray, and switches on the bedside light. "It's Thai chicken soup."

"I love Thai chicken soup!" I say in delight. "Thanks!"

Eric smiles and hands me a spoon. "Rosalie told me you two girls went to the gym today."

"Yes. It was great." I take a spoonful of soup and it's

absolutely delicious. God, I'm ravenous. "Eric, you couldn't get me a piece of bread, could you?" I raise my head. "Just to mop this up?"

"Bread?" Eric frowns, looking puzzled. "Darling, we don't keep bread in the house. We're both low-carb."

Oh, right. I'd forgotten about the low-carb thing.

"No problem!" I smile at him and take another mouthful of soup. I can be low-carb. Easy.

"Which brings me to my little gift," says Eric. "Or in fact . . . two gifts. This is the first one. . . ."

He reaches into the shopping bag and produces a laminated ring-bound booklet, which he hands to me with a flourish. The front cover is a color photograph of me and Eric in our wedding outfits, and the title reads: *Eric and Lexi Gardiner: Marriage Manual.*

"You remember the doctor suggested writing down all the details of our life together?" Eric looks proud. "Well, I've compiled this booklet for you. Any question you have about our marriage and life together, the answer should be in there."

I turn the first page, and there's a frontispiece.

Eric and Lexi
A better marriage for a better world

"We have a mission statement?" I'm slightly stunned.

"I came up with it just now." Eric shrugs modestly. "What do you think?"

"It's great!" I flip through the booklet. There are pages of print, interspersed with headings, photographs, and even some hand-drawn diagrams. I can see sections on holidays, family, laundry, weekends ...

"I've organized the entries in alphabetical order," Eric explains. "And indexed them. It should be fairly simple to use."

I flip to the index and run my eyes down the page at random.

Tomatoes—pp. 5, 23
Tongs—see Barbecue
Tongues—p. 24

Tongues? Immediately I start flipping to page twenty-four.

"Don't try and read it now." Eric gently closes the manual. "You need to eat and sleep."

I'll look up "tongues" later. When he's gone.

I finish the rest of the soup and lean back with a contented sigh. "Thank you so much, Eric. That was perfect."

"It's no trouble, my darling." Eric removes the tray and puts it on the dressing table. As he does so, he notices my shoes on the floor. "Lexi!" He flashes me a smile. "Shoes go in your dressing room."

"Oh," I say. "Sorry."

"No problem. There's a lot to learn." He comes back over to the bed and reaches into his pocket. "And this is my other gift ..." He produces a little jewelry box made of leather.

My head starts prickling in disbelief as I gaze at it.

My husband is giving me a present in a posh jewelry box. Just like grown-up people in movies.

"I'd like you to have something you actually *remember* me giving you," Eric says with a rueful smile, then nods at the box. "Open it."

I pry it open—and find a single diamond strung on a gold chain.

"Like it?"

"It's . . . it's amazing!" I stammer. "I love it! Thank you so much!"

Eric reaches over and strokes my hair. "It's good to have you home, Lexi."

"It's good to *be* home," I reply with fervor.

Which is almost true. I can't honestly say this place feels like home yet. But it feels like a really swish five-star hotel, which is even *better*. I take out the diamond and look at it in awe. Meanwhile Eric is playing idly with a strand of my hair, a tender expression on his face.

"Eric," I say, a bit shyly. "When we first met, what did you see in me? Why did you fall in love with me?"

A reminiscent smile flickers across Eric's face.

"I fell in love with you, Lexi," he says, "because you're dynamic. You're efficient. You're hungry for success, like me. People call us hard, but we're not. We're just intensely competitive."

"Right," I say after a slight pause.

To be honest, I've never thought of myself as *that* intensely competitive. But then, maybe I am in 2007.

"And I fell in love with your beautiful mouth." Eric

touches my top lip gently. "And your long legs. And the way you swing your briefcase."

He called me beautiful.

I'm listening, entranced. I want him to go on forever. No one has ever spoken to me like this, in my whole life.

"I'll leave you now." He kisses me on the forehead and picks up the tray. "You sleep well. See you in the morning."

"See you then," I murmur. "Good night, Eric. And...thank you!"

He closes the door and I'm left alone with my necklace and my marriage manual and my glow of euphoria. I have the dream husband. No, I have the *better*-than-a-dream husband. He brought me chicken soup and gave me a diamond and fell in love with the way I swing my briefcase.

I must have been Gandhi.

Chapter Eight

No way. He put in a section on *foreplay*?

I've been flicking through the marriage manual ever since I woke up this morning—and it's totally, utterly riveting. I feel like I'm spying on my own life. Not to mention Eric's. I know everything, from where he buys his cuff links to what he thinks of the government to the fact that he checks his scrotum for lumps every month. (Which is a bit more than I bargained for. Did he have to mention his scrotum?)

It's breakfast time, and we're both sitting in the kitchen. Eric's reading the *Financial Times,* and I was consulting the index to see what I normally eat. But Foreplay looks a whole lot more interesting than Food. Surreptitiously I turn to page twenty-one.

Oh my God. He seriously has written three paragraphs on foreplay! Under General Routine.

"...*sweeping, regular motion*...*normally clock-wise direction*...*gentle stimulation of the inner thighs*..."

I splutter on my coffee and Eric looks up.

"All right, darling?" He smiles. "Is the manual helpful? Are you finding everything you need?"

"Yes!" I hastily flick to another section, feeling like a kid looking up rude words in the dictionary. "I was just finding out what I usually have for breakfast."

"Gianna's left some scrambled egg and bacon in the oven," says Eric. "And you usually have some green juice." He gestures at a jug of what looks like sludgy marsh water on the counter. "It's a vitamin drink and natural appetite suppressant."

I suppress a shudder. "I think I'll give that a miss today." I take some egg and bacon from the oven and try to quell my longing for three slices of granary toast to go with it.

"Your new car should be delivered later on." Eric takes a sip of coffee. "The replacement for the one that was damaged. Although I'm guessing you won't want to drive in a hurry."

"I hadn't really thought about it," I say helplessly.

"Well, we'll see. You can't yet, anyway, until you've retaken your driving test." He wipes his mouth with a linen napkin and gets up. "There was another thing, Lexi. If you don't mind, I'd like to schedule a small dinner party for next week. Just a few old friends."

"A dinner party?" I echo, apprehensive. I've never really been the dinner-party-throwing type. Unless you count pasta on the sofa in front of *Will & Grace* as a dinner party.

"There's nothing to worry about." He puts his hands gently on my shoulders. "Gianna will do the catering. All you have to do is look wonderful. But if you're not up to it, we can forget the idea."

"Of course I'm up to it!" I say quickly. "I'm tired of everyone treating me like I'm an invalid. I feel great!"

"Well, that brings me to another subject. Work." Eric shrugs on his jacket. "Obviously you're not up to returning full-time just yet, but Simon was wondering if you'd like to go into the office for a visit. Simon Johnson," he clarifies. "Do you remember him?"

"Simon Johnson? The managing director?"

"Uh-huh." Eric nods. "He called here last night. We had a good chat. Nice guy."

"I didn't think he'd even *heard* of me!" I say in disbelief.

"Lexi, you're an important member of the senior management team," Eric says patiently. "Of course he's heard of you."

"Oh, right. Of course."

I chew my bacon, trying to look nonchalant—but inside, I want to cheer. This new life of mine gets better and better. I'm an important member of the senior management team! Simon Johnson knows who I am!

Eric is continuing. "We agreed it would be helpful for you to visit the office. It might help bring back your memory—as well as give reassurance to your department."

"I think it's a great idea," I say with enthusiasm. "I

could get to know my job again, see all the girls...We could have lunch."

"Your deputy is standing in for you at the moment," Eric says, consulting a notepad on the kitchen counter. "Byron Foster. Just till you return, obviously."

"Byron's my deputy now?" I say incredulously. "But Byron used to be my boss!"

Everything's upside down. Everything's unrecognizable. I can't *wait* to get to the office and see what's been going on.

Eric taps something into his BlackBerry, then puts it away and picks up his briefcase. "Have a good day, darling."

"You too...er...darling!" I stand up as he turns to face me—and there's a sudden frisson between us. Eric's standing only inches away from me. I can just smell his aftershave and see a little nick on his neck where he cut himself shaving.

"I haven't read the whole manual yet." I suddenly feel awkward. "Would I normally...kiss you good-bye at this point?"

"You normally would, yes." Eric sounds stiff too. "But please don't feel you—"

"No! I want to! I mean...we should do everything just like we usually do." I'm getting a bit pink in the face here. "So, would I kiss you on the cheek, or...or the lips..."

"The lips." Eric clears his throat. "That would be the usual."

"Right." I nod. "So...um..." I reach out for his

waist, trying to appear natural. "Like this? Tell me if it's not the way I normally do it..."

"Probably just one hand," Eric says after a moment's thought. "And it's usually a bit higher up."

"Okay!" I shift one hand up to his shoulder and drop the other down, feeling as if I'm ballroom dancing. Then, keeping in position as best I can, I tilt my face up.

Eric has a strange little nodule on the end of his tongue, I suddenly notice. Okay... I won't look at it. Concentrate on the kiss. He leans forward and his mouth brushes briefly against mine, and I feel... nothing.

I was hoping our first kiss would trigger all sorts of memories or sensations, maybe a sudden image of Paris or our wedding, or our first snog....But as he draws away I feel totally, one hundred percent blank. I can see the anticipation in Eric's face and quickly search for something encouraging to say.

"That was lovely! Very..."

I trail off, unable to think of a single word other than *quick,* which I'm not sure hits the right note.

"It didn't bring back any memories?" Eric is studying my face.

"Well...no," I say apologetically. "But, I mean, that doesn't mean it wasn't really...I mean it was...I feel quite turned on!" The words come out before I can stop them.

What the hell did I say that for? I don't feel turned on.

"Really?" Eric lights up and he puts his briefcase down.

Oh no. No no no. Nooo.

I cannot possibly have sex with Eric yet. Number one, I don't even know him, hardly. Number two, I haven't read what happens after gentle stimulation of the inner thighs.

"Not *that* turned on," I amend hastily. "I mean, just enough to know...to realize...I mean obviously we have a great...when it comes to the bedroom... um...arena..."

Stop. Talking. Lexi. Now.

"Anyway." I smile as brightly as I can manage. "Have a great day."

"You too." Eric touches my cheek gently, then turns and strides off. I hear the door close, and subside into a chair. That was a bit close. I reach for the marriage manual and quickly flick to the "F" section. I need to read up on Foreplay.

Not to mention Fellatio, I suddenly notice. And Frequency (Sexual).

This could take me a while.

• • •

Two hours and three cups of coffee later, I close the manual and lean back, my head bursting with information. I've read it cover to cover, and I've pretty much got the whole picture.

I've learned that Eric and I often spend weekends away at "luxury boutique hotels." I've learned that we enjoy watching business documentaries and *The West Wing*. And we had differing views on *Brokeback*

Mountain. Which I've also learned was a film about gay cowboys. (Gay *cowboys?*)

I've learned that Eric and I share a love of wine from the Bordeaux region. I've learned that I'm "driven" and "focused" and "work 24-7 to get the job done." I've learned I "don't suffer fools gladly," "despise time-wasters," and am "someone who appreciates the finer things in life."

Which is kind of news to me.

I get up and walk to the window, trying to digest everything I've read. The more I learn about twenty-eight-year-old Lexi, the more I feel like she's a different person from me. She doesn't just look different. She *is* different. She's a boss. She wears beige designer clothes and La Perla underwear. She knows about wine. She never eats bread.

She's a grown-up. That's what she is. I gaze into the mirror and my twenty-eight-year-old face stares back.

How on earth did I get from me . . . to her?

On impulse I get up and head into the bedroom, then through that into the clothes room. There have to be some clues somewhere. I sit down at my smart, minimalist dressing table, and regard it silently.

I mean, look at this, for a start. My old dressing table was painted pink and a total mess—all scarves, necklaces looped over the mirror, and jars of makeup everywhere. But this is immaculate. Silver jars in rows, a single dish containing one pair of earrings, and an art deco hand mirror.

I open a drawer at random and find a pile of neatly folded scarves, on top of which is a shiny DVD marked

Ambition: EP1 in felt-tip marker. I pick it up, puzzled—and then suddenly realize what it is. It's that program Amy was talking about. This is me on the telly!

Oh my God, I *have* to see this. First because I'm dying to know what I looked like. And second because it's another piece of the puzzle. This reality show is where Eric first saw me. It gave me my big break at work. I probably had no idea at the time how crucial it was going to be.

I hurry into the living room, eventually manage to locate the DVD player behind a translucent panel, and slot it in. Soon the program titles are rolling on all the wall-mounted screens throughout the flat. I fast-forward until my face appears onscreen, then press Play.

I'm prepared to cringe with embarrassment and duck behind the sofa. But actually . . . I don't look that bad! My teeth have already been veneered or capped or whatever—although my mouth looks much thinner than it does now. (I have *definitely* had collagen injections.) My chestnut hair's been blow-dried and tied back in a ponytail. I'm wearing a black suit and an aquamarine shirt and I look totally businesslike.

"I need to succeed," I'm saying to an off-camera interviewer. "I need to win this."

Blimey. I look so *serious*. I don't understand it. Why did I suddenly want to win a reality business show?

"Good morning, Lexi!" A voice makes me practically jump out of my skin. I jab at Stop on the remote and turn around to see a woman in her fifties. She has dark, gray-streaked hair tied back; she's wearing a flowery overall; and she's holding a plastic bucket full of cleaning things. An iPod is clipped to her overall pocket and from the speakers in her ears I can just hear the strains of opera.

"You're up!" she says in a piercing voice. "How you feeling? Any better today?" Her accent is hard to place, kind of cockney mixed with Italian.

"Are you Gianna?" I say cautiously.

"Oh my Lord in heaven." She crosses herself and kisses her fingers. "Eric warned me. You're not right in the head, poor girl."

"I'm fine, really," I say hurriedly. "I've just lost a bit of memory. So I'm having to learn everything about my life again."

"Well, I am Gianna." She hits her chest.

"Great! Er...thanks." I stand aside as Gianna moves past me and starts flicking over the glass surface of the coffee table with a feather duster, humming along to the iPod.

"Watching your TV show, are you?" she says, glancing past me at the huge screen.

"Oh. Er...I was. Just to remind myself." I hastily turn it off. Meanwhile Gianna has started polishing a display of picture frames.

I twist my fingers awkwardly. How can I just *stand* here, watching another woman clean my house? Should I offer to help?

"What would you like me to cook for dinner tonight?" she says, starting to plump up the cushions on the sofa.

"Oh," I say, looking up in horror. "Nothing! Really!"

I know Eric and I are all rich and everything, but I can't ask someone else to cook my supper. It's obscene.

"Nothing?" She pauses. "Are you going out?"

"No! I just thought...maybe I'd do the cooking myself tonight."

"Oh, I see," she says. "Well, it's up to you." Her face set, she picks up a cushion and bangs it out with more vigor. "I hope you enjoyed the soup last night," she adds, without looking at me.

"It was delicious!" I say hastily. "Thanks! Lovely... flavors."

"Good," she says in a stiff voice. "I do my best."

Oh God. She isn't offended, is she?

"Let me know what you'd like me to buy for you to cook," she continues, slapping the cushion down. "If you're after something new, or different..."

Shit. She *is* offended.

"Or...er...well." My voice is scratchy with nerves. "Actually, on second thought...maybe you could make a little something. But I mean, don't make any effort. Just a sandwich would be fine."

"A sandwich?" She raises her head incredulously. "For your dinner?"

"Or...whatever you like! Whatever *you* enjoy cooking!" Even as I say the words I know how stupid this sounds. I back away, pick up a property magazine that's lying on a side table, and open it at a piece about fountains.

How am I ever going to get used to all this? How did I turn into someone with a housekeeper, for God's sake?

"Aiee! The sofa has been damaged!" Gianna's accent suddenly sounds far more Italian than cockney. She yanks her iPod speakers out of her ears and gestures at the torn fabric in horror. "Look! Ripped! Yesterday morning it was perfect." She looks at me defensively. "I tell you—I left it in good condition, no rips, no marks..."

The blood rushes to my head. "That...that was me." I stammer. "I did it."

"*You?*"

"It was a mistake," I gabble. "I didn't mean to. I broke this glass leopard and..." I'm breathing hard. "I'll order another sofa cover, I promise. But please don't tell Eric. He doesn't know."

"He doesn't know?" Gianna seems bewildered.

"I put the cushion over the rip." I swallow. "To hide it."

Gianna stares at me for a few disbelieving moments. I stare back pleadingly, unable to breathe. Then her severe face creases into a laugh. She puts down the cushion she's holding and pats me on the arm.

"I'll sew it. Little tiny stitches. He'll never know."

"Really?" I feel a wash of relief. "Oh, thank God. That would be wonderful. I'd be so grateful."

Gianna is surveying me with a perplexed frown, her broad arms folded across her chest. "You're sure nothing happened when you bumped your head?" she says at last. "Like...personality transplant?"

"What?" I give an uncertain laugh. "I don't think so..." The door buzzer goes off. "Oh, I'd better get this." I hurry to the front door and lift the answer phone. "Hello?"

"Hello?" comes a guttural voice. "Car delivery for Gardiner."

• • •

My new car is parked in a place at the front of the building, which according to the porter is my own private spot. It's a silver Mercedes, which I can tell from the badge-thing on the front. And it's a convertible. Apart from that, I couldn't tell you much about it—except I'm guessing it cost a fortune.

"Sign here ... and here ..." The deliveryman is holding out a clipboard.

"Okay." I scribble on the paper.

"Here's your keys ... all your paperwork. Cheers, love." The guy retrieves his pen from my hand and heads out the gates, leaving me alone with the car, a bundle of papers, and a set of shiny car keys. I dangle them in my fingers, feeling a frisson of excitement.

I've never been a car person.

But then, I've never been this close to a glossy, brand-new Mercedes before. A brand-new Mercedes which is all *mine*.

Maybe I'll just check it over inside. With an instinctive gesture I hold out the key fob and press the little button—then jump as the car bleeps and all the lights flash on.

Well, I've obviously done that before. I open the door, slide into the driver's seat, and inhale deeply.

Wow. Now, *this* is a car. This knocks Loser Dave's

crappy Renault out of the park. It has the most wonderful, intoxicating scent of new leather. The seats are wide and comfortable. The dashboard is gleaming wood veneer. Cautiously I place my hands on the steering wheel. They seem to grip it quite naturally—in fact, they seem to belong there. I really don't want to take them off.

I sit there for a few moments, watching the entry gates rise and fall as a BMW drives out.

The thing is...I *can* drive. At some stage I must have passed my test, even if I don't remember doing it.

And this is such a cool car. It would be a shame not to have a go.

Experimentally I push the key into the slot beside the steering wheel—and it fits! I rotate it forward, like I've seen people do, and there's a kind of roar of protest from the engine. Shit. What did I do? I turn it forward again, more cautiously, and this time there's no roar, but a few lights pop on around the dashboard.

Now what? I survey the controls hopefully for inspiration, but none comes. I have no idea how to work this thing, is the truth. I have no memory of driving a car in my life.

But the point is...I *have* done it. It's like walking in heels—it's a skill locked away inside me. What I need is to let my body take over. If I can just distract myself enough, then maybe I'll find myself driving automatically.

I place my hands firmly on the steering wheel. Here we go. Think about other things. La la la. Don't think about driving. Just let your body do what comes naturally. Maybe I should sing a song—that worked before.

" 'Land of hope and gloree,' " I begin tunelessly, " 'mother of the freeee...' "

Oh my God. It's working. My hands and feet are moving in sync. I don't dare look at them; I don't dare register what they're doing. All I know is I've switched on the engine and pushed down on one of the pedals and there's a kind of rumbling and...I did it! I switched on the car!

I can hear the engine throbbing, as if it wants to get going. Okay, keep calm. I take a deep breath—but deep inside I'm already a bit panicky. I'm sitting at the controls of a Mercedes and the engine's running and I'm not even sure how that happened.

Right. Collect yourself, Lexi.

Hand brake. I know what that is. And the gear stick. Cautiously I release both—and at once the car moves forward.

Hastily I press my foot down on one of the pedals, to stop it, and the car bucks with an ominous grinding noise. Shit. That didn't sound good. I release my foot— and the car creeps forward again. I'm not sure I want it doing that. Trying to stay calm, I press my foot down again, hard. But this time it doesn't even stop, it just keeps going inexorably forward. I thrust again—and it revs up like a racing car.

"Shit!" I say, almost gibbering in fear. "Okay, just...stop. Stay!" I'm pulling back on the wheel, but it's making no difference. I don't know how to control this thing. We're slowly heading toward an expensive-looking sports car parked opposite and I don't know how to stop. In desperation I thrust both feet down again, hitting two pedals at once with a shrieking, engine-breaking sound.

Oh God, Oh God... My face is hot; my hands are sweating. I never should have gotten into this car. If I crash it, Eric will divorce me and I won't blame him....

"Stop!" I cry again. "Please!"

Suddenly I notice a dark-haired man in jeans coming in at the gates. He sees me gliding forward toward the sports car and his whole face jolts.

"Stop!" he yells, his voice faint through the window.

"I can't stop!" I yell back desperately.

"Steer!" He mimes steering.

The *steering wheel*. Of course. I'm a moron. I wrench it around to the right, nearly dragging my arms out of my sockets, and manage to turn the car off course. Only now I'm heading straight toward a brick wall.

"Brake!" The guy is running alongside me. "Brake, Lexi!"

"But I don't—"

"For God's sake, brake!" he yells.

The hand brake, I suddenly remember. Quick. I yank it back with both hands and the car stops with a judder. The engine is still running, but at least the car is stationary. And at least I haven't hit anything.

My breath is coming fast and hoarse; my hands are still clenched around the hand brake. I'm never driving again. Never.

"Are you okay?" The guy is at my window. After a

few moments I manage to unclench one of my hands from the hand brake. I jab randomly at the buttons on the car door until the window winds down. "What *happened*?" he says.

"I . . . panicked. I can't actually drive a car. I thought I'd remember how to, but I had a bit of a panic attack." Suddenly, with no warning, I feel a tear running down my face. "I'm sorry," I gulp. "I'm a bit freaked out. I've had amnesia, you see . . ."

I look up to see the guy just staring at me as if I'm talking a foreign language. He's got a pretty striking face, now that I come to notice it. High cheekbones, dark gray eyes, and slanted eyebrows gathered in a frown, with dark brown untidy hair. He's wearing a plain gray T-shirt over his jeans, and he looks a bit older than me, maybe early thirties.

He also seems totally dumbfounded. Which I guess is not surprising, bearing in mind he's just come into a car park, minding his own business, to find a girl crashing a car and saying she has amnesia.

Maybe he doesn't believe me, I think, suddenly alarmed. Maybe he thinks I'm drunk-driving and this is all some invented excuse.

"I was in a car crash a few days ago," I explain hurriedly. "I really was. I hit my head. Look." I point to the remaining cuts on my face.

"I know you were in a car crash," he says at last. He has a very distinctive voice, dry and kind of intense. As though every word he speaks really, really matters. "I heard about it."

"Wait a minute!" I click my tongue, suddenly realizing. "You called out my name. Do we know each other?"

A jolt of shock passes over the guy's face. I can see his eyes studying me almost as though he doesn't believe me; as though he's searching for something.

"You don't remember me?" he says at last.

"Um, no," I say with an apologetic shrug. "I'm sorry, I'm not being rude; I don't remember anyone I've met in the last three years. My friends...my husband, even. He was a total stranger to me! My own husband! Can you believe it?"

I smile—but the guy doesn't smile back or express sympathy. In fact, his expression almost makes me nervous.

"Do you want me to park that for you?" he says abruptly.

"Oh. Yes, please." I glance anxiously at my left hand, still clutching the hand brake. "Can I let go of this? Will the car roll away?"

A tiny smile flickers over his face. "No. It won't roll away. You can let go."

Cautiously I unfurl my hand, which had practically seized up, and shake out the stiffness.

"Thanks so much," I say, getting out. "This is my brand-new car. If I'd crashed it, I can't even *think*..." I wince at the idea. "My husband got it for me, to replace the other one. Do you know him? Eric Gardiner?"

"Yes," he says after a pause. "I know him."

He gets into the car, shuts the door, and signals to

me to get out of the way. The next moment he's expertly reversed the car safely back into its parking spot.

"Thanks," I say fervently as he gets out. "I really appreciate it."

I wait for the guy to say "It's no trouble" or "Any time," but he seems lost in thought.

"What did they say about the amnesia?" he says, suddenly looking up. "Have your memories gone forever?"

"They might come back anytime," I explain. "Or they might not. No one knows. I'm just trying to learn about my life again. Eric's being really helpful and teaching me all about our marriage and everything. He's the most perfect husband!" I smile again, attempting to lighten the atmosphere. "So . . . where do you fit into the picture?"

There's no response at all from the dark-haired guy. He's shoved his hands in his pockets and is staring up at the sky. I *really* don't know what his problem is.

At last he lowers his head and surveys me again, his face all screwed up, as though he's in pain. Maybe he is. Maybe he has a headache or something.

"I have to go," he says.

"Oh, right. Well, thanks again," I say politely. "And very nice to meet you. I mean, I know we've met before in my previous life, but . . . you know what I mean!" I hold out a hand to shake his—but he just looks at it as though it makes no sense to him at all.

"Bye, Lexi." He turns on his heel.

"Bye . . ." I call after him, then trail off. What a weird guy. He never even told me his name.

Chapter Nine

Fi is one of the most straightforward people I know. We met at the age of six, when I was the new girl in the school playground. She was already a head taller than me, her dark hair in bunches, her voice booming and confident. She told me my plastic skipping rope was rubbish and loudly listed all its faults. Then, just as I was about to start crying, she offered me hers to play with.

That's Fi. She can upset people with her bluntness, and she knows it. When she's said the wrong thing she rolls her eyes and claps a hand over her mouth. But underneath it all, she's warmhearted and kind. And she's great in meetings. When other people waffle on, she gets right to the point, no bullshit.

It was Fi who gave me the idea of applying to Deller Carpets. She'd been working there for two years when Frenshaws, the company I was at before, got taken over by a Spanish company and a bunch of us were laid off. There was an opening in the Flooring department, and Fi suggested I bring my CV in to show Gavin, her boss . . . and that was it. I had a job.

Since working together, Fi and I have become even closer. We have lunch together, we go to the cinema on the weekend, we send text messages to each other while Gavin is trying to give one of his "team bollockings," as he calls them. I'm close to Carolyn and Debs too—but Fi's the one I ring up first with news; the one I think of when something funny happens.

Which is why it's so weird that she hasn't been in touch. I've texted her several more times since I got out of hospital. I've left two messages on voice mail. I've sent a few jokey e-mails and even written a card thanking her for the flowers. But I haven't heard a word back. Maybe she's just busy, I keep telling myself. Or she's been on some work residential seminar thing, or she's got the flu. . . . There's a million good reasons.

Anyway, I'm going in to work today, so I'll see her. And everyone.

I stare at myself in the huge mirror in my dressing room. 2004-Lexi used to show up at the office in a pair of black trousers from Next, a shirt from the bargain bin at New Look, and a pair of loafers with chewed-up heels.

Not anymore. I'm in the crispest shirt I've ever worn in my life, all expensive Prada double cuffs. I'm wearing a black suit with a pencil skirt and a nipped-in waist. My legs are gleaming in Charnos sheer gloss tights. My shoes are patent and spiky. My hair is blow-dried and twisted up into my signature chignon. I look like an illustration from a child's picture book. Boss Lady.

Eric comes into the room and I do a twirl.

"How do I look?"

"Great!" He nods, but doesn't seem surprised at my appearance. I suppose to him this kind of outfit is normal. Whereas I can't imagine this ever feeling like anything other than dressing up.

"All set?"

"I guess!" I pick up my bag—a black Bottega Veneta tote I found in the cupboard.

I tried asking Eric about Fi yesterday—but he barely seemed to know who she was, even though she's my oldest friend and was at our wedding and everything. The only friend of mine he seems to know about is Rosalie, which is because she's married to Clive.

Anyway, it's fine. I'll see Fi today, and there'll be some explanation, and everything will fall back into place. I expect we'll all go out for a drink at lunchtime and have a good old catch-up.

"Now, don't forget this!" Eric is opening a cupboard in the corner. He retrieves a sleek black briefcase and hands it to me. "I gave it to you when we were married."

"Wow, this is beautiful!" It's made of buttery-soft calfskin and on the front are discreetly embossed initials: L.G.

"I know you still use your maiden name for work," says Eric, "but I wanted you to take a little piece of me to the office with you every day."

He is *so* romantic. He is *so* perfect.

"I must go. The car will be here to pick you up in five minutes. Have a good time." He kisses me and heads out.

As I hear the front door close I pick up my briefcase and look at it, wondering what to put in it. I've never used a briefcase before—I always just shoved everything into my bag. Eventually I take a packet of tissues and some Polos out of my bag and put them into the briefcase. Then I add a pen. I feel like I'm packing for my first day at a new school. As I'm sliding the pen into a silk pocket, my fingers bump against something thin, like a card, and I pull it out.

It's not a card; it's an old photo of me, Fi, Debs, and Carolyn. Before I had my hair done. When my teeth were still all snaggly. We're in a bar, all dressed up in glittery tops with rosy cheeks and party-popper streamers over our heads. Fi has her arm clenched around my neck and I have a cocktail umbrella in my teeth, and we're all in hysterics. I can't help grinning at the sight.

I remember that evening really well. Debs had chucked her awful banker boyfriend, Mitchell, and we were on a mission to help her forget. Halfway through the evening, when Mitchell called Debs's mobile, Carolyn answered and pretended to be a £1,000 Russian call girl who thought she was being booked. Carolyn took Russian in school, so she was quite convincing, and Mitchell got genuinely rattled, no matter what he claimed later. We were all listening on speakerphone and I thought I'd *die* of laughter.

Still smiling, I slide the photo back into the pocket and snap the briefcase shut. I pick it up and regard myself in the mirror. Boss Lady Goes to Work.

"Hi," I say to my reflection, trying to adopt a

businesslike tone. "Hi, there. Lexi Smart, Director of Flooring. Yup, hi. I'm the boss."

Oh God. I don't feel like a boss. Maybe I'll snap back into it when I get there.

. . .

Deller Carpets is the company everyone remembers from the TV ads back in the eighties. The first one showed a woman lying on some blue swirling patterned carpet in a shop, pretending it was so soft and luxurious she immediately had to have sex on it with the nerdy sales assistant. Then there was the follow-up ad where she married the nerdy assistant and had the whole aisle carpeted in flowery Deller carpet. And then they had twins, who couldn't sleep unless they had blue and pink Deller carpet in their cribs.

They were pretty tacky ads, but they did make Deller Carpets a household name. Which is part of its trouble. The company tried to change its name a few years ago, to just Deller. There was a new logo and mission statement and everything. But nobody took any notice of that. You say you work at Deller and people frown and then they say, "You mean Deller Carpets?"

It's even more ironic because carpet is only a fraction of the company these days. About ten years ago the maintenance department started producing a carpet cleaner that was sold by mail order and became incredibly popular. They expanded into all sorts of cleaning products and gadgets, and now the mail-order business is huge. So are soft furnishings and fabrics. But poor old carpets have fallen by the wayside.

Trouble is, they're not cool these days. It's all slate and laminate wood flooring. We do sell laminate flooring— but hardly anyone realizes we do, because they think we're still called Deller Carpets. It's like one big vicious circle that all leads back to shag.

I know carpets aren't cool. And I know patterned carpets are even less cool. But secretly, I really love them. Especially all the old retro designs from the seventies. I've got an old pattern book on my desk, which I always flick through when I'm in the middle of a long, tedious phone conversation. And once I found a whole box of old samples at the warehouse. No one wanted them, so I took them back to the office and pinned them up on the wall next to my desk.

That's to say, my old desk. I guess I've been upgraded now. As I head toward the familiar building on Victoria Palace Road, I feel a fizz of anticipation in my stomach. It's the same as it ever was: a tall, pale gray block with granite pillars at the entrance. I push open the glass doors to reception—and stop in surprise. The foyer is different. It looks really cool! They've moved the desk, and there are glass partitions where there used to be a wall . . . and the flooring is blue metallic-effect vinyl. There must be a new range out.

"Lexi!" A plump woman in a pink shirt and tapered black trousers is bustling toward me. She has highlights and fuchsia lipstick and pumps and she's called . . . I know her . . . head of human resources . . .

"Dana." I gasp the name in relief. "Hi."

"Lexi." She holds out a hand to shake mine.

"Welcome back! You poor thing! We were all *so* upset to hear what happened..."

"I'm fine, thanks. A lot better." I follow her over the shiny vinyl floor, take a security pass from her, and swipe my way through the security entrance. This is all new too. We didn't use to have barriers, just a guard called Reg.

"Good! Well, come this way..." Dana's ushering me along. "I thought we could have a short chat in my office, pop in on the budget meeting, and then you'll want to see your department!"

"Great! Good idea."

My department. I used to just have a desk and a stapler.

We travel up in the lift and get out at the second floor, and Dana ushers me into her office.

"Take a seat." She pulls out a plushy chair and sits down at her desk. "So now, obviously, we need to talk about your...*condition*." She lowers her voice discreetly as though I have some embarrassing ailment. "You have amnesia."

"That's right. Apart from that, I'm pretty much okay."

"Good!" She scribbles something on her pad of paper. "And is this amnesia permanent or temporary?"

"Well...the doctors said I might start remembering things at any time."

"Marvelous!" Her face brightens. "Obviously, from *our* point of view it would be great if you could remember everything by the twenty-first. That's when our sales conference is," she adds, giving me an expectant look.

"Right," I say after a pause. "I'll do my best."

"You can't do better than that!" She trills with laughter and pushes back her chair. "Now, let's go and say hello to Simon and the others. You remember Simon Johnson, the MD?"

"Of course!"

How could I not remember the boss of the whole company? I remember him giving a speech at the Christmas party. I remember him appearing in our office and asking our names while Gavin, our department head then, followed him around like a lackey. And now I go to meetings with him!

Trying to conceal my nerves, I follow Dana down the corridor and up in the lift again to the eighth floor. She leads me briskly to the boardroom, knocks on the heavy door, and pushes it open.

"Sorry to interrupt! Only Lexi's popped in for a visit."

"Lexi! Our superstar!" Simon Johnson stands up from his seat at the head of the table. He has a tall, broad-shouldered, ex-army-officer frame and thinning brown hair. He comes over, clasps my hand as if we're old friends, and kisses my cheek. "How are you feeling, my dear?"

Simon Johnson just kissed me. The MD of the whole company *kissed* me.

"Er ... fine, thanks!" I try to keep my composure. "Much better."

I glance around the room, taking in a whole bunch

of other high-powered company people in suits. Byron, who used to be my direct boss, is sitting on the other side of the conference table. He's pale and lanky with dark hair, and wearing one of his trademark retro-print ties. He gives me a pinched smile and I grin back, relieved to recognize someone else.

"You had quite a knock to the head, we understand," Simon Johnson is saying in his mellifluous public-school voice.

"That's right."

"Well, hurry back!" he exclaims with mock urgency. "Byron here is standing in for you very well." He gestures at Byron. "But whether you can trust him to safeguard your department's budget..."

"I don't know." I raise my eyebrows. "*Should* I be worried?"

There's an appreciative laugh around the table, and I notice Byron shooting me daggers.

Honestly. I was only making a joke.

"Seriously, though, Lexi. I need to talk to you about our recent...discussions." Simon Johnson gives me a meaningful nod. "We'll have lunch when you get back properly."

"Absolutely." I match his confidential tone, even though I have no idea what he's talking about.

"Simon." Dana steps forward, lowering her voice a smidgen. "The doctors don't know whether Lexi's amnesia is permanent or temporary. So she may have some problems with memory..."

"Probably an advantage, in this business," says a

balding man opposite, and there's another chuckle around the table.

"Lexi, I have every confidence in you," Simon Johnson says firmly. He turns to a red-haired guy sitting nearby. "Daniel, you two haven't met yet, have you? Daniel is our new finance controller. Daniel, you might have seen Lexi on television?"

"That's right!" I can see recognition dawning on the guy's face as we shake hands. "So you're the whiz kid I've heard about."

Whiz kid?

"Er...I don't think so," I say uncertainly, and there's a laugh.

"Don't be modest!" Simon gives me a warm smile, then turns to Daniel. "This young woman has had the most meteoric rise through this company. From associate junior sales manager to director of her department within eighteen months. As I've said many times to Lexi herself, it was a gamble, giving her the job—but I've never regretted taking that risk for a moment. She's a natural leader. She's inspirational. She puts in twenty-four hours a day; she has some exciting strategic visions for the future.... This is a very, *very* talented member of the company."

As he finishes, Simon is beaming at me; so are the balding guy and a couple of the others.

I'm in a state of total shock. My face is puce; my legs are wobbling. No one's ever spoken about me like that. Ever, my whole life.

"Well...thanks!" I stutter at last.

"Lexi." Simon gestures at an empty chair. "Can we tempt you to stay for the budget meeting?"

"Er . . ." I glance at Dana for help.

"She's not staying long today, Simon," says Dana. "We're popping down to Flooring now."

"Of course." He nods. "Well, you're missing a treat. Everyone loves a budget meeting." His eyes crinkle with humor.

"Don't you realize I *did* this to avoid the budget meeting?" I gesture at the last remaining graze on my head and there's another huge laugh around the room.

"See you soon, Lexi," Simon says. "Look after yourself."

As Dana and I leave the boardroom I'm lightheaded with exhilaration. I can't quite believe all that just happened. I bantered with Simon Johnson. I'm a whiz kid! I have strategic visions of the future!

I just hope I wrote them down somewhere.

"So, you remember where the Flooring department is?" Dana says as we descend again in the lift. "I know everyone's eager to see you."

"Me too!" I say with growing confidence. We head out of the lift and Dana's phone gives a little chirrup. "Oh dear!" she says as she glances at it. "I should take this. Do you want to pop along to your office and I'll see you in there?"

"Absolutely!" I stride down the corridor. It looks just the same as it ever did, with the same brown carpet and fire notices and plastic plants. The Flooring department is just along, to the left. And to the right is Gavin's office.

I mean *my* office.

My own private office.

I stand outside the door for a moment, psyching myself to go in. I still can't quite believe it's my office. My job.

Come on. There's nothing to be scared of. I can do this job, Simon Johnson said so. As I reach for the door handle, I see a girl of about twenty darting out of the main office. Her hands go to her mouth.

"Oh!" she says. "Lexi! You're back!"

"Yes." I peer uncertainly at her. "You'll have to forgive me. I've had this accident; my memory's gone..."

"Yeah, they said." She looks nervous. "I'm Clare. Your assistant?"

"Oh hi! Nice to meet you! So I'm in here?" I jerk my head toward Gavin's door.

"That's right. Can I bring you a cup of coffee?"

"Yes, please!" I try to hide my delight. "That would be great."

I have an assistant who brings me cups of coffee. I have really, really made it. I step into the office and let the door close behind me with a satisfying clunk.

Wow. I'd forgotten how big this room was. It has a sweeping desk and a plant and a sofa...and everything. I put my briefcase down on the desk and walk over to the window. I even have a view! Of another tall building, admittedly—but still, it's mine! I'm the boss! I can't help laughing in euphoria as I swing around and jump onto the sofa. I bounce up and down a few times, then stop abruptly as there's a knocking on the door.

Shit. If someone walked in right now and saw me...

Catching my breath, I hurry over to the desk, pick up a random piece of paper, and start perusing it with a businesslike frown.

"Come in!"

"Lexi!" Dana bustles in. "Are you making yourself at home again? Clare told me you didn't even recognize her! This is going to be tricky for you, isn't it? I hadn't quite appreciated..." She shakes her head, her brow creased. "So you don't remember *anything*?"

"Well...no," I admit. "But I'm sure it'll all come back to me, sooner or later."

"Let's hope you're right!" She still looks anxious. "Now, let's go through to the department, reacquaint yourself with everybody..."

We head out—and I suddenly see Fi coming out of the Flooring office, in a short black skirt with boots and a green sleeveless top. She looks different from the way I remember her, with a new red streak in her hair and a thinner face, somehow. But it's her. She's even wearing the same set of tortoiseshell bangles she always used to.

"Fi!" I exclaim in excitement, almost dropping my bag. "Oh my God! It's me, Lexi! Hi! I'm back!"

Fi visibly starts. She turns, and for a few seconds she just gapes at me as if I'm a lunatic. I suppose I did sound a bit overexcited. But I'm just so thrilled to see her.

"Hi, Lexi," she says at last, eyeing my face. "How're you doing?"

"I'm fine!" I say, my words tumbling out eagerly. "How are you? You look great! I love your new hair!"

Everyone's staring at me now.

"Anyway"—I force myself to sound more composed—"maybe we can catch up properly later? With the others?"

"Uh—yeah." Fi nods without looking me in the eye.

Why is she being so off? What's wrong? Coldness clenches me around the chest. Maybe that's why she never replied to any of my messages. We've had some huge row. And the others took her side. And I just don't remember. . . .

"After you, Lexi!" Dana ushers me into the main, open-plan office. Fifteen faces look up at us and I try not to gasp.

This is so weird.

I can see Carolyn, and Debs, and Melanie, and several others I know. They all look familiar . . . but three years on. Their hair and makeup and clothes all look different. Debs has super-toned arms and is tanned as though she's just got back from some exotic holiday; Carolyn's wearing new rimless glasses and her hair's cropped even shorter than before . . .

There's my desk. A girl with bleached hair in braids is sitting at it, looking totally at home.

"You all know that Lexi has been ill following her accident," Dana is announcing to the room. "We're delighted that she's back with us today for a visit. She's suffered a few side effects from her injuries, in particular amnesia. But I'm sure you'll all help her to remember her way around and give her a big welcome back." She turns to me and murmurs, "Lexi, do you want to say a few motivational words to the department?"

"Motivational words?" I echo uncertainly.

"Just something inspiring." Dana beams. "Rally the troops." Her phone chirrups again. "I'm sorry. Excuse me!" She hurries out to the corridor and I'm left alone, facing my department.

Come on. Simon Johnson says I'm a natural leader. I can do this.

"Um...hi, everyone!" I give a small wave around the office, which no one returns. "I just wanted to say that I'll be back soon, and...um...keep up the good work...." I flounder for something motivational. "Who's the best department in the company? We are! Who rocks? Flooring!" I give the air a little punch, like a cheerleader. "F! L! O! R!"

"There should be another O," interrupts a girl I don't recognize. She's standing with her arms folded, looking totally unimpressed.

"Sorry?" I stop, breathless.

"There's a double O in *flooring*." She rolls her eyes. Two girls next to her are giggling into their hands, while Carolyn and Debs are just gaping at me.

"Right," I say, flustered. "Anyway...well done, everybody...you've all done a great job..."

"So are you back now, Lexi?" demands a girl in red.

"Not exactly—"

"Only I need my expenses form signed, urgently."

"Me too!" say about six people.

"Have you spoken to Simon about our targets?" Melanie is coming forward, frowning. "Only they're totally unworkable as they are..."

"What's happening about the new computers?"

"Did you read my e-mail?"

"Have we sorted the Thorne Group order?"

Suddenly everyone in the room seems to be swarming toward me, asking questions. I can hardly follow any of them, let alone know what they mean.

"I don't know!" I'm saying desperately. "I'm sorry, I can't remember . . . I'll see you later!"

Breathing hard, I back out across the corridor and into my own office and slam the door.

Shit. What was all that about?

There's a knock at the door. "Hello?" I call out, my voice sounding strangled.

"Hi!" says Clare, coming in under a vast pile of letters and documents. "Sorry to bother you, Lexi, but while you're here, could you just have a quick run-through of these? You need to get back to Tony Dukes from Biltons and authorize the payment to Sixpack and sign these waivers, and some guy called Jeremy Northpool has rung several times, says he hopes you can resume discussions . . ."

She's holding out a pen. She's expecting me to spring into action.

"I can't authorize anything," I say in panic. "I can't sign anything. I've never heard of Tony Dukes. I don't remember any of this stuff!"

"Oh." Clare's pile of papers drops slightly as she surveys me, wide-eyed. "Well . . . who's going to run the department? Byron?"

"No! I mean . . . me. It's my job. I'll do it. I just need a bit of time . . . Look, leave all that with me." I try to pull myself together. "I'll have a read-through. Maybe it'll come back to me."

"Okay," Clare says, clearly relieved. She dumps the pile of papers on the desk. "I'll just bring your coffee through."

My head spinning, I sit down at the desk and pick up the first letter. It's all about some ongoing complaint. "As you will be aware ... expect your immediate response ..."

I turn to the next document. It's a monthly budget forecast for all the departments in the company. There are six graphs and a Post-it on which someone has scribbled: "Could I get your views, Lexi?"

"Your coffee ..." Clare taps on the door.

"Ah yes," I say, summoning a bosslike tone. "Thank you, Clare." As she puts down the cup I nod at the graphs. "Very interesting. I'll ... formulate my response to them later."

The minute she's gone I drop my head down on the desk in despair. What am I going to do? This job is really hard. I mean ... it's really, *really* hard.

How on earth do I do it? How do I know what to say and what decisions to make? There's yet another knocking at the door and I hastily sit bolt upright, grabbing a bit of paper at random.

"Everything all right, Lexi?" It's Byron, holding a bottle of water and a sheaf of papers. He leans against the door frame, his bony wrists protruding from his white shirt. Around one of them is an outsize high-tech watch, which I'm sure cost a lot, but it looks ridiculous.

"Fine! Great! I thought you were in the budget meeting."

"We've broken for lunch."

He has this sarcastic, drawling way of speaking, as though you're a total moron. Truth be told, I never got on with Byron. Now his eye is running over the pile of papers on my desk. "Back at it already, I see."

"Not really." I smile, but he doesn't return it.

"Have you decided what to do about Tony Dukes? Because Accounts were on to me yesterday."

"Well..." I hesitate. "Actually, I don't quite...I'm not..." I swallow, feeling color sweep through my face. "The thing is, I've had amnesia since my accident, and..." I trail off, twisting my fingers into knots.

Byron's face suddenly snaps in comprehension. "Jesus," he says after surveying me for a moment. "You don't know who Tony Dukes *is,* do you?"

Tony Dukes. Tony Dukes. I rack my brain frantically—but nothing.

"I...um...well...no. But if you could just remind me..."

Byron ignores me. He comes farther into the room, tapping his water bottle against his palm, his forehead creased in an appraising frown.

"Let me get this straight," he says slowly. "You remember absolutely nothing?"

All my instincts are prickling. He's like a cat prodding a mouse, working out exactly how weak its prey is...

He wants my job.

As soon as it hits me I feel like a total idiot for not

having worked that one out before. Of course he does. I leapfrogged over him. He must totally loathe me underneath that polite, pleasant veneer.

"I don't remember *nothing*!" I exclaim quickly, as if the very idea's ridiculous. "Just . . . the last three years is a bit of a blank."

"The last three years?" Byron throws back his head and laughs incredulously. "I'm sorry, Lexi, but you know as well as I do, in this business three years is a lifetime!"

"Well, I'll soon pick it all up again," I say, trying to sound robust. "And the doctors said I might remember everything at any time."

"Or presumably you might not." He adopts a concerned, sympathetic expression. "That must be a great worry for you, Lexi. That your head will be blank forever."

I meet his gaze with as much steel as I can muster. *Nice try. But you're not going to freak me out that easily.*

"I'm sure I'll be back to normal very soon," I say briskly. "Back to work, running the department . . . I was having a great chat with Simon Johnson earlier," I throw in for good measure.

"Uh-huh." He taps the water bottle thoughtfully. "So . . . what do you want to do about Tony Dukes?"

Fuck. He's outmaneuvered me. There's nothing I can say about Tony Dukes, and he knows it. I shuffle the papers on my desk, playing for time.

"Maybe . . . you could make a decision on that?" I say at last.

"I'd be happy to." He gives me a patronizing smile. "I'll take care of everything. You just look after yourself, Lexi. Get yourself better, take as much time as you need. Don't worry about a thing!"

"Well...thank you." I force a pleasant tone. "I appreciate it, Byron."

"So!" Dana appears at the door. "Are you two having a nice chat? Catching up with things, Lexi?"

"Absolutely." I smile, my teeth gritted. "Byron's being very helpful."

"Anything I can do to help..." He spreads his arms in a self-deprecating gesture. "I'm right here. Memory intact!"

"Super!" Dana glances at her watch. "Now, Lexi, I have to shoot off to lunch, but I can see you out if we leave now..."

"Don't worry, Dana," I say quickly. "I'll stay on here a bit longer and read through some paperwork."

I'm not leaving this building without talking to Fi. No way.

"Okey-doke." She beams. "Well, lovely to see you, Lexi, and let's talk on the phone about when you want to return properly." She does the phone-under-chin gesture and I find myself copying it.

"Talk soon!"

The two of them walk away, and I hear Byron saying, "Dana, may I have a word? We need to discuss this situation. With the greatest respect to Lexi..."

My office door shuts and I tiptoe toward it. I open it a chink and poke my head out.

"...she's *clearly* not fit to lead this department..."

Byron's voice is audible as he and Dana turn the corner toward the lifts.

Bastard. He didn't even bother waiting until he was out of earshot. I head back into my office, slump down at the desk, and bury my head in my hands. All my euphoria has vanished. I have no idea how I ever got this job. I lift a paper at random from the heap in front of me and stare at it. It's something about insurance premiums. How do I *know* all this stuff, anyway? When did I learn it? I feel like I've woken up clinging to the top of Mount Everest and I don't even know what a crampon is.

Heaving a huge sigh, I put the sheet down. I need to talk to someone. Fi. I lift the phone receiver and dial 352, which is her extension, unless they've changed the system.

"Flooring department, Fiona Roper speaking."

"Fi, it's me!" I say. "Lexi. Listen, can we talk?"

"Of course," Fi says in formal tones. "Do you want me to come in and see you now? Or should I make an appointment with Clare?"

My heart sinks. She sounds so . . . remote.

"I just meant we could have a chat! Unless you're busy . . ."

"Actually, I was about to go to lunch."

"Well, I'll come too!" I say eagerly. "Like old times! I could die for a hot chocolate. And does Morellis still do those great paninis?"

"Lexi . . ."

"Fi, I really need to talk to you, okay?" I clutch the phone tighter. "I . . . I don't remember anything. And it's freaking me out a bit. The whole situation." I try to laugh. "Just hang on, I'll be out in a moment..."

I thrust down the receiver and grab a piece of paper. I hesitate, then scrawl, "Please action all these, Byron. Many thanks, Lexi."

I know I'm playing right into his hands. But right now all I care about is seeing my friends. Seizing my bag and briefcase, I hurry out of my office, past Clare's desk, and into the main Flooring department.

"Hi, Lexi," says a nearby girl. "Did you want something?"

"No, it's okay, thanks, I'm just meeting Fi for lunch..." I trail off. I can't see Fi anywhere in the office. Or Carolyn. Or Debs.

The girl looks surprised. "I think they've already gone to lunch. You only just missed them, though..."

"Oh right." I try to hide my discomfiture. "Thanks. I expect they meant to meet in the lobby."

I swivel on my heel, then walk as fast as I can in my spiky shoes along the corridor—just in time to see Debs disappearing into a lift.

"Wait!" I cry out, breaking into a run. "I'm here! Debs!" But the lift doors are already closing.

She heard me. I know she did.

Thoughts are spinning wildly around in my head as I shove open the door to the stairs and clatter down. They knew I was coming. Are they avoiding me? What the fuck has gone on these last three years? We're *friends*. Okay, I know I'm boss now...but you can be friends with your boss, can't you?

Can't you?

I arrive at the ground floor and almost tumble into the foyer. The first thing I see is Carolyn and Debs heading out the main glass doors, with Fi just in front of them.

"Hi!" I cry out almost desperately. "Wait!" I pelt toward the glass doors and at last catch up with them on the front steps of the building.

"Oh, hi, Lexi." Fi gives a tiny snort that I know means she's trying not to laugh.

I suppose I do look a bit incongruous, running along red-faced in my black suit and chignon.

"I thought we were going to have lunch together!" I say, panting. "I told you I was coming!"

There's silence. No one is meeting my eyes. Debs is twiddling her long silver pendant; her blond hair is lifting in the breeze. Carolyn has taken off her glasses and is polishing them on her white shirt.

"What's going on?" I try to sound relaxed, but I can hear a throb of hurt in my own voice. "Fi, why didn't you return any of my messages? Is there some kind of . . . problem?"

None of them speaks. I can almost see the thought-bubbles traveling between them. But I can't read the thought-bubbles anymore; I'm out of the loop.

"You guys." I attempt a smile. "Please. You have to help me out. I have amnesia. I don't remember. Did we have a . . . a row or something?"

"No." Fi shrugs.

"Well, I don't understand it." I look around the faces entreatingly. "Last I remember, we were best mates! Going out on a Friday night. We had banana

cocktails, Loser Dave stood me up, we did karaoke...
remember?"

Fi exhales sharply and raises her eyebrows at
Carolyn. "That was a *long* time ago."

"So, what's happened since?"

"Look." Fi sighs. "Let's just leave it. You've had this
accident, you're ill, we don't want to upset you."

"Yes, let's just all go and get a sandwich together."
Debs glances at Fi as though to say "Humor her."

"Don't *patronize* me!" My voice is sharper than I
meant. "Forget about the accident! I'm not an invalid.
I'm fine. But I need you to tell me the truth." I look
around the group in desperation. "If we didn't have a
row, what's wrong? What happened?"

"Lexi, nothing happened." Fi sounds awkward.
"It's just...we don't really hang out with you anymore. We're not mates."

"But why not?" My heart is thudding, but I'm trying to stay calm. "Is it because I'm the boss now?"

"It's not because you're the *boss*. That wouldn't
matter if you were—" Fi breaks off. She shoves her
hands in her pockets, not meeting my eye. "If I'm honest, it's because you're a bit of a..."

"What?" I'm looking from face to face in bewilderment. "Tell me!"

Fi shrugs. "Snotty cow."

"Total bitch-boss-from-hell, more like," mutters
Carolyn.

The air seems to freeze solid in my lungs. Bitch-boss-
from-hell? Me?

"I . . . I don't understand," I stammer at last. "Aren't I a good boss?"

"Oh, you're great." Carolyn's voice drips with sarcasm. "You penalize us if we're late. You time our lunch hours. You do spot checks on our expenses. . . . Oh, it's a bundle of fun in Flooring!"

My cheeks are throbbing as though she'd hit me.

"But I would never . . . That's not what I'm like—"

Carolyn cuts me off. "Yeah. It is."

"Lexi, you asked." Fi is rolling her eyes, like she always does when she's uncomfortable. "That's why we don't hang out anymore. You do your thing and we do ours."

"I can't be a bitch," I manage at last, my voice trembling. "I can't be. I'm your friend! Lexi! We have fun together, we go out dancing together, we get pissed . . ." Tears are pricking my eyes. I look around the faces I know so well—yet kind of don't—trying desperately to spark a chord of recognition. "I'm me! Lexi. Snaggletooth. Remember *me*?"

Fi and Carolyn exchange looks.

"Lexi . . ." Fi says almost gently. "You're our boss. We do what you say. But we don't have lunch. And we don't go out." She hefts her bag on her shoulder, then sighs. "Look, come along today if you want to . . ."

"No," I say, stung. "It's okay, thanks." And with shaky legs I turn and walk away.

Chapter Ten

I'm numb with shock.

All the way home from the office, I sat in my taxi in a kind of trance. Somehow I managed to talk to Gianna about the dinner party arrangements and listen to Mum when she called to complain about her latest run-in with the council. And now it's early evening and I'm in the bath. But all the time my thoughts have been circulating around and around.

I'm a bitch-boss-from-hell. My friends all hate me. What the fuck has happened?

Every time I remember Carolyn's scathing voice, I flinch. God knows what I've done to her—but she obviously has no time for me.

Have I really turned into a bitch over the last three years? But how? *Why?*

The water is growing tepid and at last I heave myself out. I rub myself briskly, trying to energize myself. I can't keep obsessing about it. It's already six, and in an hour I have to host a dinner party.

At least I don't have to cook. When I arrived home,

Gianna was busy in the kitchen with two of her nieces—all singing along to the opera blaring out of the speakers. There were platters of sushi and canapés on every shelf in the fridge and the most amazing smell of roasting meat. I tried to join in—I'm pretty good at garlic bread—but they bustled me away. So I decided I'd be safest in the bath.

I wrap a fresh towel around myself and pad into the bedroom—then double back into the dressing room for my clothes. Jeez Louise. I know why rich people are so thin: it's from trekking around their humongous houses the whole time. In my Balham flat I could reach the wardrobe from the bed. And the TV. And the toaster.

I pick out a little black dress, some little black underwear, and some minuscule black satin shoes. There's nothing in my 2007 wardrobe that's *big*. No cuddly sweaters, no chunky shoes. Everything's slimline and tailored, to match me.

As I trail back into the bedroom I let my towel drop onto the floor.

"Hi, Lexi!"

"Aargh!" I jump in fright. The big screen at the base of the bed has lit up with a huge image of Eric's face. I clap my hands over my chest and duck behind a chair.

I'm naked. And he can see me.

He's my husband, I remind myself feverishly. He's seen it all before—it's fine.

It doesn't *feel* fine.

"Eric, can you see me?" I say in a high-pitched, strangled voice.

"Not right now." He laughs. "Put the setting to Camera."

"Oh! Okay!" I say in relief. "Just give me a sec..."

I sling on a dressing gown, then quickly start gathering the clothes I've dropped about the room. Something I've learned pretty quickly is that Eric doesn't like things lying around on the floor. Or on chairs. Or basically any kind of mess at all. I shove them all under the duvet as quickly as possible, plonk a cushion on top, and smooth it down as best I can.

"Ready!" I head to the screen and swivel the dial to Camera.

"Move back," Eric instructs me, and I back away from the screen. "Now I can see you! So, I've got one more meeting, then I'll be on my way home. Is everything set up for dinner?"

"I think so!"

"Excellent." His huge pixellated mouth spreads in a jerky beam. "And how was work?"

"It was great!" Somehow I manage a cheerful tone. "I saw Simon Johnson and all my department, and my friends..."

I trail off, suddenly feeling a burn of humiliation. Can I even describe them as friends anymore?

"Marvelous." I'm not sure Eric's even listening. "Now you really should be getting ready. I'll see you later, darling."

"Wait," I say on impulse. "Eric."

This is my husband. I may barely know him—but he knows me. He loves me. If there's anyone I should confide in about my problems, if anyone can reassure me, it's him.

"Fire away." Eric nods, his screen movements slow and jerky.

"Today, Fi said . . ." I can hardly bring myself to say the words. "She said I was a bitch. Is that true?"

"Of course you're not a bitch."

"Really?" I feel a pang of hope. "So I'm not a horrible bitch-boss-from-hell?"

"Darling, there's no way you're horrible. Or a bitch-boss-from-hell."

Eric sounds so sure, I relax in relief. There'll be an explanation. Maybe some wires have got crossed—there's been a misunderstanding, it'll all be fine—

"I'd say you were . . . tough," he adds.

My relieved smile freezes on my face. Tough? I don't like the sound of *tough*.

"Do you mean tough in a good way?" I try to sound casual. "Like, tough, but still really friendly and nice?"

"Sweetheart, you're focused. You're driven. You drive your department hard. You're a great boss." He smiles. "Now, I must go. I'll see you later."

The screen goes dark and I stare at it, totally unreassured. In fact, I'm more alarmed than ever.

Tough. Isn't that just another way of saying "bitch-boss-from-hell"?

• • •

Whatever the truth is, I can't let all this get to me. I have to keep everything in perspective. It's an hour later, and my spirits have risen a little. I've put on my new diamond necklace. I've sprayed myself with lots of expensive scent. And I've had a sneaky little glass of wine, which has made everything look a lot better.

So maybe things aren't as perfect as I thought. Maybe I've fallen out with my friends; maybe Byron is after my job; maybe I don't have a clue who Tony Dukes is. But I can put it all right. I can learn my job. I can build bridges with Fi and the others. I can google Tony Dukes.

And the point is, I'm still the luckiest girl in the world. I have a gorgeous husband, a wonderful marriage, and a stunning apartment. I mean, just look around! Tonight the place looks even more jaw-dropping than ever. The florist has been and gone—and there are arrangements of lilies and roses everywhere. The dining table has been extended and laid for dinner with gleaming silverware and crystal and a centerpiece like at weddings. There are even place cards written out in calligraphy!

Eric said it was a "casual little supper." God knows what we do when it's formal. Maybe have ten butlers in white gloves or something.

I carefully apply my Lancôme lipstick and blot it. When I've finished I can't help staring at myself in the mirror. My hair is up and my dress fits to perfection and there are diamonds at my ears and throat. I look like some elegant girl in an ad. Like any minute a caption will appear on the screen below me.

Ferrero Rocher. For the finer things in life.

British Gas. Keeping you warm in your million-billion-pound trendy loft apartment.

I step back and automatically the lights change from the mirror spotlight to more of an ambient glow. The "intelligent lighting" in this room is like magic: it figures out where you are from heat sensors and then adjusts accordingly.

I quite like trying to catch it out by running around the room and shouting, "Ha! Not so intelligent *now*, are you?"

When Eric's out, obviously.

"Darling!" I jump, and turn to see him standing at the door, in his business suit. "You look wonderful."

"Thanks!" I glow with pleasure and pat my hair.

"One tiny thing. Briefcase in the hall. Good idea?" His smile doesn't waver, but I can hear the annoyance in his voice.

Shit. I must have left it there. I was so preoccupied when I arrived home, I didn't think.

"I'll move it," I say hastily. "Sorry."

"Good." He nods. "But first, taste this." He hands me a glass of ruby-red wine. "It's the Château Branaire Ducru. We bought it on our last trip to France. I'd like your opinion."

"Right." I try to sound confident. "Absolutely."

Oh no. What am I going to say? Cautiously I take a sip and swill it around my mouth, racking my brain for all the wine-buff words I can think of. Leathery. Oaky. A fine vintage.

Come to think of it, they all just bullshit, don't they? Okay, I'll say it's a divinely full-bodied vintage with hints of strawberries. No, blackcurrants. I swallow the mouthful and nod knowledgeably at Eric.

"You know, I think this is a div—"

"It's shocking, isn't it?" Eric cuts me off. "Corked. Totally off."

Off?

"Oh! Er . . . yes!" I regain my composure. "Way past the sell-by date. Urggh." I make a face. "Revolting!"

That was a close shave. I put the glass down on a side table and the intelligent lighting adjusts again.

"Eric," I say, trying not to give away my exasperation. "Can we have a lighting mix that just stays the same all night? I don't know if that's possible—"

"*Anything* is possible." Eric sounds a bit offended. "We have infinite choice. That's what loft-style living is all about." He passes me a remote control. "Here. You can override the system with this. Pick a mood. I'll go and sort out the wine."

I head into the sitting room, find Lighting on the remote, and start experimenting with moods. Daylight is too bright. Cinema is too dark. Relax is dull. . . . I scroll much farther down. Reading . . . Disco . . .

Hey. We have disco lights? I press the remote—and laugh out loud as the room is suddenly filled with pulsating multicolored lights. Now let's try Strobe. A moment later the room is flashing black and white and I gleefully start robotic dancing around the coffee table. This is like a club! Why didn't Eric tell me we had this before? Maybe we have dry ice, too, and a mirror ball. . . .

"Jesus Christ, Lexi, what are you *doing*!" Eric's voice pierces the flashing room. "You put the whole fucking apartment on Strobe Light! Gianna nearly chopped her arm off!"

"Oh no! Sorry." Guiltily I fumble for the remote and jab it until we're back on disco. "You never told me we had disco and strobe lights! This is fantastic!"

"We never use them." Eric's face is a multicolored whirl. "Now find something sensible, for God's sake." He turns and disappears.

How can we have disco lights and never use them? What a waste! I *have* to have Fi and the others around for a party. We'll get some wine and nibbles, and we'll clear the floor and ramp up the volume—

And then my heart constricts as I remember. That won't be happening anytime soon. Or maybe ever.

Deflated, I switch the lighting to Reception Area One, which is as good as anything else. I put down the remote, walk over to the window, and stare out at the street below, suddenly determined. I'm not giving up. These are my *friends*. I'm going to find out what's been going on. And then I'm going to make up with them.

• • •

My plan for the dinner party was to memorize each guest's face and name using visualization techniques. But this scheme disintegrates almost at once when three golfing buddies of Eric's arrive together in identical suits, with identical faces and even more identical wives. Their names are things like Greg and Mick and Suki and Pooky, and they immediately start discussing a skiing holiday we all apparently went on once.

I sip my drink and smile a lot, and then about ten

more guests arrive at once and I have no idea who anyone is except Rosalie, who dashed up, introduced her husband, Clive (who doesn't seem like a monster at all, just a mild-mannered guy in a suit), and then rushed off again.

After a bit my ears are ringing and I feel dizzy. Gianna is serving drinks and her niece is handing out canapés and everything seems under control. So I murmur an excuse to the balding guy who's telling me about Mick Jagger's electric guitar, which he's just bought at a charity auction, and slip away and head out to the terrace.

I take a few lungfuls of clean air, my head still spinning. A blue-gray dusk is falling and the streetlamps are just coming on. As I gaze out over London I don't feel real. I feel like someone playing the part of a girl in a dress standing on a posh balcony with a glass of champagne in her hand.

"Darling! There you are!"

I turn to see Eric pushing the sliding doors open. "Hi!" I call back. "I was just getting some air."

"Let me introduce Jon, my architect." Eric ushers out a dark-haired man in black jeans and a charcoal linen jacket.

"Hello," I begin automatically, then stop. "Hey, we know each other!" I exclaim, relieved to have found a familiar face. "Don't we? You're the guy from the car."

An odd expression flickers across the man's face. Almost like disappointment. Then he nods.

"That's right. I'm the guy from the car."

"Jon's our creative spirit," says Eric, slapping him

on the back. "He's the talent. I may have the financial sense, but this is the man who *brings* the world"—he pauses momentously—"loft-style living." As he says the words, he does the parallel-hands-sweeping-bricks gesture again.

"Great!" I try to sound enthused. I know it's Eric's business and everything, but that phrase "loft-style living" is really starting to bug me.

"Thanks again for the other day." I smile politely at Jon. "You really saved my life!" I turn to Eric. "I didn't tell you, darling, but I tried to drive the car and nearly hit the wall. Jon helped me."

"It was my pleasure." Jon takes a sip of his drink. "So, you still don't remember anything?"

"Nothing." I shake my head.

"That must be strange for you."

"It is . . . but I'm getting used to it. And Eric's really helpful. He's made me this book to help me remember. It's like a marriage manual. With sections and everything."

"A manual?" Jon echoes, and his nose starts twitching. "You're serious. A manual."

"Yes, a manual." I stare at him suspiciously.

"Ah, there's Graham." Eric isn't even listening to the conversation. "I must just have a word. Excuse me." He heads off inside, leaving me and Jon the architect guy alone.

I don't know what it is about this man. I mean, I don't even *know* him, but he rankles me.

"What's wrong with a marriage manual?" I hear myself demanding.

"No. Nothing. Nothing at all." He shakes his head gravely. "It's a very sensible move. Because otherwise you might not know when you were supposed to kiss each other."

"Exactly! Eric's put in a whole section on—" I break off. Jon's mouth is crinkled up as if he's trying not to laugh. Does he think this is *funny*? "The manual covers all sorts of areas," I say rather stonily. "And it's been very helpful for both of us. You know, it's difficult for Eric, too, having a wife who doesn't remember the first thing about him! Or perhaps you hadn't appreciated that?"

There's silence. All the humor has melted out of his face.

"Believe me," he says at last. "I appreciate it." He drains his glass, then stares into the bottom of it for a few moments. He looks up and seems about to speak— then, as the sliding doors open, changes his mind.

"Lexi!" Rosalie comes tottering over toward us, glass in hand. "*Wonderful* canapés!"

"Oh, well...thanks!" I say, embarrassed to be receiving praise for something I had absolutely nothing to do with. "I haven't had any yet. Do they taste good?"

Rosalie appears perplexed. "I've no idea, sweetie. But they *look* marvelous. And Eric says dinner's about to begin."

"Oh God," I say guiltily. "I've just left him to it. We'd better go in. D'you two know each other?" I add as we start walking in.

"Sure," says Jon.

"Jon and I are *old* friends," Rosalie says sweetly. "Aren't we, darling?"

"See you." Jon nods, picks up his pace, and disappears through the glass doors.

"Awful man." Rosalie makes a face at his departing back.

"Awful?" I echo in surprise. "Eric seems to like him."

"Oh, Eric likes him," she says disdainfully. "And Clive thinks he's the bees' knees. He's visionary and wins prizes, blah blah blah..." She tosses her head. "But he's the rudest man I ever met. When I asked him to donate to my charity last year, he refused. In fact, he laughed."

"He *laughed*?" I say, shocked. "That's terrible! What was the charity?"

"It was called An Apple a Day," she says proudly. "I thought the whole idea up myself. The idea was, once a year we'd give an apple to every schoolchild in an inner-city borough. Full of lovely nutrients! Isn't that so simple, it's brilliant?"

"Er...great idea," I say cautiously. "So, did it work out?"

"Well, it started off well," Rosalie says rather crossly. "We gave out *thousands* of apples and we had special T-shirts and a van with an apple logo to drive about in. It was such fun! Until the council started sending us stupid letters about fruit being abandoned in the street and causing vermin."

"Oh dear." I bite my lip. The truth is, now *I* want to laugh.

"You know, this is the trouble with charity work,"

she says darkly, lowering her voice. "The local bureau-crats don't *want* you to help."

We've reached the sliding doors and I stare in at the crowd. Twenty faces I don't recognize are laughing and talking and exclaiming at each other. I can see jewels flashing and hear the rumble of men's laughter.

"Now, don't worry." Rosalie's hand is on my arm. "Eric and I have a plan. Everyone's going to stand up and introduce themselves to you at dinner." Her brow wrinkles. "Sweetie, you look freaked."

"No!" I manage a smile. "Not freaked!"

This is a lie. I'm totally freaked. As I find my place at the long glass dining table, nodding and smiling as peo-ple greet me, I feel like I'm in some weird dream. These people are allegedly my friends. They all know me. And I've never even *seen* them before.

"Lexi, *darling*." A dark woman draws me aside as I'm approaching my chair. "Can I have a quick word?" She lowers her voice almost to a whisper. "I was with you all day on the fifteenth and the twenty-first, okay?"

"Were you?" I say blankly.

"Yes. If Christian asks. Christian, my husband?" She gestures at the balding Mick-Jagger-guitar guy, who's taking his seat opposite.

"Oh, right." I digest this for a moment. "Were we really together?"

"Of course!" she says after a brief pause. "Of course we were, darling!" She squeezes my hand and moves away.

"Ladies and gentlemen." Eric is standing at the other end of the gleaming table, and the chatter dies to a hush as everyone sits down. "Welcome to our home. Lexi and I are delighted you could make it."

All eyes swivel to me, and I give an embarrassed smile.

"As you know, Lexi is suffering the aftereffects of her recent accident, which means her memory's not too hot." Eric gives a rueful smile. A man opposite laughs, then is shushed by his wife. "So what I propose is that each of you reintroduce yourselves to Lexi. Stand up, give your name, and maybe some memorable event that links you."

"Do the doctors think this will trigger Lexi's memory?" asks an earnest-looking guy to my right.

"No one knows," Eric says gravely. "But we have to try. So . . . who wants to start?"

"Me! I'll start!" Rosalie says, leaping to her feet. "Lexi, I'm your best friend, Rosalie, which you already know. And *our* memorable incident was that time we both got waxed and the girl got a bit carried away . . ." She breaks into a giggle. "Your *face* . . ."

"What happened?" says a girl in black.

"I'm not saying in public!" Rosalie looks offended. "But honestly, it was *totally* memorable." She beams around the table, then sits down.

"Right," says Eric, sounding a bit taken aback. "Who's next? Charlie?"

"I'm Charlie Mancroft." A gruff man next to Rosalie stands up and nods at me. "I suppose our memorable incident would be the time we were all at Wentworth for that corporate do. Montgomerie made a birdie on the eighteenth. Stunning play." He looks at me expectantly.

"Of course!" I have no idea what he's talking about. Golf? Or snooker, maybe. "Er . . . thanks."

He sits down and a thin girl next to him gets to her feet.

"Hi, Lexi." She gives me a little wave. "I'm Natalie. And my most memorable event would be your wedding day."

"Really?" I say, surprised and touched. "Wow."

"It was such a happy day!" She bites her lip. "And you looked so beautiful and I thought, 'That's what I want to look like when *I* get married.' I actually thought Matthew would propose to me that day, but . . . he didn't." Her smile tightens.

"Jesus, Natalie," mutters a guy across the table. "Not this again."

"No! It's fine!" she exclaims brightly. "We're engaged now! It only took three years!" She flashes her diamond at me. "I'm having your dress! Exactly the same Vera Wang, in white—"

"Well done, Natalie!" Eric chimes in heartily. "I think we should move on. . . . Jon? Your turn."

Across the table from me, Jon gets to his feet.

"Hi," he says in his dry voice. "I'm Jon. We met earlier." He lapses into silence.

"So, Jon?" prompts Eric. "What's your memorable event involving Lexi?"

Jon surveys me for a moment with those dark, intense eyes, and I find myself wondering what he's going to say. He scratches his neck, frowns, and takes a slug of wine, as though thinking hard. At last he spreads his arms. "Nothing comes to mind."

"Nothing?" I'm slightly stung, despite myself.

"Anything at all!" Eric says encouragingly. "Just some special moment the two of you shared..."

Everyone is watching Jon. He frowns again, then shrugs, apparently stumped.

"I don't recall anything," he says at last. "Nothing I could describe."

"There must be *something*, Jon," a girl opposite says eagerly. "It could trigger her memory!"

"I doubt it." He gives a brief half-smile.

"Well, all right," says Eric, sounding a bit impatient. "It doesn't matter. Let's move on."

By the time everyone around the table has stood up and recounted their anecdote, I've forgotten who the first people were. But it's a start, I suppose. Gianna and her helper serve tuna carpaccio, arugula salad, and baked pears, and I talk to someone called Ralph about his divorce settlement. And then the plates are cleared, and Gianna is making her way around the table, taking coffee orders.

"I'll make the coffee," I say, jumping up. "You've done so much tonight, Gianna. Have a break."

I've grown increasingly uncomfortable seeing her and her niece scurrying around the table with heavy plates. And the way no one even looks at them as they take their food. And the way that awful man Charlie barked at her when he wanted some more water. It's so *rude*.

"Lexi!" Eric says with a laugh. "That's hardly necessary."

"I want to," I say stubbornly. "Gianna, sit down. Have a biscuit or something. I can easily make a few cups of coffee. Really, I insist."

Gianna looks perplexed. "I'll go and turn down your bed," she says at last, and heads off toward the bedroom, her niece in her wake.

That's not exactly what I meant by having a break. But anyway.

"There." I smile around the table. "Now, who would like coffee? Hands up..." I start counting the hands. "And anyone for mint tea?"

"I'll help," Jon says suddenly, pushing his chair back.

"Oh," I say, taken aback. "Well...okay. Thanks."

I head into the kitchen, fill the kettle, and switch it on. Then I start looking in cupboards for cups. Maybe we have some special posh coffee cups for dinner parties. I briefly consult the marriage manual, but can't find anything.

Meanwhile Jon is just pacing around the kitchen, his face screwed up as though in some distant daydream, not helping at all.

"Are you okay?" I say at last, with a flash of irritation. "I don't suppose you know where the coffee cups are, do you?"

Jon doesn't even seem to hear the question.

"Hello?" I wave at him. "Aren't you supposed to be helping?"

At last he stops pacing and regards me, an even stranger expression on his face.

"I don't know how to tell you this," he says. "So I'm just going to tell you." He takes a breath—then he seems to change his mind and comes over close, studying my face. "You really don't remember? This isn't some kind of game you're playing with me?"

"Remember *what*?" I say, totally bewildered.

"Okay, okay." He turns and resumes pacing, thrusting his hands through his dark hair, leaving it spiky on top. At last he turns to face me again. "Here's the thing. I love you."

"What?" I look at him in confusion.

"And you love me," he continues, without giving me time to say anything more. "We're lovers."

"Sweetie!" The door bursts open and Rosalie's face appears. "Two more orders for mint tea and a decaf for Clive."

"Coming up!" I say, my voice sounding strangled.

Rosalie disappears and the kitchen door swings shut. There's silence between us, the most prickling silence I've ever known. I can't move or speak. My eyes keep flicking ludicrously to the marriage manual still lying on the counter, as though the answer might be in there.

Jon follows my gaze.

"I'm guessing," he says in a dry, confidential tone, "that I'm not in the manual."

Okay. I have to get a grip.

"I...don't understand," I say, trying to summon some composure. "What do you mean, lovers? You're trying to tell me we've been having an *affair*?"

"We've been seeing each other for eight months."

His dark gaze is fixed on me. "You're planning to leave Eric for me."

I can't stop a gurgle of laughter. At once I clap my hand over my mouth. "I'm sorry. I don't mean to be rude, but...leave Eric? For *you*?"

Before Jon can react, the door opens again.

"Hi, Lexi!" A red-faced man comes in. "Can I grab some more sparkling water?"

"Here." I thrust two bottles into his arms. The door closes again and Jon shoves his hands in his pockets.

"You were about to tell Eric you couldn't be with him anymore," he says, speaking faster. "You were about to leave him. We'd made plans...." He breaks off and exhales. "Then you had the accident."

His face is deadly serious. He really means all this.

"But...that's ludicrous!"

For an instant Jon looks like I've hit him. "Ludicrous?"

"Yes, ludicrous! I'm not the unfaithful type. Plus, I have a great marriage, a fantastic husband, I'm happy—"

"You're not happy with Eric." Jon interrupts me. "Believe me."

"Of course I'm happy with Eric!" I say in astonishment. "He's lovely! He's perfect!"

"*Perfect?*" Jon looks as if he's trying to stop himself from going further. "Lexi, he's not perfect."

"Well, near enough," I retort, suddenly rattled. Who does this guy think he is, interrupting my dinner party to say he's my lover? "Listen, Jon...whoever you are. I don't believe you. I would never have an affair, okay? I have the dream marriage. I have the dream life!"

"The dream life?" Jon rubs his forehead as though trying to gather his thoughts. "That's what you think?"

Something about this guy is getting under my skin.

"Of course!" I swing my arms around the kitchen. "Look at this place! Look at Eric! It's all fantastic! Why would I throw it all away on some—"

I break off abruptly as the kitchen door swings open.

"Sweetheart." Eric beams at me from the doorway. "How are those coffees going?"

"They're . . . on their way," I say, flustered. "Sorry, darling." I turn away to hide the blood pumping through my cheeks, and start spooning coffee messily into the cafetiere. I just want this man to *leave*.

"Eric, I'm afraid I have to go," Jon says behind me, as though reading my mind. "Thanks for a great evening."

"Jon! Good man." I can hear Eric clapping Jon on the back. "We should hook up tomorrow, talk about the planning meeting."

"Let's do it," Jon replies. "Good-bye, Lexi. Nice to make your acquaintance again."

"Good-bye, Jon." Somehow I force myself to turn and present a hostessy smile. "Lovely to see you." He bends forward and kisses me lightly on the cheek.

"You don't know anything about your life," he murmurs in my ear, then strides out of the kitchen without looking back.

Chapter Eleven

It can't be true.

Morning light is creeping in around the blinds and I've been awake for a while, but I haven't got out of bed. I'm gazing straight up at the ceiling, breathing evenly in and out. My theory is that if I lie still enough, maybe the maelstrom of my mind will calm down and everything will fall neatly into place.

So far it's turning out to be a pretty crap theory.

Every time I replay the events of yesterday I feel giddy. I thought I was coming to grips with this new life of mine. I thought it was all falling into place. But now it's like everything is slipping and sliding away. Fi says I'm a bitch-boss-from-hell. Some guy says I'm his secret lover. What next? I discover I'm an FBI agent?

It cannot be true. End of story. Why would I cheat on Eric? He's good-looking and caring and a multimillionaire and knows how to drive a speedboat. Whereas Jon is scruffy. And kind of . . . spiky.

As for saying "You don't know anything about your life"—what a nerve! I know *plenty* about my life, thank you. I know where I get my hair done, I know what dessert I had at my wedding, I know how often Eric and I have sex . . . It's all in the manual.

And anyway, how rude is that? You don't just pitch up in someone's house and say "We're lovers" when they're trying to host a dinner party with their husband. You . . . you choose a different moment. You write a note.

No, you don't write a note. You—

Anyway. Stop thinking about it.

I sit up, press the button for the window blinds to retract, and run my fingers through my hair, wincing at the tangles. The screen in front of me is blank and the room is eerily silent. I still find it weird, after my drafty bedroom in Balham, to be living in such a hermetically sealed box. According to the manual we're not supposed to open the windows because it messes up the air-conditioning system if you do.

This Jon guy is probably a psycho. He probably makes a habit of targeting people with amnesia and telling them he's their lover. There's no evidence we're having an affair. None. I haven't seen any mention of him, no scribbled notes, no photos, no mementos.

But then . . . I'd hardly leave them around for Eric to find, would I? says a tiny voice at the back of my brain.

I sit perfectly still for a moment, letting my thoughts swirl around. Then on impulse I get up and head into my clothes room. I hurry to the dressing table and wrench open the top drawer. It's full of Chanel makeup, arranged in neat rows by Gianna. I shut the drawer and pull open the next, which is full of folded scarves. The next contains a jewelry roll and a suede photo album, both empty.

Slowly I shut the drawer. Even here, in my very own private sanctum, everything's so tidy and sterile and kind of nothing-y. Where's the mess? Where's the stuff? Where's the letters and the photos? Where's all my studded belts and free lipsticks off crappy magazines? Where's... *me*?

I lean forward on my elbows, chewing my nail for a moment. Then inspiration hits me. Underwear drawer. If I was going to hide anything, it would be there. I open the wardrobe and pull open my knicker drawer. I reach down among the satiny sea of La Perla—but I can't feel anything. Nor in my bra drawer...

"Looking for something?" Eric's voice makes me jump. I turn my head to see him standing at the door, watching me search, and at once my cheeks stain pink.

He knows.

No, he doesn't. Don't be stupid. There's nothing *to* know.

"Hi, Eric!" I withdraw my hands from the cupboard as nonchalantly as I can. "I just thought I'd look for... some bras!"

Okay, this is the main reason why I can't be having an affair. I'm the most crap liar in the world. Why would I need "some bras"? Do I suddenly have six boobs?

"Actually, I was wondering," I continue hastily. "Is there any more of my stuff anywhere?"

"Stuff?" Eric wrinkles his brow.

"Letters, diaries, that kind of thing?"

"There's your desk in the office. That's where you keep all your work files."

"Of course." I'd forgotten about the office. Or rather, I thought it was more Eric's domain than mine.

"It was a marvelous evening last night, I thought." Eric comes a couple of steps into the room. "Bravo, darling. Can't have been easy for you."

"It was good fun." I sit back on my haunches, fiddling with my watch strap. "There were some . . . interesting people there."

"You weren't too overwhelmed?"

"A little." I shoot him a bright smile. "There's still so much to learn."

"Well, you know you can ask me anything about your life. That's what I'm here for." Eric spreads his arms. "Is there anything particular on your mind?"

I stare back at him for a moment, speechless.

Have I been shagging your architect, do you happen to know?

"Well." I clear my throat. "Since you ask, I was just wondering. We are happy together, aren't we? We do have a happy . . . faithful . . . marriage?"

I'm thinking I dropped in *faithful* quite subtly there, but Eric's keen ears pick it up straightaway.

"Faithful?" He frowns. "Lexi, I've never been unfaithful to you. I would never *think* of being unfaithful to you. We made vows. We made a commitment."

"Of course!" I exclaim quickly. "Absolutely."

"I can't even imagine how such an idea came to you." He looks quite shocked. "Has someone been saying otherwise? One of our guests? Because whoever it was—"

"No! No one said anything! I just…everything's still so new and strange." I'm floundering, my face hot. "I just…thought I'd ask. Just out of interest."

Okay, so we don't have some open, groovy marriage. Just in case I needed that point clarified.

I shut the bra drawer, open another at random, and stare at three rows of rolled-up tights, my mind whirling. I should move away from this whole subject area. But I can't help it, I have to probe.

"So, um, that guy…" I wrinkle my brow artificially as though I can't remember his name. "The architect guy."

"Jon."

"*Jon*. Of course. He seems like a pretty good guy." I shrug, trying to appear as casual as possible.

"Oh, one of the best," says Eric firmly. "He's been a massive part of our success. That guy has more imagination than anyone I know."

"Imagination?" I seize on this with slight hope. "So is he maybe *over*imaginative sometimes? Like…a bit of a fantasist?"

"No." Eric seems puzzled. "Not at all. He's my right-hand man. You'd trust Jon with your life."

To my relief, the phone suddenly gives a shrill ring, before Eric can ask why I'm so interested in Jon.

Eric disappears into the bedroom to answer it and I shut the tights drawer. I'm about to give up on searching in my cupboard when suddenly I see something I never noticed before. A concealed drawer, at the base of the unit, with a tiny keypad located to the right.

I have a secret drawer?

My heart starts to thump. Slowly I reach down and punch in the PIN number I've always used—4591. There's a tiny click—and the drawer opens. Glancing at the door to make sure Eric isn't there, I gingerly stretch out my hand and clasp my hand around something hard, like the handle of a . . .

It's a whip.

For a moment I'm too gobsmacked to move. It's a little whip, with strands of black leather, like something straight out of a bondage shop. I'm totally transfixed by the sight of it in my hand. Is this my adultery whip? Have I turned into a completely different person? Am I now a fetishist and go to S&M bars to drag men around while wearing a studded corset?

Suddenly I can feel eyes on me and turn to see Eric leaning in the doorway. His gaze falls on the whip and he raises his eyebrows quizzically.

"Oh!" I say, starting in panic. "I just . . . I found that here! I didn't know . . ."

"You'd better not leave that around for Gianna to find." He sounds amused.

I stare back, my befuddled brain working overtime. Eric knows about the whip. He's smiling. That, therefore, would mean . . .

No. Way.

No way no way no way.

"This wasn't in the manual, Eric!" I'm aiming to sound light and jokey, but my voice is shrill.

"Not everything's in the manual." His eyes twinkle.

Okay, this is changing the rules. I thought *everything* was supposed to be in the manual.

I glance at the whip nervously. So ... what happens? Do I whip him? Or does he—

No. I can't think about it anymore. I shove it back in the drawer and bang it shut, my hands sweaty.

"That's right." Eric gives me a tiny wink. "Keep it safe. See you later." He heads out and a few moments later I hear the front door bang.

I think I might need a small vodka.

• • •

In the end I settle for a cup of coffee and two biscuits Gianna gives me from her private stash. God, I've missed biscuits. And bread. And *toast*. I could die for some toast, all chewy and golden, slathered in butter ...

Anyway, stop fantasizing about carbs. And stop thinking about the whip. One teeny whip. So what?

Mum's coming over to visit at eleven, and I have nothing to do till then. I wander into the sitting room, sit down on the arm of the immaculate sofa, and open a magazine. After two minutes I close it again. I'm too edgy to read. It's as if tiny cracks are appearing in my perfect life. I don't know what to believe. I don't know what to do.

I put down my coffee cup and stare at my immaculate nails. I was a normal girl with frizzy hair and snaggle teeth and a crap boyfriend. And a fairly crap job, and friends who I had a laugh with, and a cozy little flat.

And now . . . I still do a double take whenever I catch my reflection in the mirror. I don't see my personality reflected anywhere in this apartment. The TV show . . . the high heels . . . my friends refusing to hang out with me . . . a guy saying he's my secret lover . . . I just don't know who I've turned into. I don't get what the fuck's *happened* to me.

On impulse I head into the office. There's my desk, all spick-and-span with the chair pushed under tidily. I've never owned a desk that looked like that in my life; no wonder I didn't realize it was mine. I sit down and open the first drawer. It's full of letters, tidily clipped together in plastic files. The second is full of bank statements, threaded onto a piece of blue string.

Jeez Louise. Since when did I become so *anal*?

I open the last, biggest drawer, expecting to find neatly stacked bottles of Wite-Out or something—but it's empty except for two scraps of paper.

I pull the bank statements out of the other drawer and flick through them, my eyes widening as I clock my monthly salary, which is at least three times what I used to earn. Most of my money seems to be going out of my single account into the joint account I hold with Eric, except one big sum every month, going to something called "Unito Acc." I'll have to find out what that is.

I put the bank statements away and reach into the bottom drawer for the scraps of paper. One is covered in my own handwriting—but so abbreviated I can't make anything out. It's almost in code. The other is torn out of a foolscap pad and has my writing scrawled across it, only three words in pencil.

I just wish

I stare at it, riveted. What? What did I wish?

As I turn the scrap over in my fingers I try to imagine myself writing those words. I even try—though I know it's pointless—to remember myself writing them. Was it a year ago? Six months? Three weeks? What was I talking about?

The buzzer rings, interrupting my thoughts. I fold the scrap of paper carefully and put it in my pocket. Then I bang the empty drawer shut and head out.

• • •

Mum has brought three of the dogs along with her. Three huge, energetic whippets. To an immaculate apartment full of immaculate things.

"Hi, Mum!" I take her tatty quilted jacket and try to kiss her as two of the dogs slip out of her grasp and bound toward the sofa. "Wow. You brought...dogs!"

"The poor things looked so lonely as I was leaving." She embraces one of them, rubbing her cheek against its face. "Agnes is feeling rather *vulnerable* at the moment."

"Right," I say, trying to sound sympathetic. "Poor old Agnes. Could she maybe go in the car?"

"Darling, I can't just abandon her!" Mum raises her eyes with a martyred air. "You know, it wasn't easy organizing this trip to London."

Oh for God's sake. I knew she didn't really want to come today. This whole visit arose out of cross-purposes. All I said on the phone was that I felt a bit weird being surrounded by strangers, and the next thing Mum was getting all defensive and saying of *course* she was planning to visit. And we ended up making this arrangement.

To my horror I notice a dog putting its paws up on the glass coffee table, while the other is on the sofa grabbing a cushion in its jaws.

Jesus. If the sofa's worth ten grand, then that cushion is probably worth about a thousand quid on its own.

"Mum...could you possibly get that dog off the sofa?"

"Raphael won't do any harm!" says Mum, looking hurt. She lets go of Agnes, who bounces over to join Raphael and whatever the other one is called.

There are now three whippets romping joyfully on Eric's sofa. He'd better not turn on the cameras.

"Have you got any diet Coke?" Amy has sauntered in behind Mum, hands in her pockets.

"In the kitchen, I think," I say distractedly, holding out my hand. "Here, dogs! Off the sofa!"

All three dogs ignore me.

"Come here, darlings!" Mum produces some dog biscuits out of her cardigan pockets, and the dogs magically stop chewing the upholstery. One sits at her feet and the other two snuggle up beside her, resting their heads on her faded print skirt.

"There," says Mum. "No harm done."

I look at the mangled cushion that Raphael has just dropped. It's really not worth saying anything.

"There's no diet Coke." Amy reappears from the kitchen, unwrapping a Chupa Chups lollipop, her legs endless in white skinny jeans tucked into boots. "Have you got any Sprite?"

"We might have..." I look at her, suddenly distracted. "Shouldn't you be at school?"

"No." Amy pops the lolly in her mouth with a defiant shrug.

"Why not?" I look from her to Mum, sensing a sudden tension in the air.

No one answers immediately. Mum is adjusting her velvet Alice band on her hair, her eyes distant, as though positioning it just right is her absolute priority.

"Amy's in a teeny bit of trouble," she says at last. "Isn't she, Raphael?"

"I've been suspended from school." With a swagger, Amy heads over to a chair, sits down, and puts her feet up on the coffee table.

"*Suspended?* Why?"

There's silence. Mum doesn't appear to have heard me. "Mum, *why?*"

"I'm afraid Amy's been up to her old tricks again," Mum says with a little wince.

"Old tricks?"

The only tricks I can ever remember Amy doing are card tricks from a magic set she once got in her Christmas stocking. I can see her now, in her pink gingham pajamas and bunny slippers in front of the fireplace, asking us to pick a card while we all pretended not to notice the one she had hidden up her sleeve.

I feel a pang of nostalgia. She was such a sweet little thing.

"What did you do, Ame?"

"It was nothing! They so *totally* overreacted." Amy takes her lolly out of her mouth and sighs with exaggerated patience. "All I did was bring this psychic into school."

"A psychic?"

"Well." Amy meets my eye with a smirk. "This woman I met in a club. I don't know exactly how psychic she is. But everyone believed us. I charged ten quid each and she told all the girls they'd meet a boy tomorrow. Everyone was happy. Until some teacher found out."

"Ten quid each?" I stare at her in disbelief. "No wonder you got in trouble!"

"I'm on my final warning," she says proudly.

"Why? Amy, what else have you done?"

"Nothing much! Just...over the holidays I collected money for this math teacher, Mrs. Winters, who was in the hospital." Amy shrugs. "I said she was on the way out and everyone gave loads. I raised over five hundred quid." She snuffles with laughter. "It was so cool!"

"Darling, it's extorting money under false pretenses." Mum's twisting her amber beads obsessively with one hand, while stroking one of the dogs with the other. "Mrs. Winters was very upset."

"I gave her some chocolates, didn't I?" retorts Amy, unrepentant. "And anyway, I wasn't lying. You *could* die from liposuction."

I'm trying to find something to say, but I'm too gob-smacked. How did my sister turn from cute, innocent little Amy into...*this*?

"I need some lip salve," Amy says, swinging her legs down off the sofa. "Can I get some off your dressing table?"

"Um, sure." As soon as she's out of the room I turn to Mum. "What's going on? How long has Amy been getting into trouble?"

"Oh...for the last couple of years." Mum doesn't look at me and instead addresses the dog on her lap. "She's a good, sweet girl, really, *isn't* she, Agnes? She just gets led astray. Some older girls encouraged her into the stealing; that really wasn't her fault...."

"Stealing?" I echo in horror.

"Yes. Well." Mum looks pained. "It was an unfortunate incident. She took a jacket from a fellow pupil and sewed her own name-tape into the back. But she really was very repentant."

"But...*why*?"

"Darling, nobody knows. She took her father's death quite badly and ever since then...it's been one thing after another."

I don't know what to say to that. Maybe all teens who lose their fathers go off the rails for a bit.

"That reminds me. I've got something for you, Lexi." Mum reaches into her canvas bag and produces a DVD in a plain plastic case. "This is the last message from your father. He did a farewell recording before the operation, just in case. It was played at the funeral. If you don't remember it, you should probably see it." She hands it over with two fingers as though it's contaminated.

I take the DVD and stare at it. The last surviving message from Dad. I still can't quite believe he's been dead for over three years.

"It'll be like seeing him again." I turn the disc over in my hands. "How amazing that he did a recording."

"Yes. Well." Mum's got that twitchy look again. "You know your father. Always had to be the center of attention."

"Mum! It's fair enough to be the center of attention at your own *funeral*."

Again Mum appears not to have heard. That's always her trick whenever anyone starts talking about a topic she doesn't like. She just blanks the whole conversation and changes the subject. Sure enough, a moment later she looks up and says, "Maybe *you* could help Amy, darling. You were going to find her an internship at your office."

"An internship?" I frown doubtfully. "Mum, I'm not sure about that."

My work situation is complicated enough right now without Amy flouncing around the place.

"Just for a week or two. You said you'd spoken to the right people about it and it was all set up—"

"Maybe I did." I cut her off hastily. "But everything's different now. I'm not even back at work yet. I need to relearn my job—"

"You've done so well in your career," says Mum persuasively.

Yup, I've done great. From junior sales manager to bitch-boss-from-hell, in one seamless leap.

There's silence for a few moments, apart from the sound of dogs skittering in the kitchen. I dread to think what they're doing.

"Mum, I was wondering about that," I say. "I'm trying to put all the pieces of my life together ... and it doesn't make sense. *Why* did I go on that TV show? Why did I become all hard and ambitious overnight? I don't get it."

"I have no idea." Mum seems preoccupied, searching in her bag for something. "Natural career advancement."

"But it *wasn't* natural." I lean forward, trying to get her attention. "I was never a high-powered career woman—you know I wasn't. Why would I suddenly change?"

"Darling, it was all so long ago, I really can't remember.... *Aren't* you a good girl? *Aren't* you the most beautiful girl in the world?"

She's addressing one of the dogs, I suddenly realize. She isn't even listening to me. Typical.

I look up to see Amy coming back into the room, still sucking her lollipop.

"Amy, Lexi was just talking about you doing an internship at her office!" Mum says brightly. "Would you like that?"

"Maybe," I put in quickly. "When I've been back at work for a while."

"Yeah. S'pose."

She doesn't even look grateful.

"There'd have to be some ground rules," I say. "You can't rip off my colleagues. Or steal from them."

"I don't steal!" Amy looks stung. "It was one jacket, and there was a mix-up. *Jesus*."

"Sweetheart, it wasn't just the jacket, was it?" says Mum, after a pause. "It was the makeup, too."

"Everyone thinks the worst of me. Every time anything goes missing, I'm the scapegoat." Amy's eyes are glittering in her pale face. She hunches her thin shoulders and suddenly I feel bad. She's right. I've judged her without even knowing the facts.

"I'm sorry," I say awkwardly. "I'm sure you don't steal."

"Whatever." Her face is averted. "Just blame me for everything, like everyone else."

"No. I won't." I head over to where she's standing by the window. "Amy, I really want to apologize. I know things have been hard for you since Dad died.... Come here." I hold my arms out for a hug.

"Leave me alone," she says almost savagely.

"But Amy—"

"Go away!" She backs away urgently, raising her arms as though to fend me off.

"But you're my little sister!" I lean forward and give her a tight hug—then draw back almost immediately, rubbing my ribs. "Ow! What the hell...You're all lumpy!"

"No, I'm not," Amy says after a fraction of a beat.

"Yes, you are!" I peer at her bulky denim jacket. "What on earth have you got in your pockets?"

"Tins of food," says Amy seamlessly. "Tuna and sweet corn."

"Sweet corn?" I stare at her, baffled.

"Not again." Mum shuts her eyes. "Amy, what have you taken from Lexi?"

"Give me a break!" Amy yells. "I haven't taken anything!" She throws her hand up in a defensive motion and two Chanel lipsticks fly out of the sleeve of her jacket, followed by a powder compact. They land on the floor with a clatter and we all stare at them.

"Are those mine?" I say at last.

"No," Amy says belligerently, but she's turned pink.

"Yes, they are!"

"Like you'd even *notice*." She shrugs sulkily. "You've got thousands of bloody lipsticks."

"Oh, Amy," Mum says sorrowfully. "Turn out your pockets."

Shooting Mum a murderous glance, Amy starts unpacking her pockets, laying all the contents on the coffee table with a series of little crashes. Two unopened moisturizers. A Jo Malone candle. A load of makeup. A Christian Dior perfume gift set. I watch her in silence, goggling at her haul.

"Now take off your T-shirt," Mum orders, like some kind of immigration official.

"This is *so* unfair," mutters Amy. She struggles out of the T-shirt and my jaw drops. Underneath, she's wearing an Armani slip dress that I recognize from my wardrobe, all scrunched up under her jeans. She has about five La Perla bras worn around her middle, and dangling from them, like charms from a bracelet, are two beaded evening bags.

"You took a *dress*?" I suppress a giggle. "And *bras*?"

"*Fine*. You want your dress back. *Fine*." She peels everything off and dumps it on the table. "Satisfied?" She looks up and catches the expression on my face. "It's not *my* fault. Mum won't give me any money for clothes."

"Amy, that's nonsense!" Mum exclaims sharply. "You have plenty of clothes!"

"They're all out of date!" she instantly yells back at Mum, in a way that suggests they've had this argument before. "We don't all live in a bloody fashion time-warp like you do! When are you going to realize it's the twenty-first century?" She gestures at Mum's dress. "It's tragic!"

"Amy, stop it!" I say hastily. "That's not the point. And anyway, those bras don't even fit you!"

"You can sell bras on eBay," she retorts scathingly. "Fancy overpriced bras, that is."

She shoves on her T-shirt, sinks down onto the floor, and starts texting something on her phone.

I'm totally flummoxed by all of this. "Amy," I say at last, "maybe we should have a little talk. Mum, why don't you go and make some coffee or something?"

Mum looks totally flustered, and seems grateful to head out to the kitchen. When she's gone I sit down on the floor, across from where Amy has plonked herself. Her shoulders are tensed angrily and she doesn't look up.

Okay. I have to be understanding and sympathetic. I know there's a big age gap between me and Amy. I know I can't even remember a whole chunk of her life. But surely we have a sisterly rapport?

"Amy, listen," I say in my best understanding-grown-up-sister-but-still-pretty-cool voice. "You can't steal, okay? You can't extort money from people."

"Fuck off," Amy says without raising her head.

"You'll get in trouble. You'll get chucked out of school!"

"Fuck," Amy says conversationally. "Off. Fuck off, fuck off, fuck off..."

"Look!" I say, trying to keep my patience. "I know things can be difficult. And you're probably lonely with just you and Mum at home. But if you ever want to talk about anything, if you've got any problems, I'm here for you. Just call me, or text me, anytime. We could go out for a coffee, or see a film together..." I trail away.

Amy's still texting with one hand. With the other she has slowly moved her thumb and index finger into the "Loser" sign.

"Oh fuck off, yourself!" I exclaim furiously, and hug my knees. Stupid little cow. If Mum thinks I'm having her in my office on some internship, she has to be *joking*.

We sit there in grouchy silence for a bit. Then I reach for the DVD of Dad's funeral message, slide across the floor, and plug it into the machine. The huge screen opposite lights up, and after a few moments my father's face appears.

I stare at the screen, gripped. Dad's sitting in an armchair, wearing a red plushy dressing gown. I don't recognize the room—but then, I never did get to see many of Dad's homes. His face is gaunt, the way I remember it after he got ill. It was as though he was slowly deflating. But his green eyes are twinkling and there's a cigar in his hand.

"Hello," he says, his voice hoarse. "It's me. Well, you know that." He gives a little laugh, then breaks into a hacking cough, which he relieves by taking a puff on his cigar as if it was a drink of water. "We all know this operation has a fifty-fifty chance of survival. My own fault for buggering up my body. So I thought I'd do a little message to you, my family, just in case."

He pauses and takes a deep slug from a tumbler of whisky. His hand is shaking as he puts it down, I notice. Did he know he was going to die? Suddenly there's a hard lump in my throat. I glance over at Amy. She's let go of her phone and is watching, too, transfixed.

"Live a good life," Dad is saying to the camera. "Be happy. Be kind to one another. Barbara, stop living your life through those bloody dogs. They're not human. They're never going to love you or support you or go to bed with you. Unless you're *very* desperate."

I clap my hand over my mouth. "He *didn't* say that!"

"He did." Amy gives a little snort of laughter. "Mum walked out of the room."

"You only get one life, loves. Don't waste it." He looks at the camera with glittering green eyes, and I suddenly remember him when I was much younger, picking me up from school in a sports car. I was pointing him out to everyone: *That man there is my daddy!* All the kids were gasping at the car and all the mothers were shooting surreptitious glances at him, in his smart linen jacket and Spanish tan.

"I know I've fucked up here and there," Dad's saying. "I know I haven't been the best family man. But hand on heart, I did my best. Cheers, m'dears. See you on the other side." He raises his glass to the camera and drinks. Then the screen goes blank.

The DVD clicks off, but neither Amy nor I moves. As I gaze at the blank screen I feel even more marooned than before. My dad's dead. He's been dead three years. I can never talk to him again. I can never give him a birthday present. I can never ask him for advice. Not that you'd ask Dad's advice on anything except where to buy sexy underwear for a mistress—but still. I glance over at Amy, who meets my gaze with a tiny shrug.

"That was a really nice message," I say, determined not to be sentimental or cry or anything. "Dad came good."

"Yeah." Amy nods. "He did."

The frostiness between us seems to have melted. Amy reaches in her bag for a tiny makeup case with *Babe* embossed on the lid in diamante. She takes out a lip pencil and expertly outlines her lips, peering into a tiny mirror. I've never seen her put on makeup before, except as a dressing-up game.

Amy's not a child anymore, I think as I watch her. She's on the brink of being an adult. I know things haven't gone that well between us today—but maybe in the past she's been my friend.

My confidante, even.

"Hey, Amy," I say in a low, cautious voice. "Did we talk much before the accident? The two of us, I mean. About . . . stuff." I glance toward the kitchen to make sure Mum can't hear.

"A bit." She shrugs. "What stuff?"

"I was just wondering." I keep my voice natural. "Out of interest, did I ever mention anyone called . . . Jon?"

"Jon?" Amy pauses, lipstick in hand. "You mean the one you had sex with?"

"*What?*" My voice shoots out like a rocket. "Are you sure?"

Oh my God. It's true.

"Yeah." Amy seems surprised by my reaction. "You told me at New Year's Eve. You were quite pissed."

"What else did I tell you?" My heart is thumping wildly. "Tell me everything you can remember."

"You told me everything!" Her eyes light up. "All the gory details. It was your first-ever time, and he lost the condom, and you were freezing to death on the school field . . ."

"School field?" I stare at Amy, my mind trying to make sense of this. "Do you mean . . . are you talking about *James*?"

"Oh yeah!" She clicks her tongue in realization. "That's who I meant. James. The guy in the band when you were at school. Why, who are you talking about?"

She finishes her lipstick and regards me with fresh interest. "Who's Jon?"

"He's no one," I say hastily. "Just ... some guy. He's nothing."

• • •

You see—there's no evidence. If I was really having an affair I would have left a trail. A note, or a photo, or a diary entry. Or Amy would know, or something ...

And the point is, I'm happily married to Eric. *That's* the point.

It's much later that evening. Mum and Amy left a while ago, after we finally managed to cajole one whippet off the balcony and another out of Eric's Jacuzzi, where it was having a fight with one of the towels. And now I'm in the car with Eric, zipping along the Embankment. He's having a meeting with Ava, his interior designer, and suggested I come along and see the show flat of his latest development, Blue 42.

All Eric's buildings are called "Blue" and then some number. It's the company's brand. It turns out that having a brand is a crucial part of selling loft-style living, as is having the right music on when you walk in, and the right cutlery on the show table. Apparently Ava is a genius at choosing the right cutlery.

I learned about Ava from the marriage manual. She's forty-eight, divorced, worked in LA for twenty years, has written a series of books called things like *Tassel* and *Fork,* and designs all the show homes for Eric's company.

"Hey, Eric," I say as we drive along. "I was looking

at my bank statement today. I seem to pay all this regular money to something called Unito. I rang up the bank, and they said it's an offshore account."

"Uh-huh." Eric nods as though he's not remotely interested. I wait for him to say something else, but he turns on the radio.

"Don't you know anything about it?" I say over the sound of the news.

"No." He shrugs. "Not a bad idea, though, putting some of your money offshore."

"Right." I'm dissatisfied by his response; I almost feel like I want to pick a fight about it. But I don't know why.

"I just need to get some petrol." Eric swings off the road into a BP station. "I won't be a moment..."

"Hey," I say as he opens the door. "Could you get me some chips in the shop? Salt 'n' vinegar if they have them."

"Chips?" He turns back and stares at me as though I've asked for some heroin.

"Yes, chips."

"Darling." Eric looks perplexed. "You don't eat chips. It was all in the manual. Our nutritionist has recommended a low-carb, high-protein diet."

"Well ... I know. But everyone's allowed a little treat once in a while, aren't they? And I really feel like some chips."

For a moment Eric seems lost for an answer.

"The doctors warned me you might be irrational, and make odd, out-of-character gestures," he says, almost to himself.

"It's not irrational to eat a packet of chips!" I protest. "They're not *poison*."

"Sweetheart ... I'm thinking of you." Eric adopts a loving tone. "I know how hard you've worked at reducing those two dress sizes. We invested a lot in your personal trainer. If you want to throw it away on a bag of chips, then that's your choice. Do you still want the chips?"

"Yes," I say, a bit more defiantly than I meant to.

I see a flash of annoyance pass over Eric's face, which he manages to convert into a smile.

"No problem." He shuts the car door with a heavy clunk. A few minutes later I see him walking briskly back from the garage, holding a packet of chips.

"Here you are." He drops them on my lap and starts the engine.

"Thank you!" I smile gratefully, but I'm not sure he notices. As he drives off, I try to open the packet—but my left hand is still clumsy after the accident and I can't get a proper grip on the plastic. At last I put the packet between my teeth, yank as hard as I can with my right hand ... and the entire packet explodes.

Shit. There are chips everywhere. All over the seats, all over the gear stick, and all over Eric.

"Jesus!" He shakes his head in annoyance. "Are those in my *hair*?"

"Sorry," I gasp, brushing at his jacket. "I'm really, really sorry ..."

The reek of salt and vinegar has filled the car. Mmm. That's a good smell.

"I'll have to have the car valeted." Eric's nose is

wrinkled in distaste. "And my jacket will be covered in grease."

"I'm sorry, Eric," I say again, humbly, brushing the last crumbs off his shoulder. "I'll pay for the dry cleaning." I sit back, reach for a massive chip that landed on my lap, and put it in my mouth.

"Are you *eating* that?" Eric sounds like this is the last straw.

"It only landed on my lap," I protest. "It's clean!"

We drive on awhile in silence. Surreptitiously I eat a few more chips, trying to crunch them as quietly as possible.

"It's not your fault," says Eric, staring ahead at the road. "You had a bump on the head. I can't expect normality yet."

"I feel perfectly normal," I say.

"Of course you do." He pats my hand patronizingly and I stiffen. Okay, I may not be totally recovered. But I do know that eating one packet of chips doesn't make you mentally ill. I'm about to tell that to Eric, when he signals and turns in at a pair of electric gates that has opened for us. We drive into a shallow forecourt and Eric turns off the engine.

"Here we are." I can hear the pride crackling in his voice. He gestures out the window. "This is our latest baby."

I stare up, totally overcome, forgetting all about chips. In front of us is a brand-new white building. It has curved balconies, an awning, and black granite steps up to a pair of grand silver-framed doors.

"You built this?" I say at last.

"Not personally." Eric laughs. "Come on." He opens his door, brushing the last few chips off his trousers, and I follow, still in awe. A uniformed porter opens the door for us. The foyer is all palest marble and white pillars. This place is a *palace*.

"It's amazing. It's so glamorous!" I keep noticing tiny details everywhere, like the inlaid borders and the sky-painted ceiling.

"The penthouse has its own lift." With a nod to the porter, Eric ushers me to the rear of the lobby and into a beautiful marquetry-lined lift. "There's a pool in the basement, a gym, and a residents' cinema. Although of course most apartments have their own private gyms and cinemas as well," he adds.

I look up sharply to see if he's joking—but I don't think he is. A private gym and cinema? In a flat?

"And here we are . . ." The lift opens with the tiniest of pings and we walk into a circular, mirrored foyer. Eric presses gently on one of the mirrors, which turns out to be a door. It swings open and I just gape.

I'm looking at the most massive room. No, *space*. It has floor-to-ceiling windows, a walk-in fireplace on one wall—and on another wall there's a gigantic steel sheet down which are cascading endless streams of water.

"Is that real water?" I say stupidly. "Inside a house?" Eric laughs.

"Our customers like a statement. It's fun, huh?" He picks up a remote and jabs it at the waterfall—and at once the water is bathed in blue light. "There are ten pre-programmed light shows. Ava?" He raises his voice, and a moment later a skinny blond woman in rimless glasses, gray trousers, and a white shirt appears from some recessed doorway next to the waterfall.

"Hi there!" she says in a mid-Atlantic accent. "Lexi! You're up and about!" She grasps my hand with both of hers. "I heard all about it. You poor thing."

"I'm fine, really." I smile. "Just piecing my life back together again." I gesture around the room. "This place is amazing! All that water..."

"Water is the theme of the show apartment," says Eric. "We've followed feng shui principles pretty closely, haven't we, Ava? Very important for some of our ultra-high net worths."

"Ultra-what?" I say, confused.

"The very rich," Eric translates. "Our target market."

"Feng shui is vital for ultra-highs." Ava nods earnestly. "Eric, I've just taken delivery of the fish for the master suite. They're stunning!" She adds to me, "Each fish is worth three hundred pounds. We hired them especially."

Ultra-high whatevers. Fish for hire. It's a different world. Lost for words, I look around again at the massive apartment: at the curved cocktail bar and the sunken seating area and the glass sculpture hanging from the ceiling. I have no idea how much this place costs. I don't *want* to know.

"Here you are." Ava hands me an intricate scale model made of paper and tiny wooden sticks. "This is the whole building. You'll notice I've mirrored the curved balconies in the scalloped edges of the scatter pillows," she adds. "Very art deco meets Gaultier."

"Er...excellent!" I rack my brains for something to say about art deco meets Gaultier, and fail. "So, how did you think of it all?" I gesture at the waterfall, which is now bathed in orange light. "Like, how did you come up with this?"

"Oh, that wasn't me." Ava shakes her head emphatically. "My area is soft furnishings, fabrics, sensual details. The big concept stuff was all down to Jon."

I feel a tiny lurch inside.

"Jon?" I tilt my head, adopting the vaguest expression I can muster, as if *Jon* is some unfamiliar word from an obscure foreign language.

"Jon Blythe," Eric prompts helpfully. "The architect. You met him at the dinner party, remember? In fact, weren't you asking me about him earlier on?"

"Was I?" I say after an infinitesimal pause. "I... don't really remember." I start turning over the model in my fingers, trying to ignore the slight flush rising up my neck.

This is ridiculous. I'm *behaving* like a guilty adulterous wife.

"Jon, there you are!" Ava calls out. "We were just talking about you!"

He's *here*? My hands clench involuntarily around the model. I don't want to see him. I don't want him to see me. I have to make an excuse and leave—

But too late. Here he is, loping across the floor, wearing jeans and a navy V-neck and consulting some bit of paper.

Okay, stay calm. Everything's fine. You're happily married and have no evidence of any secret fling, affair, or liaison with this man.

"Hi, Eric, Lexi." He nods politely as he approaches—then stares at my hands. I look down and feel a jerk of dismay. The model's totally crushed. The roof's broken and one of the balconies has become detached.

"*Lexi!*" Eric has just noticed it. "How on earth did that happen?"

"Jon." Ava's brow crumples in distress. "Your model!"

"I'm really sorry!" I say, flustered. "I don't know how it happened. I was just holding it, and somehow..."

"Don't worry." Jon shrugs. "It only took me a month to make."

"A *month*?" I echo, aghast. "Look, if you give me some Scotch tape I'll fix it...." I'm patting at the crushed roof, desperately trying to prod it back into shape.

"Maybe not quite a month," Jon says, watching me. "Maybe a couple of hours."

"Oh." I stop patting. "Well, anyway, I'm sorry."

Jon shoots me a brief glance. "You can make it up to me."

Make it up to him? What does that mean? Without quite meaning to I slip my arm through Eric's. I need some reassurance. I need ballast. I need a sturdy husband by my side.

"So, the apartment's very impressive, Jon." I adopt a bland, corporate-wife-type manner, sweeping an arm around the space. "Many congratulations."

"Thank you. I'm pleased with it," he replies in equally bland tones. "How's the memory doing?"

"Pretty much the same as before."

"You haven't remembered anything new?"

"No. Nothing."

"That's a shame."

"Yeah."

I'm trying to stay natural—but there's an electric atmosphere growing between us as we face each other. My breath is coming just slightly short. I glance up at Eric, convinced he must have noticed something—but he hasn't even flickered. Can't he feel it? Can't he *see* it?

"Eric, we need to talk about the Bayswater project," says Ava, who has been riffling through her soft leather handbag. "I went to see the site yesterday and made some notes—"

"Lexi, why don't you look around the apartment while Ava and I talk?" Eric cuts her off, loosening his arm from mine. "Jon will show you."

"Oh." I stiffen. "No, don't worry."

"I'd be happy to show you." Jon's voice is dry and kind of bored. "If you're interested."

"Really, there's no need..."

"Darling, Jon designed the whole building," Eric says reprovingly. "It's a great opportunity for you to find out the vision of the company."

"Come this way and I'll explain the initial concept." Jon gestures toward the other side of the room.

I can't get out of this.

"That would be great," I say at last.

Fine. If he wants to talk, I'll talk. I follow Jon across the room and we pause next to the tumbling streams of the waterfall. How could anyone live with water thundering down the wall like this?

"So," I say politely. "How do you think of all these ideas? All these 'statements' or whatever they are."

Jon frowns thoughtfully and my heart sinks. I hope he's not going to come up with a load of pretentious stuff about his artistic genius. I'm really not in the mood.

"I just ask myself, what would a wanker like?" he says at last. "And I put it in."

I can't help a half-laugh of shock. "Well, if I were a wanker I'd love this."

"There you go." He takes a step nearer and lowers his voice beneath the sound of the water. "So you really haven't remembered anything?"

"No. Nothing at all."

"Okay." He exhales sharply. "We have to meet. We have to talk. There's a place we go, the Old Canal House in Islington." In a much louder voice he adds, "You'll notice the high ceilings, Lexi. They're a trademark feature of all our developments." He glances over and catches my expression. "What?"

"Are you crazy?" I hiss, glancing over to make sure Eric can't hear. "I'm not meeting you! For your information, I haven't found a single piece of evidence that you and I are having an affair. Not one. What a great sense of space!" I add at full volume.

"Evidence?" Jon looks as if he doesn't understand. "Like what?"

"Like ... I don't know. A love note."

"We didn't write each other love notes."

"Or trinkets."

"Trinkets?" Jon looks like he wants to laugh. "We weren't much into trinkets, either."

"Well, it couldn't have been much of a love affair, then!" I retort. "I've looked in my dressing table—nothing. I looked in my diary—nothing. I asked my sister—she'd never even *heard* of you."

"Lexi." He pauses as though working out how to explain the situation to me. "It was a secret affair. That would mean *an affair that you keep secret*."

"So you have no proof. I knew it."

I turn on my heel and stride away toward the fireplace, Jon following closely behind.

"You want proof?" I can hear him muttering in low, incredulous tones. "What, like ... you have a strawberry mark on your left buttock?"

"I *don't*—" I swivel around in triumph, then stop abruptly as Eric glances across the room at us. "I don't know how you came up with this amazing use of light!" I wave at Eric, who waves back and continues his conversation.

"I *know* you don't have a birthmark on your buttock." Jon rolls his eyes. "You don't have any birthmarks at all. Just a mole on your arm."

I'm briefly silenced. He's right. But so what?

"That could be a lucky guess." I fold my arms.

"I know. But it's not." He looks at me steadily. "Lexi, I'm not making it up. We're having an affair. We love each other. Deeply and passionately."

"Look." I thrust my hands through my hair. "This is just . . . mad! I wouldn't have an affair. Not with you or anyone. I've never been unfaithful to anybody in my life—"

"We had sex on that floor four weeks ago," he cuts me off. "Right there." He nods at a huge fluffy white sheepskin.

I stare at it speechlessly.

"You were on top," he adds.

"Stop it!" Flustered, I wheel around and stride away toward the far end of the space, where a trendy Lucite staircase rises to a mezzanine level.

"Let's take a look at the wet room complex," Jon says loudly as he follows me up. "I think you'll like it . . ."

"No, I won't," I shoot over my shoulder. "Leave me alone."

We both reach the top of the staircase and turn to look over the steel balustrade. I can see Eric on the level below, and beyond, the lights of London through the massive windows. I have to hand it to him, it's a staggering apartment.

Beside me, Jon is sniffing the air.

"Hey," he says. "Have you been eating salt and vinegar chips?"

"Maybe." I give him a suspicious look.

Jon's eyes open wide. "I'm impressed. How did you sneak those past the food fascist?"

"He's not a food fascist," I say, feeling an immediate need to defend Eric. "He just . . . cares about nutrition."

"He's Hitler. If he could round up every loaf of bread and put it in a camp, he would."

"Stop it."

"He'd gas them all. Finger rolls first. Then croissants."

"*Stop* it." My mouth twists with an urge to giggle and I turn away.

This guy is funnier than I thought at first. And he's kind of sexy, close up, with his rumpled dark hair.

But then, lots of things are funny and sexy. *Friends* is funny and sexy. It doesn't mean I'm having an affair with it.

"What do you want?" At last I turn to face Jon, helpless. "What do you expect me to do?"

"What do I want?" He pauses, his brow knitted as though he's thinking it through. "I want you to tell your husband you don't love him, come home with me, and start a new life together."

He's serious. I almost want to laugh.

"You want me to come and live with you," I say, as though to clarify arrangements. "Right now. Just like that."

"In, say, five minutes." He glances at his watch. "I have a few things to do first."

"You're a total psycho." I shake my head.

"I'm not a psycho," he says patiently. "I love you. You love me. Really. You have to take my word on that."

"I don't have to take your word on anything!" I suddenly resent his confidence. "I'm *married*, okay? I have a husband whom I love, whom I've promised to love forever. Here's the proof!" I brandish my wedding ring at him. "This is proof!"

"You love him?" Jon ignores the ring. "You feel love for him? Right deep down here?" He thumps his chest.

I want to snap "Yes, I'm desperately in love with Eric" and shut him up for good. But for some ridiculous reason I can't quite bring myself to lie.

"Maybe it's not quite there yet . . . but I'm sure it will be," I say, sounding more defiant than I meant to. "Eric's a fantastic guy. Everything's wonderful between us."

"Uh-huh." Jon nods politely. "You haven't had sex since the accident, have you?"

I stare at him mistrustfully.

"Have you?" There's a glint in his eye.

"I . . . we . . ." I flounder. "Maybe we have, maybe we haven't! I'm not in the habit of discussing my private life with you."

"Yeah, you are." There's a sudden wryness in his face. "You are. That's the point." To my surprise he reaches for one of my hands. He just holds it for a moment, looking at it. Then, very slowly, he starts tracing over the skin with his thumb.

I can't bring myself to move. My skin is fizzing; his thumb is leaving a trail of delicious sensation wherever it goes. I can feel tiny prickles up the back of my neck.

"So what do you think?" Eric's booming voice heralds us from below and I jump a mile, whipping my hand away. What was I *thinking*?

"It's great, darling!" I trill back over the balustrade, my voice unnaturally high. "We'll just be a couple more seconds . . ." I draw back, out of sight of the floor below, and beckon Jon to follow. "Look, I've had enough," I say in a swift undertone. "Leave me alone. I don't know you. I don't love you. Things are hard enough for me right now. I just want to get on with my life, with my husband. Okay?" I make to head down the stairs.

"No! Not okay!" Jon grabs hold of my arm. "Lexi, you don't know the whole picture. You're unhappy with Eric. He doesn't love you, he doesn't *understand* you—"

"Of course Eric loves me!" Now I'm really rattled. "He sat by my hospital bed night and day, he brought me these amazing taupe roses..."

"You think *I* didn't want to sit by your hospital bed night and day?" Jon's eyes darken. "Lexi, it nearly killed me."

"Let me go." I try to pull my arm free, but Jon holds firm.

"You can't throw us away." He's scanning my face desperately. "It's in there. It's all in there somewhere, I know it is—"

"You're wrong!" With a huge effort I wrench my arm out of his grasp. "It's not!" I clatter down the stairs without looking back, straight into Eric's arms.

"Hi!" He laughs. "You seem in a rush. Is everything all right?"

"I...don't feel too good." I put a hand to my brow. "I've got a headache. Can we go now?"

"Of course we can, darling." He squeezes my shoulders and glances up at the mezzanine level. "Have you said good-bye to Jon?"

"Yes. Let's just . . . go."

As we head to the door I cling to his expensive jacket, letting the feel of him soothe my jangled nerves. This is my husband. This is who I'm in love with. This is reality.

Chapter Twelve

Okay, I need my memory back. I've *had* it with amnesia. I've had it with people telling me they know more about my life than I do.

It's *my* memory. It belongs to me.

I stare into my eyes, reflected an inch away in the mirrored wardrobe door. This is a new habit of mine, to stand right up close to the mirror so the only bit I can see is my eyes. It's comforting. It makes me feel as if I'm looking at the old me.

"Remember, you moron," I instruct myself in a low, fierce voice. *"Re-mem-ber."*

My eyes stare back at me as though they know everything but won't tell. I sigh, and lean my head against the glass in frustration.

In the days since we got back from the show apartment, I've done nothing but immerse myself in the last three years. I've looked through photo albums, watched movies I know I've "seen," listened to songs that I know the old Lexi heard a hundred times.... But nothing's worked. Whichever mental filing cabinet my missing memories are locked into, it's pretty sturdy. It's not about to fly open just because I listen to a song called "You're Beautiful" by James . . . someone or other.

Stupid secretive brain. I mean, who's in charge here? Me or it?

Yesterday I went to see that neurologist, Neil. He nodded sympathetically as I poured everything out, and scribbled loads of notes. Then he said it was all fascinating and he might write a research paper on me. When I pressed him, he added that maybe it would help to write out a timeline, and I could go and see a therapist if I liked.

But I don't need therapy. I need my *memory*. The mirror is misting up from my breath. I'm pressing my forehead harder against the mirror, as though the answers are all inside the mirror-me, as though I can get them if I concentrate enough . . .

"Lexi? I'm off." Eric comes into the bedroom, holding a DVD, out of its box. "Darling, you left this on the rug. Sensible location for a DVD?"

I take the disc from him. It's the *Ambition EP 1* DVD that I started watching the other day.

"I'm sorry, Eric," I say quickly, taking it from him. "I don't know how it got there."

That's a lie. It got there when Eric was out and I had about fifty DVDs all scattered over the rug, together with magazines and photo albums and candy wrappers. If he'd seen it, he'd have had a heart attack.

"Your taxi will be here at ten," says Eric. "I'm off now."

"Great!" I kiss him, like I do every morning now. It's actually starting to feel quite natural. "Have a good day!"

"You too." He squeezes my shoulder. "Hope it goes well."

"It will," I say with confidence.

I'm going back to work today, full-time. Not to take over the department—obviously I'm not ready to do that. But to start relearning my job, catching up on what I've missed. It's five weeks since the accident. I can't just sit around at home anymore. I have to *do* something. I have to get my life back. And my friends.

On the bed, all ready, are three glossy gift bags with presents inside for Fi, Debs, and Carolyn, which I'm going to take in today. I spent ages choosing the perfect gifts; in fact, every time I think about them I want to hug myself with pleasure.

Humming, I head into the sitting room and slot the *Ambition* DVD into the player. I never did watch the rest of this. Maybe it'll help me get back into office mode. I fast-forward through the introductory shots, until I come to a bit with me in a limo with two guys in suits, and press Play.

"Lexi and her teammates won't be taking it easy to-night," explains a male voice-over. The camera focuses in on me, and I hold my breath with anticipation.

"We're going to win this task!" I'm saying in a sharp voice to the guys, slapping the back of one hand on the other palm. "If we have to work around the clock, we're going to win. Okay? No excuses."

My jaw drops slightly. Is that fierce, scary business-woman me? I've never spoken like that in my *life*.

"As ever, Lexi is taking her team to task," says the voice-over. "But has the Cobra gone too far this time?"

I don't quite understand what he's talking about. What cobra?

The picture now flashes to one of the guys from the limo. He's sitting in an office chair, a night sky visible through the plate-glass window behind him.

"She isn't human," he's muttering. "There's only so many fucking hours in the day. We're all doing our best, you know, but does she fucking care?"

As he's talking, an image of me striding around some warehouse has appeared on the screen. I feel a sudden dismay. Is he talking about *me*? Now the picture cuts to a full, stand-up row between me and the same guy. We're standing on a London street and he's trying to defend himself, but I'm not letting him get a word in.

"You're sacked!" I snap at last, my voice so scathing that I wince. "You're sacked from my team!"

"And the Cobra has struck!" the jaunty voice-over comes again. "Let's see that moment again!"

Hang on a minute. Is he saying—

I'm the Cobra?

To menacing music, a slow-motion replay has begun onscreen, zooming right into my face.

"You're sssssacked!" I'm hissing. "You're sssss-sacked from my team."

I stare, light-headed with horror. What the fuck

have they done? They've manipulated my voice. It sounds like I'm a snake.

"And Lexi's in top venomous form this week!" says the voice-over. "Meanwhile, over on the other team..."

A different group of people in suits appears on the screen and starts arguing about a price negotiation. But I'm too shell-shocked to move.

Why— How—

Why didn't anyone tell me? Why didn't anyone *warn* me about this? On autopilot, I reach for my phone and jab in Eric's number.

"Hi, Lexi."

"Eric, I just watched the DVD of that TV show!" My voice comes shooting out in agitation. "They called me the Cobra! I was a total bitch to everyone! You never told me about that!"

"Sweetheart, it was a great show," says Eric soothingly. "You came across really well."

"But they named me after a *snake*."

"So what?"

"So I don't want to be a snake!" I know I sound almost hysterical, but I can't help it. "No one likes snakes! I'm more like a . . . a squirrel. Or a koala."

Koalas are soft and furry. And a bit snaggly.

"A *koala*? Lexi!" Eric laughs. "Darling, you're a cobra. You have timing. You have attack. That's what makes you a great businesswoman."

"But I don't *want* to be—" I break off as the buzzer sounds. "My taxi's here. I'd better go."

I head into the bedroom and pick up my three glossy gift bags, trying to regain my former optimism, trying to be excited about the day again. But suddenly all my confidence has evaporated.

I'm a snake. No wonder everyone hates me.

• • •

As my taxi wends its way toward the Victoria Palace Road, I sit rigid on the backseat, clutching my gift bags, giving myself a pep talk. First of all, everyone knows the TV skews things. No one really thinks I'm a snake. Besides which, that TV show was ages ago—everyone's probably forgotten about it.

Oh God. The trouble with giving yourself a pep talk is, deep down you know it's all bullshit.

The taxi deposits me outside the building and I take a deep breath, tugging my beige Armani suit straight. Then, with trepidation, I make my way up to the third floor. As I step out of the lift the first thing I see is Fi, Carolyn, and Debs standing by the coffee machine. Fi is gesturing to her hair and talking with animation while Carolyn chips in, but as I appear the conversation instantly stops, as though someone pulled the plug on the radio.

"Hi, you guys!" I look around with the warmest, friendliest smile I can muster. "I'm back again!"

"Hi, Lexi." There's a general muted reply and Fi makes a kind of acknowledging shrug. Okay, it wasn't a smile—but at least it was a reaction.

"You look really nice, Fi! That top's great." I gesture at her cream shirt and she follows my gaze in surprise. "And Debs, you look fab too. And Carolyn! Your hair looks so cool, all cropped like that and...and those boots are fantastic!"

"These?" Carolyn snorts with laughter and kicks one brown suede boot against the other. "I've had them for years."

"Well, still...they're really striking!"

I'm gabbling with nerves, talking a load of bollocks. No wonder they all seem unimpressed. Fi's arms are folded and Debs looks like she wants to giggle.

"So, anyway..." I force myself to slow down a bit. "I got you all a little something. Fi, this is for you, and Debs..."

As I hand over the gift bags they suddenly look ridiculously shiny and conspicuous.

"What's this for?" Debs says blankly.

"Well, you know! Just to...um..." I falter slightly. "You guys are my friends, and...Go on. Open them!"

Giving each other uncertain looks, all three start ripping at their wrapping paper.

"*Gucci?*" Fi says in disbelief as she pulls out a green jewelry box. "Lexi, I can't accept—"

"Yes, you can! Please. Just open it, you'll see..."

Silently, Fi snaps it open to reveal a gold bangle watch.

"D'you remember?" I say eagerly. "We always used to look at them in the shop windows. Every weekend. And now you've actually got one!"

"Actually..." Fi sighs, looking uncomfortable. "Lexi, I got it two years ago."

She lifts up her sleeve and she's wearing exactly the same watch, only a little duller and older-looking.

"Oh," I say, my heart sinking. "Oh, right. Well, never mind. I can take it back, or exchange it, we can get something else..."

"Lexi, I can't use this," Carolyn chimes in, and hands back the perfume gift set I bought her, together with the leather tote it came in. "That smell makes me gag."

"But it's your favorite," I say in bewilderment.

"Was," she corrects me. "Before I fell pregnant."

"You're *pregnant*?" I stare at her, overwhelmed. "Oh my God! Carolyn, congratulations! That's so wonderful! I'm *so* happy for you. Matt will be the best dad ever—"

"It's not Matt's baby." She cut me off flat.

"It's not?" I say stupidly. "But what...Did you two break *up*?"

They can't have broken up. It's impossible. Everyone assumed Carolyn and Matt would be together forever.

"I don't want to talk about it, okay?" Carolyn says almost in a whisper. To my horror I see her eyes have turned pink behind her glasses and she's breathing hard. "See you." She thrusts all the wrapping paper and ribbon at me, then turns and strides off, back toward the office.

"Great, Lexi," says Fi sarcastically. "Just when we thought she'd finally got over Matt."

"I didn't know!" I say, aghast. "I had no idea. I'm so sorry..." I rub my face, feeling hot and flustered. "Debs, open your present."

I bought Debs a cross studded with tiny diamonds.

She's so crazy about jewelry, and you can't go wrong with a cross. She *has* to love it.

In silence Debs pulls off the wrapping.

"I know it's quite extravagant," I say nervously. "But I wanted to get something really special—"

"This is a cross!" Debs thrusts the box back at me, her nose wrinkled as though it smells of something rancid. "I can't wear this! I'm Jewish."

"You're *Jewish*?" My mouth hangs open. "Since when?"

"Since I've been engaged to Jacob," she says as though it's obvious. "I've converted."

"Wow!" I say joyfully. "You're *engaged*?" And of course now I can't miss the platinum ring on her left hand, with a diamond lodged right in the center of the band. Debs wears so many rings, I hadn't noticed it. "When's the wedding?" My words spill out in excitement. "Where's it happening?"

"Next month." She looks away. "In Wiltshire."

"Next *month*! Oh my God, Debs! But I haven't got—"

I break off abruptly into a kind of hot, thudding silence. I was about to say "But I haven't got an invitation."

I haven't got an invitation because I haven't been invited.

"I mean...um...congratulations!" Somehow I keep a bright smile plastered on my face. "I hope it all goes brilliantly. And don't worry, I can easily return the cross...and the watch...and the perfume...." With trembling fingers I start stuffing all the ripped wrapping paper into one of the gift bags.

"Yeah," Fi says in an awkward voice. "Well, see you, Lexi."

"Bye." Debs still can't look me in the eye. They both walk off and I watch them go, my chin stiff from wanting to cry.

Great work, Lexi. You didn't win your friends back—you just fucked up everything even more.

"A present for me?" Byron's sarcastic voice hits the back of my head and I turn to see him loping along the corridor, coffee in hand. "How sweet of you, Lexi!"

God, he gives me the creeps. *He's* the snake.

"Hi, Byron," I say as briskly as I can. "Good to see you."

Summoning all my strength, I lift my chin high and sweep a stray hair back off my face. I can't crumble.

"It's very brave of you to come back, Lexi," Byron says as we head down the corridor. "Very admirable."

"Not really!" I say as confidently as I can. "I'm looking forward to it."

"Well, any questions, you know where I am. Although today I'll be with James Garrison most of the day. You remember James Garrison?"

Bloody bloody bloody. *Why* does he pick the people I've never heard of?

"Remind me," I say reluctantly.

"He's head of our distributor, Southeys? They distribute stock around the country? Like, carpet, flooring, the stuff we sell? They drive it around in lorries?" His tone is polite, but he's smirking.

"Yes, I remember Southeys," I say cuttingly. "Thanks. Why are you seeing them?"

"Well," says Byron after a pause. "The truth is, they've lost their way. It's crunch time. If they can't improve their systems, we're going to have to look elsewhere."

"Right." I nod in as bosslike a way as I can. "Well, keep me posted." We've reached my office and I open the door. "See you later, Byron."

I close the door, dump my gift bags on the sofa, open the filing cabinet, and take out an entire drawer's worth of files. Trying not to feel daunted, I sit down at the desk and open the first one, which contains minutes of departmental meetings.

Three years. I can catch up on three years. It's not *that* long.

• • •

Twenty minutes later, my brain is already aching. I haven't read anything serious or heavy for what seems like months—and this stuff is as dense as treacle. Budget discussions. Contracts up for renewal. Performance evaluations. I feel like I'm back at college, doing about six degrees at once.

I've started a sheet of paper: *Questions to ask,* and already I'm onto the second side.

"How are you doing?" The door has opened silently and Byron is looking in. Doesn't he *knock*?

"Fine," I say defensively. "Really well. I just have a couple of tiny questions..."

"Fire away." He leans against the doorjamb.

"Okay. First, what's QAS?"

"That's our new accounting system software. Everyone's been trained in it."

"Well, I can get trained too," I say briskly, scribbling on my sheet. "And what's Services.com?"

"Our online customer service provider."

"What?" I wrinkle my brow, confused. "But what about the customer services department?"

"All made redundant years ago," says Byron, sounding bored. "The company was restructured and a load of departments were contracted out."

"Right." I nod, trying to take all this in, and glance down at my sheet again. "So what about BD Brooks? What's that?"

"They're our ad agency," Byron says with exaggerated patience. "They make advertisements for us, on the radio and the TV—"

"I know what an ad agency is!" I snap, more hotly than I intended. "So, what happened to Pinkham Smith? We've had such a great relationship with them—"

"They don't exist anymore." Byron rolls his eyes. "They went bust. Jesus, Lexi, you don't know a bloody thing, do you?"

I open my mouth to retort—but I can't. He's right. It's as if the landscape I knew has been swept away by some kind of hurricane. Everything's been rebuilt and I don't recognize any of it.

"You're never going to pick all this up again." Byron is surveying me pityingly.

"Yes, I am!"

"Lexi, face it. You're mentally ill. You shouldn't be putting your head under this kind of strain—"

"I'm not *mentally ill*!" I exclaim furiously, and get to my feet. I push roughly past Byron and out the door, and Clare looks up in alarm, snapping her mobile phone shut.

"Hi, Lexi. Did you want something? A cup of coffee?"

She looks terrified, like I'm about to bite her head off or fire her or something. Okay, now is my chance to show her I'm not a bitch-boss-from-hell. I'm *me*.

"Hi, Clare!" I say in my most friendly, warm manner, and perch on the corner of her desk. "Everything okay?"

"Um . . . yes." Her eyes are wide and wary.

"I just wondered if you'd like me to get you a coffee?"

"You?" She stares as though suspecting a trick. "Get me a coffee?"

"Yes! Why not?" I beam, and she flinches.

"It's . . . it's okay." She slides out of her chair, her eyes fixed on me as though she thinks I really *am* a cobra. "I'll get one."

"Wait!" I say almost desperately. "You know, Clare, I'd like to get to know you better. Maybe one day we could have lunch together . . . hang out . . . go shopping . . ."

Clare looks even more pole-axed than before.

"Um . . . yeah. Okay, Lexi," she mumbles, and scuttles down the corridor. I turn to see Byron still in the doorway, cracking up.

"What?" I snap.

"You really are a different person, aren't you?" He raises his eyebrows in wonder.

"Maybe I just want to be friendly with my staff and treat them with respect," I say defiantly. "Anything wrong with that?"

"No!" Byron lifts his hands. "Lexi, that's a great idea." He runs his eyes over me, that sarcastic smile still at his lips, then clicks his tongue as though remembering something. "That reminds me. Before I shoot off, there's one thing I left for you to deal with as director of the department. I thought it only right."

At last. He's treating me like the boss.

"Oh, yes?" I lift my chin. "What is it?"

"We've had an e-mail from on high about people abusing lunch hours." He reaches into his pocket and produces a piece of paper. "SJ wants all directors to give their teams a bollocking. Today, preferably." Byron raises his eyebrows innocently. "Can I leave that one to you?"

• • •

Bastard. *Bastard*.

I'm pacing about my office, sipping my coffee, my stomach churning with nerves. I've never told anyone off before. Let alone a whole department. Let alone while simultaneously trying to prove that I'm really friendly and not a bitch-boss-from-hell.

I look yet again at the printed-out e-mail from Natasha, Simon Johnson's personal assistant.

Colleagues. It has come to Simon's attention that members of staff are regularly pushing the limit of lunchtime well beyond the standard hour. This is unacceptable. He would be grateful if you could make this plain to your teams ASAP, and enforce a stricter policy of checks.

Thanks.
Natasha

Okay. The point is, it doesn't actually *say* "give your department a bollocking." I don't need to be aggressive or anything. I can make the point while still being pleasant.

Maybe I can be all jokey and friendly! I'll start off, "Hey, guys! Are your lunch hours long enough?" I'll roll my eyes to show I'm being ironic and everyone will laugh, and someone will say, "Is there a problem, Lexi?" And I'll smile ruefully and say, "It's not me, it's the stuffed shirts upstairs. So let's just try and make it back on time, yeah?" And a few people will nod as though to say "fair enough." And it'll all be fine.

Yes. That sounds good. Taking a deep breath, I fold the paper and put it away in my pocket, then head out of my office, into the open-plan main Flooring office.

There's the chatter and buzz of people on the phone and typing and chatting to each other. For about a minute no one even notices me. Then Fi looks up and nudges Carolyn, and she prods a girl I don't recognize, who brings her phone conversation to an end. Around the room, receivers go down and people look up from their screens and chairs swivel around, until gradually the whole office has come to a standstill.

"Hi, everyone!" I say, my face prickling. "I... um...Hey, guys! How's it going?"

No one replies, or even acknowledges that I've spoken. They're all just staring up with the same mute, get-on-with-it expression.

"Anyway!" I try to sound bright and cheerful. "I just wanted to say...Are your lunch hours long enough?"

"What?" The girl at my old desk looks blank. "Are we allowed longer ones?"

"No!" I say hurriedly. "I mean...they're *too* long."

"I think they're fine." She shrugs. "An hour's just right for a bit of shopping."

"Yeah," agrees another girl. "You can just make it to the King's Road and back."

Okay, I am really not getting my point across here. And now two girls in the corner have started talking again.

"Listen, everyone! Please!" My voice is becoming shrill. "I have to tell you something. About lunch hours. Some people in the company...um...I mean, not necessarily any of *you*—"

"Lexi," says Carolyn clearly. "What the fuck are you talking about?" Fi and Debs explode with laughter and my face flames with color.

"Look, guys," I try to keep my composure. "This is serious."

"Seriousssss," someone echoes, and there are sniggers about the room. "It's sssserioussssss."

"Very funny!" I try to smile. "But listen, seriously..."

"Sssseriousssly..."

Now almost everyone in the room seems to be hissing or laughing or both. All the faces are alive; everyone's enjoying the joke, except me. All of a sudden a paper airplane flies past my ear and lands on the floor. I jump with shock and the entire office erupts with gales of laughter.

"Okay, well, look, just don't take too long over lunch, okay?" I say desperately.

No one's listening. Another paper airplane hits me on the nose, followed by an eraser. In spite of myself, tears spring to my eyes.

"Anyway, I'll see you guys!" I manage. "Thanks for...for all your hard work." With laughter following me I turn and stumble out of the office. In a daze, I head toward the ladies' room, passing Dana on the way.

"Going to the bathroom, Lexi?" she says in surprise as I'm pushing my way in. "You know, you have a key to the executive washroom! Much nicer!"

"I'm fine in here." I force a smile. "Really."

I head straight for the end cubicle, slam the door shut, and sink down with my head in my hands, feeling the tension drain from my body. That was the single most humiliating experience of my life.

Except for the white swimsuit episode.

Why did I ever want to be a boss? *Why?* All that happens is you lose your friends and have to give people bollockings and everyone hisses at you. And for what? A sofa in your office? A posh business card?

At last, wearily, I lift my head, and find myself focusing on the back of the cubicle door, which is covered in graffiti as usual. We've always used this door like a kind of message board, to vent, or make jokes or just silly conversation. It gets fuller and fuller, then someone scrubs it clean and we start again. The cleaners have never said anything, and none of the executives ever comes in here—so it's pretty safe.

I'm running my eye down the messages, smiling at some libelous story about Simon Johnson, when a new message in blue marker catches my eye. It's in Debs's handwriting and it reads: "The Cobra's back."

And underneath, in faint black Biro: "Don't worry, I spat in her coffee."

• • •

There's only one way to go. And that's to get really, really, *really* drunk. An hour later and I'm slumped at the bar at the Bathgate Hotel, around the corner from work, finishing my third mojito. Already the world has turned a little blurry—but that's fine by me. As far as I'm concerned, the blurrier the better. Just as long as I can keep my balance on this bar stool.

"Hi." I lift my hand to get the attention of the barman. "I'd like another one, please."

The barman raises his eyebrows very slightly, then says, "Of course."

I watch him a touch resentfully as he gets out the mint. Isn't he going to ask me *why* I want another one? Isn't he going to offer me some homespun barman wisdom?

He puts the cocktail on a coaster and adds a bowl of peanuts, which I push aside scornfully. I don't want anything soaking up the alcohol. I want it right in my bloodstream.

"Can I get you anything else? A snack, perhaps?"

He gestures at a small menu, but I ignore it and take a deep gulp of the mojito. It's cold and tangy and limey and perfect.

"Do I look like a bitch to you?" I say as I look up. "Honestly?"

"No." The barman smiles.

"Well, I am, apparently." I take another slug of mojito. "That's what all my friends say."

"Some friends."

"They used to be." I put my cocktail down and stare at it morosely. "I don't know where my life went wrong."

I sound slurred, even to my own ears.

"That's what they all say." A guy sitting at the end of the bar looks up from his *Evening Standard*. He has an American accent and dark, receding hair. "No one knows where it went wrong."

"No, but I *really* don't know." I lift a finger impressively. "I have a car crash . . . and boom! I wake up and I'm trapped in the body of a bitch."

"Looks like you're trapped in the body of a babe to me." The American guy edges along to the next bar stool, a smile on his face. "I wouldn't trade that body for anything."

I gaze at him in puzzlement for a moment—until realization dawns.

"Oh! You're *flirting* with me! Sorry. But I'm already married. To a guy. My husband." I lift up my left hand, locate my wedding ring after a few moments, and point at it. "You see. Married." I think intently for a moment. "Also, I may have a lover."

There's a muffled snort from the barman. I look up suspiciously, but his face is straight. I take another gulp of my drink and feel the alcohol kicking in, dancing around my head. My ears are buzzing and the room is starting to sway.

Which is a good thing. Rooms *should* sway.

"You know, I'm not drinking to forget," I say conversationally to the barman. "I already forgot everything." This suddenly strikes me as being so funny, I start giggling uncontrollably. "I had one bang on the head and I forgot everything." I'm clutching my stomach; tears are edging out of my eyes. "I even forgot I had a husband. But I do!"

"Uh-huh." The barman is exchanging glances with the American guy.

"And they said there isn't a cure. But you know, doctors can be wrong, can't they?" I appeal to the bar. Quite a few people seem to be listening now, and a couple of them nod.

"Doctors are always wrong," the American guy says emphatically. "They're all assholes."

"Exactly!" I swivel to him. "You are so right! Okay." I take a deep gulp of my mojito, then turn back to the barman. "Can I ask you a small favor? Can you take that cocktail shaker and hit me over the head with it? They said it wouldn't work, but how do they *know*?"

The barman smiles, as if he thinks I'm joking.

"Great." I sigh impatiently. "I'll have to do it my-self." Before he can stop me, I grab the cocktail shaker and whack myself on the forehead. "Ow!" I drop the shaker and clutch my head. "Ouch! That hurt!"

"Did you see that?" I can hear someone exclaiming behind me. "She's a nutter!"

"Miss, are you all right?" The barman looks alarmed. "Can I call you a—"

"Wait!" I lift a hand. For a few moments I'm poised, completely still, waiting for memories to flood into my brain. Then I subside in disappointment. "It didn't work. Not even one. Bugger."

"I'd get her a strong black coffee," I can hear the American guy saying in an undertone to the barman. Bloody nerve. I don't *want* a coffee. I'm about to tell him this, when my phone beeps. After a small struggle with the zipper of my bag I get my phone out—and it's a text from Eric.

Hi, on my way home. E

"That's from my husband," I inform the barman as I put away my phone. "You know, he can drive a speedboat."

"Great," says the barman politely.

"Yeah. It is." I nod emphatically, about seven times. "It *is* great. It's the perfect, perfect marriage . . ." I con-sider for a moment. "Except we haven't had sex."

"You haven't had sex?" the American guy echoes in astonishment.

"We have *had* sex." I take a slug of mojito and lean toward him confidentially. "I just don't remember it."

"That good, huh?" He starts to laugh. "Blew your mind, huh?"

Blew my mind. His words land in my mind like a big neon flashing light. *Blew my mind.*

"You know what?" I say slowly. "You may not realize it, but that's very sig . . . sigficant . . . significant."

I'm not sure that word came out quite right. But *I* know what I mean. If I have sex, maybe it'll blow my mind. Maybe that's just what I need! Maybe Amy was right all along, it's nature's own amnesia-cure.

"I'm going to do it." I put my glass down with a crash. "I'm going to have sex with my husband!"

"You go, girl!" says the American, laughing. "Have fun."

• • •

I'm going to have sex with Eric. This is my mission. As I ride home in a taxi I'm quite excited. As soon as I get back, I'll jump him. And we'll have amazing sex and my mind will be blown and suddenly everything will be clear.

The only tiny snag I can think of is I don't have the marriage manual on me. And I can't *totally* remember the order of foreplay.

I close my eyes, trying to ignore my dizzy head and recall exactly what Eric wrote. Something was in a clockwise direction. And something else was with "gentle, then urgent tongue strokes." Thighs? Chest? I should have memorized it. Or written it on a Post-it; I could have stuck it on the headboard.

Okay, I think I have it. Buttocks first, then inner thighs, *then* scrotum...

"Sorry?" says the taxi driver.

Oops. I didn't realize I was speaking aloud.

"Nothing!" I say hastily.

Earlobes came in somewhere, I suddenly remember. Maybe *that* was the urgent tongue strokes. Anyway, it doesn't matter. What I can't remember I'll make up. I mean, it can't be that we're some boring old married couple and do it *exactly the same way* each time, can it?

Can it?

I feel a tiny qualm, which I ignore. It's going to be great. Plus, I have fantastic underwear on. Silky and matching, and everything. I don't even *possess* anything scaggy anymore.

We draw up in front of the building and I pay the taxi driver. As I travel up in the lift I remove the chewing gum that I've been chewing for fresh breath, and unbutton my shirt a bit.

Too far. You can see my bra.

I do it up again, let myself into the apartment, and call out, "Eric!"

There's no answer, so I head toward the office. I am quite drunk, to tell the truth. I'm lurching on my heels, and the walls are going backward and forward in my field of vision. We'd better not try and do it standing up.

I arrive at the door of the office and look for a few

moments at Eric, who's working at his computer. On the screen I can see the brochure for Blue 42, his new building. The launch party is in a few days, and he's spending all his time preparing his presentation.

Okay, what he should do now is sense the charged sexual vibe in the room, turn around, and see me. But he doesn't.

"Eric," I say in my most husky, sensual voice—but still he doesn't move. Suddenly I realize he's wearing earphones. "Eric!" I yell, and at last he turns around. He pulls out his earphones and smiles.

"Hi. Good day?"

"Eric...take me." I push a hand through my hair. "Let's do it. Blow my mind."

He peers at me for a few seconds. "Sweetheart, have you been drinking?"

"I may have had a couple of cocktails. Or three." I nod, then hold on to the door frame for balance. "The point is, they made me realize what I want. What I *need*. Sex."

"Oooo-kay." Eric raises his eyebrows. "Maybe you should sober up, have something to eat. Gianna made us a great seafood stew—"

"I don't want seafood stew!" I feel like stamping my foot. "We have to *do* it! It's the only way I'll ever remember!"

What's wrong with him? I was expecting him to leap on me, but instead he's rubbing his forehead with the back of his fist.

"Lexi, I don't want to rush you into anything. This is a big decision. The doctor at the hospital said we should only go to whatever stage you're comfortable with...."

"Well, I'm comfortable with us doing it right now." I undo two more buttons, exposing my La Perla under-wire plunge bra. *God*, my boobs look great in this.

I mean, they ought to, for sixty quid.

"Come on." I lift my chin in a challenging way. "I'm your wife."

I can see Eric's mind working as he stares at me.

"Well...okay!" He closes his document and turns off the computer, then walks over, puts his arms around me, and starts kissing me. And it's...nice.

It is. It's...pleasant.

His mouth is quite soft. I noticed that before. It's a bit weird for a man. I mean, it's not exactly *un*sexy, but—

"Are you comfortable, Lexi?" Eric's breathy voice comes in my ear.

"Yes!" I whisper back.

"Shall we move to the bedroom?"

"Okay!"

Eric leads the way out of the office and I follow him, stumbling slightly on my heels. It all seems a bit oddly formal, like he's showing me in to a job interview.

In the bedroom, we resume kissing. Eric seems really into it, but I have no idea what I'm supposed to do next. I glimpse the marriage manual on the ottoman and wonder if I could quickly nudge it open with my toe. Except Eric might notice.

Now he's pulling me down onto the bed. I have to reciprocate. But with what? Eeny-meeny-miney— No.

Stop it. I'm going to go with...chest. Unbutton the shirt. Sweeping strokes. Clockwise.

He does have a good chest. I'll give him that. Firm and muscled from the hour he spends in the gym every day.

"Are you comfortable with me touching your breast?" he murmurs as he starts undoing my bra.

"I guess so," I murmur back.

Why is he squeezing me? It's like he's buying fruit. He's going to give me a bruise in a minute.

Anyway. Stop being picky. This is all great. I have a fab husband with a fab body and we're in bed and—

Ouch. That was my *nipple.*

"I'm sorry," whispers Eric. "Listen, sweetheart, are you comfortable with me touching your abdomen?"

"Er...I guess!"

Why did he ask that? Why would I be comfortable with the breast and not the abdomen? That doesn't make sense. And to be absolutely honest, I don't know if *comfortable* is the word. This is all a bit surreal. We're moving around and panting and doing it all like in a book, but I don't feel like I'm *going* anywhere.

Eric's breath is hot on my neck. I think it's time for me to do something else. Buttocks, maybe, or...Oh, right. From the way Eric's hands are moving, looks like we're jumping straight to inner thighs.

"You're hot," he's saying, his voice urgent. "Jesus, you're hot. This is so hot."

I don't believe this! He says *hot* the whole time too! He should *so* have sex with Debs.

Oh. No. Obviously he shouldn't have sex with Debs. Erase that thought.

Suddenly I realize I'm about three steps behind on the whole foreplay thing, not to mention the sex talk. But Eric doesn't even seem to have noticed.

"Lexi, sweetheart?" he murmurs breathily, right in my ear.

"Yes?" I whisper back, wondering if he's about to say "I love you."

"Are you comfortable with me putting my penis into your—"

Uurk!

Before I can stop myself, I've pushed him off me and rolled away.

Oops. I didn't mean to shove quite so hard.

"What's wrong?" Eric sits up in alarm. "Lexi! What happened? Are you okay? Did you have a flashback?"

"No." I bite my lip. "I'm sorry. I just suddenly felt a bit ... um ..."

"I knew it. I *knew* we were rushing things." Eric sighs and takes both my hands. "Lexi, talk to me. Why weren't you comfortable? Was it because of some ... traumatic memory resurfacing?"

Oh God. He looks so earnest. I have to lie.

No. I can't lie. Marriages only work if you're totally honest.

"It wasn't because of a traumatic memory," I say at last, carefully looking past him at the duvet. "It was because you said 'penis.' "

"Penis?" Eric looks utterly stumped. "What's wrong with 'penis'?"

"It's just . . . you know. Not very sexy. As words go."

Eric leans back against the headboard, his brow knitted in a frown.

"I find 'penis' sexy," he says at last.

"Oh, right!" I backtrack quickly. "Well, I mean, obviously it is *quite* sexy . . ."

How can he find the word "penis" sexy?

"Anyway, it wasn't just that." I hastily change the subject. "It was the way you kept asking me every two seconds if I was comfortable. It made things a bit . . . formal. Don't you think?"

"I'm just trying to be considerate," says Eric stiffly. "This is a pretty strange situation for both of us." He turns away and starts pulling on his shirt with jerky gestures.

"I know!" I say quickly. "And I appreciate it, I really do." I put a hand on his shoulder. "But maybe we can loosen up. Be more . . . spontaneous?"

Eric's silent for a while, as though weighing up what I've said.

"So . . . should I sleep here tonight?" he says at last.

"Oh!" In spite of myself I recoil.

What's *wrong* with me? Eric's my husband. A moment ago I was all for having sex with him. But still, the idea of him sleeping here with me all night seems . . . too intimate.

"Maybe we could leave it a while. I'm sorry, it's just . . ."

"Fine. I understand." Without meeting my eye he gets up. "I think I'll take a shower."

"Okay."

Left alone, I slump back on the pillows. Great. I didn't have sex. I didn't remember anything. My mission totally failed.

I find "penis" sexy.

I give a sudden gurgle and clap my hand over my mouth in case he can hear me. Beside the bed the phone starts ringing, but at first I don't move—it's bound to be for Eric. Then I realize he must be in the shower. I reach over and pick up the state-of-the-art Bang & Olufsen receiver.

"Hello?"

"Hi," comes a dry, familiar voice. "It's Jon."

"Jon?" I feel a white-hot thrill. Eric's nowhere in sight, but even so, I dart into the adjoining bathroom with the phone, then shut the door and lock it.

"Are you crazy?" I hiss in lowered, furious tones. "What are you ringing here for? It's so risky! What if Eric picked up?"

"I was expecting Eric to pick up." Jon sounds a bit baffled. "I need to speak with him."

"Oh." I halt in sudden realization. I'm so *stupid.* "Oh . . . right." Trying to remedy the situation, I put on a formal, wifely voice. "Of course, Jon. I'll just fetch him—"

Jon cuts me off. "But I need to speak with you more. We have to meet. We have to talk."

"We can't! You have to stop this. This whole . . . talking thing. On the phone. And also not on the phone."

"Lexi, are you drunk?" says Jon.

"No." I survey my bloodshot reflection. "Okay . . . maybe a tad."

There's a snuffling sound at the end of the phone. Is he *laughing*?

"I love you," he says.

"You don't know me."

"I love the girl . . . you were. You are."

"You love the Cobra?" I retort sharply. "You love the bitch from hell? Well then, you must be nuts."

"You're not a bitch from hell." He's definitely laughing at me.

"Everyone else seems to think I am. Was. Whatever."

"You were unhappy. And you made some pretty big mistakes. But you weren't a bitch."

Beneath my drunken haze, I'm absorbing every word. It's like he's rubbing salve on some raw part of me. I want to hear more.

"What . . ." I swallow. "What kind of mistakes?"

"I'll tell you when we meet. We'll talk about everything. Lexi, I've missed you so much. . . ."

Suddenly his intimate, familiar tone is making me uneasy. Here I am, in my own bathroom, whispering to a guy I don't know. What am I getting into here?

"Stop. Just . . . stop!" I cut across him. "I need to . . . think."

I pace to the other side of the room, thrusting my hand through my hair, trying to force some rational thoughts into my giddy head. We could meet, and just talk . . .

No. *No.* I can't start seeing someone behind Eric's back. I want my marriage to work.

"Eric and I just had sex!" I say defiantly.

I'm not even quite sure why I said that.

There's silence down the line and I wonder whether Jon is so offended he's gone. Well, if he has, that's a *good* thing.

"Your point would be?" His voice comes down the line.

"You know. That changes things, surely."

"I'm not following. You think I won't be in love with you anymore because you had sex with Eric?"

"I...I don't know. Maybe."

"Or you think having sex with Eric somehow proves you love him?" He's relentless.

"I don't know!" I say again, rattled. I shouldn't even be having this conversation. I should be marching straight out of the bathroom, holding the phone aloft, calling, "Darling? It's Jon for you."

But something's keeping me here, the receiver clamped to my ear.

"I thought it might trigger my memories," I say at last, sitting on the side of the bath. "I just keep thinking, maybe my memory's all there, all locked up, and if only I could get to it...It's so *frustrating*..."

"Tell me about it," Jon says wryly, and I suddenly imagine him standing in his gray T-shirt and jeans, scrunching his face up in that way he does, holding the phone with one hand, the other elbow bent with his hand behind his head, a glimpse of armpit—

The image is so vivid that I blink.

"So, how was it? The sex." His tone has changed, is easier.

"It was..." I clear my throat. "You know. Sex. You know about sex."

"I do know about sex," he agrees. "I also know about sex with Eric. He's adept...considerate...He has quite the imagination..."

"Stop it! You're making all of those sound like *bad* qualities—"

"We have to meet," Jon cuts in. "Seriously."

"We can't." I feel a fearful quake deep inside me. Like I'm about to step over an edge. Like I have to stop myself.

"I miss you so much." His voice is lower, softer. "Lexi, you have no idea how much I miss you, it's tearing me up, not being with you—"

My hand is damp around the phone. I can't listen to him anymore. It's confusing me; it's shaking me up. Because if it was true, if everything he was saying was really true—

"Look, I have to go," I say in a rush. "I'll get Eric for you." My legs wobbly, I unlock the bathroom door and head out, holding the phone away from me like it's contaminated.

"Lexi, wait." I can hear his voice coming from the phone, but I ignore it.

"Eric!" I call brightly as I approach his door and he comes out, dressed in a towel. "Darling? It's Jon for you. Jon the architect."

Chapter Thirteen

I've tried. I really have tried. I've done everything I can think of to show the department that I'm not a bitch.

I've put up a poster asking for suggestions for a fun department outing—but no one's filled any in. I've put flowers on the windowsills, but no one's even mentioned them. Today I brought in a massive basket of blueberry, vanilla, and chocolate-chip muffins and put it on the photocopier, together with a sign saying *From Lexi—Help Yourself!*

I took a stroll into the office a few minutes ago and not a single muffin had been taken. But never mind, it's still early. I'll leave it another ten minutes before I go and check again.

I turn a page in the file I've been reading, then click on the onscreen document. I'm working through paper files and computer files at the same time, trying to cross-reference everything. Without meaning to, I give an enormous yawn and lean my head on the desk. I'm tired. I mean, I'm *knackered.* I've been coming in every morning at seven, just to get through some more of this mountain of paperwork. My eyes are red from all the endless reading.

I nearly didn't come back here at all. The day after Eric and I "kind of" had sex, I woke up with a pale face, the most crashing headache, and absolutely no desire to go to work again, ever. I staggered into the kitchen, made a cup of tea with three spoonfuls of sugar, then sat down and wrote out on a sheet of paper, wincing at every movement:

OPTIONS
1. Give up.
2. Don't give up.

I stared at it for ages. Then at last I put a line through *Give up*.

The thing with giving up is you never know. You never know whether you could have done the job. And I'm sick of not knowing about my life. So here I am, in my office, reading through a debate on carpet-fiber cost trends, dating from 2005. Just in case it's important.

No. Come on. It can't be important. I close the file, stand up, shake out my legs, then tiptoe to my door. I open it a crack and peek hopefully out at the main office. I can just glimpse the basket through the window. It's still intact.

I feel totally squashed. What's *wrong*? Why is no one taking any? Maybe I'll just make it absolutely clear that these muffins are for everyone. I head out of my room, into the main open-plan office.

"Hi there!" I say brightly. "I just wanted to say,

these muffins are from me to all of you. Fresh from the bakery this morning. So...go ahead! Help yourself!"

No one answers. No one even acknowledges my presence. Did I suddenly become invisible?

"So, anyway." I force myself to smile. "Enjoy!" I swivel on my heel and walk out.

I've done my bit. If they want the muffins, they want them. If they don't, they don't. End of subject. I really don't care either way. I sit back down at my desk, open a recent financial report, and start running my finger down the relevant columns. After a few moments I lean back, rubbing my eyes with my fists. These figures are just confirming what I already know: the department performance is terrible.

Sales went up in the last year by a bit, but they're still far, far too low. We're going to be in real trouble if we don't turn things around. I mentioned it to Byron the other day—and he didn't even seem bothered. How can he be so blasé? I make a memo on a Post-it— "Discuss sales with Byron." Then I put my pen down.

Why don't they want my muffins?

I was really optimistic when I bought them this morning. I imagined everyone's faces lighting up at the sight, and people saying "What a nice thought, Lexi. Thanks!" But now I'm crestfallen. They must totally hate me. I mean, you'd have to loathe someone to refuse a muffin, wouldn't you? And these are really deluxe ones. They're fat and fresh and the blueberry ones have even got lemon icing on them.

A tiny, sensible voice in my head is telling me to

leave it. Forget about it. It's only a basket of muffins, for God's sake.

But I can't. I can't just sit here. On impulse I leap to my feet again and head into the main office. There's the basket, still untouched. Everyone is typing away or on the phone, ignoring both me and the muffins.

"So!" I try to sound relaxed. "Nobody wants a muffin? They're really nice ones!"

"Muffin?" Fi says at last, her brow wrinkled. "I can't see any muffins." She looks around the office as though baffled. "Anyone seen any muffins?"

Everyone shrugs, as though equally baffled.

"Do you mean an English muffin?" Carolyn's brow is wrinkled. "Or a French muffin?"

"They do muffins at Starbucks. I could send out if you like," Debs says, barely hiding her giggles.

Ha-ha. Really funny.

"Fine!" I say, trying to hide my hurt. "If you want to be childish about it, then that's fine. Just forget it. I was only trying to be nice."

Breathing hard, I stalk out again. I can hear the sniggers and giggles behind me, but I try to block my ears. I have to keep my dignity; I have to be calm and bosslike. I mustn't rise. I mustn't react.

Oh God. I can't help it. Hurt and anger are rising through me like a volcano. How can they be so mean?

"Actually, it's not fine." I march back into the office, my face burning. "Look, I went to a lot of time and trouble to get these muffins, because I thought it would be nice to give you a treat, and now you're pretending you can't even *see* them..."

"I'm sorry, Lexi." Fi appears blank and apologetic. "I honestly don't know what you're talking about."

Carolyn snorts with laughter—and something inside me snaps.

"I'm talking about this!" I grab a chocolate-chip muffin and brandish it at Fi's face, and she shrinks away. "It's a muffin! It's a bloody muffin! Well, fine! If you're not going to eat it, then I will!" I stuff the muffin into my mouth and start chewing it furiously, then take another bite. Huge crumbs are falling all over the floor, but I don't care. "In fact, I'll eat all of them!" I add. "Why not?" I grab an iced blueberry muffin and cram that in my mouth too. "Mmm, yum!"

"Lexi?" I turn and my insides shrivel up. Simon Johnson and Byron are standing at the door to the office.

Byron looks like he wants to burst with delight. Simon's regarding me as though I'm the crazy gorilla throwing its food around at the zoo.

"S-Simon!" I splutter muffin crumbs in horror. "Um...hi! How are you?"

"I just wanted a quick word, if you're not...busy?" Simon raises his eyebrows.

"Of course not!" I smooth my hair down, desperately trying to swallow my mouthful. "Come through to my office."

As I pass by the glass door I catch my reflection and wince at my eyes, all red from tiredness. My hair looks a bit all over the place too. Maybe I should have put it up. Oh well, nothing I can do about it now.

"So, Lexi," Simon says as I close the door and dump

my half-eaten muffins on the desk. "I just had a good meeting with Byron about June '07. I'm sure he's been filling you in on developments."

"Sure." I nod, trying to look like I know what he's referring to. But "June '07" means absolutely nothing to me. Is something happening then?

"I'm scheduling in a final decision meeting for Monday. I won't say any more just now. Obviously discretion is crucial...." Simon breaks off, his forehead suddenly furrowed. "I know you've had reservations, Lexi. We all have. But really, there are no more options."

What's he talking about? *What?*

"Well, Simon, I'm sure we can work it out," I bluff, desperately hoping he won't ask me to elaborate.

"Good girl, Lexi. Knew you'd come around." He raises his voice again, sounding more cheerful. "I'm seeing James Garrison later on, the new guy at Southeys. What do you make of him?"

Thank God. At last, something I've heard of.

"Ah yes," I say briskly. "Well, unfortunately I gather Southeys isn't up to scratch, Simon. We'll have to look elsewhere for a distributor."

"I beg to differ, Lexi!" Byron cuts in with a laugh. "Southeys has just offered us an improved rate and service package." He turns to Simon. "I was with them all day last week, along with Keith from Soft Furnishings. James Garrison has turned the place around. We were impressed."

My face is burning. *Bastard.*

"Lexi, don't you agree with Byron?" Simon turns to me in surprise. "Have you met James Garrison?"

"I...um...no, I haven't." I swallow. "I'm...I'm sure you're right, Byron."

He has completely shafted me. On purpose.

There's a horrible pause. I can see Simon regarding me with puzzled disappointment. "Right," he says at last. "Well, I must be off. Good to see you, Lexi."

"Bye, Simon." I usher him out of my office, trying my best to sound confident and senior-management-like. "Look forward to catching up again soon. Maybe we can do that lunch sometime..."

"Hey, Lexi," Byron says suddenly, gesturing at my bum. "There's something on your skirt." I grope behind me, and find myself peeling off a Post–it. I look at it—and the ground seems to swivel beneath me like quicksand. Someone's printed, in pink felt-tip: *I fancy Simon Johnson.*

I can't look at Simon Johnson. My head feels like it's about to explode.

Byron snorts with laughter. "There's another one." He jerks his head and numbly I peel off a second Post-it: *Simon, do it to me!*

"Just a silly prank!" I crumple up the Post-its desperately. "The staff having a bit of...fun...."

Simon Johnson doesn't look amused.

"Right," he says after a pause. "Well, I'll see you, Lexi."

He turns on his heel and heads away, down the corridor, with Byron. After a moment I hear Byron saying, "Simon, *now* do you see? She's absolutely..."

I stand there, watching them go, still quivering in shock. That's it. My career's ruined before I've even had a chance to try it out. In a daze I walk back into my office and sink into my chair. I can't do this job. I'm knackered. Byron's shafted me. No one wants my muffins.

At that last thought I feel an enormous pang of hurt—and then suddenly I can't help it, a tear is running down my face. I bury my face in my arms and soon I'm convulsing with sobs. I thought it was going to be so great. I thought being boss would be fun and exciting. I never realized...I never thought...

"Hi." A voice pierces my thoughts and I raise my head to see Fi standing just inside the doorway.

"Oh. Hi." I wipe my eyes roughly. "Sorry. I was just..."

"Are you okay?" she says awkwardly.

"I'm fine. Fine." I scrabble in my desk drawer for a tissue and blow my nose. "Can I do anything for you?"

"Sorry about the Post-its." She bites her lip. "We never thought Simon would come down. It was just supposed to be a laugh."

" 'S all right." My voice is shaky. "You weren't to know."

"What did he say?"

"He wasn't impressed." I sigh. "But he's not impressed with me anyway, so what's the difference?" I tear off a bit of chocolate-chip muffin, stuff it in my mouth, and feel immediately better. For about a nanosecond.

Fi is just staring at me.

"I thought you didn't eat carbs anymore," she says at last.

"Yeah, right. Like I could live without chocolate." I take another massive bite of muffin. "Women need chocolate. It's a scientific fact."

There's silence, and I look up to see Fi still gazing at me uncertainly. "It's so strange," she says. "You sound like the old Lexi."

"I *am* the old Lexi." I feel suddenly weary at having to explain all over again. "Fi...imagine you woke up tomorrow and it was suddenly 2010. And you had to slot into some new life and be some new person. Well, that's what this is like for me." I break off another piece of muffin and survey it for a few moments, then put it down again. "And I don't recognize the new person. I don't know why she is like she is. And it's kind of...it's hard."

There's a long silence. I'm staring fixedly at the desk, breathing hard, crumbling the muffin into little pieces. I don't dare look up, in case Fi says something else sarcastic or laughs at me and I burst into tears again.

"Lexi, I'm sorry." When she speaks, her voice is so quiet, I barely hear it. "I didn't...we didn't realize. I mean, you don't *look* any different."

"I know." I give her a rueful smile. "I look like a brunette Barbie." I lift a strand of chestnut hair and let it fall. "When I saw myself in the mirror in hospital, I nearly died of shock. I didn't know who I was."

"Look..." She's chewing her lip and twisting her bangles. "I'm sorry. About the muffins, and the Post-its and...everything. Why don't you have lunch with us today?" She comes toward the desk with a sudden eagerness. "Let's start again."

"That'd be nice." I give her a grateful smile. "But I can't today. I'm seeing Loser Dave for lunch."

"Loser *Dave*?" She sounds so shocked, I can't help laughing. "Why are you seeing him? Lexi, you're not thinking of—"

"No! Of course not! I'm just trying to work out what's happened in my life during the last three years. Put the pieces together." I hesitate, suddenly realizing that Fi probably has the answers to all my questions. "Fi, do you know how it ended with me and Loser Dave?"

"No idea." Fi shrugs. "You never told us how you broke up. You shut us all out. Even me. It was like... all you cared about was your career. So in the end we stopped trying."

I can see a flicker of hurt in her face.

"I'm sorry, Fi," I say awkwardly. "I didn't mean to shut you out. At least, I don't *think* I did...." It's surreal, apologizing for something I have no memory of. Like I'm a werewolf or something.

"Don't worry. It wasn't you. I mean, it *was* you.... but it *wasn't* you...." Fi trails off. She seems pretty confused too.

"I'd better go." I glance at my watch and get to my feet. "Maybe Loser Dave will have some answers."

"Hey, Lexi," says Fi, looking embarrassed. "You missed one." She jerks her thumb at my skirt. I reach behind and pull off yet another Post-it. It reads *Simon Johnson: I would.*

"I so *wouldn't*," I say, crumpling it.

"Wouldn't you?" Fi grins wickedly. "I would."

"No, you wouldn't!" I can't help a giggle at her expression.

"I reckon he's quite fit."

"He's ancient! He probably can't even do it anymore." I catch her eye and suddenly we're both laughing helplessly, like in the old days. I drop my jacket and sit on the arm of the sofa, clutching my stomach, unable to stop. I don't think I've laughed like this since the accident. It's like all my strains and tensions are coming out; everything's being laughed away.

"God, I've missed you," Fi says at last, still gulping.

"I've missed you too." I take a deep breath, trying to collect my thoughts. "Fi, really. I'm sorry for whatever I was like . . . or whatever I did—"

"Don't be a sap." Fi cuts me off kindly but firmly, handing me my jacket. "Go and see Loser Dave."

. . .

Loser Dave's done really well for himself, it turns out. I mean, *really* well. He now works for Auto Repair Workshop at their head office, and has some quite senior sales role. As he gets out of the lift, he's all dapper in a pin-striped suit, with much longer hair than the buzz cut he used to have, and rimless glasses. I can't help jumping up from my seat in the lobby and exclaiming, "Loser Dave! Look at *you*!"

Immediately he winces, and looks warily around the lobby. "No one calls me Loser Dave anymore," he snaps in a low voice. "I'm David, okay?"

"Oh, right. Sorry...er...David. Not Butch?" I can't resist adding, and he shoots me a glare.

His paunch has disappeared too, I notice as he leans against the foyer desk to talk to the receptionist. He must be working out properly these days, as opposed to his old routine, which was five heaves of a dumbbell, followed by cracking open a beer and turning on the soccer.

Now I look back, I can't believe I put up with him. Scuzzy boxer shorts littered over his flat. Crude, anti-feminist jokes. Complete paranoia that I was desperate to trap him into marriage and three kids and domestic drudgery.

I mean. *He* should be so lucky.

"You're looking good, Lexi." As he turns away from the reception desk he eyes me up and down. "It's been a while. Saw you on the telly, of course. That *Ambition* show. Kind of program I might have wanted to take part in once." He shoots me a pitying glance. "But I've leapfrogged over that level now. I'm on the fast track. Shall we go?"

I'm sorry, I just can't take Loser Dave seriously as "David the fast-track businessman." We head out of the office toward what Loser Dave calls a "good local eatery," and all the while he's on his phone, talking loudly about "deals" and "mill," his eyes constantly sliding toward me.

"Wow," I say as he puts his phone away at last. "You're really senior now."

"Got a Ford Focus." He casually shoots his cuffs. "Company AmEx card. Use of the corporate ski chalet."

"That's great!" We've reached the restaurant now, which is a small Italian place. We sit down and I lean forward, resting my chin on my hands. Loser Dave seems a bit edgy, fiddling with the plastic menu and endlessly checking his phone.

"David," I begin. "I don't know if you got the message about why I wanted to meet up?"

"My secretary told me you wanted to talk over old times?" he says cautiously.

"Yeah. The thing is, I had this car accident. And I'm trying to piece together my life, work out what happened, talk about our breakup..."

Loser Dave sighs.

"Sweetheart, is this really a good idea, dredging all that up again? We both had our say at the time."

"Dredging up all what?"

"You know..." He looks around and catches the eye of a nearby lounging waiter. "Could we get some service here? Some vino? Bottle of house red, please."

"But I *don't* know! I have no idea what happened!" I lean farther forward, trying to get his attention. "I have amnesia. Didn't your secretary explain? I don't remember anything."

Very slowly Loser Dave turns back and stares at me, as though suspecting a joke.

"You've got *amnesia*?"

"Yes! I've been in hospital, everything."

"Fuck me." He shakes his head as a waiter comes over and goes through the rigamarole of pouring and tasting. "So you don't remember anything?"

"Nothing from the last three years. And what I want

to know is, why did we split? Did something happen...or did we drift apart...or what?"

Loser Dave doesn't answer straightaway. He's eyeing me over his glass. "So is there anything you *do* remember?"

"The last thing is the night before my dad's funeral. I was in this nightclub, and I was really pissed off with you because you didn't turn up...and then I fell down some steps in the rain.... And that's all I remember."

"Yeah, yeah." He's nodding thoughtfully. "I remember that night. Well, in fact...that's why we split up."

"Why?" I say, puzzled.

"Because I never turned up. You chucked me. Finito." He takes a gulp of wine, visibly relaxing.

"*Really?*" I say, astonished. "I chucked you?"

"Next morning. You'd had enough, so that was it. We were over."

I frown as I try to imagine the scene. "So, did we have a big row?"

"Not so much a row," Loser Dave says after a moment's consideration. "More like a mature discussion. We agreed it was right to end things and you said you might be making the biggest mistake in the world, but you couldn't stop your jealous, possessive nature."

"Really?" I say dubiously.

"Yeah. I offered to come along to your dad's funeral, show support, but you turned me down, said you couldn't bear the sight of me." He takes a gulp of wine. "I didn't bear you a grudge, though. I said, 'Lexi, I will always care for you. Whatever you want, I want.'

I gave you a single rose and a final kiss. Then I walked away. It was beautiful."

I put my glass down and survey him. His gaze is as open and blameless as it used to be when he conned customers into taking extra-premium total-scam insurance on their cars.

"So that's exactly what happened?" I say.

"Word for word." He picks up the menu. "Fancy some garlic bread?"

Is it my imagination or does he seem a whole lot more cheerful since he's heard I have amnesia?

"Loser Dave...is that *really* what happened?" I give him my severest, most penetrating look.

"Of course," he says in an injured tone. "And stop calling me Loser Dave."

"Sorry." I sigh, and start unwrapping a bread stick. Maybe he's telling the truth. Or a Loser-Dave version of it, at least. Maybe I did chuck him. I was certainly pissed off with him.

"So...did anything else happen back then?" I snap the bread stick in two and start nibbling it. "Is there anything you can remember? Like, why did I suddenly get so career-oriented? Why did I shut my friends out? What was going on in my head?"

"Search me." Loser Dave is perusing the specials menu. "D'you fancy sharing the lasagne for two?"

"It's all just so...confusing." I rub my brow. "I feel like I've been plonked in the middle of a map, with one of those big arrows pointing to me. 'You Are Here.' And what I want to know is, how did I *get* here?"

At last Loser Dave lifts his eyes from the specials menu.

"What you want is GPS," he says, like the Dalai Lama making a pronouncement on top of a mountain.

"That's it! Exactly!" I lean forward eagerly. "I feel lost. And if I could just trace the path, if I could navigate back somehow..."

Loser Dave is nodding wisely. "I can do you a deal."

"What?" I say, not understanding.

"I can do you a deal on GPS." He taps his nose. "We're branching out at Auto Repair."

For a moment I think I might explode with frustration.

"I don't literally need GPS!" I almost yell. "It's a metaphor! Me-ta-phor!"

"Right, right. Yeah, of course." Loser Dave nods, his brow furrowed as though he's digesting my words and mulling them over. "Is that a built-in system?"

I don't believe it. Did I actually go out with this guy?

"Yeah, that's right," I say finally. "Honda makes it. Let's have the garlic bread."

• • •

When I arrive home later, I'm planning to ask Eric what he knows about my breakup with Loser Dave. We must have talked about all our old relationships, surely. But when I walk into the loft, I sense straightaway that this isn't the moment. He's striding around, on the phone, looking stressed.

"Come on, Lexi." He puts his hand briefly over the phone. "We'll be late."

"For what?"

"For *what*?" echoes Eric, looking as though I've asked him what gravity is. "For the launch!"

Shit. It's the Blue 42 launch party tonight. I did know that; it just slipped my mind.

"Of course," I say hurriedly. "I'll just go and get ready."

"Shouldn't your hair be up?" Eric casts a critical eye over me. "It looks unprofessional."

"Oh. Er . . . right. Yes."

Totally flustered, I change into a black silk tailored suit, put on my highest black pumps, and quickly shove my hair up into its chignon. I accessorize with diamonds, then turn to survey myself.

Aargh. I look so boring. Like an actuary or something. I need . . . something else. Don't I have any brooches anymore? Or any silk flowers or scarves or sparkly hair clips? Anything *fun*? I root around for a bit in my drawers, but can't find anything except a plain quilted beige hair band. Great. That's a real style statement.

"Ready?" Eric strides in. "You look fine. Let's go."

Jeez Louise. I've never seen him so tense and hyper before. All the way there, he's on the phone, and when at last he puts it away, he taps his fingers on it, staring out the car window.

"I'm sure it'll go really well," I say encouragingly.

"It has to," he says without turning toward me. "This is our big sales push. Lots of ultra-highs. Lots of press. This is where we turn Blue 42 into the talk of the city."

As we turn in at the entrance gates I can't help gasping. Burning torches lead the way to the front doors. Lasers are sweeping the night sky. There's a red carpet for guests to walk down and even a couple of photographers waiting. It looks like a film premiere.

"Eric, this is amazing." Impulsively I squeeze his hand. "It's going to be a triumph."

"Let's hope." For the first time Eric turns to give me a quick, tight smile. The driver opens my door, and I pick up my bag to leave.

"Oh, Lexi." Eric is feeling in his pocket. "Before I forget. I've been meaning to give you this." He hands me a piece of paper.

"What's this?" I smile as I unfold it. Then my smile kind of melts away. It's an invoice. At the top is Eric's name, but he's crossed it out and written "Assigned to Lexi Gardiner." I scan the words in disbelief. *Chelsea Bridge Glass Objets. Large Blown Leopard: quantity 1. To pay: £3,200.*

"I ordered a replacement," Eric is saying. "You can settle up anytime. Check is fine, or just put a transfer into my bank account..."

He's *invoicing* me?

"You want me to pay for the leopard?" I force a little laugh, just to see if he's joking. "Out of my own money?"

"Well, you broke it." Eric sounds surprised. "Is there a problem?"

"No! That's...that's fine." I swallow. "I'll write you a check. As soon as we get home."

"No hurry." Eric smiles, and gestures at the waiting driver, holding the door. "We'd better get going."

It's fine, I tell myself firmly. It's fair for him to invoice me. It's obviously how our marriage works.

That's not how a marriage should work.

No. Stop it. It's fine. It's lovely.

I stuff the paper into my bag and smile as brightly as I can at the driver, then get out and follow Eric along the red carpet.

Chapter Fourteen

Bloody hell. This is a real, serious, glitzy party. The whole building is alive with light and thudding music. The penthouse loft looks even more spectacular than before, with flowers everywhere, and waiters in cool black outfits holding trays of champagne, and gift bags ready for people to take. Ava and Jon, and a few other people I don't recognize, are gathered by the window, and Eric strides straight over to them.

"People," he says. "Have we done the rundown on the guests? Sarah, you've got the press list? All under control?"

"They're here." A young girl in a wrap dress comes hurrying in, almost tripping over her stilettos. "The van Gogens are early. And they've brought friends. And there's another lot right behind them!"

"Good luck, guys." Eric is high-fiving his entire team. "Let's sell this building."

The next moment a couple in expensive-looking coats enters, and Eric springs into full-charm offensive, ushering them to meet Ava, handing them champagne, and taking them over to see the view. More people are arriving, and soon there's a small crowd chattering and leafing through the brochure and eyeing the waterfall.

Jon is about ten yards away, to my left, wearing a dark suit, frowning as he talks to the van Gogens. I haven't spoken to him yet. I have no idea if he's noticed me. Occasionally I glance over at him, then quickly look away as my stomach pops over.

It's like I'm thirteen again and he's my crush. All I'm aware of in this entire roomful of people is him. Where he is, what he's doing, who he's talking to. I dart another glance at him and this time he meets my eye. Cheeks flaming, I turn away and swig my wine. Great, Lexi. Not at all obvious.

Deliberately, I swivel right away so he's out of my line of vision. I'm watching everyone arrive, almost in a trance, when Eric arrives beside me.

"Lexi, darling." He has a fixed, disapproving smile. "You look awkward, standing there on your own. Come with me."

Before I can stop him, he's leading me firmly over to Jon, who's talking to another rich-looking couple. The woman is in a Dior-print trouser suit, with dyed red hair and severely overdone lipliner. She bares her porcelain teeth at me, and her gray-haired husband grunts, his hand clamped possessively on her shoulder.

"Let me introduce my wife, Lexi." Eric beams at them. "One of the greatest fans of"—he pauses, and I tense up, waiting for it—"loft-style living!"

If I hear that phrase one more time I'm going to *shoot* myself.

"Hi, Lexi." Jon meets my eye briefly as Eric heads off again. "How are you?"

"I'm fine, thanks, Jon." I try to sound calm, like he's any other person at the party; like I haven't been fixating on him since I arrived. I turn to the Dior woman. "So . . . how do you like the loft?"

The couple exchange doubtful glances. "We have one concern," says the man, in a European accent I can't quite place. "The space. Whether it is *big* enough."

I'm stumped. This place is like a bloody aircraft hangar. How can it not be big enough?

"We think five thousand square feet is a generous size," says Jon. "However, you could knock two or even three units together if you need a larger space."

"Our other problem is the design," says the man.

"The design?" echoes Jon politely. "Is something wrong with the design?"

"At our home we have touches of gold," says the man. "Gold paintings. Gold lamps. Gold . . ." He seems to run out of steam.

"Carpets," the woman puts in, rolling the "rrr" heavily. "Gold carrr-pets."

The man jabs at the brochure. "Here I see a lot of silver. Chrome."

"I see." Jon nods, deadpan. "Well, obviously the loft can be customized to your own individual taste. We could, for example, have the fireplace gold-plated."

"A gold-plated fireplace?" says the woman uncertainly. "Would that be . . . too much?"

"Is there such a thing as too much gold?" Jon replies pleasantly. "We could also add solid gold light-fittings. And Lexi could help you with the gold carpet. Couldn't you, Lexi?"

"Of course." I nod, praying desperately I don't suddenly snort with laughter.

"Yes. Well, we will think about it." The couple moves off, talking in some foreign language I don't recognize. Jon knocks back his drink.

"Not big enough. Jesus Christ. *Ten* of our units at Ridgeway would fit into this space."

"What's Ridgeway?"

"Our affordable-housing project." He sees my blank look. "We only get planning permission for a place like this if we put up some affordable units."

"Oh, right," I say in surprise. "Eric's never even mentioned affordable housing."

A flicker of amusement passes over Jon's face. "I'd say his heart isn't totally in that aspect of the job," he says, as Eric steps up onto a small podium in front of the mantelpiece. The ambient lighting dims, a spotlight falls on Eric, and gradually the hum of chatter dies away.

"Welcome!" he says, his voice ringing out around the space. "Welcome to Blue 42, the latest in the Blue series of projects dedicated to . . ."

I hold my breath. *Please don't say it, please don't say it . . .*

"Loft-style living!" His hands sweep along and all the members of his staff applaud vigorously.

Jon glances at me and takes a step back, away from

the crowd. After a moment I move back too, my eyes fixed firmly ahead. My whole body is crackling with apprehension. And ... excitement.

"So, have you remembered anything yet?" he says in a casual undertone.

"No."

Behind Eric, a massive screen is lighting up with images of lofts from all angles. Punchy music fills the air and the room becomes even darker. I have to hand it to Eric—this is a fantastic presentation.

"You know, we first met each other at a loft launch like this one." Jon's voice is so low, I can barely hear it above the music. "The minute you spoke I knew."

"Knew what?"

"Knew I liked you."

I'm silent for a few moments, curiosity prickling at me.

"What did I say?" I whisper back at last.

"You said, 'If I hear that phrase *loft-style living* again, I'm going to shoot myself.'"

"*No.*" I stare at him, then splutter with laughter. A man in front turns around with a frown, and as if in sync, Jon and I back away a few more paces, till we're right in the shadows.

"You shouldn't be hiding away," I say. "This is your moment. Your loft."

"Yeah, well," he says dryly. "I'll let Eric take the glory. He's welcome to it."

For a few moments we watch Eric onscreen in a hard hat, striding over a building site.

"You make no sense," I say quietly. "If you think lofts are for rich wankers, why do you design them?"

"That's a good question." Jon takes a gulp of his drink. "Truth is, I should move on. But I like Eric. He believed in me, he gave me my first chance, he runs a great company...."

"You *like* Eric?" I shake my head in disbelief. "Of course you do. That's why you keep telling me to leave him."

"I do. He's a great guy. He's honest, he's loyal..." For a while Jon's silent beside me, his eyes flickering in the dim light. "I don't *want* to fuck Eric's life up," he says finally. "It wasn't in the plan."

"So why..."

"He doesn't understand you." Jon looks directly at me. "He has no idea who you are."

"And you do, I suppose?" I retort, just as the lights come up and applause breaks out around the room. Instinctively I take a step away from Jon, and we both watch as Eric mounts the podium again, glowing with an aura of success and money and on-top-of-the-world-ness.

"So, have you encountered Mont Blanc yet?" Jon says, clapping vigorously, his mood lighter.

"What's Mont Blanc?" I give him a suspicious glance.

"You'll find out."

"Tell me."

"No, no." He shakes his head, pressing his mouth together as though trying not to laugh. "I couldn't spoil the surprise."

"Tell me!"

"Jon! There you are. Emergency!" We both start in surprise as Ava appears behind us. She's dressed in a black trouser suit, holding a burlap sack, and appears flustered. "The ornamental rocks for the master bedroom fish tank have only just arrived from Italy. But I've got to see to the kitchen place-settings—some fucking *idiot's* been fiddling with them—so can you do it?" She shoves the burlap sack into Jon's arms. "Just arrange the rocks in the tank. There should be time before the presentation finishes."

"No problem." Jon hefts the sack in his arms, then looks at me, his eyes opaque and impenetrable. "Lexi, want to come with me and help?"

My throat tightens up so hard, I can't breathe. This is an invitation. A challenge.

No. I have to say no.

"Um . . . yes." I swallow. "Sure."

I feel almost light-headed as I follow Jon through the crowd, up the stairs onto the mezzanine level, and into the bedroom. No one even notices us. All attention is on the presentation.

We head into the main bedroom and Jon closes the door.

"So," he says.

"Look." My voice is sharp with nerves. "I can't carry on like this! All this whispering, creeping around, trying to . . . to sabotage my marriage. I'm happy with Eric!"

"No." He shakes his head. "You won't be with him in a year." He sounds so sure of himself, I'm nettled.

"Yes, I will," I shoot back. "I expect I'll be with him in fifty years!"

"You'll try your best, you'll try to mold yourself... but your spirit's too free for him. At last you won't be able to stand it anymore." He exhales, pressing his meshed hands outward. "I've watched it happen once. I don't want to see it again."

"Thanks for the warning," I snap. "Well, when it does happen, I'll give you a call, how's that? We should do the rocks." I jerk my head toward the sack, but Jon ignores me.

He puts it down on the floor and comes toward me, his eyes intense and questioning. "You really, *really* don't remember anything?"

"No," I say almost wearily. "For the millionth time, I don't remember anything."

He's only inches away from me now, studying my face, searching for something. "All the time we spent together, all the things we said.... There has to be *something* to trigger your memory." He briefly rubs his brow, frowning. "Do sunflowers mean anything to you?"

In spite of myself I rack my brain. Sunflowers. Sunflowers. Didn't I once...

No, it's gone.

"Nothing," I say at last. "I mean, I *like* sunflowers, but..."

"e.e. cummings? Mustard on fries?"

"I don't know what you're talking about," I say helplessly. "None of this means anything to me."

He's so close I can feel his gentle breath on my skin. His eyes haven't left mine.

"Does this mean anything to you?" He's moved his hands up to my face, cradling my cheeks, rubbing my skin with his thumbs.

"No." I swallow.

"This?" He leans down and brushes a kiss against my neck.

"Stop it," I say feebly, but I can barely get the words out. And besides, I don't mean them. My breathing is getting shorter and shorter. I've forgotten about everything else. I want to kiss him. I want to kiss him in a way I didn't want to kiss Eric.

And then it's happening—his mouth is on mine and my entire body's telling me this is the right thing to do. He smells right. He tastes right. He feels right. I can feel his arms wrapping themselves tightly around me; the roughness of his five-o'clock shadow. My eyes are closed, I'm losing myself, this is so right. . . .

"Jon?" Ava's voice comes through the door and it's like someone electrocuted me. I fly away from Jon, tripping over my wobbly legs, cursing under my breath, "Fuck!"

"Shh!" He looks thrown too. "Stay cool. Hi, Ava. What's up?"

Rocks. Yes. That's what we're supposed to be doing. I grab the sack and start pulling rocks out, chucking them into the fish tank as fast as I can with a series of splashes. The poor fish are swimming about like lunatics, but I don't have any choice.

"Everything okay?" Ava puts her head around the

door. "I'm about to lead a party of guests up here for the tour..."

"No problem," Jon says reassuringly. "Nearly done."

As soon as Ava disappears, he kicks the door shut and comes back to me.

"Lexi." He grasps my face as though he wants to devour me, or hug me, or maybe both. "If you only knew, this has been *torture*..."

"Stop it!" I draw away, my mind spinning like a kaleidoscope. "I'm married! We can't— You can't just—" I gasp and clap a hand to my mouth. "Oh shit. Shit!"

I'm not looking at Jon anymore. I'm looking at the fish tank.

"What?" Jon stares, uncomprehending, then follows my gaze. "Oh. Oops."

The tank has quieted down. All the tropical fish are swimming peacefully among the marble rocks. Except one blue stripy one, which is floating on top.

"I've killed a fish!" I let out a horrified giggle. "I've brained it with one of the rocks."

"So you have," Jon says, going over to survey the tank. "Nice aim."

"But it cost three hundred pounds! What am I going to do? The guests will be in here any moment!"

"That's pretty bad feng shui." Jon grins. "Okay, I'll go and delay Ava. You flush it away." He reaches for my hand and holds it a moment. "We haven't finished." He kisses the tips of my fingers—then heads out of the room, leaving me alone with the tank. Wincing, I reach into the warm water and pick up the fish by the very edge of its fin.

"I'm really sorry," I say in a tiny voice. Trying to catch the dripping water with my other hand, I hurry into the high-tech bathroom. I drop the fish in the gleaming white loo and look for the flush. There isn't one. This must be an intelligent loo.

"Flush," I say aloud, waving my arms to set off the sensors. "Flush!"

Nothing happens.

"Flush!" I say, with more desperation. "Go on, flush!" But the loo is totally dead. The fish is floating around, looking even more lurid blue against the white porcelain.

This cannot be happening. If anything is going to put a customer off a high-end luxury apartment, it's a dead fish in the loo. I pull out my phone from my pocket and scroll down my contacts until I find J. That must be him. I press speed-dial, and a moment later he answers.

"Jon here."

"The fish is in the loo!" I hiss. "But I can't flush it!"

"The sensors should set it off automatically."

"I know! But they're not setting anything off! There's a dead blue fish staring up at me! What am I going to do?"

"It's fine. Go to the panel next to the bed. You can override it and flush it from there. Hey, Eric! How are you doing?" The phone abruptly cuts off. I hurry over to the bed and locate a flip-down panel set into the wall. A scary digital display blinks back at me and I can't help a small moan. How can anyone live in a house that's more complicated than NASA? Why does a house have to be intelligent, anyway? Why can't it be nice and stupid?

My fingers fumbling, I press Menu, then Override, then Options. I scan down the list. Temperature... Lighting... Where's Bathroom? Where's Flush Loo? Do I even have the right panel?

Suddenly I notice another flip-up panel on the other side of the bed. Maybe that's it. I rush to it, wrench it open, and start jabbing at random. In a minute I'm going to have to scoop the stupid fish out of the water with my bare hands....

A sound draws me up short. It's a wail. A kind of distant siren. What on earth...

I stop jabbing and look more carefully at the panel I've been hitting. It's flashing words at me in red. *Panic Alert—Secure Space.* A sudden movement from the window attracts my attention and I look up to see a metal grille descending steadily over the glass.

What the—

Frantically I jab again at the panel, but it flashes back at me *Unauthorized,* then returns to *Panic Alert—Secure Space.*

Oh...my God. What have I done?

I dart to the door of the bedroom and look down to the space below.

I don't believe it. It's mayhem.

The siren is even louder out here. Metal grilles are descending everywhere, over the windows, the paintings, the waterfall. All the rich guests are clinging to each other in the middle of the space like hostages, apart from one portly man who's trapped next to the waterfall.

"Is it a robbery? Do they have guns?" a woman in a white trouser suit is exclaiming hysterically, wrenching at her hands. "George, swallow my rings!"

"That's a helicopter!" A gray-haired man is cocking his ear. "Listen! They're on the roof! We're sitting targets!"

I'm staring at the scene, my heart hammering, frozen with panic.

"It's coming from the master bedroom!" shouts one of Eric's staff, who has been consulting a panel by the fireplace. "Someone's set off the panic alarm. The police are on their way."

I've ruined the party. Eric will kill me, he'll *kill* me . . .

And then, with no warning, the noise stops. The sudden quiet is like the sun coming out.

"Ladies and gentlemen." A voice comes from the stairs, and my head whips around. It's Jon. He's holding a remote control, and he glances briefly up at me before addressing the crowd. "We hope you enjoyed our security demonstration. Rest assured, we are not under attack from robbers."

He pauses, and a few people laugh nervously. Around the room the grilles have already started retracting. "However," Jon continues, "as all of you know, in London today, security is of prime consideration. Many developments talk about security; we wanted you to see it firsthand. This system is MI5 quality—and it's here for your protection."

My legs are so weak with relief, they're barely holding me up. He's saved my life.

As he continues talking, I totter back into the bedroom suite and find the blue fish still floating in the loo. I count to three—then plunge my hand in, grab the fish, and, with a shudder, stuff it in my bag. I wash my hands, then head out to see that Eric has taken over from Jon.

"From this adventure you'll see even more clearly that we at Blue Developments understand you and your concerns better even than you yourselves do," he's saying. "You're not our customers...you're our *partners* in a perfect lifestyle." He lifts up his glass. "Enjoy your tours."

As he steps aside, a relieved babble of chatter and laughter breaks out. I can see the woman in the white trouser suit grabbing three massive diamond rings back from her husband and pushing them back onto her fingers.

I wait a few minutes, then unobtrusively slip down the stairs. I grab a glass of champagne from a passing waiter and take a deep swig. I am never touching any panels again, ever. Or fish. Or loos.

"Sweetie!" Rosalie's voice makes me jump. She's wearing a skimpy beaded dress in turquoise, and high feathered shoes. "*Oh* my God. Wasn't that genius? That'll make a few diary pieces tomorrow. Everyone's talking about the state-of-the-art security. You know it cost three hundred grand? Just for the system!"

Three hundred grand, and the loo doesn't even flush.

"Yes," I say. "Great!"

"Lexi." Rosalie is giving me a thoughtful look. "Sweetie...can I have a little word? About Jon. I saw you talking to him earlier."

I feel suddenly apprehensive. Did she see something?

"Oh, right!" I aim for a careless tone. "Yes, well, he's Eric's architect, so we just got chatting about the design, as you do..."

"Lexi." She takes me by the arm and draws me away from the hubbub. "I know you had your bump on the head and everything." She leans forward. "But do you *remember* anything about Jon? From your past?"

"Um...not really."

Rosalie pulls me still nearer. "Sweetie, I'm going to give you a bit of a shock," she says in a low, breathy voice. "A while ago you told me something in confidence. Girlfriend to girlfriend. I didn't say a word to Eric..."

I'm transfixed, my fingers frozen around the stem of my champagne flute. Does Rosalie *know*?

"I know this may seem really hard to believe, but something was going on between you and Jon, behind Eric's back."

"You're joking!" My face is burning. "Like...what, exactly?"

"Well, I'm afraid to say...." Rosalie glances around the room and hustles closer. "Jon kept pestering you. I just thought I should warn you in case he tried it on again."

For a moment I'm too dumbstruck to reply. *Pestering* me?

"Wh-what do you mean?" I stammer at last.

"What do you think? He's tried it on with all of us." Her nose wrinkles disparagingly.

"You mean..." I can't quite process this. "You mean he's tried it on with you too?"

"*Oh* my God, yes." She rolls her eyes. "He told me Clive doesn't understand me. Which is true," she adds after a moment's thought. "Clive's a *total* dimwit. But that doesn't mean I'm going to rush off and be a notch on his bedpost, does it? And he went after Margo, too," she adds, waving merrily at a woman in green across the room. "*Such* a nerve. He said he knew her better than her own husband and she deserved more, and he could tell she was a sensual woman.... All kinds of ridiculous stuff!" She clicks her tongue dismissively. "Margo's theory is he targets married women and tells them whatever they want to hear. He probably gets some kind of weird kick out of it—" She breaks off as she sees my frozen face. "Sweetie! Don't *worry*. He's like an irritating fly, you just have to swat him away. But he was quite persistent with you. You were, like, the big challenge. You know, being Eric's wife and everything?" She peers at me. "Don't you remember any of this?"

Ava walks past us with some guests, and Rosalie beams at them, but I can't move.

"No," I say at last. "I don't remember any of it. So...what did I do?"

"You kept telling him to leave you alone. It was

awkward. You didn't want to wreck his relationship with Eric, you didn't want to rock the boat.... You were very dignified, sweetie. I would have poured a drink over his head!" She suddenly focuses over my shoulder. "Darling, I must just dash and have a word with Clive about our dinner arrangements. He's booked completely the wrong table, he's an absolute *nightmare*..." She breaks off and looks at me again, suddenly anxious. "Are you okay? I just thought I should warn you...."

"No." I come to. "I'm glad you did."

"I mean, I know you'd never fall for his bullshit." She squeezes my arm.

"Of course not!" Somehow I manage to laugh. "Of course I wouldn't!"

Rosalie trips away into the party, but my feet are rooted to the ground. I've never felt so humiliated in my life, so gullible, so *vain*.

I believed it all. I fell for his blarney.

We've been having a secret affair....I know you better than Eric does....

It's all bullshit. He took advantage of my memory loss. He flattered me, turned my head. And all he wanted was to get me into bed like a . . . a trophy. I feel hot with mortification. I *knew* I would never have an affair! I'm not the unfaithful type. I'm just not. I have a decent husband who loves me. And I allowed my head to be swayed. I nearly ruined everything.

Well, not anymore. I know where my priorities are. I take a few deep gulps of champagne. Then I lift my head high, walk forward through the crowd until I find Eric, and slip my arm through his.

"Darling. The party's going wonderfully. You're brilliant."

"I think we've pulled it off." He looks more relaxed than he has all evening. "Narrow escape with that alarm. Trust Jon to save the day. Hey, there he is! Jon!"

I clutch Eric's arm even more tightly as Jon walks toward us. I can't even bear to look at him. Eric claps him on the back and hands him a glass of champagne from a nearby tray. "Here's to you," he exclaims. "Here's to Jon."

"To Jon," I echo tightly, taking the smallest possible sip of champagne. I'm just going to pretend he doesn't exist. I'm going to blank him out.

A beep from my bag disturbs my thoughts, and I pull out my phone to see a new message.

From Jon.

I do not *believe* this. He's texting me in front of Eric? I quickly press View and the message comes up.

Old Canal House in Islington, any evening from 6.
We have so much to talk about.
I love you.
J
PS Delete this message.
PPS What did you do with the fish??

My face is burning with fury. Rosalie's words ring in my head. *You just have to swat him away.*

"It's a text from Amy!" I say to Eric, my voice shrill. "I might just quickly reply . . ."

Without looking at Jon, I start texting, my fingers charged up with adrenaline.

Yeah. Right. I suppose you thought it was a laugh, taking advantage of the girl who lost her memory. Well, I know your stupid game, okay? I'm a married woman. Leave me alone.

I send the text and put my phone away. A moment later, Jon frowns at his watch and says casually, "Is that the right time? I think I'm fast." He takes his cell phone out and squints at the display as though checking, but I can see his thumb moving over the keys and I can see him reading the message and I can see his face jerk with shock.

Ha. Got him.

After a few moments, he seems to recover. "I'm six minutes out," he says, tapping at the phone. "I'll just change the clock . . ."

I don't know why he's bothering with an excuse. Eric's not even paying any attention. Three seconds later my phone beeps again and I pull it out.

"Another text from Amy," I say disparagingly. "She's such a pain." I dart a glance at Jon as I put my finger on Delete, and his eyes widen with consternation. Huh. Now that I know the truth, it's *obvious* he's putting it all on.

"Is that a good idea?" he says quickly. "Deleting a message without even reading it?"

"I'm really not interested." I shrug.

"But if you haven't read it, you don't know what it says..."

"Like I say"—I shoot him a sweet smile—"I'm not interested." I press Delete, switch off my phone, and drop it into my bag.

"So!" Eric turns back to us, glowing and ebullient. "The Clarksons want a repeat viewing tomorrow. I think we have another sale. That's six units, just tonight."

"Well done, my darling, I'm so proud of you!" I exclaim, putting an arm around him in an extravagant gesture. "I love you even more now than I did on our wedding day."

Eric frowns, confused. "But you don't remember our wedding day. So you don't know how much you loved me."

For God's sake. Does he have to be so *literal*?

I try to control my impatience. "Well, however much I loved you then...I love you more now. Much more." I put my champagne glass down, and with a defiant glance at Jon, pull Eric in for a kiss. The longest, most slurpy, look-how-much-I-love-my-husband-and-by-the-way-we-have-great-sex kiss. At one point Eric tries to draw back, but I clamp tighter, pinning his face to mine. At last, when I think I might suffocate, I release him, wipe my mouth with the back of my hand, and look around the emptying room.

Jon has gone.

Chapter Fifteen

My marriage. That's my priority. From now on I'm going to focus on my relationship with Eric, and nothing else.

I'm still a bit shaken the next morning, as I go into the kitchen for breakfast and take the jug of green juice out of the fridge. I must have been crazy last night. I have the dream husband, handed to me on a plate. Why would I jeopardize that? Why would I kiss some guy in the back bedroom, whatever his story was?

I pour a little green juice into a glass and swirl it around to look like dregs, which is what I do every morning. (I can't drink that pond-weed stuff. But neither can I disappoint Eric, who thinks green juice is almost as great as loft-style living.) Then I take a boiled egg from the pan and pour myself a cup of tea from the pot that Gianna made earlier. I'm really getting into this low-carb start to the day. I have a boiled egg, bacon, or egg-white omelette every morning without fail.

And then sometimes a bagel on the way to work. Just if I'm starving.

As I sit down, the kitchen seems calm and tranquil. But I'm still jittery. What if I'd taken things further with Jon? What if Eric had found out? I could have wrecked everything. I've only had this marriage for a few weeks—and already I'm risking it. I need to *cherish* it. Like a yucca plant.

"Morning!" Eric breezes into the kitchen in a blue shirt, looking ebullient. I'm not surprised. Last night's launch was the best they've ever had, apparently. "Sleep well?"

"Great, thanks!"

We're not sharing a bedroom yet, nor have we tried sex again. But if I'm going to cherish my marriage, maybe we should be getting more physical. I stand up to get the pepper and brush deliberately against Eric.

"You look great this morning." I smile up at him.

"So do you!"

I run my hand down his jawline. Eric's eyes meet mine questioningly, and he puts a hand up to meet mine. I glance quickly at the clock. There isn't time, thank God.

No. I didn't think that.

I need to be *positive*. Sex with Eric is going to be great, I know it is. Maybe we just need to do it in the dark. And not talk to each other.

"How are you...feeling?" Eric says with a cryptic little smile.

"I'm feeling fine! In a bit of a hurry, though." I flash him a smile, move away, and gulp at my tea before he can suggest a quickie against the oven. Thank goodness, he seems to get the message. He pours himself a cup of tea, then takes out his BlackBerry as it beeps.

"Ah!" he says, sounding pleased. "I've just won a case of '88 Lafite Rothschild at auction."

"Wow!" I say enthusiastically. "Well done, darling!"

"Eleven hundred quid," he continues. "Bit of a steal."

Eleven hundred quid?

"For ... how many bottles?" I ask.

"A case." He frowns as though it's obvious. "Twelve."

I can't speak. Eleven hundred quid for twelve bottles of wine? I'm sorry, that's just ... wrong. Does he know how much eleven hundred quid *is*? I could buy a hundred bottles of wine for that. And they'd still be posh ones. And I'd have money left over.

"Lexi, are you okay?"

"I'm fine." I come to. "Just thinking ... what a great deal!" With a final gulp of tea I put on my jacket and pick up my briefcase. "Bye, darling."

"Bye, sweetheart." Eric comes over and we kiss each other good-bye. It's actually starting to feel quite natural. I shrug on my jacket and am at the door when something hits me.

"Hey, Eric," I say as casually as possible. "What's ... Mont Blanc?"

"Mont Blanc?" Eric turns, his face searching mine in disbelief. "You're kidding. Do you remember Mont Blanc?"

Okay. I really fell into this one. I can't say "No, Jon told me."

"I don't *remember,* exactly," I improvise. "But the

name 'Mont Blanc' came back to me, and it seemed significant, somehow. Does it mean something... special?"

"You'll find out, darling." I can see the suppressed pleasure in Eric's face. "It'll all come back to you. I won't say any more for now. This has to be a good sign!"

"Maybe!" I try to match his excitement. "Well... see you later!" I head out of the kitchen, racking my brain. *Mont Blanc*. Skiing? Those posh fountain pens? A great big snowy mountain?

I have absolutely no idea.

I get off the tube at Victoria, buy a bagel, and nibble it as I walk along. But as I get near the office, I'm suddenly not hungry anymore. I have a nasty churning in my stomach. That kind of sinking, I-don't-want-to-go-to-school sensation.

Fi might be my friend again, but no one else is. And I messed up in front of Simon Johnson, and I still don't feel on top of anything... As the building comes in sight I stop, heavy with dread.

Come on, I tell myself firmly. It'll be fun.

No, it won't.

Well, okay, it won't. But I don't have any choice.

Summoning all my determination, I chuck the rest of the bagel in a bin and push my way through the main glass doors. I head straight up to my office without bumping into anyone, sit down, and pull my pile of papers toward me. As I do so, I notice the Post-it I wrote yesterday: *Discuss sales with Byron*. Maybe I'll do that now. I lift the phone to dial his extension, but put it down again when there's a knock at the door.

"Hello?"

"Hi, Lexi?" Debs edges her way into the room. She's wearing a turquoise beaded cardigan and denim skirt, and holding an envelope.

"Oh," I say apprehensively. "Hi, Debs."

"How are you?" She sounds awkward.

"I'm ... fine." The door widens to reveal Fi and Carolyn, both looking ill at ease too. "Hi!" I exclaim in surprise. "Is everything okay?"

"I told them what you told me," says Fi. "Last night we went out for a drink and I told them."

"We didn't realize," says Debs, looking worried. "We didn't give you a chance. We just assumed you were still ..." She casts around for the word.

"A power-crazed nightmare," supplies Carolyn, deadpan.

"We feel bad." Debs bites her lip as she looks at the others. "Don't we?"

"Don't worry." I force a smile. But all of a sudden, as I regard the three of them, I feel more lonely than ever. These were my mates; we were always a foursome. But now they've had three years of nights out and talking and laughs that I've missed out on. They're banded together in a trio and I'm the stranger.

"So, I just wanted to give you this." Debs advances toward the desk, her face pinkening, and hands me the envelope. I rip it open and pull out a stiff white engraved card. A wedding invitation.

"Hope you can come." Debs has shoved her hands into her pockets. "You and Eric."

I feel a rush of humiliation. Her body language is obvious. The last thing she wants is us at her wedding.

"Look, Debs, you don't have to ask me. It's really kind of you . . ." I'm trying to stuff the card back into the envelope, my face hot. "But I know you don't really—"

"Yes, I do." She puts her hand on mine, stopping me, and I look up. Her eyes are just the same as they ever were—deep blue with long mascaraed lashes. "You were one of my best friends, Lexi. I know things changed. But . . . you should be there."

"Well . . . thanks," I mumble at last. "I'd love to come." I turn the invitation over, running a finger over the engraving. "How did you get your mother to agree to such a late guest?"

"She nearly killed me," Debs says bluntly, and I can't help laughing.

"Did she threaten to stop your allowance?"

"*Yes!*" Debs exclaims, and this time we all break into giggles. Debs's mum has been threatening to stop her allowance ever since I've known her—even though she stopped giving Debs an allowance about ten years ago.

"We've bought some muffins, too," says Fi. "To say sorry for yesterday . . ." She stops as there's a tapping at the door. Simon Johnson is standing in the doorway.

"Simon!" I start in shock. "I didn't see you there!"

"Lexi." He smiles. "Available for a quick chat?"

"We'll go," Fi says hurriedly, and hustles the others out. "Thanks for that . . . er . . . information, Lexi. Very useful."

"Bye, Fi!" I smile at her gratefully.

"I won't take up your time," Simon says, shutting the door as they leave. "Just wanted to give you the final rundown for Monday's meeting. Obviously keep it close to your chest. Within this department, only you and Byron have this information." He comes toward the desk, holding out a folder.

"Absolutely." I nod in a businesslike manner. "Thanks."

As I take the folder from him, I see *June '07* typed discreetly in the top right-hand corner and feel a twinge of foreboding. I still have no idea what June '07 means. I searched through all my files yesterday afternoon, but found nothing. No computer files, no paperwork, nothing.

I know I should have asked Byron. But I was too proud. I wanted to figure it out for myself.

"Looking forward to it!" I pat the folder, hoping I look convincing.

"Good. It's Monday, twelve noon sharp, in the boardroom. A couple of the nonexecutive directors have to shoot off promptly."

"See you there," I say with a confident smile. "Thanks, Simon."

The minute Simon has left, I sit down and whip open the folder. The first page is entitled Summary, and I run my eyes down the text. *June '07 ... major restructuring ... realignment in the market ... overall rethink ...*

After a few seconds I sink down into my chair, feeling overwhelmed. No wonder this is a big secret. The whole company's being changed around. We're acquiring a home technology company...we're amalgamating several departments...I flick my eyes farther down.

...*context of its current sales performance...plans to disband...*

What?

I read the words again. And again.

My spine has gone cold. I'm frozen on my chair, reading the lines over and over. That can't...it *can't* mean what I think it means...

With a surge of adrenaline I leap to my feet and hurtle out the door and down the corridor. There's Simon, by the lifts, talking to Byron.

"Simon!" I'm gulping air in my panic. "Could I possibly have a quick word?"

"Lexi." As he looks up I can see a wrinkle of irritation in his brow.

"Hi." I look around, checking there's no one around to overhear. "I just wanted to...to...clarify a couple of things. These plans to disband the Flooring section." I tap the folder. "That can't mean...you can't really mean..."

"She's finally twigged." Byron folds his arms, shaking his head with such amusement that I want to punch him. He *knew* about this?

Simon sighs. "Lexi, we've been through this many times, as you know. It's a tough market out there. You've done marvels with your sales force—we all appreciate that. And you yourself will be rewarded. But the department is unsustainable."

"But you can't get rid of Flooring! Deller Carpets is all about flooring! This is how the company started!"

"Keep your voice down!" Simon snaps sotto voce, glancing around the floor. All the pleasantness has disappeared from his veneer. "Lexi, I cannot have this level of disruption. It's highly unprofessional."

"But—"

"There's nothing to worry about. You and Byron will both have new roles in senior management. It's all been worked out very carefully. I don't have time for this." The lift arrives and he steps into it.

"But, Simon," I say desperately. "You can't just *fire* the whole department...."

It's too late. The lift doors have closed.

"It's not called firing," Byron's sardonic voice comes behind me. "It's called making redundant. Get your terms right."

"How can you just *stand* there?" I wheel around, incensed. "And how come I didn't know anything about this?"

"Oh, didn't I tell you?" Byron clicks his tongue in mock self-reproach. "I'm sorry, Lexi. It's hard to know where to start when you've forgotten...let's see. Everything."

"Where are the files? Why didn't I see this before?"

"I may have borrowed them." He shrugs and heads toward his office. "*Ciao.*"

"No! Wait!" I push my way in behind him and close the door. "I don't understand. Why are they axing the department?"

"Have you *looked* at our sales recently?" Byron rolls his eyes.

"They went up!" I retort before I can stop myself, already knowing this is the wrong tack.

"By three percent?" Byron scoffs. "Lexi, carpet is old news. We've failed to penetrate the other flooring markets. We've only got a couple of contracts to see out. Face it. The party's over."

"But we can't just lose the department. Those original carpet designs are classics! What about...rugs?"

Byron stares at me incredulously for a moment, then bursts into laughter.

"You're hilarious, you know that?"

"What?"

"You do know you're repeating yourself? You said all this at the first crisis meeting. 'We could make the carpets into rugs!'" he imitates me in a shrill voice. "Give up."

"But they'll all be out of a job! The whole team!"

"Yeah. Shame." He sits at his desk and motions toward the door. "I have work to do?"

"You're a *bastard*," I say, my voice shaking. I stride out of his office and slam the door, still clutching the folder, breathing harder and harder until I think I might hyperventilate. I have to read all this information, I have to think....

"Lexi!" My head jerks up and instinctively I clasp the folder closer to my chest. Fi is standing at the door of the main Flooring office, beckoning me. "Come in! Have a muffin."

For a moment I just stare speechlessly at her.

"Come on!" She laughs. "Simon Johnson's gone now, hasn't he?"

"Um . . . yes," I say huskily. "He has."

"Well, come on, then! We're all waiting!"

I can't refuse. I have to appear normal; I have to appear friendly, even though I'm in a state of meltdown . . .

Fi grabs my arm—and as I follow her into the main office, I feel an almighty shock. A banner has been strung up between two window latches, reading *Welcome Back, Lexi!!!* A plate of fresh muffins is on the filing cabinet, along with an Aveda gift basket.

"We never gave you a proper welcome back," says Fi, her face slightly pink. "And we just wanted to say we're glad you're okay after the car crash." She addresses the room. "To those of you who didn't know Lexi way back when . . . I just want to say that I think this accident has changed things. I know she's going to be the most fantastic boss and we should all get right behind her. Here's to you, Lexi."

She lifts her coffee mug and the whole room breaks into applause.

"Thanks, everyone," I manage, my face puce. "You're . . . all great."

They're all about to lose their jobs. They have no idea. And they've bought me muffins and a gift basket.

"Have a coffee." Fi brings a mug over. "Let me take that folder for you . . ."

"No!" I gasp, clutching it tighter. "It's . . . fairly confidential . . ."

"It's all our bonuses, isn't it?" Debs says with a grin, and then gives me a nudge. "Make sure they're all nice and big, Lexi! I want a new handbag!"

Somehow I raise a sick smile. I'm in a bad dream.

• • •

As I finally leave work at six-thirty, the nightmare hasn't lifted. I have the weekend to put together a defense of the Flooring department somehow. And I barely know what the problem is, let alone the answer. As I'm jabbing the ground-floor button in the lift, Byron slips in, wearing his overcoat.

"Working at home?" He raises his eyebrows as he sees my stuffed briefcase.

"I have to save the department," I say shortly. "I'm going to work all weekend until I find a solution."

"You have to be kidding." Byron shakes his head incredulously. "Lexi, haven't you read the proposal? This is going to be *better* for you and me. They're creating a new strategic team, we're going to have more power, more scope . . ."

"That's not the point!" I cry in a blaze of fury. "What about all our friends who won't have anything?"

"Sob, sob, let me just mop up my bleeding heart," Byron drawls. "They'll find jobs." He hesitates, eyeing me closely. "You know, you weren't bothered before."

It takes a second or two for his words to register. "What do you mean?"

"Before you had that car crash, you were all for getting rid of Flooring. Once you saw your new package. More power for us, more money . . . what's not to love?"

A coldness creeps over me.

"I don't believe you." My voice is jerky. "I don't believe you. I would *never* have sold out my friends."

Byron just looks at me pityingly.

"Yeah, you would. You're not a saint, Lexi. Why should you be?" The doors open and he strides out of the lift.

• • •

I arrive at Langridge's department store, and travel up to the personal shopping department as though in a daze. I have an appointment at seven o'clock with my shopper, Ann. According to the manual, I see her every three months and she picks out some "pieces" and we work on that season's "look."

"Lexi! How *are* you?" A voice greets me as I approach the reception area. Ann is very petite, with close-cropped dark hair, slim black cigarette pants, and a distinct perfume that turns my stomach instantly. "I was so devastated to hear about your accident!"

"I'm fine, thanks. All recovered now." I attempt a smile.

I should have canceled this appointment. I don't know what I'm doing here.

"Good! Now, I have some *fabulous* pieces for you to see." Ann ushers me into a cubicle and presents a rail of clothes to me with a flourish. "You'll see some new shapes and styles here, but I think you can carry them off..."

What is she talking about, new shapes and styles? They're all suits in neutral colors. I have a cupboard full of these already.

Ann is showing me jacket after jacket, talking about pockets and lengths, but I can't hear a word. Something is buzzing in my head like a trapped insect; it's getting louder and louder. . . .

"Do you have anything different?" I cut her off abruptly. "Do you have anything . . . *alive*?"

"Alive?" Ann echoes uncertainly. She hesitates, then reaches for another beige jacket. "This is full of flair . . ."

I stride out of the cubicle onto the main shop floor, feeling like I need to gasp for air. Blood is rushing in my ears. I feel a bit deranged, to be honest.

"This." I seize a purple minidress with bright splodges on it. "This is great. I could go clubbing in this."

Ann looks like she wants to pass out.

"Lexi," she says at last. "That's . . . not what I would call your style."

"Well, I would." Defiantly I grab a silver miniskirt. "And this."

It's exactly like what I'd pick up at New Look, only a million times more expensive, obviously.

"Lexi." Ann places her fingers on the bridge of her nose and breathes in a couple of times. "I am your stylist. I know what suits you. You have a very workable, attractive, professional look that we've spent some time honing—"

"It's boring. It's stultifying." I pluck a beige sleeveless dress out of her arms and hold it up. "I'm not this person, I'm just not."

"Lexi, you are."

"I'm not! I need fun. I need color."

"You've existed perfectly well for several years in beige and black." Ann's face has tightened. "Lexi, you told me *specifically* at our first meeting that what you required was a working capsule wardrobe in neutral colors—"

"That was then, okay?" I'm trying to curb my agitation, but it's as if all the events of the day are bubbling up in a rush of distress. "Maybe things have changed. Maybe *I've* changed."

"This." Ann comes up with another beige suit, with tiny pleats. "*This* is you."

"It's not."

"It is."

"It's not me! It's not! I'm not this person! I won't be her!" Tears are stinging my eyes. I start tugging pins out of my chignon, suddenly desperate to get rid of it. "I'm not the kind of person who wears beige suits! I'm not the kind of person who wears her hair in a bun every day. I'm not the kind of person who pays a thousand quid for wine. I'm not the kind of person who... who sells out her friends..."

I'm gulping with sobs by now. My chignon won't come loose, so strands of hair are sticking out all over my head like a scarecrow. My whole face is wet with tears. I wipe my eyes with the back of my hand, and Ann whips the beige dress away in horror.

"Don't get tears on the Armani!" she snaps.

"Here." I shove it back to her. "You're welcome to it." And without saying any more, I leave.

• • •

I head to the café on the ground floor, order a hot chocolate, and drink it while I take the rest of the pins out of my chignon. Then I order another, together with a doughnut. After a while, all the carbs have settled in my stomach like a warm, comforting cushion, and I feel better. There has to be a way, there *has* to. I'll work all weekend, I'll find the solution, I'll save the department....

A beep from my pocket interrupts my thoughts. I pull out my phone and see it's a text from Eric.

How are you doing? Working late?

As I stare at the words I'm suddenly touched. Overwhelmingly touched, in fact. Eric cares about me. He's thinking about me.

On my way home now, I type back. I missed you today!!

It's not exactly true, but it has the right sound to it.

I missed you too! comes back instantly.

I knew there was a point to marriage. And this is it. Someone to care about you when everything's crap. Someone to cheer you up. Just texting Eric is making me feel a million times warmer than the hot chocolate did. I'm composing a reply in my head when the phone beeps once more.

Fancy a Mont Blanc?? :) :)

Again with the Mont Blanc. What *is* this? A cocktail, maybe?

Well, it's obviously really special to Eric. And there's only one way I'll find out.

Great! I text back. Can't wait!

Then I pick up my bag, head out of Langridges, and hail a taxi.

It only takes about twenty minutes to arrive home, during which time I reread three files, each more depressing than the last. Carpet sales have never been worse in the whole history of the company, whereas every other department is booming. At last I close the files and stare out the taxi window, my mind working overtime. If I could just put a rescue package together ... I *know* there's still value in the Deller Carpet brand—

"Love?" The taxi driver breaks me out of my reverie. "We're here."

"Oh, right. Thanks." I'm fumbling for my purse when my phone beeps yet again.

I'm ready!

Ready? This gets more and more mysterious.

Just got home! See you in a minute!

I text back briskly, and hand the money to the taxi driver.

As I let myself into the flat, the lights are dim, in a setting that I recognize as Seduction. Music is playing so quietly I can barely hear it; other than that it's totally silent.

"Hi!" I call out cautiously, hanging up my coat.

"Hi!"

Eric's distant voice seems to be coming from the bedroom. My bedroom.

Well ... I guess, officially, our bedroom.

I check my reflection in the mirror and hastily give my disheveled hair a comb. Then I head to the other side of the living area and through to the bedroom. The door is only slightly ajar; I can't see inside the room. I stand there for a moment, wondering what on earth this is all about. Then I push the door open. And at the sight before me I nearly scream out loud.

This is Mont Blanc? *This* is Mont Blanc?

Eric is lying on the bed. Totally naked. Except for the most massive mound of whipped cream on his genital region.

"Hi, darling." He raises his eyebrows with a knowing twinkle, then glances downward. "Dive in!"

In?

Dive?

Dive *in*?

I'm paralyzed with horror as I survey the creamy, whippy mountain. Every cell in my body is telling me that I do not want to dive in.

But I can't just turn and run away, can I? I can't reject him. This is my husband. This is obviously ... what we do.

Oh God, oh God...

Gingerly I edge forward toward the creamy edifice. Barely knowing what I'm doing, I extend a finger and take a tiny scoop from the top of the mound, then put it in my mouth.

"It's...it's sweetened!" My voice is grainy from nerves.

"Low calorie." Eric beams back at me.

No. No. I'm sorry. This just...This isn't happening. Not in my lifetime. I have to come up with an excuse....

"I feel dizzy!" The words come out of nowhere. I clap a hand to my eyes and back away from the bed. "Oh my God. I'm having a flashback."

"A *flashback*?" Eric sits up, alert.

"Yes! I had a sudden memory of...the wedding," I improvise. "It was just a brief image, of you and me, but it was really vivid, it took me by surprise..."

"Sit down, darling!" Eric is frowning anxiously. "Take it easy. Maybe some more memories will come back."

He seems so hopeful, I feel terrible for lying. But it's better than saying the truth, surely?

"I might just go and lie down quietly in the other room, if you don't mind." I head swiftly toward the door, my hand still shielding my eyes from the sight of the cream mountain. "I'm sorry, Eric, after you went to so much...trouble..."

"Darling, it's fine! I'll come too—" Eric makes to get up from the bed.

"*No!*" I cut him off a bit too shrilly. "You just... sort yourself out. I'll be fine."

Before he can say anything else, I hurry out and flop down on the big cream sofa. My head is spinning, whether from the Mont Blanc shocker or the whole day . . . I don't know. All I know is, I feel like curling up under a duvet and pretending the world doesn't exist. I can't cope with this life of mine. Any of it.

Chapter Sixteen

I can't look at Eric without seeing whipped cream. Last night I dreamed he was *made* of whipped cream. It wasn't a great dream.

Thankfully we've barely seen each other this weekend. Eric's been doing corporate entertaining and I've been trying desperately to come up with a plan to save Flooring. I've read through all the contracts of the last three years. I've looked at our supplier information. I've analyzed customer feedback. To be honest, it's a crap situation. We did have a small triumph last year, when I negotiated a good deal with a new software company. I guess that's what impressed Simon Johnson. But it masked our real position.

Not only are orders too low, no one even seems *interested* in Flooring anymore. We have a fraction of the advertising and marketing budget that other departments do. We're not running any special promotions. In the weekly directors' meeting, Flooring always appears last on the agenda. It's like the Cinderella of the company.

But all that will change, if I have anything to do with it. Over the weekend I've devised a total relaunch. It'll need a bit of money and faith and cost-trimming—but I'm positive we can kick-start sales. Cinderella went to the ball, didn't she? And I'm going to be the fairy godmother. I *have* to be the fairy godmother. I can't let all my friends lose their jobs.

Oh God. My stomach heaves yet again with nerves. I'm sitting in the taxi on the way to work, my hair firmly up, my presentation folder in my lap. The meeting is in an hour. All the other directors are expecting to vote to disband Flooring. I'm going to have to argue my socks off. Or else...

No. I can't think about "or else." I have to succeed, I just *have* to.... My phone rings and I nearly jump off the seat, I'm so on edge.

"Hello?"

"Lexi?" I hear a small voice. "It's Amy. Are you free?"

"Amy!" I say in astonishment. "Hi! Actually, I'm on my way somewhere—"

"I'm in trouble." She cuts me off. "You have to come. Please."

"Trouble?" I say, alarmed. "What kind of trouble?"

"Please come." Her voice is quivering all over the place. "I'm in Notting Hill."

"Notting *Hill*? Why aren't you at school?"

"Hang on." The sound is muffled and I can just hear Amy saying, "I'm talking to my big sister, okay? She's coming." Then she's back on the line. "Please, Lexi. Please come. I've got myself into a bit of a mess."

I've never heard Amy like this. She sounds desperate.

"What have you *done*?" My mind's racing, trying to think what trouble she could have got into. Drugs? Loan sharks?

"I'm on the corner of Ladbroke Grove and Kensington Gardens. How long will you be?"

"Amy..." I clutch my head. "I can't come now! I have a meeting, it's really important. Can't you phone Mum?"

"No!" Amy's voice rockets in panic. "Lexi, you said. You said I could ring whenever I wanted, that you were my big sister, that you'd be there for me."

"But I didn't mean... I have this presentation..." I trail off, suddenly aware of how feeble this sounds. "Look, any other time..."

"Fine." Her voice is suddenly tiny. She sounds about ten years old. "Go to your meeting. Don't worry."

Guilt drenches me, mixed with frustration. Why couldn't she have phoned last night? Why pick the very minute I need to be somewhere else?

"Amy, just tell me, what's *happened*?"

"It doesn't matter. Go to your meeting. Sorry I bothered you."

"Stop it! Just let me think a second." I stare blindly out the window, wired up with stress, with indecision.... There's forty-five minutes until the meeting. I don't have time, I just don't.

I might, if I went straight now. It's only ten minutes to Notting Hill.

But I can't risk being late for the meeting, I just *can't*—

And then suddenly, against the crackly background of the phone line, I can hear a man's voice. Now he's shouting. I stare at the phone, feeling a nasty chill. I can't leave my little sister in trouble. What if she's got in with some street gang? What if she's about to be beaten up?

"Amy, hold on," I say abruptly. "I'm coming." I lean forward and knock on the driver's window. "We need to make a quick detour to Notting Hill. As fast as you can, please."

As we head up Ladbroke Grove, the taxi roaring with the effort, I'm leaning forward, peering desperately out the window, trying to glimpse Amy...and then suddenly I see a police car. On the corner of Kensington Gardens.

My heart freezes. I'm too late. She's been shot. She's been knifed.

Weak with terror, I thrust the cash at the driver and get out of the cab. There's a throng of people in front of the police car, masking my view, all peering and gesturing at something and talking agitatedly to each other. Bloody rubberneckers.

"Excuse me." My voice isn't working properly as I approach the crowd. "It's my sister, can I get through...." Somehow I manage to push my way in between the anoraks and denim jackets, steeling myself for what I might see...

And there's Amy. Not shot or knifed. Sitting on a wall, wearing a policeman's hat, looking totally cheery.

"Lexi!" Amy turns to the policeman standing next to her. "There she is. I told you she'd come."

"What's been going on?" I demand, shaky with relief. "I thought you were in trouble!"

"Is this your sister?" The policeman chimes in. He's stocky and sandy-haired, with large freckled forearms, and has been making notes on a clipboard.

"Er . . . yes." My heart is sinking. Has she been shop-lifting or something? "What's wrong?"

"I'm afraid this young lady's in trouble. She's been exploiting tourists. A lot of angry people here." He gestures at the crowd. "Nothing to do with you, is this?"

"No! Of course not! I don't even know what you're talking about!"

"Celebrity tours." He hands me a leaflet, his eyebrows raised sky-high. "So-called."

In disbelief I read the leaflet, which is fluorescent yellow and has obviously been put together on some crappy word-processor.

Undercover Celebrity Tour of London

Many Hollywood stars have settled in London. See them on this unique tour. Catch glimpses of:

★ Madonna putting out her washing ★
★ Gwyneth in her garden ★
★ Elton John relaxing at home ★

Impress your friends with all the insider gossip!
£10 per person including souvenir A–Z

Important note:
If you challenge the stars, they may deny their identities.
Do not be fooled! This is part of their Undercover Secret!

I look up in a daze. "Is this serious?" The policeman nods.

"Your sister's been leading people around London, telling them they're seeing celebrities."

"And who are they seeing?"

"Well, people like her." He gestures across the road, where a thin blond woman is standing on the steps of her big white stucco house in jeans and a peasant top, holding a little girl of about two on her hip.

"I'm not bloody Gwyneth Paltrow!" she's snapping irately at a pair of tourists in Burberry raincoats. "And no, you can't have an autograph."

Actually, she *does* look rather like Gwyneth Paltrow. She has the same long blond straight hair and a similar kind of face. Just a bit older and more haggard.

"Are you with her?" The Gwyneth look-alike suddenly spots me and comes down her steps. "I want to make an official complaint. I've had people taking pictures of my home all week, intruding into my life—*For the last time, she's not called fucking Apple!*" She turns to a young Japanese woman who is calling "Apple! Apple!" to the little girl, trying to get a picture.

This woman is furious. And I don't blame her.

"The more I tell people I'm not Gwyneth Paltrow, the more they think I am her," she's saying to the policeman. "I can't win. I'll have to move!"

"You should be flattered!" Amy says insouciantly. "They think you're an Oscar-winning movie star!"

"You should be put in jail!" snarls not-Gwyneth. She looks like she wants to hit Amy over the head.

To be honest, I'd be right behind her.

"I'm going to have to reprimand your sister officially." The policeman turns to me as a policewoman tactfully steps in and leads not-Gwyneth back to her house. "I can release her into your custody, but only when you've filled in these forms and arranged an appointment at the station."

"Fine," I say, and shoot a murderous look at Amy. "Whatever."

"Piss off!" Not-Gwyneth is rounding on a young geeky guy who is tagging along behind her hopefully, holding out a CD. "No, I can't get that to Chris Martin! I don't even *like* bloody Coldplay!"

Amy is sucking in her cheeks as though she's trying not to laugh.

Yeah. This is so funny. We're all having a great time. I don't have to be somewhere else really important, or anything.

I fill in all the forms as quickly as I can, stamping a furious full stop after my signature.

"Can we go now?"

"All right. Try and keep tabs on her," the policeman adds, handing me back a duplicate form and leaflet entitled "Your Guide to a Police Reprimand."

Keep tabs on her? Why should *I* have to keep tabs on her?

"Sure." I give a tight smile and stuff the documents into my bag. "I'll do my best. Come on, Amy." I glance at my watch and feel a spasm of panic. It's already ten to twelve. "Quick. We need to find a taxi."

"But I want to go to Portobello—"

"*We need to find a fucking taxi!*" I yell. "I need to

get to my meeting!" Her eyes widen and she obediently starts scanning the road. At last I flag one down and bundle Amy into it.

"Victoria Palace Road, please. Quick as you can."

There's no way I'll make it for the start. But I can still get there. I can still say my piece. I can still do it.

"Lexi...thanks," says Amy in a small voice.

"It's fine." As the taxi heads back down Ladbroke Grove my eyes are glued to the road, desperately willing lights to change, willing traffic to move over. But everything's suddenly solid. I'm *never* going to get there for midday.

Abruptly I pull out my phone, dial Simon Johnson's office number, and wait for his PA, Natasha, to answer.

"Hi, Natasha?" I say, trying to sound calm and professional. "It's Lexi. I'm having a slight holdup, but it's really vital that I speak at the meeting. Could you tell them to wait for me? I'm on my way in a taxi."

"Sure," Natasha says pleasantly. "I'll tell them. See you later."

"Thanks!"

I ring off and lean back in my seat, a tiny bit more relaxed.

"Sorry," Amy says suddenly.

"Yeah, whatever."

"No, really, I am."

I sigh, and look at Amy properly for the first time since we got in the cab. "*Why*, Amy?"

"To make money." She shrugs. "Why not?"

"Because you'll get in serious trouble! If you need money, can't you get a job? Or ask Mum?"

"Ask Mum," she echoes scornfully. "Mum doesn't have any money."

"Okay, maybe she doesn't have loads of money—"

"She doesn't have *any*. Why d'you think the house is falling down? Why d'you think the heating's never on? I spent half of last winter at my friend Rachel's house. At least they put on the radiators. We're skint."

"But that's weird," I say, puzzled. "How come? Didn't Dad leave Mum anything?"

I know some of Dad's businesses were a bit dodgy. But there were quite a few of them, and I know she was expecting a windfall when he died. Not that she ever would have admitted it.

"Dunno. Not much, anyway."

"Well, whatever, you can't carry on like this. Seriously, you'll end up in jail or something."

"Bring it on." Amy tosses back her blue-streaked hair. "Prison's cool."

"Prison's not *cool*!" I stare at her. "Where d'you get that idea? It's gross! It's manky! Everyone has bad hair, and you can't shave your legs or use cleanser."

I'm making all this up. Probably these days they have in-prison spas and blow dryers.

"And there aren't any boys," I add for good measure. "And you're not allowed an iPod, or any chocolate or DVDs. You just have to march around a yard." That bit I'm sure isn't true. But I'm on a roll now. "With chains around your legs."

"They don't have *leg chains* anymore," Amy says scornfully.

"They brought them back," I lie without missing a

beat. "Especially for teenagers. It was a new experimental government initiative. Jeez, Amy, don't you read the papers?"

Amy looks slightly freaked. Ha. That pays her back for Moo-mah.

"Well, it's in my genes." She regains some of her defiance. "To be on the wrong side of the law."

"It's not in your genes—"

"Dad was in prison," she shoots back triumphantly.

"*Dad?*" I stare at her. "What do you mean, Dad?" The idea's so preposterous, I want to laugh.

"He was. I heard some men talking about it at the funeral. So it's, like, my fate." She shrugs and takes out a pack of cigarettes.

"Stop it!" I grab the cigarettes and throw them out the window. "Dad didn't go to prison. You're not going to prison. And it's not cool; it's lame." I break off and think for a moment. "Look, Amy . . . come and be an intern at my office. It'll be fun. You can get some experience, and earn some money."

"How much?" she shoots back.

God, she's annoying sometimes.

"Enough! And maybe I won't tell Mum about this." I flick the yellow leaflet. "Deal?"

There's a long silence in the taxi. Amy is peeling at the chipped blue varnish on her thumbnail, as though it's the most important thing in the world.

"Okay," she says at last, shrugging.

The taxi pulls up at a red light and I feel a spasm as I consult my watch for the millionth time. It's twenty past. I just hope they started late. My gaze drifts to the yellow leaflet again and a grin reluctantly creeps over my face. It was a pretty ingenious scheme.

"So, who were your other celebrities?" I can't help asking. "You didn't *really* have Madonna."

"I did!" Amy's eyes light up. "This woman in Kensington looked just like Madonna, only fatter. Everyone totally fell for it, especially when I said that proved how much airbrushing they did. And I had a Sting, and a Judi Dench, and this really nice milkman in Highgate who looked the spitting image of Elton John."

"Elton John? A milkman?" I can't help laughing.

"I said he was doing community service on the quiet."

"And how on earth did you find them?"

"Just went looking. Gwyneth was my first—she gave me the idea." Amy grins. "She *really* hates me."

"I'm not surprised! She probably gets more hassle than the real Gwyneth Paltrow."

The taxi moves off again. We're nearing Victoria Palace Road now. I open my presentation folder and scan my notes, just to make sure all the important points are fresh in my mind.

"You know, they *did* say Dad had been in prison." Amy's quiet voice takes me by surprise. "I didn't make it up."

I don't know what to say. I can't get my head around this. Our dad? In prison? It seems . . . impossible.

"Did you ask Mum about it?" I venture at last.

"No." She shrugs.

"Well, I'm sure it wouldn't have been for anything—" I flounder, feeling out of my depth—"you know, bad."

"D'you remember how he used to call us the girls?" All trace of bolshiness has vanished from Amy's face. "His three girls. You, Mum, and me."

I smile reminiscently. "And he used to dance with each of us."

"Yeah." Amy nods. "And he always bought those massive boxes of chocolates—"

"And you used to get sick..."

"Deller Carpets, ladies." The taxi has drawn up in front of the Deller Building. I hadn't even noticed.

"Oh, right. Thanks." I root in my bag for some money. "Amy, I have to rush. I'm sorry, but this is really, really important."

"What's up?" To my surprise she actually looks interested.

"I have to save my department." I wrench open the handle and scramble out of the cab. "I have to talk eleven directors into doing something they've already decided not to do. And I'm late. And I don't know what the fuck I'm doing."

"Wow." Amy makes a dubious face. "Well...good luck with that."

"Thanks. And...we'll talk more." I give her a brief hug, then skitter up the steps and crash into the lobby. I'm only half an hour late. It could be worse.

"Hi!" I call to Jenny the receptionist as I run past the desk. "I'm here! Can you let them know?"

"Lexi—" Jenny starts to call something out to me, but I haven't got time to stop. I hurry to a waiting lift, jab the button for the eighth floor, and wait the agonizing thirty or so seconds it takes to get to the top. We need express lifts in this place. We need emergency, late-for-a-meeting instant lifts...

At last. I burst out, run toward the boardroom... and stop.

Simon Johnson is standing in the corridor outside the boardroom, talking cheerfully to three other guys in suits. A man in a blue suit is shrugging on his raincoat. Natasha is milling around, pouring cups of coffee. There's a hubbub of chatter.

"What's..." My chest is bursting with adrenaline. I can barely speak. "What's going on?"

All the faces turn toward me in surprise.

"Don't panic, Lexi." Simon shoots me the same disapproving frown he had before. "We're having a break. We've finished the crucial part of the meeting and Angus has to leave." He gestures toward the guy in the raincoat.

"*Finished?*" I feel an almighty lurch of horror. "Do you mean—"

"We've voted. In favor of the reorganization."

"But you can't!" I hurry toward him in panic. "I've found a way to save the department! We just have to trim a few costs; and I had some ideas about marketing—"

Simon cuts me off firmly. "Lexi, we've made our decision."

"But it's the *wrong* decision!" I cry desperately. "There's value in the brand—I know there is! Please." I appeal directly to Angus. "Don't leave. Hear me out. Then you can vote again..."

"Simon." Angus turns away from me, looking embarrassed. "Good to see you. I have to run."

"Absolutely."

They aren't even acknowledging me. No one wants to know. I watch, my legs watery, as the directors file back into the boardroom.

"Lexi." Simon is in front of me. "I admire your loyalty to your department. But you *cannot* behave like this at directors' meetings."

There's steel beneath his pleasant voice; I can tell he's furious.

"Simon, I'm sorry..." I swallow.

"Now, I know things have been tricky for you since your accident." He pauses. "So what I suggest is you take three months' paid leave. And when you return, we'll find you a more...suitable role within the company. All right?"

All the blood drains from my face. He's demoting me.

"I'm fine," I say quickly. "I don't need any leave—"

"I think you do." He sighs. "Lexi, I'm truly sorry about how things have gone. If you recovered your memory, then things would be different, but Byron's been filling me in on your situation. You're not up to a senior position right now."

There's an absolute finality in his voice.

"Fine," I manage at last. "I understand."

"Now, you might want to go down to your department. Since you weren't here"—he pauses meaningfully—"I gave Byron the task of breaking the unfortunate news to them."

Byron?

With a final curt nod, Simon disappears into the boardroom. I watch the door as though pinioned to the floor, then with a sudden burst of panic, run to the lift. I can't let Byron tell them the bad news. I have to do that myself, at least.

In the lift, I punch Byron's direct line into my cell phone and get his voice mail.

"Byron!" I say, my voice quivering with urgency. "Don't tell the department about the redundancies yet, okay? I want to do it myself. Repeat, do *not* tell them."

Without looking right or left I pelt out of the lift, into my office, and close the door. I'm shaking all over. I've never been so petrified in my life. How am I going to break the news? What am I going to say? How do you tell all your friends they're losing their jobs?

I pace around my office, twisting my hands, feeling like I might throw up. This is worse than any exam, any test, anything I've ever done. . . .

And then a sound alerts me. A voice outside the door. "Is she in there?"

"Where's Lexi?" chimes in another voice.

"Is she *hiding*? Bitch."

For an instant I consider diving under the sofa and never coming out.

"Is she still upstairs?" The voices are getting louder outside my door.

"No, I saw her! She's in there! Lexi! Come out here!" Someone bangs on the door, making me flinch. Somehow I force myself to move forward across the carpet. Gingerly I stretch out a hand and open the door.

They know.

They're all standing there. All fifteen members of the Flooring department, silent and reproachful. Fi is at the front, her eyes like stone.

"It . . . it wasn't me," I stammer desperately. "Please listen, everyone. Please understand. It wasn't my decision. I tried to . . . I was going to . . ." I trail off.

I'm the boss. The bottom line is, it was down to me to save the department. And I failed.

"I'm sorry," I whisper, tears filling my eyes, looking from face to unrelenting face. "I'm so, so sorry . . ."

There's silence. I think I might melt under the hatred of their gazes. Then, as though at a signal, they all turn and silently walk away. My legs like jelly, I back toward my desk and sink into my chair. How did Byron break it to everybody? What did he *say*?

And then suddenly I spot it in my inbox. A round-robin e-mail under the heading: *COLLEAGUES— SOME BAD NEWS*.

With trepidation I click on the e-mail, and as I read the words, I give a whimper of despair. This went out? Under *my* name?

To all colleagues in Flooring,

As you may have noticed, the performance of Flooring has been appalling of late. It has been decided by senior management to disband the department.

You will all therefore be made redundant in June. In

the meantime, Lexi and I would be grateful if you would work with improved efficiency and standards. Remember, we'll be giving your references, so no slacking or taking the piss.

Yours,
Byron and Lexi

OK. Now I want to shoot myself.

When I arrive home Eric is sitting on the terrace in the evening sun. He's reading the *Evening Standard* and sipping a gin and tonic. He looks up from the paper. "Good day?"

"To be honest . . . no," I say, my voice quivering. "It was a pretty terrible day. The entire department is being fired." As I say the words out loud I can't help it— I dissolve into tears. "All my friends. They're all losing their jobs. And they all hate me . . . and I don't blame them. . . ."

"Darling." Eric puts down his paper. "It's business. These things happen."

"I know. But these are my *friends*. I've known Fi since I was six."

Eric seems to be thinking as he sips his drink. At last he shrugs and turns back to the paper. "Like I say, these things happen."

"They don't just happen." I shake my head vehemently. "You stop them from happening. You fight."

"Sweetheart." Eric appears amused. "You still have your job, don't you?"

"Yes."

"The company's not collapsing, is it?"

"No."

"Well, then. Have a gin and tonic."

How can he respond like that? Isn't he human?

"I don't want a gin and tonic, okay?" I feel like I'm spiraling out of control. "I don't want a bloody gin and tonic!"

"A glass of wine, then?"

"Eric, don't you understand?" I almost shout. "Don't you *get* how terrible this is?"

All my rage toward Simon Johnson and the directors is swiveling direction like a twister, channeling toward Eric, with his calm roof terrace and his Waterford glass and his complacent life.

"Lexi—"

"These people need their jobs! They're not all... ultra-high rich bloody billionaires!" I gesture around at our glossy balcony. "They have mortgages. Rent to find. Weddings to pay for."

"You're overreacting," Eric says shortly, and turns a page of his paper.

"Well, you're underreacting! And I don't understand. I just don't *understand* you." I'm appealing to him directly. Wanting him to look up, to explain his view, to talk about it.

But he doesn't. It's like he didn't even hear me.

My whole body is pulsating with frustration. I feel like throwing his gin and tonic off the balcony.

"Fine," I say at last. "Let's not talk about it. Let's just pretend everything's okay and we agree, even though we don't." I wheel around and draw a sharp breath.

Jon is standing at the doors to the terrace. He's wearing black jeans and a white T-shirt and shades, so I can't see his expression.

"Hi." He steps down onto the terrace. "Gianna let me in. I'm not . . . intruding?"

"No!" I turn away swiftly so he can't see my face. "Of course not. It's fine. Everything's fine."

Of all the people to show up. Just to make my day complete. Well, I'm not even going to look at him. I'm not going to *acknowledge* him.

"Lexi's a little upset," Eric says to Jon in a man-to-man undertone. "A few people at her work are losing their jobs."

"Not just a few people!" I can't help expostulating. "A whole department! And I didn't do anything to save them. I'm supposed to be their boss and I fucked up." A tear creeps down my cheek and I roughly wipe it away.

"Jon." Eric isn't even listening to me. "Let me get you a drink. I've got the Bayswater plans right here. There's a lot to talk about. . . ." He gets up and steps into the sitting room. "Gianna! Gianna, are you there?"

"Lexi." Jon comes across the terrace to where I'm standing, his voice low and urgent.

He's trying it on again. I don't believe this.

"Leave me *alone*!" I round on him. "Didn't you get the message before? I'm not interested! You're just a . . . a womanizing bullshitter. And even if I were interested, it's not a good time, okay? My whole department has just crumbled to nothing. So unless you have the answer to that, piss off."

There's silence. I'm expecting Jon to come back with some cheesy chat-up line, but instead he takes off his shades and rubs his head as though perplexed.

"I don't understand. What happened to the plan?"

"Plan?" I say aggressively. "What plan?"

"Your big carpet deal."

"What carpet deal?"

Jon's eyes snap open in shock. For a few moments he just stares at me as though I have to be joking. "You're not serious. You don't *know* about it?"

"Know about *what*?" I exclaim, at the end of my tether. "I have no idea what the fuck you're talking about!"

"Jesus Christ." Jon exhales. "Okay, Lexi. Listen to me. You had this massive carpet deal all lined up in secret. You said it was going to change everything, it was going to bring in big bucks, it was going to transform the department. . . . So! You enjoy the view, huh." He seamlessly switches track as Eric appears at the door, holding a gin and tonic.

Massive carpet deal?

My heart is beating fast as I stand there, watching Eric give Jon his drink and pull out a chair under the huge sunshade.

Ignore him, says a voice in my head. *He's making it up. He's playing you—this is all part of the game.*

But what if it's not?

"Eric, darling, I'm sorry about earlier." My words

come out almost too fluently. "It's just been a difficult day. Could you possibly get me a glass of wine?"

I'm not even looking at Jon.

"No problem, sweetheart." Eric disappears inside again and I wheel around.

"Tell me what you're talking about," I say in low tones. "Quickly. And this better not be a windup."

As I meet his gaze I feel the sting of humiliation. I have no idea if I can trust anything he says or not. But I have to hear more. Because if there's just a *one* percent chance that what he's saying is true...

"This isn't a windup. If I'd *realized* before that you didn't know..." Jon shakes his head incredulously. "You'd been working on this thing for weeks. You had a big blue file that you used to carry around. You were so excited about it you couldn't sleep—"

"But what *was* it?"

"I don't know the exact details. You were too superstitious to tell me. You had this theory I was a jinx." His mouth twists briefly as though he's sharing a private joke. "But I know it was using retro carpet designs from some old pattern book. And I know it was going to be huge."

"But why don't I know about it? Why doesn't anyone know about it?"

"You were keeping it quiet until the last moment. You said you didn't trust everyone at the office and it was safer not to." He lifts his voice. "Hey, Eric. How's it going?"

I feel like I've been slapped in the face. He can't stop there.

"Here you are, Lexi," Eric says cheerfully, handing me a glass of wine. Then he heads to the table, sits down, and gestures at Jon to sit. "So the latest is, I spoke to the planning officer again..."

I'm standing perfectly still as they talk, my mind racing, torn apart with uncertainty. It could all be bullshit. Maybe I'm a gullible fool, listening to even a word.

But how would he know about the old pattern book? What if it's true? My chest constricts with a deep, painful spasm of hope. If there's still a chance, even a *tiny* chance...

"Are you all right, Lexi?" Eric shoots me an odd look, and I realize I'm standing stock-still in the middle of the terrace, my hands clasped to my face.

"Fine." Somehow I gather myself, retreat to the other end of the terrace, and sit down in a galvanized-steel swing seat. The sun is hot on my face. I'm barely aware of the distant roar of traffic below. Over at the table, Jon and Eric are studying an architect's drawing.

"We might have to rethink the parking completely." Jon is sketching on the paper. "It's not the end of the world."

"Okay." Eric sighs heavily. "If you think it can be done, Jon, I trust you."

I take a deep swig of wine—then pull out my phone. I cannot believe I'm about to do this. With fumbling hands I find Jon's number and type a text.

Can we meet? L

I press Send, then immediately slip my phone into my bag and stare rigidly out at the view.

A moment later, still sketching and without looking anywhere near me, Jon takes his phone out of his pocket with his other hand. He checks it briefly and types back a return text. Eric doesn't even seem to notice.

I force myself to count to fifty—then casually flip open my phone.

Sure. J

Chapter Seventeen

We've agreed to meet in a café called Fabian's in Holland Park, a small, cozy place with terra-cotta painted walls and prints of Tuscany and shelves full of Italian books. As I walk in and look around at the granite bar, the coffee machine, the battered sofa . . . I have the weirdest feeling—like I've been there before.

Maybe I'm just having déjà vu. Maybe it's wishful thinking.

Jon is already sitting at a table in the corner, and as he looks up I feel my guard rising. Against all my better instincts, after all my protests, here I am, meeting him illicitly. Just like he wanted all along. I feel like I'm falling into some kind of trap . . . but I don't know what the trap is.

Anyway, I'm meeting him for business reasons. As long as I remember that, I'll be fine.

"Hi." I join him at the table, where he's drinking coffee, and drop my briefcase on an adjoining chair. "So. We're both busy people. Let's talk about this deal."

Jon is just staring at me, as though trying to work something out.

"Is there anything more you can tell me?" I add, trying to ignore his expression. "I think I'll have a cappuccino."

"Lexi, what *is* this? And what the fuck happened at the party?"

"I...I don't know what you mean." I pick up the menu and pretend to be studying it. "Maybe I'll have a latte."

"Come on." Jon pulls the menu down so he can see my face. "You can't hide. What happened?"

He thinks this is funny. I can tell it from his voice. With a jag of wounded pride, I slap the menu down on the table.

"If you must know," I say tightly, "I spoke to Rosalie at the party, and she told me about your... predilections. I know it was all bullshit. And I don't appreciate being bullshitted, thanks."

"Lexi—"

"Don't try and pretend, okay? I know you tried it on with her and Margo." An edge of bitterness has crept into my voice. "You're just some smooth operator who tells married women what they want to hear. What you *think* they want to hear."

Jon's expression doesn't flicker.

"I did try it on with Rosalie and Margo. And I might have gone"—he hesitates—"a tad too far. But you and I agreed I should. That was our cover."

Well, of *course* he'd bloody well say that.

I glare at him in impotent fury. He can say anything

he likes, and there's no way for me to know whether he's speaking the truth or not.

"You have to understand." He leans across the table. "It was all fake. We cooked up a story that would fool everyone, so if we were ever spotted together, that could be the explanation. Rosalie fell for it, just like we wanted her to."

"You *wanted* to be portrayed as a womanizer?" I retort, rolling my eyes.

"Of course not!" There's a sudden heat to his voice. "But we had a couple of...near misses. Rosalie, in particular—she's sharp. She would have cottoned on."

"So you chat her up." I can't help the sarcasm. "Nice. Really classy."

Jon meets my look steadfastly. "You're right. This hasn't all been pretty. It's not a perfect situation and we've made mistakes." He reaches a hand toward mine. "But you have to trust me, Lexi. Please. You have to let me explain everything."

"Stop it!" I whip my hands away. "Just...stop! We're not here to talk about that, anyway, it's irrelevant. Let's stick to the subject." A waitress approaches the table and I look up. "A cappuccino, please." As soon as the waitress moves away, I say briskly, "So, this deal. It doesn't exist. I've looked everywhere. I went into the office and searched every tiny corner, every computer file. I've looked at home, nothing. The only thing I've found is this." I reach into the briefcase and produce the piece of paper with the coded scribbles on it. "There was an empty drawer in my desk. This was in there."

I'm half-hoping Jon's eyes will light up and he'll say, "Aha! The key!" like we're in *The Da Vinci Code*. Instead he glances at it and shrugs. "That's your handwriting."

"I know it's my handwriting." I try to keep my patience. "But I don't know what it means!" In frustration I throw the paper down. "Why on earth didn't I keep my notes on the computer?"

"There's a guy at work, Byron?"

"Yes," I say guardedly. "What about him?"

"You didn't trust him. You thought he actually *wanted* the department to be disbanded. You thought he'd try and screw things up for you. So you were going to present the whole thing to the board when it was already done."

The door to the café swings open and I jump in guilt, imagining it's Eric. I'm all ready with an excuse at the tip of my tongue, *I was just out shopping and guess what, I bumped into Jon! By total coincidence!* But of course it's not Eric, it's a cluster of teenagers who start talking in French.

"So you don't know anything else." My guilt makes me sound aggressive, almost accusing. "You can't help me."

"I didn't say that," Jon replies calmly. "I've been thinking back, and I did remember something. Your contact was Jeremy Northam. Northwick. Something like that."

"Jeremy Northpool?" The name pops into my head. I can remember Clare thrusting a Post-it at me with his name on it. Along with the other thirty-five Post-its.

"Yes." Jon nods. "That could be it. Northpool."

"I think he called while I was in hospital. Several times."

"Well." Jon raises his eyebrows. "Maybe you should call him back."

"But I can't." I drop my hands on the table in despair. "I can't say 'Hi, this is Lexi Smart, do we have a deal, oh and by the way, what's your business?' I don't know enough! Where's all the information?"

"It's there." Jon is stirring his coffee. "It's there somewhere. You must have moved the file. Hidden it somewhere, or put it somewhere for safekeeping..."

"But *where*?"

The waitress arrives and puts a cappuccino down in front of me. I pick up the little freebie biscuit and distractedly start unwrapping it. Where would I have put a file? Where would I hide it? What was I thinking?

"I remember something else." Jon drains his cup and gestures to the waitress for another. "You went down to Kent. You went to your mother's house."

"Really?" I look up. "When?"

"Just before the accident. Maybe you took the file down."

"To my mum's house?" I say skeptically.

"It's worth a chance." He shrugs. "Call her up and ask her."

I stir my cappuccino moodily as the waitress brings over another coffee for Jon. I don't want to ring up Mum. Ringing Mum is bad for my health.

"Come on, Lexi, you can do it." Jon's mouth twitches

with amusement at my expression. "What are you, woman or walrus?"

I raise my head, stunned. For a moment I wonder whether I heard that right.

"That's what Fi says," I say at last.

"I know. You told me about Fi."

"What did I tell you about Fi?" I say suspiciously.

Jon takes a sip of coffee. "You told me you met in Mrs. Brady's class. You had your first and last cigarette with her. You went to Ibiza together three times. Losing her friendship has been really traumatic." He nods at my phone, sticking out of my bag. "Which is why you should make the call."

This is so *spooky*. What the hell else does he know? Sliding him wary glances, I take the phone out of my bag and key in Mum's number.

"Lexi, I'm not magic." Jon looks even more as if he wants to laugh. "We had a relationship. We talked."

"Hello?" Mum's voice on the line tears me away from Jon.

"Oh, Mum! It's me, Lexi. Listen, did I bring some papers down any time recently? Or like . . . a folder?"

"That big blue folder?"

I feel an almighty thrust of disbelief. It's true. It exists. I can feel the excitement rising inside me. And the hope.

"That's right." I try to stay calm. "Do you have it? Is it still there?"

"It's in your room, exactly where you left it." Mum sounds defensive. "One corner may be *slightly* damp . . ."

I don't believe it. A dog's peed on it.

"But it's still okay?" I say anxiously. "It's still legible?"

"Of course!"

"Great!" I clutch the phone tighter. "Well, just hold on to it, Mum. Keep it safe and I'll come and get it today." I flip my phone shut and turn to Jon. "You were right! It's there. Okay, I have to go down there straightaway. I have to get to Victoria—there's bound to be a train in the next hour..."

"Lexi, calm down." Jon drains his coffee. "I'll drive you, if you like."

"What?"

"I'm not busy today. It'll have to be in your car, though. I don't have one."

"You don't have a car?" I say disbelievingly.

"I'm between cars at the moment." He shrugs. "I use my bike or taxis. But I *do* know how to drive a swanky Mercedes open-top." Again he looks like he's sharing a private joke with someone.

With me, it suddenly hits me. With the girl I used to be.

I open my mouth to speak—but I'm too confused. My head is teeming with thoughts.

"Okay," I say at last. "Okay. Thanks."

· · ·

We have our story totally worked out. At least I do. If anyone asks, Jon is giving me a driving lesson. He just happened to drop by when I was getting into the car, and just happened to offer.

But no one does ask.

It's a sunny day, and as Jon reverses the car out of its parking space, he retracts the roof. Then he reaches in his pocket and hands me a black hair elastic. "You'll need this. It's windy."

I take the hair elastic in surprise. "How come you have this in your pocket?"

"I have them everywhere. They're all yours." He rolls his eyes, signaling left. "I don't know what you do, *shed* them?"

Silently, I put my hair up into a ponytail before it can get windswept. Jon turns onto the road and heads to the first junction. "It's in Kent," I say as we pull up at the lights. "You have to head out of London on the—"

"I know where it is."

"You know where my mother's house is?" I say a touch incredulously.

"I've been there."

The lights turn green and we move on. I stare out at the grand white houses passing by, barely noticing them. He's been to Mum's house. He knows about Fi. He has my hair elastic in his pocket. He was right about the blue folder. Either he's really, *really* done his research, or...

"So...hypothetically," I say at last. "If we were once lovers..."

"Hypothetically." Jon nods without turning his head.

"What exactly happened? How did we..."

"Like I told you, we met at a launch party. We kept bumping into each other through the company. I came over to your place more and more. I'd arrive early, while Eric was still tied up. We'd chat, hang out on the terrace. . . . It was innocuous." He pauses, negotiating a tricky lane-change. "Then Eric went away one week-end. And I came over. And after that . . . it wasn't so in-nocuous."

I'm starting to believe. It's like the world is sliding— a screen is going back. Colors are becoming sharper and clearer.

"So what else happened?" I say.

"We saw each other as often as we could."

"I know *that*." I cast around. "I mean . . . what was it like? What did we say, what did we do? Just . . . tell me stuff."

"You crack me up." Jon shakes his head, his eyes crinkled in amusement. "That's what you always said to me in bed. 'Tell me stuff.' "

"I like hearing stuff." I shrug defensively. "Any old stuff."

"I know you do. Okay. Any old stuff." He drives silently for a while and I can see a smile pushing at his mouth as he thinks. "Everywhere we've been together, we've ended up buying you socks. Same thing every time, you rip off your shoes to be barefoot on the sand or the grass or whatever, and then you get cold and we need to find you socks." He pulls up at a crosswalk. "What else? You've got me into putting mustard on fries."

"French mustard?"

"Exactly. When I first saw you, I thought it was an evil perversion. Now I'm addicted." He pulls away from the crossing and turns onto a big dual carriageway. The car is speeding up; he's harder to hear over traffic noise. "One weekend it rained. Eric was away playing golf and we watched every single episode of *Doctor Who,* back to back." He glances at me. "Should I keep going?"

Everything he's saying is resonating. My brain is tuning up. I don't remember what he's talking about, but I'm feeling stirrings of recognition. It feels like me. This feels like my life.

"Keep going." I nod.

"Okay. So . . . we play table tennis. It's pretty brutal. You're two games ahead, but I think you're about to crack."

"I am *so* not about to crack," I retort automatically.

"Oh, you are."

"Never!" I can't help grinning.

"You met my mum. She instantly guessed. She knows me too well to kid her. But that's okay. She's cool, she'd never say anything." Jon pulls into another lane. "You always sleep on the left. We've had five whole nights together in eight months." He's silent for a moment. "Eric's had two hundred and thirty-five."

I don't know how to reply to that. Jon's gaze is focused ahead; his face is intent. "Should I keep going?" he says at last.

"Yeah." I clear my throat huskily. "Keep going."

• • •

As we drive through the Kent countryside, Jon has exhausted all the details he can give me about our relationship. Obviously I can't supply any of my own, so we're sitting in silence as the hop fields and oast houses pass by. Not that I'm looking at them. I grew up in Kent, so I don't even notice the picturesque, garden-of-England scenery. Instead I'm watching the GPS screen in a trance; following the arrow with my gaze.

Suddenly it reminds me of my conversation with Loser Dave, and I heave a sigh.

"What's up?" Jon glances over.

"Oh, nothing. I just still keep wondering, how did I get to where I am? What made me go after my career, get my teeth done, turn into this...*other* person?" I gesture at myself.

"Well," says Jon, squinting up at a sign. "I suppose it started with what happened at the funeral."

"What do you mean?"

"You know. The thing with your dad."

"What about my dad?" I say, puzzled. "I don't know what you're talking about."

With a screech of brakes, Jon stops the Mercedes right next to a field full of cows, and turns to face me. "Didn't your mother tell you about the funeral?"

"Of course she did!" I say. "It happened. Dad was...cremated or whatever."

"That's it?"

I rack my brain. I'm sure Mum didn't say anything else about the funeral. She changed the subject when I brought it up, I suddenly recall. But, I mean, that's normal for Mum. She changes every subject.

Shaking his head in disbelief, Jon puts the car back

into gear. "This is unreal. Do you know *anything* about your life?"

"Apparently not," I say, a bit rattled. "Well, tell me! If it's so important."

"Uh-uh." Jon shakes his head as the car moves off again. "Not my call. Your mum has to tell you this one." He turns off the road and pulls into a gravel drive. "We're here."

So we are. I hadn't even noticed. The house is looking pretty much as I remember it: a redbrick house dating from the 1900s, with a conservatory on one side and Mum's ancient Volvo parked in front. The truth is, the place hasn't changed since we moved in twenty years ago; it's just got more crumbly. A length of gutter is hanging off the roof and ivy has crept even farther up the walls. Under a moldy tarpaulin at the side of the drive is a pile of paving stones that Dad once dumped there. He was going to sell them and start a business, I think. That was . . . eight years ago? Ten?

Through the gate I can just glimpse the garden, which used to be quite pretty, with raised flower beds and a herb patch. Before we got the dogs.

"So . . . you're saying Mum lied to me?"

Jon shakes his head. "Not lied. Edited." He opens the car door. "Come on."

• • •

The thing about whippets is they look quite slight, but when they stand on their hind legs they're huge. And when about ten of them are trying to jump up on you at once, it's like being mugged.

"Ophelia! Raphael!" I can just about hear Mum's voice over the scrabbling and yelping. "Get down! Lexi, darling! You really did rush down here. What *is* all this?" She's wearing a corduroy skirt and blue-striped shirt with fraying hems at the sleeves, and she's holding an ancient "Charles and Diana" tea towel.

"Hi, Mum," I say breathlessly, manhandling a dog off me. "This is Jon. My...friend." I gesture at Jon, who is gazing a whippet straight in the eyes and saying, "Put your paws on the floor. Step *away* from the humans."

"Well!" Mum seems flustered. "If I'd realized, I would have rustled up some lunch. *How* you expect me to cater at this late notice—"

"Mum, we don't expect you to cater. All I want is that folder. Is it still there?"

"Of course." She sounds defensive. "It's perfectly all right."

I hurry up the creaky green-carpeted stairs and into my bedroom, which still has the floral Laura Ashley wallpaper it always did.

Amy's right—this place *stinks*. I can't tell if it's the dogs or the damp or the rot...but it should get sorted. I spot the folder on top of a chest of drawers and grab it—then recoil. Now I know why Mum was defensive. This is so gross. It totally smells of dog pee.

Wrinkling my nose, I gingerly extend two fingers and open it.

There's my writing. Lines and lines of it, clear as day. Like a message from me to...me. I scan the first page, trying to glean as quickly as possible what I was doing, what I was planning, what this is all about.... I can see I had written some sort of proposal, but *what* exactly? I turn the page, my brow wrinkled in bewilderment, then turn another page. And that's when I see the name.

Oh. My God.

In an instant, I understand. I've got the whole picture. I raise my head, my heart thudding with excitement. That is such a good idea. I mean, that is *such* a good idea. I can already see the potential. It could be huge, it could change everything....

Filled with adrenaline, I grab the folder, not caring how it smells, and rush out of the room, taking the stairs two steps at a time.

"Got it?" Jon is waiting at the bottom of the stairs.

"Yes!" A smile licks across my face. "It's brilliant! It's a brilliant idea!"

"It was your idea."

"*Really?*" I feel a glow of pride, which I try to quell. "You know, this is what we needed all along. This is what we should have been doing. If this works out, they *can't* give up carpeting. They'd be mad."

A dog jumps up and tries to chew my hair, but even that can't dent my mood. I can't believe I put together this deal. Me, Lexi! I can't wait to tell everyone—

"Now!" Mum is approaching bearing a tray of coffee cups. "I can at least offer you a cup of coffee and a biscuit."

"Really, Mum, it's okay," I say. "I'm afraid we have to dash off—"

"I'd like a coffee," says Jon pleasantly.

He *what*? Shooting him daggers, I follow him into the sitting room and we sit down on a faded sofa. Jon takes his seat like he feels totally at home there. Maybe he does.

"So, Lexi was just talking about piecing her life together," he says, crunching a biscuit. "And I thought, maybe knowing the events that happened at her dad's funeral would help."

"Well, of course, losing a parent is always traumatic..." Mum is focused on breaking a biscuit in two. "*Here* you are, Ophelia." She feeds half to a whippet.

"That's not what I'm talking about," Jon says. "I'm talking about the other events."

"Other events?" Mum looks vague. "Now, Raphael, that's naughty! Coffee, Lexi?"

The dogs are all over the biscuit plate, slobbering and grabbing. Are we supposed to eat those now?

"Lexi doesn't seem to have the fullest of pictures," Jon persists.

"Smoky, it's *not* your turn..."

"*Stop talking to the fucking dogs!*" Jon's voice makes me leap off my seat.

Mum looks almost too shocked to speak. Or even move.

"*This* is your child." Jon gestures at me. "Not that." He jerks a thumb at a dog and gets up from the sofa in an abrupt movement. Both Mum and I gaze up at him, transfixed, as he walks over to the fireplace, ruffling his hair, ignoring the dogs clustering around him. "Now, I care about your daughter. She may not realize it, but I do." He focuses directly on Mum. "Maybe you want to get through life in a state of denial. Maybe it helps you. But it doesn't help Lexi."

"What are you talking about?" I say helplessly. "Mum, what happened at the funeral?"

Mum's hands are fluttering around her face as though to protect herself. "It was rather . . . unpleasant."

"Life can be unpleasant," Jon says bluntly. "It's even more unpleasant if you don't know about it. And if you don't tell Lexi, I will. Because she told me, you see." He crunches the last of his biscuit.

"All right! What happened was . . ." Mum's voice descends into a whisper.

"*What?*"

"The bailiffs came!" Her cheeks are growing pink with distress. "Right in the middle of the party."

"Bailiffs? But . . ."

"They came with no warning. Five of them." She's staring straight ahead, stroking the dog on her lap with an obsessive repetitive motion. "They wanted to repossess the house. Take all the furniture, everything. It turned out your father hadn't been . . . totally honest with me. Or anybody."

"Show her the second DVD," says Jon. "Don't tell me you don't know where it is."

There's a pause, then without looking at either of us, Mum gets up, roots in a drawer, and finds a blank, shiny disc. She puts it into the machine and the three of us sit back.

"Darlings." Dad is on the screen again, in the same room as in the other DVD, in the same plushy dressing gown. The same charming twinkle as he faces the camera. "If you're watching this, I've popped it. And there's something you should know. But this one's not for...public consumption, shall we say." He takes a deep puff on his cigar, frowning regretfully. "There's been a bit of a catastrophe on the old moolah front. Didn't mean to land you in it. You girls are clever— you'll find a way to sort it out." He considers for a moment. "But if you're stuck, ask old Dickie Hawford. He should be good for a bit. Cheers, m'dears." He lifts his glass up—then the screen goes dark. I wheel around to Mum.

"What did he mean, 'catastrophe'?"

"He meant he'd remortgaged the entire house." Her voice is trembling. "That was his real message. That DVD arrived in the post a week after the funeral. But it was too late! The bailiffs had visited! What were we supposed to do?" She's stroking the whippet harder and harder, until, with a sudden yelp, it escapes from her grasp.

"So...what did we do?"

"We would have had to sell up. Move to another area. Amy would have been taken out of school..." Her hands are fluttering around her face again. "So my brother very kindly stepped in. And so did my sister. And...and so did you. You said you'd pay off the mortgage. As much as you could afford."

"*Me?*"

I sink back into the sofa, my mind reeling with shock, trying to fit this into the picture. *I agreed to pay off Dad's debts.*

"Is it an offshore mortgage?" I say suddenly. "Is the bank called Uni...something?"

She nods. "Most of Daddy's dealings were offshore. Trying to avoid the tax man. I don't know *why* he couldn't just be honest—"

"Said the woman who kept her daughter in the dark!" expostulates Jon. "How can you even *say* that?"

I can't help catching some of his exasperation.

"Mum, you knew I couldn't remember the funeral. You didn't tell me *any* of this. Can't you see how it might have...made things clearer for me? I had no idea where that money was going."

"It's been very difficult!" Mum's eyes are swiveling from side to side. "I've been trying to keep it quiet for Amy's sake."

"But—" I break off as something else even darker occurs to me. "Mum...I have another question. Was Dad ever in prison?"

Mum winces as though I've trodden on her toe.

"Briefly, darling. A long time ago...It was a misunderstanding. Let's not dwell on that. I'll make some more coffee."

"No!" In frustration I leap to my feet and stand right in front of her, trying to get her single-minded attention. "Mum, listen! You can't just live in a bubble, pretending nothing's happened. Amy's right! You have to break out of this...this time warp."

"Lexi!" Mum says sharply, but I ignore her.

"Amy *heard* about Dad going to prison. She got the idea it's cool. No wonder she's been getting in so much trouble.... Jesus!" Suddenly the pieces of my life are slotting together like a Tetris puzzle. "*That's* why I suddenly got ambitious. That's why I was so single-minded. That funeral changed everything."

"You told me what happened," Jon says. "When the bailiffs arrived, she went to bits." He glances scornfully at Mum. "You had to hold them off, Lexi; you had to make the decisions. You took it all on yourself."

"Stop looking at me as though it's all my fault!" Mum suddenly cries out, her voice shrill and quivering. "Stop heaping blame on me! You have no idea about my life, none! Your father, that *man*—"

She breaks off, the words hanging in the air, and I catch my breath as her blue eyes meet mine. For the first time that I can remember, my mother sounds... true.

The room is totally still. I hardly dare speak.

"What about Dad?" My sotto voce whisper still feels too loud. "Mum, tell me."

But it's too late. Already the moment's over. Mum's eyes are shifting sideways, avoiding me. With a sudden pang I see her as though for the first time: her hair girlish in its Alice band, her hands wrinkled, Dad's ring still on her finger. Even as I watch, she's feeling for a dog's head and starting to pat it.

"It's nearly lunchtime, Agnes!" Her voice is bright and brittle. "Let's see what we can find you—"

"Mum, please." I take a step forward. "You can't stop there. What were you going to say?"

I don't know what exactly I'm hoping for—but as

she looks up I can tell I'm not going to get it. Her face is opaque again, as though nothing just happened.

"I was *simply* going to say"—already she's regaining her old martyred spirit—"that before you start blaming me for everything in your life, Lexi, that chap had a lot to answer for. That boyfriend of yours at the funeral. Dave? David? *He's* the one you should be accusing."

"Loser Dave?" I stare at her, thrown. "But...Loser Dave wasn't at the funeral. He told me he offered to come but I turned him down. He said..." I peter out as I see Jon just shaking his head, his eyes raised to heaven.

"What else did he tell you?"

"He said we broke up that morning, and that it was beautiful, and that he gave me a single rose..." Oh God. What was I thinking, even *half*-believing him? "Excuse me."

I march outside into the drive, fueled with frustration at Mum, at Dad, at myself for being so gullible. Whipping my mobile phone from my pocket, I direct-dial Loser Dave's office.

"Auto Repair Workshop," comes his businesslike voice down the line. "Dave Lewis at your service."

"Loser Dave, it's me," I say, my voice steely. "Lexi. I need to hear about our breakup again. And this time I need to hear the truth."

"Babe, I told you the truth." He sounds supremely confident. "You're going to have to trust me on this one."

I want to *wallop* him.

"Listen, you fuckhead," I say in slow, furious tones. "I'm at the neurological specialist's office right now, okay? They say someone has been giving me wrong information and it's messing up my neural memory pathways. And if it isn't corrected, I'll get permanent brain damage."

"Jesus." He sounds shaken. "Straight up?"

He really is stupider than one of Mum's whippets.

"Yeah. The specialist's with me right now, trying to correct my memory circuits. So maybe you want to try again with the truth? Or maybe you'd like to speak to the doctor?"

"No! Okay!" He sounds totally unnerved. I can just picture him breathing harder, running a finger around his collar. "Maybe it wasn't *exactly* like I told you. I was trying to protect you."

"Protect me from what? Did you come to the funeral?"

"Yeah, I came along," he says after a pause. "I was handing out canapés. Being helpful. Giving you support."

"And then what happened?"

"Then I . . ." He clears his throat.

"*What?*"

"Shagged one of the waitresses. It was the emotional stress!" he adds defensively. "It makes us all do crazy things. I thought I'd locked the door—"

"I walked *in* on you?" I say in disbelief.

"Yeah. We weren't naked or anything. Well, obviously a bit—"

"Stop!" I thrust the phone away from me.

I need a few moments to take all this in. Breathing hard, I crunch over the gravel, sit down on the garden wall, and look at the field of sheep opposite, ignoring the "Lexi! Lexi!" coming from the phone.

I caught Loser Dave two-timing me. Well, of course I did. I'm not even that surprised.

At last I lift the phone back to my ear. "So, how did I react? And *don't* say I gave you a rose and it was beautiful."

"Well." Loser Dave breathes out. "To be honest, you went ballistic. You started yelling about your life. Your whole life had to change, it was all crap, you hated me, you hated everything.... I'm telling you, Lexi, it was extreme. I tried to calm you down, give you a prawn sandwich. But you weren't interested. You stormed out."

"Then what?"

"Then I didn't see you again. Next time I clapped eyes on you, you were on the telly, looking totally different."

"Right." I watch two birds circling in the sky. "You know, you could have told me the truth, first time around."

"I know. I'm sorry."

"Yeah, right."

"No, I am." He sounds as genuine as I've ever heard him. "And I'm sorry I shagged that girl. And I'm sorry for what she called you, that was well out of order."

I sit up, suddenly alert. "What did she call me?"

"Oh. You don't remember," he says hastily. "Er... nothing. I don't remember either."

"What was it?" I stand up, clutching the phone tighter. "Tell me what she called me! Loser Dave!"

"I gotta go. Good luck with the doctor." He rings off. I immediately redial his number, but it's busy. Little sod.

I march into the house to find Jon still sitting on the sofa, reading a copy of *Whippet World*.

"Hi!" His face lights up. "How did it go?"

"What did the waitress call me at the funeral?"

At once Jon looks evasive. "I don't know what you mean. Hey, have you ever read *Whippet World*?" He holds it up. "Because it's a surprisingly good—"

"You *do* know what I mean." I sit down beside him and pull his chin around so he has to look at me. "I know I told you. Tell me."

Jon sighs. "Lexi, it's a tiny detail. Why does it matter?"

"Because . . . it just does. Look, Jon, you can't lecture my mum about denial and then not tell me something which happened in *my* own life, which I deserve to know. Tell me what that waitress called me. *Now*." I glare at him.

"All right!" Jon lifts his hands as though in defeat. "If you have to know, she called you . . . Dracula."

Dracula? In spite of myself—in spite of the fact that I *know* my teeth aren't snaggly anymore—I can feel my cheeks staining with mortification.

"Lexi—" Jon's wincing, as he reaches for my hand.

"No." I shake him off. "I'm fine."

My face still hot, I stand up and head over to the window, trying to picture the scene, trying to put myself back in my own chewed-up, flat-heeled Lexi shoes. It's 2004. I didn't get a bonus. It's my dad's funeral. The bailiffs have just arrived to bankrupt us. I come across my boyfriend screwing a waitress . . . and she takes one look at me and calls me Dracula.

Okay. Things are starting to make sense.

Chapter Eighteen

On the way back, I sit in silence for a long, long while. I'm clutching the blue folder tightly on my lap as if it might try to run away. The fields are whizzing past outside. Jon glances at me every now and then but doesn't speak.

I'm going around and around it all in my head, trying to digest everything I've just learned. I feel like I've done a degree in Lexi Smart, in the space of half an hour.

"I still can't believe my dad left us in trouble like that," I say at last. "With no warning or anything."

"Oh no?" Jon sounds noncommittal.

Kicking off my shoes, I draw my feet up onto the seat and rest my chin on my knees, gazing out at the road. "You know, everyone loved my dad. He was so good-looking, and fun, and sparky, and he loved us. Even though he fucked up a few times, he really did love us. He used to call us his three girls."

"His three girls." Jon's voice is drier than ever. "A dog-obsessive in denial, a teenage extortionist, and a screwed-up amnesiac. And all of them in debt. Good work, Michael. Nicely done."

I shoot him a look. "You don't think much of my dad, do you?"

"I think he had a good time and left the pieces for all of you to deal with," says Jon. "I think he was a selfish prick. But hey, I never met the guy." Abruptly he signals and pulls into another lane. His hands are gripping the wheel tightly, I suddenly notice. He seems almost angry.

"At least I *get* myself a bit more." I chew on my thumbnail. "Did I ever talk to you about it? The funeral?"

"Once or twice." Jon gives me a wry smile.

"Oh, right." I color. "All the time. I must have bored you to death."

"Don't be stupid." He takes a hand off the wheel and squeezes mine briefly. "One day, really early on, when we were still just friends, it all came out. The whole story. How that day changed your life. How you took on your family's debt, booked a cosmetic dentistry appointment the next day, went on a crash diet, decided to change everything about yourself. Then you went on TV and everything became even more extreme. You rocketed up the career ladder, you met Eric, and he seemed like the answer. He was solid, rich, stable. A million miles away from . . ." He breaks off into silence.

"My dad," I say eventually.

"I'm no psychologist. But I would guess."

There's silence. I watch a small plane heading higher

and higher into the sky, leaving a double trail of white smoke.

"You know, when I woke up, I thought I'd landed the dream life," I say slowly. "I thought I was Cinderella. I was *better* than Cinderella. I thought I must be the happiest girl in the world..." I break off as Jon shakes his head.

"You were living your whole life under a strain. You went too far too soon; you didn't know how to handle it; you made mistakes." He hesitates. "You alienated your friends. You found that the hardest of all."

"But I don't *understand*," I say helplessly. "I don't understand why I became a bitch."

"You didn't mean to. Lexi, give yourself a break. You were thrust into this boss position. You had a big department to run, you wanted to impress senior management, not be accused of favoritism...and you floundered. You did some things the wrong way. Then you felt trapped. You'd built up this tough persona. It was part of your success."

"The *Cobra*," I say, wincing. I still can't believe I got nicknamed after a snake.

"The Cobra." He nods, a smile pushing at his mouth again. "You know, that was the TV producers' idea. That wasn't you. Although they had something— you *are* pretty cobra-like when it comes to business."

"No, I'm not!" I lift my head in horror.

"In a good way." He grins.

A good way? How can you be like a cobra in a good way?

We drive on for a while without speaking, golden

fields sprawling into the distance on either side of us. At length Jon turns on the radio. The Eagles are playing "Hotel California" and as we zip along, sunlight glinting off the windshield, I suddenly feel like we could be in another country. Another life.

"You once said to me, if you could go back in time and do everything differently, you would." Jon's voice is softer than before. "With everything. Yourself... your job... Eric... Everything looks different when the gloss is gone."

I feel a sudden sting at the mention of Eric. Jon's talking like everything's in the past—but this is now. I'm married. Nor do I like what he's implying.

"Look, I'm not some shallow gold-digger, okay?" I say hotly. "I must have loved Eric. I wouldn't just marry a guy because of the gloss."

"At first you thought Eric was the real deal," Jon agrees. "He's charming, he ticks the boxes... In fact, he's like one of the intelligent systems from our lofts. Put him on 'Husband' setting and away he goes."

"Stop it."

"He's state-of-the-art. He has a range of mood settings; he's touch sensitive..."

"*Stop* it." I'm trying not to laugh. I lean forward and turn the radio up higher, as though to block Jon out. A moment later I've worked out what I want to say, and turn it down again.

"Okay, look. Maybe we did have an affair. In the past. But that doesn't mean... Maybe I want to make my marriage *work* this time around."

"You can't make it work." Jon doesn't miss a beat. "Eric doesn't love you."

Why does he have to be such a bloody *know-it-all*?

"Yes, he does." I fold my arms. "He told me so. In fact, it was really romantic, if you want to know."

"Oh yeah?" Jon doesn't sound remotely fazed. "What'd he say?"

"He said he fell in love with my beautiful mouth and my long legs and the way I swing my briefcase." I can't help coloring with self-consciousness. I've always remembered Eric saying that, in fact I memorized it on the spot.

"That's a crock of shit." Jon doesn't even turn.

"It's not a crock of shit!" I retort indignantly. "It's romantic!"

"Oh, really? So would he love you if you *didn't* swing your briefcase?"

I'm momentarily stumped. "I . . . don't know. That's not the point."

"How can it not be the point? It's exactly the point. Would he love you if your legs weren't long?"

"I don't know!" I say crossly. "Shut up! It was a lovely, beautiful moment."

"It was bullshit."

"Okay." I jut out my chin. "So what do *you* love about me?"

"I don't know. The essence of you. I can't turn it into a *list*," he says, almost scathingly.

There's a long pause. I'm staring straight ahead, my arms still folded tightly. Jon's focused on the road, as though he's already forgotten the conversation. We're getting nearer London now, and the traffic is thickening up around us.

"Okay," he says finally, as we draw to a halt in a queue of cars. "I like the way you squeak in your sleep."

"I squeak in my sleep?" I say disbelievingly.

"Like a chipmunk."

"I thought I was supposed to be a cobra," I retort. "Make up your mind."

"Cobra by day." He nods. "Chipmunk by night."

I'm trying to keep my mouth straight and firm, but a smile is edging out.

As we crawl along the dual carriageway, my phone beeps with a text and I pull it out.

"It's Eric," I say after reading it. "He's arrived safely in Manchester. He's scoping out some possible new sites for a few days."

"Uh-huh. I know." Jon swings around a roundabout.

We're into the outskirts of the city now. The air seems grayer and a spot of rain suddenly hits me on the cheek. I shiver, and Jon puts the roof of the Mercedes back up. His face is set as he negotiates the lanes of the dual carriageway.

"You know, Eric could have paid off your dad's debt in his sleep," he suddenly says, his voice matter-of-fact. "But he left you to it. Never even mentioned it."

I feel at a loss. I don't know how to reply to that; I don't know what to think.

"It's his money," I say at last. "Why should he? And anyway, I don't *need* anyone's help."

"I know. I offered. You wouldn't take anything.

You're pretty stubborn." He reaches a big junction, draws up behind a bus, and turns to look at me. "I don't know what you're planning now."

"Now?"

"The rest of today." He shrugs. "If Eric's away."

Deep within me, something starts stirring. A gentle pulsing, which I don't want to admit to. Even to myself.

"Well." I try to sound businesslike. "I wasn't planning anything. Just go home, have some supper, read through this folder..." I force myself to leave a natural pause before I add, "Why?"

"Nothing." Jon leaves a pause too, and frowns ahead at the road before he adds casually, "It's just there's some stuff of yours at my flat. You might want to pick it up."

"Okay." I shrug noncommittally.

"Okay." He swings the car around and we travel the rest of the way in silence.

• • •

Jon lives in the most beautiful flat I've ever seen.

Okay, it's in a daggy street in Hammersmith. And you have to ignore the graffiti on the wall opposite. But the house is big and pale brick, with massive old arched windows, and it turns out that the flat runs into the next-door building too, so it's a million times wider than it seems from the outside.

"This is...*amazing.*"

I'm standing, looking around his workspace, almost speechless. The ceiling is high and the walls are white and there's a tall, sloped desk covered in paper, next to a workstation bearing a massive Apple Mac. In the corner is a drawing easel, and opposite is an entire wall covered in books, with an old-fashioned library ladder on wheels.

"This whole row of houses was built as artists' studios." Jon's eyes are gleaming as he walks around, picking up about ten old coffee cups and disappearing with them into a tiny kitchen.

The sun has come out again and is glinting through the arched windows onto the reclaimed floorboards. Discarded pieces of paper are on the floor, covered in lines, drawings, sketches. Plonked in the middle of all the work is a bottle of tequila next to a packet of almonds.

I look up to see Jon standing in the kitchen doorway, watching me soundlessly. He ruffles his hair as though to break some mood, and says, "Your stuff's through here."

I walk where he's pointing, through an archway into a cozy sitting room. It's furnished with big blue cotton sofas and a massive leather bean bag and an old TV balanced on a chair. Behind the sofa are battered wooden shelves, haphazardly filled with books and magazines and plants and...

"That's my mug." I stare at a hand-painted red pottery mug that Fi once gave me for my birthday, sitting on the shelves like it belongs there.

"Yeah." Jon nods. "That's what I mean. You left stuff here." He picks it up and hands it to me.

"And...my sweater!" There's an old ribbed polo

neck draped over one of the sofas. I've had it forever, since I was about sixteen. How come—

I look around in disbelief as more things spring into my vision, like a Magic Eye. That furry fake-wolf throw that I always used to wrap around myself. Old college photos in their beaded frames. My pink retro *toaster*?

"You used to come here and eat toast." Jon follows my astonished gaze. "You used to cram it in like you were starving."

I'm suddenly seeing the other side of me; the side I thought had disappeared forever. For the first time since I woke up in hospital I feel like I'm at home. There's even a string of fairy lights draped around the plant in the corner; the same fairy lights I had in my little flat in Balham.

All this time, all my stuff was here. Suddenly I have a memory of Eric's words, that first time I asked him about Jon. *You'd trust Jon with your life.*

Maybe that's what I did. Trusted him with my life.

"Do you remember anything?" Jon sounds casual, but I can sense the hope underneath.

"No." I shake my head. "Just the stuff that came from my life before..." I break off as I notice a beaded frame I don't recognize. I move closer to see the picture—and feel a tiny jolt. It's a photo of me. And Jon. We're sitting on a tree trunk and his arms are around me and I'm wearing old jeans and sneakers. My hair is streaming down my back; my head is tossed back. I'm laughing as though I'm the happiest girl there ever was.

It was real. It was really real.

My head is prickling as I stare at our faces, bleached by the sunshine. All this time, he had proof.

"You could have shown me this," I say almost accusingly. "This photo. You could have brought it along the first time we met."

"Would you have believed me?" He sits on the arm of the sofa. "Would you have wanted to believe me?"

I'm halted. Maybe he's right. Maybe I would have explained it away, rationalized it, clung to my perfect husband, my dream life.

Trying to lighten the atmosphere, I walk over to a table cluttered with old novels belonging to me and a bowl of seeds.

"Sunflower seeds." I grab a handful. "I love sunflower seeds."

"I know you do." Jon has the oddest, most unfathomable expression on his face.

"What?" I look at him in surprise, seeds halfway to my mouth. "What's wrong? Are these okay?"

"They're fine. There was something..." He breaks off and smiles, as though to himself. "No. It doesn't matter. Forget it."

"What?" I frown, bewildered. "Something from our relationship? You have to tell me. Go on."

"It's nothing." He shrugs. "It was stupid. We just had this...tradition. The first time we had sex you'd been munching on sunflower seeds. You planted one in a yogurt pot and I took it home. It was like our own private joke. Then we started doing it every time. As a memento. We called them our children."

"We planted sunflowers?" I wrinkle my brow with interest. That rings a tiny bell.

"Uh-huh." Jon nods, like he wants to change the subject. "Let me get you a drink."

"So where are they?" I say as he pours out two glasses of wine. "Did you keep any of them?" I'm looking around the room for signs of seedlings in yogurt pots.

"It doesn't matter." He hands me a glass.

"Did you throw them away?"

"No, I didn't throw them away." He heads over to a CD player and puts on some low music, but I won't be put off.

"Where are they, then?" A challenging note creeps into my voice. "We must have had sex a few times, if everything you say is true. So there should be a few sunflower plants."

Jon takes a sip of his wine. Then without saying a word he turns on his heel and gestures for me to walk along a small corridor. We head through a sparsely decorated bedroom. There he pushes open double doors to a wide, decked balcony. And I catch my breath.

There's a wall of sunflowers all the way around. From huge yellow monsters reaching up to the sky, down to young flowers, tethered to canes, down to spindly green shoots in tiny pots, just starting to open. Everywhere I look, I can see sunflowers.

This was it. This was us. From the very beginning to the latest scrappy seedling in a pot. My throat is suddenly tight as I gaze around at the sea of green and yellow. I had no idea.

"So, how long ago . . . I mean . . ." I jerk my head at the tiniest seedling, in a tiny painted pot, propped up with sticks. "Since we last . . ."

"Six weeks ago. The day before the crash." Jon pauses, an unreadable expression on his face. "I'm kind of looking after that one."

"Was that the last time I saw you before . . ." I bite my lip.

There's a beat of silence, then Jon nods. "That's the last time we were together."

I sit down and gulp at my wine, feeling totally overwhelmed. There's a whole story here. A whole relationship. Growing and thickening and turning into something so strong I was going to leave Eric.

"What about . . . the first time?" I say eventually. "How did it all start?"

"It was that weekend Eric was away. I was over and we were chatting. We were out on the balcony, drinking wine. Kind of like we are now." Jon gestures around. "And then halfway through the afternoon we fell silent. And we knew."

He lifts his dark eyes to mine and I feel a lurch, deep inside. He gets up and starts walking toward me. "We both knew it was inevitable," he says softly.

I'm transfixed. Gently he removes the wineglass from my hand and takes hold of both my hands.

"Lexi . . ." He brings my hands up to his mouth, closing his eyes, gently kissing them. "I knew . . ." His voice is muffled against my skin. "You'd come back. I knew you'd come back to me."

"Stop it!" I whip my hands away, my heart thudding in distress. "You don't . . . you don't know anything!"

"What's wrong?" Jon looks as shell-shocked as though I'd hit him.

I almost don't know what's wrong myself. I want him so badly; my entire body's telling me to go for it. But I can't.

"What's wrong is . . . I'm freaked."

"By what?" He looks dumbfounded.

"By all this!" I gesture at the sunflowers. "It's too much. You're presenting me with this . . . this fully fledged relationship. But for me, it's just the beginning." I take a deep gulp of wine, trying to keep my cool. "I'm too many steps behind. It's too unbalanced."

"We'll balance it," he says quickly. "We'll work it out. I'll go back to the beginning too."

"You can't go back to the beginning!" I thrust my hands hopelessly through my hair. "Jon, you're a guy who's attractive and witty and cool. And I really like you. But I don't love you. How could I? I haven't done all this. I don't remember all this."

"I don't expect you to *love* me—"

"Yes, you do. You do! You expect me to be her."

"You *are* her." There's a sudden streak of anger in his voice. "Don't give me this bullshit. You're the girl I love. Believe it, Lexi."

"I don't know!" My voice rises in agitation. "I don't *know* if I am, okay? Am I her? Am I me?"

To my horror, tears are streaming down my face; I

have no idea where they came from. I turn away and wipe my face, gulping, unable to stop the torrent.

I want to be her, I want to be the girl laughing on the tree trunk. But I'm not.

At last I manage to get a grip on myself and turn around. Jon is standing in exactly the same place as he was before, a bleakness on his face that makes my heart constrict.

"I look around at these sunflowers." I swallow hard. "And the photos. And all my things here. And I can see that it happened. But it looks like a wonderful romance between two people I don't know."

"It's you," says Jon in a quiet voice. "It's me. You know both of us."

"I know it in my head. But I don't feel it. I don't *know* it." I clench a fist on my chest, feeling the tears rising again. "If I could just remember *one thing*. If there was one memory, one thread..." I trail off in silence. Jon is gazing at the sunflowers as though rapt by every petal.

"So, what are you saying?"

"I'm saying...I don't know! I don't know. I need time...I need..." I break off helplessly.

Spots of rain are starting to fall on the balcony. A breeze gusts past and the sunflowers sway against each other as though they're nodding.

At last Jon breaks the silence. "A lift home?" He lifts his eyes to meet mine—and there's no anger anymore.

"Yes." I wipe my eyes and push my hair back. "Please."

• • •

It only takes fifteen minutes to reach home. We don't chat. I sit holding on to the blue folder and Jon changes gear, his jaw set. He pulls the Mercedes into my parking space, and for a moment neither of us moves. Rain is thundering against the roof by now and there's a sudden crash of lightning.

"You'll have to run straight in," Jon says, and I nod.

"How will you get back?"

"I'll be fine." He hands me my keys, avoiding my eye. "Good luck with that." He nods at the folder. "I mean it."

"Thanks." I run a hand over the cardboard, biting my lip. "Although I don't know how I'm going to get to Simon Johnson to talk about it. I've been demoted. I've lost all my credibility. He won't be interested."

"You'll do it."

"If I can get in to speak to him, it'll be fine. But I know I'll be fobbed off. They have no time for me anymore." I sigh and reach for the car door. The rain is totally sheeting down, but I can't sit here all night.

"Lexi . . ."

I feel a flurry of nerves at Jon's tone.

"Let's . . . talk," I say hurriedly. "Sometime."

"Okay." He holds my gaze for a moment. "Sometime. It's a deal." He gets out, lifting his hands ineffectually against the rain. "I'm going to find a cab. Go on, run." He hesitates, then drops a kiss on my cheek and strides away.

I pelt through the rain to the entrance, nearly

dropping the precious folder, then stand under the portico, gathering the papers together, feeling a fresh spasm of hope as I remember the details. Although what I said was true. If I can't see Simon Johnson it will all be for nothing.

And all of a sudden I sag as the reality of my situation hits home. I don't know what I've been thinking. Whatever I have in this folder, he's never going to give me another chance, is he? I'm not the Cobra anymore. I'm not Lexi the talented whiz kid. I'm the memorily challenged, embarrassment-to-the-firm, total fuckup. Simon Johnson won't even give me five minutes, let alone a full hearing.

I'm not in the mood for the lift. To the obvious astonishment of the doorman, I head for the stairwell and trudge up the gleaming steel-and-glass stairs that not a single resident of this block ever uses. Once inside, I put on the remote-control fire and try to hunker up on the cream sofa. But the cushions are all shiny and awkward, and I'm afraid of my rain-damp head leaving a stain on the fabric, so in the end I get up and head to the kitchen to make a cup of tea.

After all the adrenaline of the day I'm leaden with disappointment. So I learned a few things about myself. So what? I got totally carried away, with Jon, with the deal, with everything. This whole day has been a pipe dream. I'm never going to save the Flooring department. Simon's never going to usher me into his office and ask me what I think, let alone pitch a deal. Never in a million years. Not unless . . .

Not unless . . .

No.

I *couldn't*. Could I?

I'm frozen in a disbelieving excitement, thinking through the implications, with Simon Johnson's voice running through my head like a soundtrack.

If you recovered your memory, Lexi, then things would be different.

If I recovered my memory, then things would be different.

The kettle is coming to the boil, but I don't even notice. As though in a dream, I pull out my mobile phone and direct dial.

"Fi," I say as soon as it's answered. "Don't say anything. Listen."

Chapter Nineteen

Think bitch. Think boss. Think Cobra.

I survey myself in the mirror and put on some more lipstick. It's a pale gray-pink shade that could practically be called "Bitch-boss-from-hell." My hair's scraped back and I'm wearing the most severe outfit I could find in my wardrobe: the slimmest pencil skirt; the pointiest pumps; a white shirt striped with gray. There's no mistaking the message this outfit conveys: *I mean business.*

I spent two hours with Jeremy Northpool yesterday, at his office in Reading, and every time I think of it, I experience a tiny thrill. Everything's in place. We both want this deal to work out. Now it's up to me.

"You don't look mean enough." Fi, standing by my side in a navy trouser suit, surveys me critically. "Try scowling more."

I screw my nose up—but now I just look like I want to sneeze.

"Nope." Fi shakes her head. "That's still not right. You used to have this really chilling stare. Like, 'You are an insignificant minion, get out of my way instantly.'" She narrows her eyes and puts on a hard, dismissive voice. "I'm the boss and I'll have things done *my* way."

"That's really good!" I turn in admiration. "You should do this. We'll swap."

"Yeah, right." She pushes my shoulder. "Go on, do it again. Scowl."

"Get out of my way, you minion," I snarl in a Wicked Witch of the West voice. "I'm the boss and I'll have things done *my* way."

"Yes!" She applauds. "That's better. And kind of flick your eyes past people, like you can't even waste time acknowledging they're there."

I sigh and flop down on the bed. All this bitchy behavior is exhausting. "I was a real cow, wasn't I?"

"You weren't as bad as that *all* the time." Fi relents. "But we can't run any risks of people guessing. The meaner the better."

Fi has been coaching me for the last twenty-four hours. She took a sick day yesterday and came over, bringing breakfast with her. In the end we were so engrossed, she stayed all day, and the night. And she's done the most brilliant job. I know *everything*. I know what happened at last year's Christmas party. I know that at a meeting last year, Byron stormed out and called me an arrogant nobody. I know that vinyl sales went up two percent last March, due to an order from a school in Wokingham, which then complained that the color was wrong and tried to sue us.

My head is so crammed full of facts it's ready to burst. And that's not even the most important bit.

"When you go into your office, always slam the door." Fi is still instructing me. "*Then* come out and demand a coffee. In that order."

The most important bit is that I come across like the old bitch-boss Lexi and fool everyone. I put away my lipstick and pick up my briefcase.

"Get me a coffee," I bark at myself. "At once!"

"Narrow your eyes even more." Fi surveys me, then nods. "You're set."

"Fi...thanks." I turn and give her a hug. "You're a star."

"If you pull this off you'll be a star." She hesitates, then adds, a little gruffly, "Even if you don't pull it off. You didn't have to make all this effort, Lexi. I know they're offering you a big job, even if they close the department."

"Yeah, well." I rub my nose awkwardly. "That's not the point. Come on, let's go."

As we travel to the office in a cab, my stomach is clenched up with nerves and I can't make small talk. I'm crazy, doing this. I know I'm crazy. But it's the only way I can think of.

"Jesus, I've got stage fright," Fi murmurs as we draw up. "And it's not even me doing it. I don't know *how* I'm going to keep a straight face in front of Debs and Carolyn."

We haven't told the others what I'm up to. We reckon the fewer people that know, the safer.

"Well, Fi, you'll just have to make an effort, okay?"

I snap in my new-Lexi voice, and nearly giggle as her face jerks in shock.

"God, that's scary. You're *good*."

We get out of the cab, and I hand the driver the fare, practicing my mean-eyed glare as I collect my change.

"Lexi?" A voice comes from behind me. I look around, all ready to launch my scary-Lexi face on some unsuspecting person—but instead feel it drop in astonishment.

"*Amy?* What the hell are you doing here?"

"I've been waiting for you." She smooths a strand of hair back a little defiantly. "I'm here to be your intern."

"You...*what*?"

As the taxi drives away, I goggle at her. She's dressed in teetering high heels, fishnets, a tiny pin-striped miniskirt with a matching waistcoat, and her blue-streaked hair in a ponytail. On her lapel is a badge reading *You don't have to be crazy to work here but it helps if you're a hot lesbian.*

"Amy..." I put my hand to my head. "Today really isn't a good day—"

"You said!" Her voice quivers. "You said you'd sort it out. I've made a real effort to get here. I got up early and everything. Mum was really pleased. She said you'd be pleased too."

"I am pleased! But of all the days..."

"That's what you said last time. You're not really interested." She turns away and yanks her ponytail free. "Fine. I don't want your stupid crappy job anyway."

"She might be a distraction," Fi says beside me in a

low voice. "It might actually be a good idea. Can we trust her?"

"Trust me?" Amy's voice sharpens with interest. "With what?" She comes over, her eyes shining. "Have you guys got a secret?"

"Okay." I make a snap decision. "Listen, Amy." I lower my voice. "You can come in, but here's the thing. I'm telling everyone I've recovered my memory and I'm my old self, to get a deal done. Even though I haven't. Got it?"

Amy doesn't bat an eyelid. I can see her mind working furiously, taking all this in. There are some advantages to having a scam artist as a little sister.

"So you're trying to make out you're the old Lexi," she says.

"Yes."

"Then you should look meaner."

"That's what I said," agrees Fi.

"Like you think everyone is just a . . . worm."

"Exactly."

They both sound so sure, I feel a pang of hurt. "Was I *ever* nice?" I say, a bit plaintively.

"Er . . . yes!" Fi says unconvincingly. "Plenty of times. Come on."

As I push open the glass doors to the building, I adopt my meanest scowl. Flanked by Fi and Amy, I stride over the marble, toward the reception desk. Here we go. Showtime.

"Hi," I snarl at Jenny. "This is my temporary intern, Amy. Please make her out a pass. For your information, I'm fully recovered and if you've got any mail for me I want to know why it isn't upstairs already."

"Excellent!" whispers Fi by my side.

"There's nothing for you, Lexi." Jenny seems taken aback as she fills out a pass for Amy. "So . . . you remember everything now, do you?"

"Everything. Come on, Fi. We're late enough already. I need to talk to the team. They've been slacking."

I stride away, toward the lifts. A moment later I can hear Jenny behind me, saying in an excited undertone, "Guess what? Lexi's got her memory back!" I turn back—and sure enough, she's already on the phone to someone.

The lift pings. Fi, Amy, and I walk in—and as soon as the doors close, dissolve into giggles.

"High five!" Fi lifts her hand. "That was great!"

We all get out at the eighth floor, and I head straight to Natasha's desk outside Simon Johnson's office, my head high and imperious.

"Hi, Natasha," I say curtly. "I assume you got my message about my memory returning? Obviously I'll need to see Simon as soon as possible."

"Yes, I got your message." Natasha nods. "But I'm afraid Simon's quite booked up this morning—"

"Then juggle things around! Cancel someone else! It's essential I see him."

"Okay!" Natasha types hastily at her keyboard. "I could do you a slot at . . . ten-thirty?"

"Fantast—" I stop as Fi nudges me. "That'll be fine," I amend, shooting Natasha my meanest scowl for good measure. "Come on, Fi."

God, this barking and snapping is a strain. It's getting me down and I've only been doing it for ten minutes.

"Ten-thirty," Amy says as we get back in the lift. "That's cool. Where do we go now?"

"To the Flooring department." I feel a stab of nerves. "I'll have to keep this act up till ten-thirty."

"Good luck." Fi squeezes my shoulder briefly, and the lift doors open.

As we head along the corridor to the main office I feel slightly sick. *I can do this,* I tell myself, over and over. *I can be a bitch boss.* I arrive at the door and stand there for a few moments, surveying the scene before me. Then I draw a breath.

"So." I summon a harsh, sarcastic voice. "Reading *Hello!* magazine is work, is it?"

Melanie, who had been flicking through *Hello!* with a telephone receiver under her chin, jumps as though she's been scalded and flames red.

"I was just...waiting to be put through to Accounts." She hastily closes *Hello!*

"I'll be speaking to you all about attitude later." I glare around the room. "And that reminds me. Didn't I ask everyone to provide full written travel-expense breakdowns two months ago? I want to see them."

"We thought you'd forgotten," Carolyn says, looking dumbstruck.

"Well, I've remembered." I give her a sweet, scathing smile. "I've remembered everything. And *you* might all remember that you're relying on me for references."

I sweep out, almost straight into Byron.

"Lexi!" He nearly drops his cup of coffee. "What the fuck—"

"Byron. I need to talk to you about Tony Dukes," I say crisply. "How did you handle the discrepancy in his calculations? Because we all know his reputation for pulling a fast one. Remember the trouble we had in October 2006?"

Byron's mouth is hanging open stupidly.

"And I want to talk to you about our annual strategy conference. Last year's was a shambles." I head to my office, then turn around. "Speaking of which, where are the minutes of our last product meeting? You were doing them, as I remember."

"I'll...get those to you." He looks utterly gobsmacked.

Everything I'm saying is hitting right home. Fi is a total genius!

"So, are you recovered?" Byron says as I open my office door. "Are you back?"

"Oh yes. I'm back." I usher Amy in and slam the door. I count to three, then I look out again. "Clare, a coffee. And one for my temp, Amy. Fi, can you come in here?"

As Fi closes the door behind her, I collapse on the sofa, breathless.

"You should be on the stage!" Fi exclaims. "That was so great! That's just the way you used to be!"

I'm still cringing inside. I can't *believe* I said those things.

"So now we just have to sit it out till ten-thirty." Fi

glances at her watch as she perches on my desk. "It's past ten now."

"You were a real bitch out there," says Amy admiringly. She's taken out mascara and is applying yet another coat. "That's what I'll be like when I go into business."

"Then you won't make any friends."

"I don't want to make friends." She tosses her head. "I want to make money. You know what Dad always said? He said—"

Suddenly I really *don't* want to hear what Dad always said.

"Amy, we'll talk later." I cut her off. "About Dad." There's a knock on the door and we all freeze.

"Quick!" says Fi. "Get behind the desk. Sound cross and impatient."

I scuttle to the office chair, and she quickly pulls up a chair opposite.

"Come in," I call, trying to muster the most impatient tone I can. The door opens and Clare appears, holding a tray of coffee. Irritably I jerk my head at the desk. "So, Fi . . . I've had just enough of your attitude!" I improvise as Clare unloads the coffee cups. "It's unacceptable. What have you got to say for yourself?"

"Sorry, Lexi," Fi mumbles, her head bowed. Suddenly I realize she's in fits of giggles.

"Yes, well." I'm trying desperately to keep a straight face. "I'm the boss. And I won't have you . . ." Oh God, my brain is blank. What's she done? "I won't have you . . . sitting on the desk!"

A kind of spluttery snort comes from Fi.

"Sorry," she gasps, and clutches a hanky to her eyes.

Clare looks absolutely petrified. "Um...Lexi," she says, backing toward the door. "I don't want to interrupt, but Lucinda is here? With her baby?"

Lucinda.

That means nothing to me.

Fi sits up, her giggles vanished. "Lucinda who worked for us last year, do you mean?" she says quickly, glancing at me. "I didn't know she was coming in today."

"We're giving her a baby gift and we wondered if Lexi could present it to her?" Clare gestures out the door and I see a small cluster around a blond woman holding a baby carrier. She looks up and waves.

"Lexi! Come and see the baby!"

Shit. There's no way out of this one. I can't refuse to look at a baby—it'll seem too weird.

"Well...all right," I say at last. "Just for a moment."

"Lucinda was with us about eight months," Fi murmurs frantically as we head out of the office. "Took care of European accounts, mainly. Sat by the window, likes peppermint tea..."

"Here we are." Clare hands me a huge gift-wrapped parcel crowned with a satin bow. "It's a baby gym."

As I draw near, the others back away. To be honest, I don't blame them.

"Hi, Lexi." Lucinda looks up, glowing at all the attention.

"Hi there." I nod curtly at the baby, which is dressed

in a white onesie. "Congratulations, Lucinda. And this is...a girl? A boy?"

"He's called Marcus!" Lucinda appears offended. "You've met him before!"

Somehow I force myself to shrug disparagingly. "I'm afraid I'm not into babies."

"She eats them!" I hear someone whisper.

"Anyway, on behalf of the department, I'd like to give you this." I hand the parcel over.

"Speech!" says Clare.

"That's not necessary," I say with a forbidding glare. "Everyone back to—"

"Yes it is!" Debs objects defiantly. "This is like Lucinda's leaving-do too. She can't not have a speech."

"Speech!" calls someone at the back. "Speech!" A couple of others start banging the desks.

Oh God. I can't refuse. Bosses give speeches about their employees. This is what they do.

"Of course," I say at last, and clear my throat. "We're all very pleased for Lucinda on the birth of Marcus. But sad to say good-bye to such a valued member of our team."

I notice Byron joining the cluster of people, surveying me closely over his *Lost* mug.

"Lucinda was always..." I take a sip of coffee, playing for time. "She was always...by the window. Sipping her peppermint tea. Managing her European accounts."

I glance up and see Fi at the back, frantically miming some kind of activity.

"We all remember Lucinda for her love of...biking," I say uncertainly.

"Biking?" Lucinda looks puzzled. "Do you mean riding?"

"Yes. Exactly. Riding," I amend hastily. "And we all appreciated your efforts with those...French clients."

"I didn't deal with France." Lucinda is gazing at me in outrage. "Did you ever even notice what I *did*?"

"Tell the story about Lucinda and the snooker table!" calls out someone at the back, and there's a chorus of laughter.

"No," I snap, rattled. "So...here's to Lucinda." I raise my coffee cup.

"Don't you remember the story, Lexi?" Byron's bland voice comes from the side. I glance at him—and feel a sudden hollowness inside. He's guessed.

"Of course I *remember* it." I summon my most cutting tones. "But it's not the time for silly, irrelevant stories. We should all be at work. Get back to your desks, everyone."

"God, she's a hard bitch," I can hear Lucinda muttering. "She's even worse than before!"

"Wait!" Byron's voice rises smoothly over the disgruntled muttering. "We forgot Lucinda's other present! The mother and baby spa voucher." He brings a slip of paper up to me with an overdeferential air. "It just needs Lucinda's name filled in, Lexi. You should do that, being head of the department."

"Right." I take the pen.

"You need to put the surname too," he adds casually as I take off the cap. I look up and his eyes are gleaming.

Fuck. He's got me.

"Of course," I say briskly. "Lucinda . . . remind me what name you're using these days."

"The same as before," she says resentfully, cradling her baby. "My maiden name."

"Right."

As slowly as I can, I write *Lucinda* on the dotted line.

"And the surname?" Byron says, like a torturer turning the screw. I look up desperately at Fi, to see her mouthing something at me. Dobson? Dodgson?

Holding my breath, I carefully write a *D*. Then I pause and stretch out my arm as though limbering it up. "I've had problems with my wrist," I say to no one in particular. "The muscles sometimes get a bit . . . stiff."

"Lexi, face it," says Byron, shaking his head. "The pantomime's over."

"Nothing's *over*," I say cuttingly. "I'll just take this back to my office—"

"Give me a break!" He sounds incredulous. "I mean, for God's sake! Do you *really* think you're kidding—"

"Hey!" Amy's high-pitched voice shoots across the office, drawing everyone's attention. "Look! That's Jude Law! With no shirt on!"

"Jude *Law*?"

"Where is he?"

Byron's voice is drowned out under an instant stampede to the window. Debs is pushing Carolyn out of the way, and even Lucinda is craning to see.

I love my little sister.

"Right," I say in a businesslike way. "Well, I must get on. Clare, could you finish this up, please?" I thrust the voucher at her.

"It is Jude Law!" I can hear Amy insisting. "I just saw him kissing Sienna! We should call *OK!* magazine!"

"She hasn't remembered a bloody thing!" Byron is saying furiously, trying to make his voice heard. "This is all a bloody act!"

"I need to go to my meeting with Simon. Get back to work." I swivel on my heel in my best scary-Lexi manner and walk rapidly out of the office before he can reply.

• • •

The door of Simon Johnson's office is closed as I arrive upstairs, and Natasha gestures to me to take a seat. I sink down onto the sofa, still a bit shaky from Byron's near-confrontation. "Are you both seeing Simon Johnson?" she says in surprise, looking at Fi.

"No. Fi's just here . . ."

I can't say, "As moral support."

"Lexi needed to consult me on a sales document," Fi says smoothly, and raises her eyebrows at Natasha. "She really is back to her old self."

"Understood." Natasha raises her own eyebrows back.

A moment later the phone rings and Natasha listens

for a moment. "All right, Simon," she says at length. "I'll tell her." She puts down the receiver and looks at me. "Lexi, Simon's in with Sir David and a few other directors."

"Sir David Allbright?" I echo apprehensively.

Sir David Allbright is chairman of the board. He's the total bigwig, even bigger and wiggier than Simon. And he's really fierce, everyone says so.

"That's right." Natasha nods. "Simon says you should just go in, join the meeting and see all of them. In about five minutes, okay?"

Panic is sending little shooters through my chest. I wasn't counting on Sir David and the directors.

"Of course! Fine. Um . . . Fi, I need to powder my nose. Let's just continue our discussion in the Ladies'."

"Fine." Fi looks surprised. "Whatever."

I push my way into the empty Ladies' and sit down on a stool, breathing hard. "I can't do this."

"What?"

"I can't do it." I hug my folder helplessly. "This is a stupid plan. How am I going to impress Sir David Allbright? I've never given a presentation to important people like that. I'm no good at giving speeches—"

"Yes, you are!" retorts Fi. "Lexi, you've given speeches to the whole company. You were excellent."

"Really?" I stare at her blankly.

"I wouldn't lie," she says firmly. "At the last sales conference you were brilliant. You can do this standing on your head. You just have to believe it."

I'm silent for a few seconds, trying to picture it, *wanting* to believe it. But it doesn't chime in my brain.

It's not registered anywhere. She could be telling me I'm fabulous at the circus trapeze, or have a great triple axel.

"I don't know." I rub my face hopelessly, my energy dissipating. "Maybe I'm just not cut out to be a boss. Maybe I should just give up—"

"No! You're totally meant to be a boss!"

"How can you *say* that?" My voice trembles. "When I was promoted to director, I couldn't cope! I alienated all of you, I didn't manage the department well...I fucked it up. And they realize that." I jerk my head toward the door. "That's why they demoted me. I don't know why I'm even bothering." I sink my head into my hands.

"Lexi, you didn't fuck it up." Fi speaks in a rush, almost brusque with embarrassment. "You were a good boss."

"Yeah." I look up briefly and roll my eyes. "Right."

"You *were*." Her cheeks have reddened. "We... weren't fair. Look, we were all pissed off at you, so we gave you a hard time." She hesitates, twisting a paper towel into a plait. "Yes, you were too impatient some of the time. But you did some really great things. You are good at motivating people. Everyone felt alive and kicking. People wanted to impress you. They admired you."

As I take in her words I can feel an underlying tension slowly slipping off me, like a blanket onto the floor. Except I can't quite trust what I'm hearing.

"But you made me sound like such a bitch. All of you."

Fi nods. "You were a bitch some of the time. But sometimes you needed to be." She hesitates, weaving the towel through her fingers. "Carolyn was taking the piss with her expenses. She deserved a bit of a rocket. I didn't say that," she adds quickly, with a grin, and I can't help smiling back.

The door to the Ladies' opens and a cleaner starts coming in with a mop.

"Could you give us two minutes?" I say at once in my best crisp, don't-argue-with-me voice. "Thanks." The door closes again.

"Thing is, Lex..." Fi abandons her mangled paper towel. "We were jealous." She looks at me frankly.

"Jealous?"

"One minute you were Snaggletooth. Next thing, you've got this amazing hair and teeth and your own office, and you're in charge and telling us what to do."

"I know." I sigh. "It's...mad."

"It's not mad." To my surprise. Fi comes over to where I'm sitting. She crouches down and takes both my shoulders in her hands. "They made a good decision, promoting you. You can be boss, Lexi. You can do this. A million times better than fucking *Byron*." She swivels her eyes derisively.

I'm so touched by her belief in me, I can't quite speak for a moment.

"I just want to be...one of you," I say at last. "With everybody."

"You will be. You are. But *someone* has to be out there." Fi sits back on her heels. "Lexi, remember when we were at primary school? Remember the sack race on sports day?"

"Don't remind me." I roll my eyes. "I fucked that up too. Fell flat on my face."

"That's not the point." Fi shakes her head vigorously. "The point is, you were winning. You were way out in front. And if you'd kept going, if you hadn't waited for the rest of us . . . you would have won." She gazes almost fiercely at me, with the same green eyes I've known since I was six years old. "Just keep going. Don't think about it, don't look back."

The door opens again and we both start.

"Lexi?" It's Natasha, her pale brow wrinkling as she sees me and Fi. "I wondered where you'd got to! Are you ready?" I give one final glance at Fi, then get to my feet and lift my chin high. "Yes. Ready."

• • •

I can do this. I can. As I walk into Simon Johnson's room, my back is ramrod stiff and my smile rigid.

"Lexi." Simon beams. "Good to see you. Come and take a seat."

Everyone else looks totally at ease. Four directors are clustered around a small table, in comfortable leather chairs. Cups of coffee are on the go. A thin, graying man whom I recognize as David Allbright is talking to the man on his left about a villa in Provence.

"So, your memory is recovered!" Simon hands me a cup of coffee. "Tremendous news, Lexi."

"Yes. It's great!"

"We're just going through the implications of June

'07." He nods at the papers spread over the table. "This is very good timing, because I know you had some strong views about the amalgamation of departments. You know everyone here?" He pulls out a chair, but I don't sit down.

"Actually..." My hands are damp and I curl them around the folder. "Actually, I wanted to speak to you. All of you. About... something else."

David Allbright looks up with a frown. "What?"

"Flooring."

Simon winces. Someone else mutters, "For God's sake."

"Lexi." Simon's voice is tight. "We've discussed this before. We've moved on. We're no longer dealing in Flooring."

"But I've done a deal! That's what I want to talk about!" I take a deep breath. "I've always felt the archive prints that Deller owns are one of its biggest assets. For several months I've been trying to find a way to harness these assets. Now I have a deal in place with a company that would like to use one of our old designs. It'll raise Deller's profile. It'll turn the department around!" I can't help sounding exhilarated. "I know I can motivate my department. This can be the beginning to something big and exciting! All we need is another chance. Just one more chance!"

I stop breathlessly and survey the faces.

I can see it at once. I have made precisely no impact whatsoever. Sir David has the same impatient frown on his face. Simon looks murderous. One guy is checking his BlackBerry.

"I thought the decision on Flooring had been made," Sir David Allbright says testily to Simon. "Why are we raising it again?"

"It has been decided, Sir David," he says hurriedly. "Lexi, I don't know *what* you're doing—"

"I'm doing business!" I retort with a clench of frustration.

"Young lady," Sir David says. "Business is forward-looking. Deller is a new-millennium, high-tech company. We have to move with the times, not cling to the old."

"I'm not clinging!" I try not to yell. "The old Deller prints are fabulous. It's a *crime* not to use them."

"Is this to do with your husband?" Simon says, as though he suddenly understands. "Lexi's husband is a property developer," he explains to the others, then turns back to me. "Lexi, with all due respect, you're not going to save your department by carpeting a couple of show flats."

One of the men laughs and I feel a knife of fury. Carpeting a couple of show flats? Is that all they think I'm capable of? Once they hear what this deal is, they'll...they'll...

I'm drawing myself up, ready to tell them; ready to blow them away. I can feel the bubbling of triumph, mixed with a bit of venom. Maybe Jon's right, maybe I am a bit of a cobra.

"If you *really* want to know..." I begin, eyes blazing.

And then all of a sudden I change my mind. I halt,

mid-sentence, thinking furiously. I can feel myself retreating, fangs going back in.

Biding my time.

"So . . . you've really made your decision?" I say in a different, more resigned voice.

"We made our decision a long time ago," says Simon. "As you well know."

"Right." I sink as though in massive disappointment and chew at one of my nails. Then I perk up as though an idea's just hit me. "Well, if you're not interested, maybe I could buy the copyright of the designs? So I can license them as a private venture."

"Jesus Christ," mutters Sir David.

"Lexi, please don't waste your time and money," says Simon. "You have a position here. You have prospects. There's no need for this kind of gesture."

"I want to," I say stubbornly. "I really believe in Deller Carpets. But I need it soon, for my deal."

I can see the directors exchanging glances.

"She had a bump to the head in a car crash," Simon murmurs to the guy I don't recognize. "She hasn't been right since. You have to feel sorry for her, really."

"Let's just sort it out." Sir David Allbright waves an impatient hand.

"I agree." Simon heads to his desk, lifts his phone, and punches in a number. "Ken? Simon Johnson here. One of our employees will be coming to see you about the copyright of some old Deller Carpets design. We're closing down the department, as you know, but she's got some idea of licensing it." He listens for a moment. "Yes, I know. No, she's not a company, just a single operator. Work out a nominal fee and the paperwork, could you? Thanks, Ken."

He puts the phone down, then scribbles a name and number on a piece of paper.

"Ken Allison. Our company lawyer. Call him to make an appointment."

"Thanks." I nod and pocket the paper.

"And Lexi." Simon pauses. "I know we talked about a three-month leave. But I think that by mutual agreement your employment here should be terminated."

"Fine." I nod. "I... understand. Good-bye. And thanks."

I turn on my heel and walk out. As I open the door I can hear Simon saying, "It's a *terrific* shame. That girl had such potential..."

Somehow I get out of the room without skipping.

• • •

Fi is waiting for me as I step out of the lift at the third floor, and raises her eyebrows. "Well?"

"Didn't work," I murmur as we head to the main Flooring office. "But it's not all over."

"There she is." Byron heads out of his office as I pass by. "The miracle recovery girl."

"Shut up," I say over my shoulder.

"So, are we really supposed to believe that you've recovered your memory?" His sarcastic drawl follows me. "You're really going to snap back into it?"

I turn and regard him with a blank, perplexed gaze.

"Who's he?" I say at last to Fi, who snorts with laughter.

"Very funny," snaps Byron, whose cheeks have colored. "But if you think—"

"Oh, leave it out, Byron!" I say wearily. "You can *have* my fucking job." I've arrived at the door to the main office, and clap my hands to get everyone's attention.

"Hi," I say, as everyone looks up. "I just wanted to let you know, I'm not cured. I haven't got my memory back, that was a lie. I tried to pull off a massive bluff, to try to save this department. But . . . I failed. I'm really sorry."

As everyone watches, agog, I take a few steps into the office, looking around at the desks, the wall charts, the computers. They'll all be pulled down and disposed of. Sold, or chucked into skips. This whole little world will be over.

"I did everything I could, but . . ." I exhale sharply. "Anyway. The other news is, I've been fired. So Byron, over to you." I register the jolt of shock on Byron's face and can't help a half-smile. "And to all of you who hated me or thought I was a total hard-as-nails bitch . . ." I swivel around, taking in all the silent faces. "I'm sorry. I know I didn't get it right. But I did my best. Cheers, and good luck, everyone." I lift a hand.

"Thanks, Lexi," says Melanie awkwardly. "Thanks for trying, anyway."

"Yeah . . . thanks," chimes in Clare, whose eyes have been like saucers through my speech.

To my astonishment someone starts clapping. And suddenly the whole room is applauding.

"Stop it." My eyes start stinging and I blink hard. "You idiots. I didn't do anything. I *failed*."

I glance at Fi and she's clapping hardest of all.

"Anyway." I try to keep my composure. "As I say, I've been fired, so I'll be going to the pub immediately to get pissed." There's a laugh around the room. "I know it's only eleven o'clock...but anyone care to join me?"

● ● ●

By three o'clock, my bar bill is over three hundred quid. Most of the Flooring employees have drifted back to the office, including a fractious Byron, who has been in and out of the pub, demanding that everyone return, for the last four hours.

It was one of the best parties I've ever been to. When I produced my platinum AmEx, the pub people whacked up the music for us and provided hot nibbles, and Fi gave a speech. Amy did a karaoke version of "Who Wants to Be a Millionaire," then got chucked out by the bar staff, who suddenly realized she was underage. (I told her to go back to the office and I'd see her there, but I think she's gone to TopShop.) And then two girls I barely know did a fantastic sketch of Simon Johnson and Sir David Allbright meeting on a blind date. Which apparently they did at Christmas, only of course I don't remember it.

Everyone had a great time; in fact, the only one who

didn't get totally pissed was me. I couldn't, because I have a meeting with Ken Allison at four-thirty.

"So." Fi lifts her drink. "To us." She clinks glasses with me, Debs, and Carolyn. It's just the four of us sitting around a table now. Like the old days.

"To being unemployed," Debs says morosely, picking a bit of party popper out of her hair. "Not that we blame you, Lexi," she adds hastily.

I take a swig of wine, then lean forward. "Okay, you guys. I have something to tell you. But you can't let on to anyone."

"What?" Carolyn is bright-eyed. "Are you pregnant?"

"No, you dope!" I lower my voice. "I've done a deal. That's what I was trying to tell Simon Johnson about. This company wants to use one of our old retro carpet designs. Like a special, high-profile limited edition. They'll use the Deller name, we'll get huge PR... it'll be amazing! The details are all sorted out, I just need to finalize the contract."

"That's great, Lexi," says Debs, looking uncertain. "But how can you do it now you're fired?"

"The directors are letting me license the old designs as an independent operator. For a song! They're so *short-sighted*." I pick up a samosa—then put it down again, too excited to eat. "I mean, this could be just the start! There's so much archive material. If it grows, we could expand, employ some more of the old team... turn ourselves into a company..."

"I can't believe they weren't interested." Fi shakes her head incredulously.

"They've totally written off carpet and flooring. All they care about is bloody home entertainment systems. But that's good! It means they're going to let me license all the designs for practically nothing. Then all the profits will come to me. And...whoever works with me."

I look from face to face, waiting for the message to hit home.

"*Us?*" says Debs, her face suddenly glowing. "You want us to work with you?"

"If you're interested," I say a little awkwardly. "I mean, think about it first, it's just an idea."

"I'm in," Fi says firmly. She opens a packet of chips and crunches a handful into her mouth. "But, Lexi, I still don't understand what happened up there. Didn't they get excited when you told them who the deal was with? Are they *crazy*?"

"They didn't even ask who it was with." I shrug. "They assumed it was one of Eric's projects. 'You're not going to save your department by carpeting a couple of show flats!' " I imitate Simon Johnson's patronizing voice.

"So, who *is* it?" asks Debs. "Who's the company?"

I glance at Fi—and can't help a tiny smile as I say, "Porsche."

Chapter Twenty

So that's it. I am the official licenser of Deller Carpets designs. I had a meeting with the lawyer yesterday and another one this morning. Everything's signed and the bank draft has gone through. Tomorrow I meet with Jeremy Northpool again, and we sign the contract for the Porsche deal.

As I arrive home I'm still powered up by adrenaline. I need to call all the girls, fill them in on developments. Then I need to think where we're going to base ourselves. We need an office, somewhere cheap and convenient. Maybe Balham.

We could have fairy lights in the office, I think in sudden glee. Why not? It's our office. And a proper makeup mirror in the loos. And music playing while we work.

There are voices coming from Eric's office as I walk into the flat. Eric must have arrived home from Manchester while I was with the lawyer. I peep around the open door to see a roomful of his senior staff grouped around the coffee table, with an empty cafetiere at the center. Clive is there, and the head of HR, Penny, and some guy called Steven, whose role I've never been able to work out.

"Hi!" I smile at Eric. "Good trip?"

"Excellent." He nods, then gives a puzzled frown. "Shouldn't you be at work?"

"I'll...explain that later." I look around the faces, feeling generous after my successful morning. "Can I bring you all some more coffee?"

"Gianna will do it, darling," says Eric reprovingly.

"It's okay! I'm not busy."

I head into the kitchen, humming as I make a fresh pot, sending quick texts to Fi, Carolyn, and Debs to let them know all went well. We'll have a meeting this evening, and talk everything through. I've already had an e-mail from Carolyn this morning, saying how excited she is, and listing a load of new ideas and possible contacts for more exclusive deals. And Debs is gagging to take on PR.

We're going to make a good team, I know we are.

I head back to Eric's office with a full pot and discreetly start pouring it out while listening to the discussion. Penny is holding a list of personnel names, with figures scribbled in pencil at the side.

"I'm afraid I don't think Sally Hedge deserves a raise *or* a bonus," she's saying as I pour her a cup of coffee. "She's very average. Thanks, Lexi."

"I like Sally," I say. "You know her mum's been ill recently?"

"Really?" Penny makes a face as though to say "So what?"

"Lexi made friends with all the secretaries and junior staff when she came into the office." Eric gives a little laugh. "She's very good at that kind of thing."

"It's not a 'kind of thing'!" I retort, a little rankled by his tone. "I just got talking to her. She's really interesting. You know, she nearly made the British gymnastics squad for the Commonwealth games? She can do a front somersault on the beam."

Everyone looks at me blankly for a second.

"Anyway." Penny turns back to her paper. "We're agreed, no bonus or raise this time, but perhaps a review after Christmas. Moving on, Damian Greenslade..."

I know this isn't my business. But I can't bear it. I can just imagine Sally waiting for the news of the bonuses. I can just imagine her thud of disappointment.

"Excuse me!" I dump the coffeepot on a handy shelf and Penny stops talking in surprise. "I'm sorry, can I just say something? The thing is... a bonus may not be much to the company. It's peanuts to the bottom line. But it's huge to Sally Hedge. Do *any* of you remember what it was like to be young and poor and struggling?" I look around at Eric's managers, all dressed in smart, grown-up clothes with their smart, grown-up accessories. "Because I do."

"Lexi, we know you're a tenderhearted soul." Steven rolls his eyes. "But what are you saying—we should all be poor?"

"I'm not saying you have to be poor!" I try to control my impatience. "I'm saying you have to remember what it's like, being at the bottom of the ladder. It's a lifetime away for all of you." I sweep my hand around the room. "But that was me. And it feels like it was about six weeks ago. I was that girl. No money, hoping for a bonus, wondering if I'd ever get a break, standing in the pouring rain..." Suddenly I realize I'm getting a bit carried away. "Anyway, I can tell you that if you give it to her, she really will appreciate it."

There's a pause. I glance at Eric, and he has a fixed, livid smile on his face.

"Right." Penny raises her eyebrows. "Well...we'll come back to Sally Hedge." She marks her paper.

"Thanks. I didn't mean to interrupt. Carry on." I pick up the coffeepot and try to creep out of the room silently, only stumbling briefly on a Mulberry briefcase that someone's left on the floor.

Maybe they'll give a bonus to Sally Hedge and maybe they won't. But at least I said my bit. I pick up the paper and am just flicking through to see if there's an "Offices to Rent" section, when Eric appears out of his office.

"Oh hi," I say. "Having a break?"

"Lexi. A word." He walks me swiftly to my bedroom and closes the door, that horrible smile still on his face. "Please don't ever interfere with my business again."

Oh God, I *thought* he seemed pissed off.

"Eric, I'm sorry I interrupted the meeting," I say quickly. "But I was only expressing an opinion."

"I don't need any opinions."

"But isn't it *good* to talk about things?" I say in

astonishment. "Even if we disagree? I mean, that's what keeps relationships alive! Talking!"

"I don't agree."

His words are coming out like bullet fire. He's still got that smile on, like a mask, as if he has to hide how angry he really is. And all of a sudden, it's like a filter falls off my eyes. I don't know this man. I don't love him. I don't know what I'm doing here.

"Eric, I'm sorry. I . . . won't do it again." I walk over to the window, trying to gather my thoughts. Then I turn around. "Can I ask you a question, since we're talking? What do you really, genuinely think? About us? Our marriage? Everything?"

"I think we're making good progress." Eric nods, his mood instantly better, as though we've moved on to a new subject on the agenda. "We're becoming more intimate . . . you've started having flashbacks . . . you've learned everything from the marriage manual . . . I think it's all coming together. All good news."

He sounds so businesslike. Like he might suddenly produce a PowerPoint presentation with a graph going up to show how happy we are. How can he think that, when he's not interested in what I think or any of my ideas or who I really am?

"Eric, I'm sorry." I heave a deep sigh and slump down on a suede armless chair. "But I don't agree. I don't think we are becoming more intimate, not really. And . . . I have something to confess. I invented the flashback."

Eric stares at me in shock. "You invented it? Why?"

Because it was that or the whipped cream mountain.

"I suppose I just . . . really wanted it to be true," I improvise vaguely. "But the truth is, I've remembered nothing this whole time. You're still just a guy I met a few weeks ago."

Eric sits down heavily on the bed and we lapse into silence. I pick up a black-and-white photograph of us at our wedding. We're toasting each other and smiling, and outwardly blissful. But now I look more carefully, I can see the strain in my eyes.

I wonder how long I was happy for. I wonder when it hit me that I'd made a mistake.

"Eric, let's face it, it's not working out." I sigh as I replace the picture. "Not for either of us. I'm with a man I don't know. You're with a woman who remembers nothing."

"That doesn't matter. We're building a new marriage. Starting again!" He's sweeping his hands around for emphasis. Any minute he's going to say we're enjoying "marriage-style living."

"We're not." I shake my head. "And I can't do it anymore."

"You can, darling." Eric switches instantly into "concerned husband of deranged invalid" mode. "Maybe you've been pushing yourself too hard. Take a rest."

"I don't need a rest! I need to be *myself*!" I get to my feet, my frustration bubbling to the surface. "Eric, I'm not the girl you think you married. I don't know who I've been these last three years, but it hasn't been me. I like color. I like mess. I like . . ." I flail my arms around. "I like pasta! All this time, I wasn't hungry for success, I was *hungry*."

Eric looks totally bemused.

"Darling," he says carefully. "If it means that much to you, we can buy some pasta. I'll tell Gianna to order some—"

"It's not about the pasta!" I cry out. "Eric, you don't understand. I've been acting for the last few weeks. And I can't do it anymore." I gesture at the massive screen. "I'm not into all this high-tech stuff. I don't feel relaxed. To be honest, I'd rather live in a house."

"A *house*?" Eric looks as horrified as if I've said I want to live with a pack of wolves and have their babies.

"This place is fantastic, Eric." I suddenly feel bad for slagging off his creation. "It's stunning and I really admire it. But it's not me. I'm just not made for...loft-style living."

Aargh. I can't believe it. I actually did the sweeping, parallel-hands gesture.

"I'm...shocked, Lexi." Eric looks truly pole-axed. "I had no idea you felt that way."

"But the most important thing is, you don't love me." I meet his eye straight on. "Not *me*."

"I do love you!" Eric seems to regain his confidence. "You know I do. You're talented and you're beautiful..."

"You don't think I'm beautiful."

"Yes, I do!" He seems affronted. "Of course I do!"

"You think my collagen job is beautiful," I correct him gently, shaking my head. "And my tooth veneers and my hair dye."

Eric is silenced. I can see him eyeing me up incredulously. I probably told him it was all natural.

"I think I should move out." I take a few steps away, focusing on the carpet. "I'm sorry, but it's just...too much of a strain."

"I guess we rushed things," Eric says at last. "Maybe a break *would* be a good idea. After a week or two you'll see things differently, and we can think again."

"Yeah." I nod. "Maybe."

• • •

It feels weird, packing up this room. This isn't my life—it's another girl's life. I'm stuffing the absolute minimum into a Gucci suitcase that I found in a cupboard—some underwear, jeans, a few pairs of shoes. I don't feel I have any right to all the beige designer suits. Nor, to be honest, do I want them. As I'm finishing, I sense a presence in the room and look up to see Eric in the doorway.

"I have to go out," he says stiffly. "Will you be all right?"

"Yes, I'll be fine." I nod. "I'll take a cab to Fi's house. She's coming home early from work." I zip up the suitcase, wincing at its sound of finality. "Eric... thanks for having me. I know this has been hard for you too."

"I care for you deeply. You must know that." There's genuine pain in Eric's eyes, and I feel a stab of guilt. But you can't stay with people because of guilt. Or because they can drive a speedboat. I stand up, rubbing my stiff back, and survey the massive, immaculate room. The designer state-of-the-art bed. The built-in screen. The dressing-room for all those millions of clothes. I'm sure I'll never live in such a luxurious place again in my life. I must be crazy.

As my gaze sweeps over the bed, something crosses my mind.

"Eric, do I squeak in my sleep?" I ask casually. "Have you ever noticed?"

"Yes, you do." He nods. "We went to a doctor about it. He suggested you douche your nasal passages with salt water before retiring, and prescribed a nose clip." He heads to a drawer, brings out a box, and produces a gross-looking plastic contraption. "Do you want to take it with you?"

"No," I manage after a pause. "Thanks anyway."

Okay. I'm making the right decision.

Eric puts the nose clip down. He hesitates—then comes over and gives me an awkward hug. I feel like we're obeying instructions from the marriage manual: *Separation (parting embrace)*.

"Bye, Eric," I say against his expensive scented shirt. "I'll see you."

Ridiculously, I feel near tears. Not because of Eric . . . but because it's over. My whole, amazing, perfect dream life.

At last, he pulls away. "Bye, Lexi." He strides out of the room and a moment later I know he's gone.

• • •

An hour later, I really have finished packing. In the end, I couldn't resist stuffing another suitcase full of La

Perla and Chanel makeup and body products. And a third full of coats. I mean, who else will want them? Not Eric. And I've kept my Louis Vuitton bag, for old times' sake.

Saying good-bye to Gianna was pretty hard. I gave her a huge good-bye hug, and she muttered something in Italian while she patted my head. I think she kind of understood.

And now it's just me. I drag my cases to the living room, then glance at my watch. There's still a few minutes till the taxi's due. I feel like I'm checking out of a posh boutique-style hotel. It's been a great place to stay, and the facilities were amazing. But it was never home. Even so, I can't help a massive pang as I step out onto the huge terrace for the very last time, shading my eyes against the afternoon sun. I can remember arriving here and thinking I'd landed in heaven. It seemed like a palace. Eric seemed like a Greek god. I can still conjure up that amazing, lottery winner's euphoria.

With a sigh, I turn on my heel and head back inside. I guess I didn't have the perfect life handed to me on a plate, after all.

Which probably means I was never Gandhi.

As I'm locking the terrace door it occurs to me I should say good-bye to my pet. I flick on the screen and click onto "Pet Corner." I summon up my kitten and watch it for a minute, patting a ball, cute and ageless forever.

"Bye, Arthur," I say. I know it's not real, but I can't help feeling sorry for it, trapped in its virtual world.

Maybe I should say good-bye to Titan, too, just to

be fair. I click on "Titan" and at once a six-foot spider appears on the screen, rearing up at me like some kind of monster.

"Jesus!"

In horror I recoil backward, and the next moment I hear a loud crash. I wheel around, still shaken—to see a mess of glass, earth, and greenery on the floor.

Oh *great*. Stunning work. I've knocked over one of those bloody posh-plant things. Orchids, or whatever they are. As I'm staring at the wreckage in dismay, a message flashes up on the screen, bright blue on green, over and over.

Disruption. Disruption.

This place is really trying to tell me something. Maybe it is pretty intelligent, after all.

"I'm sorry!" I say aloud to the screen. "I know I've disrupted things, but I'm going! You won't have to put up with me anymore!"

I fetch a broom from the kitchen, sweep up all the mess, and dump it in the bin. Then I find a piece of paper and write Eric a note.

Dear Eric,
I broke the orchid. I'm sorry.
Also, I ripped the sofa. Please send me an
invoice.

Yours, Lexi.

The doorbell rings, just as I'm signing, and I prop the page up against the new glass leopard.

"Hi," I say into the phone. "Can you possibly come up to the top floor?"

I might need some help with my cases. God knows what Fi will say; I told her I was only taking a shoebox full of essentials. I head to the outside landing and listen to the lift coming up to the penthouse floor.

"Hello!" I begin as the doors start opening. "I'm sorry, I've got quite a lot of—" And then my heart stops dead.

It's not the taxi driver standing in front of me.

It's Jon.

He's wearing off-duty jeans and T-shirt. His dark hair is sticking up unevenly and his face looks all scrumpled as though he slept on it wrong. He's the opposite of Eric's immaculate, Armani-model groomedness.

"Hi," I say, my throat suddenly dry. "What..."

His face is almost austere; his dark eyes as intense as ever. I'm suddenly reminded of the very first time I met him, down in the car park, when he kept studying me as if he couldn't believe I didn't remember him.

Now I can understand why he looked so desperate when I told him about my marvelous husband Eric. I can understand...a lot of things.

"I called you at work," he says. "But they said you were at home."

"Yeah." I manage a nod. "Some stuff has happened at work."

I'm all twisted up inside. I can't meet his eyes. I don't know why he's here. I take a step away, staring at the floor, winding my hands around each other tightly; holding my breath.

"I need to say something to you, Lexi." Jon takes a deep breath and every muscle in my body tightens in apprehension. "I need...to apologize. I shouldn't have pestered you; it was unfair."

I feel a jolt of shock. That's not what I was expecting.

"I've thought about it a lot," Jon continues rapidly. "I realize this has been an impossible time for you. I haven't helped. And...you're right. You're right." He pauses. "I'm not your lover. I'm a guy you just met."

He sounds so matter-of-fact, there's a sudden lump in my throat.

"Jon, I didn't mean..."

"I know." He lifts a hand, his voice gentler. "It's okay. I know what you meant. This has been hard enough for you." He takes a step closer, his eyes searching for mine. "And what I want to say is...don't beat yourself up, Lexi. You're doing your best. That's all you can do."

"Yeah." My voice is clotted with unshed tears. "Well...I'm trying."

Oh God, I'm going to cry. Jon seems to realize this, and moves away as though to give me space.

"How'd it go at work with the deal?"

"Good." I nod.

"Great. I'm really pleased for you."

He's nodding like this is the windup, like he's about to turn and leave. And he doesn't even know yet.

"I'm leaving Eric." I blurt it out like a release. "I'm leaving right now. I've got my suitcases packed, the taxi's coming..."

I don't mean to look for Jon's reaction, but I can help it. And I see it. The hope rushing into his face like sunshine. Then out again.

"I'm...glad," he says at last, carefully measured. "You probably need some time to think everything over. This is all still pretty new for you."

"Uh-huh. Jon..." My voice is all thick. I don't even know what I want to say.

"Don't." He shakes his head, somehow managing a wry smile. "We just missed our time."

"It's not fair."

"No."

Through the glass behind Jon, I suddenly see a black taxi turning into the entrance. Jon follows my gaze, and I see a sudden bleakness in the cast of his cheekbone. But as he turns back, he's smiling again. "I'll help you down."

When the bags are all packed into the taxi and I've given the driver Fi's address, I stand opposite Jon, my chest tight, not knowing how to say good-bye.

"So."

"So." He touches my hand briefly. "Look after yourself."

"You..." I swallow. "You too."

With slightly stumbling legs I get into the cab and pull the door to. But I can't yet bring myself to close it properly. I can't yet hear that horrible final clunk.

"Jon." I look up to where he's still standing. "Were we...really good together?"

"We were good." His voice is so low and dry it's

…e; his face full of mingled love and sadness …s. "We were really, really good."

…d now tears are spilling down my cheeks; my …omach is wrenched with pain. I'm almost weakening. I could fling open the door; say I've changed my mind ...

But I can't. I can't just run straight from one guy I don't remember into the arms of another.

"I have to go," I whisper, turning my head away so I can't see him anymore; rubbing furiously at my eyes. "I have to go. I have to go."

I pull the heavy door shut. And slowly the taxi pulls away.

Chapter Twenty-one

The world has finally gone mad. This is the proof.

As I walk into Langridge's and unwind my bright pink scarf, I have to rub my eyes. It's only October 16, and already tinsel is up everywhere. There's a Christmas tree covered in baubles, and a choir is standing on the mezzanine, belting out "Hark the Herald."

Soon they'll be starting the run-up to Christmas on January 1. Or they'll start having an extra "midseason" Christmas. Or it'll just be Christmas the whole time, even in the summer holidays.

"Special-offer festive Calvin Klein pack?" drones a bored-looking girl in white, and I dodge her before I can get sprayed. Although, on second thought, Debs quite likes that perfume. Maybe I'll get it for her.

"Yes, please," I say, and the girl nearly falls over in surprise.

"Festive gift wrap?" She scurries around behind the counter before I can change my mind.

"Gift wrap, please," I say. "But not festive."

As she ties up the parcel, I survey myself in the

mirror behind her. My hair's still long and glossy, though not quite as bright a shade as before. I'm wearing jeans and a green cardigan and my feet are comfortable in suede sneakers. My face is bare of makeup; my left hand is bare of a ring.

I like what I see. I like my life.

Maybe I don't have the dream existence anymore. Maybe I'm not a millionairess living in penthouse glory, overlooking London.

But Balham's pretty cool. What's even cooler is, my office is on the floor above my flat, so I have the world's shortest commute. Which is maybe why I don't fit into the skinniest of my jeans anymore. That, and the three slices of toast I have for breakfast every morning.

Three months on, the business has all worked out so well, sometimes I have to pinch myself. The Porsche contract is all happening and has already had interest from the media. We've done another deal supplying carpet to a restaurant chain—and just today, Fi sold my favorite Deller design—an orange circle print—to a trendy spa.

That's why I'm here, shopping. I reckon everyone in the team deserves a present.

I pay for the perfume, take my bag, and walk on into the store. As I pass a rack of teetering high heels I'm reminded of Rosalie, and can't help smiling. As soon as she heard Eric and I were splitting up, Rosalie announced that she wasn't going to take sides and I was her closest friend and she was going to be my rock, my absolute *rock*.

She's come to visit once. She was an hour late because she claimed her GPS didn't go south of the river, and then got traumatized by what she said was a street disturbance by Yardie gangs. (Two kids messing with each other. They were eight.)

Still, she's done better than Mum, who's managed to cancel each planned visit with some dog ailment or other. We still haven't talked since I went to see her that day, not properly.

But Amy's kept me posted. Apparently, the day after I visited, without a word to anyone, Mum gathered up a whole load of her frilly clothes and sent them to Oxfam. Then she went to the hairdresser. Apparently she has a bob now, which really suits her, and she's bought some quite modern-looking trousers. She also got a man in to sort the dry rot—and paid him to take away Dad's paving slabs.

I know it doesn't sound very much. But in Mum's world, that's huge strides.

And on the completely positive and fantastic front, Amy is doing spectacularly at school! Somehow she's wangled a place in Business Studies A-level, alongside all the sixth-formers, and her teacher is bowled over by her progress. She's coming to intern with us in the Christmas holidays—and I'm actually looking forward to it.

As for Eric . . . I sigh whenever I think of him.

He still thinks we're on a temporary separation, even though I've contacted his lawyer about a divorce. About a week after I moved out, he sent me a typed-out document entitled *Lexi and Eric: Separation*

Manual. He suggested we have what he called a "milestone meeting" every month. But I haven't made a single one. I just . . . can't see Eric right now.

Nor can I bring myself to look at his section entitled *Separation Sex: Infidelity, Solo, Reconciliation, Other.*

Other? What on earth—

No. Don't even think about it. The point is, there's no point dwelling on the past. There's no point brooding. It's like Fi said, you have to keep looking forward. I'm getting pretty good at that. Most of the time, it's as if the past is a whole other area, sealed off in my head, taped down at the edges.

I pause in the accessories department and buy a funky purple patent bag for Fi. Then I head upstairs and find a cool seventies-style T-shirt for Carolyn.

"Festive mulled wine?" A guy in a Santa hat offers a tray full of tiny glasses, and I take one. As I wander on, I realize I've got slightly lost in the new layout of this floor, and seem to have strayed into menswear. But it doesn't matter; I'm in no hurry. I meander for a few moments, sipping the hot spiced wine, listening to the carols and watching the fairy lights twinkle . . .

Oh God, they've got me. I'm starting to feel Christmasy. Okay, this is *bad.* It's only October. I have to leave, before I start buying jumbo packs of mince pies and Bing Crosby CDs and wondering if *The Wizard of Oz* will be on. I'm just looking for somewhere to put my empty glass down, when a bright voice greets me.

"Hello again!"

It's coming from a woman with a blond bob who's

folding pastel-colored sweaters in the men's Ralph Lauren department.

"Er . . . hello," I say uncertainly. "Do I know you?"

"Oh no." She smiles. "I just remember you from last year."

"Last year?"

"You were in here, buying a shirt for your . . . chap." She glances at my hand. "For Christmas. We had quite a long conversation as I gift-wrapped it. I've always remembered it."

I stare back at her, trying to imagine it. Me, here. Christmas shopping. The old Lexi, probably in a beige business suit, probably in a terrible rush; probably frowning with stress.

"I'm sorry," I say at length. "I've got a terrible memory. What did I say?"

"Don't worry!" She laughs gaily. "Why should you remember? I just remembered it, because you were so . . ." She pauses, mid-sweater-fold. "This will seem silly, but you seemed so *in love*."

"Right." I nod. "Right." I brush back a strand of hair, telling myself to smile and walk away. It's a tiny coincidence, that's all. No big deal. Come on, smile and go.

But as I'm standing there, with the fairy lights twinkling and the choir singing "The First Nowell," and a strange blond woman telling me what I did last Christmas, all sorts of buried feelings are emerging; thrusting their way up like steam. The sealing tape is peeling up at the corner; I can't keep the past in its place anymore.

"This might seem like an . . . an odd question." I rub my damp top lip. "But did I say what his name was?"

"No." The woman eyes me curiously. "You just said he brought you alive. You hadn't been alive before. You were bubbling over with it, with the happiness of it." She puts the sweater down and eyes me with genuine curiosity. "Don't you *remember*?"

"No."

Something is clenching at my throat. It was Jon.

Jon, who I've tried not to think about every single day since I walked away.

"What did I buy him?"

"It was this shirt, as I recall." She hands me a pale green shirt, then turns away to another customer. "Can I help you?"

I hold the shirt, trying to picture Jon in it; myself choosing it for him. Trying to conjure up the happiness. Maybe it's the wine; maybe it's just the end of a long day. But I can't seem to let go of this shirt. I can't put it down.

"Could I buy it, please?" I say as soon as the woman's free. "Don't bother wrapping it."

• • •

I don't know what's wrong with me. As I walk out of Langridge's and hail a taxi I've still got the green shirt, clasped to my face like a comfort blanket. My whole head is buzzing; the world is receding, like I'm getting the flu or something.

A taxi draws up and I get in, on autopilot.

"Where to?" asks the driver, but I barely hear him. I

can't stop thinking about Jon. My head's buzzing harder; I'm clutching the shirt . . .

I'm humming.

I don't know what my head is doing. I'm humming a tune I don't know. And all I know is it's Jon.

This tune is Jon. It means Jon. It's a tune I know from him.

I close my eyes desperately, chasing it, trying to flag it down. . . . And then, like a flash of light, it's in my head.

It's a memory.

I have a memory. Of him. Me. The two of us together. The smell of salt in the air, his chin scratchy, a gray sweater . . . and the tune. That's it. A fleeting moment, nothing else.

But I have it. I *have* it.

"Love, where to?" The driver has turned around and opened the partition.

I stare at him as though he's talking a foreign language. I can't let anything else into my mind; I have to keep hold of this memory, I have to cherish it . . .

"For Chrissake." He rolls his eyes. "Where-do-you-want-to-go?"

There's only one place I can go. I have to go.

"To . . . to . . . Hammersmith." He turns around, puts the taxi in gear, and we roar off.

As the taxi moves through London, I sit bolt upright, tensed up, clutching the straps. I feel as though my head contains a precious liquid and if it's jolted it'll be spilled. I can't think about it or I'll wear it out. I can't talk, or look out the window, or let anything into my brain at all. I have to keep this memory intact. I have to tell him.

As we arrive in Jon's road I thrust some money at the driver and get out, immediately realizing I should have called first. I whip out my mobile and dial his number. If he's not here I'll go to wherever he is.

"Lexi?" he answers the phone.

"I'm here," I gasp. "I remembered."

There's silence. The phone goes dead and I can hear swift footsteps inside. The next minute the front door swings open at the top of the steps and there he is, in a polo neck and jeans, old Converse sneakers on his feet.

"I remembered something," I blurt out before he can say anything. "I remembered a tune. I don't know it, but I know I heard it with you, at the beach. We must have been there one time. Listen!" I start humming the tune, avid with hope. "Do you remember?"

"Lexi..." He pushes his hands through his hair. "What are you talking about? Why are you carrying a shirt?" He focuses on it again. "Is that mine?"

"I heard it with you at the beach! I know I did." I know I'm babbling incoherently, but I can't help it. "I can remember the salty air and your chin was scratchy and it went like this..." I start humming again, but I know I'm getting more inaccurate, scrabbling for the right notes. At last I give up and stop expectantly. Jon's face is screwed up, perplexed.

"I don't remember," he says.

"*You* don't remember?" I stare at him in outraged disbelief. "*You* don't remember? Come on! Think back! It was cold, but we were warm somehow, and you hadn't shaved . . . you had a gray sweater on . . ."

Suddenly his face changes. "Oh God. The time we went to Whitstable. Is that what you're remembering?"

"I dunno!" I say helplessly. "Maybe."

"We went to Whitstable for the day." He's nodding. "To the beach. It was fucking freezing, so we wrapped up and we had a radio with us . . . hum the tune again?"

Okay, I should never have mentioned the tune. I'm such a crap singer. Mortified, I start humming it again. God knows what I'm singing now . . .

"Wait. Is it that song that was everywhere? 'Bad Day.'" He starts humming and it's like a dream coming to life.

"Yes!" I say eagerly. "That's it! That's the tune!"

There's a long pause, and Jon rubs his face, looking bemused. "So that's all you remember. A tune."

When he says it like that it makes me feel utterly stupid for dashing across London. And all of a sudden, cold reality is crashing into my bubble. He's not interested anymore, he's moved on. He's probably got a girlfriend by now.

"Yes." I clear my throat, trying unsuccessfully to seem nonchalant. "That's all. I just thought I'd let you know that I'd remembered something. Just out of interest. So . . . um . . . anyway. Nice to see you. Bye."

I pick up my shopping bags with clumsy hands. My cheeks are flaming miserably as I turn to leave. This is so embarrassing. I need to get out of here, as quick as I can. I don't know what I was *thinking*—

"Is it enough?"

Jon's voice takes me by surprise. I swivel, to see he's come halfway down the steps, his face taut with hope. And at the sight of him, all my pretense falls away. The last three months seem to fall away. It's just us again.

"I . . . I don't know," I manage at last. "Is it?"

"It's your call. You said you needed a memory. A thread linking us to . . . us." He takes another step down toward me. "Now you have one."

"If I do, it's the thinnest thread in the world. One tune." I make a sound that was supposed to be a laugh. "It's like . . . a cobweb. Gossamer-thin."

"Well then, hold on to it." His dark eyes never leaving mine, he's coming down the rest of the steps, breaking into a run. "Hold on, Lexi. Don't let it snap." He reaches me and wraps me tightly in his arms.

"I won't," I whisper, and grab him. I don't ever want to let him go again. Out of my arms. Out of my head.

When at last I resurface, three children are staring at me from the next-door steps.

"Ooh," says one. "Sex-eee."

I can't help laughing, even though my eyes are shiny with tears.

"Yeah," I agree, nodding at Jon. "Sexy."

"Sexy." He nods back at me, his hands spanning my waist; his thumbs gently caressing my hip bones like they belong there.

"Hey, Jon." I clap my hand over my mouth as though in sudden inspiration. "Guess what? I suddenly remember something else."

"What?" His face lights up. "What do you re-member?"

"I remember going into your house...taking the phones off the hooks...and having the best sex of my life for twenty-four hours solid," I say seriously. "I even remember the exact date."

"Really?" Jon smiles, but looks a bit puzzled. "When?"

"October 16, 2007. At about..." I consult my watch. "Four fifty-seven p.m."

"*Aaah.*" Jon's face clicks in understanding. "Of course. Yes, I remember that too. It was a pretty awe-some time, wasn't it?" He runs a finger down my back and I feel a delicious shiver of anticipation. "Only I think it was forty-eight hours solid. Not twenty-four."

"You're right." I click my tongue in mock reproof. "How could I have forgotten?"

"Come on." Jon leads me up the stairs, his hand firm in mine, to the cheers and jeers of the children.

"By the way," I say as he kicks the door shut behind us. "I haven't had good sex since 2004. Just so you know."

Jon laughs. He peels off his polo neck in one move-ment and I feel a bolt of instant lust. My body remem-bers this, even if I don't.

"I'll accept that challenge." He comes over, takes my face in his two hands, and just surveys me for a mo-ment, silent and purposeful until my insides are melt-ing with want. "So remind me...what happened after the forty-eight hours were over?"

I can't hold out anymore. I have to pull his face down to me for a kiss. And this one I'll never forget; this one I'll keep forever.

"I'll tell you," I murmur at last, my mouth against Jon's hot, smooth skin. "I'll tell you when I remember."

Acknowledgments

While writing this book I had many questions about amnesia; my thanks go to Liz Haigh-Reeve, Sallie Baxendale, and in particular Trevor Powell, for all their help.

I am so lucky to be supported and published by such a crack team of experts. My endless thanks go to Susan Kamil, Irwyn Applebaum, Nita Taublib, Barb Burg, Sharon Propson, Carolyn Schwartz, Betsy Hulsebosch, Cynthia Lasky, Paolo Pepe, Cathy Paine, and Noah Eaker. I'm also eternally grateful to my agents, Araminta Whitley and Kim Witherspoon; also to David Forrer and Lucy Cowie. And to those who keep me sane along the way: the Board and my family, Henry, Freddy, Hugo, and Oscar.

About the Author

SOPHIE KINSELLA is a former financial journalist and the author of the best-selling novels *Confessions of a Shopaholic, Shopaholic Takes Manhattan, Shopaholic Ties the Knot, Shopaholic & Sister, Shopaholic & Baby, Can You Keep a Secret?, The Undomestic Goddess,* and *Remember Me?* She lives in England, where she is at work on her next book.